Rushing the GOAL

Rushing the GOAL

THE ASSASSINS SERIES

TONI ALEO

Editing by Lisa A. Hollett, Silently Correcting Your Grammar.
Cover by Regina Wamba
Cover photo by Sara Eirew
Interior design and formatting by

www.emtippettsbookdesigns.com

Books in
THE ASSASINS SERIES

This book is for any single mom who wants to give up.
Your prince is coming.
Just keep being a great mom. And take care of yourself.

Chapter ONE

Lucy Sinclair was no stranger to pain.

She grew up with three younger brothers. Very rough, tough, hockey-playing brothers and, of course, she had to watch out to make sure none of them killed themselves. Not an easy job, mind you. Especially when she was convinced Jude and Jayden were going to kill each other and Jace was going to get lost in the woods trying to keep up with them. Those three should have done her in a long time ago, but somehow she had survived.

She also survived the pain of having her heart broken many times growing up. Those teenage boys sure do a number on young girls, and she was a victim plenty. But she did fall in love young…and then she had a baby.

Enough said.

She also made it through a nasty marriage that turned into an even nastier divorce. Which now resulted in co-parenting with the King of Dicks, aka Rick, her ex-husband. Again, not easy since Rick was hell-bent on ruining Lucy's life by using their daughter against her, but she was surviving.

And to top off the pain train, she also hadn't had sex in a good long while. Lord knew, she needed a release from a man something serious. So, yes, she knew pain. Embraced it. Only knew that feeling most of the time, well, except when Angie was smiling at her. That brought happiness, but still, she knew pain.

But as she held the couch, her eyes squeezed tightly shut while her toe throbbed, she was convinced this was the kind of pain that was going to kill her.

Stubbing her toe.

Her fucking toe was going to kill her.

What a way to go.

"Momma!"

"Just a minute, sweetheart," she clenched out as she opened her eyes to glance down at her foot.

Thankfully, the toe was still there.

Nail polish chipped to hell, but her toe was still intact.

She guessed that was good, but then, losing a toe would be her luck. Her week had been shit. She had lost a potential client at her interior design firm because she couldn't fit them into her schedule fast enough to suit them. She needed to hire someone to help out, but she couldn't really afford it, or, better yet, didn't want to let go of that money. But still, she was losing money, so something had to change. She also needed to find a sitter since her baby brother and his wife had moved to Florida after he was drafted by the NHL to the Panthers. She could really use a good thing to happen, but she didn't see light at the end of the tunnel at that particular moment.

But then, her toe was still intact.

Little things.

When Angie came barreling around the corner, Lucy cringed when her daughter came to a halt inches from her throbbing foot as she held the phone out, shaking it violently at her. "Avery and baby Ashlyn want to see you now!"

Shaking Lucy's phone even harder, causing her sister-in-law to laugh while her baby niece cooed sweetly, Angie showed a face full of delight. She loved her aunt and cousin so much and, like Lucy, missed them a lot.

"Thank you," Lucy breathed out, taking the phone and looking at her sister-in-law on FaceTime. Then Angie was gone, her long, brown hair flying in the wind she was causing. Kid was a running motor. As Lucy held the phone out, Avery laughed.

"What's wrong with you?"

"I'm pretty sure I almost just died," Lucy breathed, sitting on the couch and propping her foot up.

Avery grinned, her eyes bright as Ashlyn moved her fingers along her chin. It still stunned Lucy to see Avery with Ashlyn. Not only were they just two beautiful girls, but seeing Avery with Ashlyn, her being so young at barely nineteen, reminded her of herself when she had Angie. She had only been eighteen, but unlike Avery, who was in a beautiful and loving marriage, Lucy had been lost, scared, and getting knocked around by Rick, the King of Dicks.

"How?" Avery asked, her turquoise eyes set on Lucy.

"Stubbed my toe."

Avery cringed. "That sucks."

"Girl, I seriously thought I was dying a slow death."

Giggling, Avery kissed Ashlyn's palm. "A toe can't take you out."

Lucy scoffed. "The jury's still out on that."

Rolling her eyes, Avery laughed softly. "Anyway, Angie seems good. She's excited for hockey."

Groaning, Lucy let her head fall back. She had completely forgotten about that. "Fuck me."

Avery laughed louder. "You forgot."

"I did. When does it start?"

"Tomorrow."

"Ugh," she moaned. "Curse Jayden for making me do this. He demands it, but he can't even commit to taking her. Rick already said he won't take her, which means she's gonna miss almost half the damn games. Can't I just bail on it?"

Avery shook her head. "But she's excited."

She was.

"Okay, I guess I can get Mom to help since you decided to leave me."

Avery's smile dropped. "Don't remind me. I hate that we aren't there anymore. We miss you guys."

Lucy smiled. "But Jace is doing awesome."

"He is." She beamed, doing a little wiggle as Ashlyn tried to type on the computer keyboard. "It's hard, though, just me and Boogie."

"I hear ya," Lucy agreed. "But at least your man comes home. "

Avery gave her a small smile of sympathy, and Lucy hated that. She didn't want anyone to pity her. Yeah, she hadn't dated in a good long while. Yeah, she had cobwebs growing in her vagina, but, hey, she was busy. Or at least, that's what she told herself. It was probably because she was a total bitch and didn't trust anything that had a dick.

Well, except her brothers. Those guys were good.

"Momma, I found a sword," Angie called from down the hall of their small apartment above Lucy's interior design office. Small wasn't the right word, really; it was more like tiny. It was one room bigger than a studio apartment and compact. But after her mom moved her boyfriend into the house, there was no way Lucy was still living there. Seeing Coach's ass once as he banged her mother was one time too many, and it had Lucy hightailing it out of her childhood home.

She'd get a bigger place soon; she just had to make more money.

"That's great, honey," she called before shaking her head. "I need to find a man. I need to get laid."

Avery's face lit up. This was an ongoing conversation, one that never really went anywhere. "Yes, you do!"

"Whoa, don't get excited. I was thinking out loud. Let's be honest, I don't want a man."

Letting out a long breath, Avery rolled her eyes. "Then find a woman."

"Um, no," she scoffed before shaking her head. "Maybe I can find a one-night stand when Angie goes to Rick's house this weekend. I need to come or something. I hate life right now."

Avery laughed and Lucy grinned. It had been a long time since she'd had a true "girlfriend." It had always been her and her mom, but when she met Avery, something about her just clicked for them. She was a great girl and Jace loved her something insane. Since Lucy felt kind of responsible for Jace, him being the baby and all, she immediate clung to Avery. She loved her other two sisters-in-law, of course, but she and Avery had a bond.

One she needed.

Since she was becoming a hermit.

Shooting Lucy a bored look, Avery said, "But that means you have to leave the house, put pants on, and turn off Netflix. Let's be honest, your love affair with Netflix is stronger than your desire to go find someone to lay you."

She shrugged. "This is true, but in all fairness, Netflix has never let me down."

"It also can't lay you."

"No, but it still satisfies me."

"Not in the way you want," Avery supplied and Lucy shrugged.

"Shut up, you," she complained as something hard fell onto her chest.

"Oh my God! Is that a dildo?" Avery squawked, and when Lucy looked down to her neon yellow dildo, horror filled her from the tip of her head to the bottom of her feet.

"No, silly! It's a sword! Come on, Momma, fight me!" Angie demanded, holding Lucy's sparkly Edward Cullen vibrator.

"Jesus take the wheel!" Lucy shrieked before snatching the other dildo from her daughter, panic roaring through her system. "Let me call you back," she yelled before hanging up on Avery and throwing her phone down. "Angie! Stay out of my drawer!"

Getting up, she rushed down the hall with Angie chasing her. "Why? What is that? Isn't it a sword?"

"No! It's Mommy's. Please don't touch it," she cried, embarrassment consuming her as she went back into her room. "Please go wash your hands and go watch TV or something."

"Why? Why can't I play with your swords?" Angie shot at her, and Lucy closed her eyes.

Lord, please take me now.

"'Cause they are Mommy's toys. Now, go," she yelled, and as soon as the words left her mouth, she regretted them.

Like Lucy knew she would, Angie glared. "Why can't I play with your toys? You say sharing is caring. You're not caring, Momma!"

At her wits' end, she spun around and set her rambunctious seven-year-old with a look. Angie's big green eyes held Lucy's, her little mouth in a pout, looking every bit like Lucy. Lucy wasn't sure what Angie got from Rick, but she was thankful her little baby looked nothing like him. God, she hated him. But then, hate wasn't even a good enough word to describe her feelings toward Rick. She couldn't even think of a word to express her feelings toward her ex-husband. She did know, though, that if he were on fire, she wouldn't even piss on him to put out the flames. He may have given her the greatest gift in the world, their daughter, but that was it.

Everything else was pain.

Sucking in a breath, she glared as her mom voice came out in full force. "Angela Lynn, I said no. These are mine, and you cannot play with them. Now, go on!"

"That's not fair," she complained. "It's the perfect sword!"

"Jesus," she muttered before shaking her head and throwing the dildos back in her drawer. Reminding herself that she needed to find another place for her toys, she looked back at her daughter. She didn't even have time to use them, hence, why she was a walking billboard for resting bitch face. Swallowing hard, she bit out, "I said no. Now go find something to do before I take away your iPad."

Angie glared. "You're mean."

Lucy glared back. "Oh, really? Mean is not taking you to hockey tomorrow, missy. Remember that."

Angie's brows scrunched together, her eyes deepening in a scowl, every bit as strong-willed as Lucy was. Growing up, Lucy's mom had said one day she would have a kid just like her. Well, ladies and gentlemen, here was that child: Angela Lynn.

Thanks, Mom.

Lucy wanted to smack the look that mirrored her own, but Angie huffed before turning around and stomping out of the room, her ponytail swishing from side to side. When she was out of view, Lucy dropped down onto the bed she shared with her angry daughter and slammed her drawer shut as she shook her head. Man, couldn't she catch a break?

Any other day, she'd probably laugh, but not this day. This day, she wanted to quit. Along with the week from hell, Rick had sent a text asking how she felt about exchanging Angie week-to-week instead of him getting her only every other weekend. She knew Angie wouldn't go for it, and when she told Rick that, he accused her of brainwashing her. Nothing new, dude had shit for brains, but it still bothered her.

She felt she was being fair when it came to Angie. She kept her daughter's best interests in mind, and Angie didn't like it at Rick and his wife, Heidi's, house. She wanted to be with Lucy, and no matter how hard it was being a single parent, Lucy hated when Angie was gone too. She kind of turned into a recluse. Not leaving the house because she worried so much about her daughter. It just didn't feel right that Angie didn't like it there, and that scared her. If he could raise a hand to Lucy, what stopped him from raising one to Angie out of anger?

It was such a fucking headache, and she wished he would just disappear.

But she wasn't that lucky.

Nope. Instead, she stubbed her toe and her daughter waved her dildos around like they were swords.

Classic.

Shaking her head, she fell back onto the bed and squeezed her eyes shut. She had so much work to do but no desire to do it. She wanted to cuddle with Angie and watch a movie. But knowing she had to make money to feed her, clothe her, and one day, give Angie a bigger house, she got up to get to work. Before she could reach the table where all her work stuff waited, her phone rang.

It was her brother, Jayden.

"Hey."

"Hey," he said, a car door slamming. "Just making sure Angie will be there tomorrow."

She groaned. "I could kill you for this."

Jayden laughed. "Oh, hush, you know she's excited, and it's gonna be great."

"You know she's gonna miss half the games."

He growled. "Seriously? Rick the Dick won't bring her?"

"He said no."

"Man, I hate him."

"Join the club. I'm the awesome president of it," she said as he let out a long breath.

"Whatever. Hopefully, Angie will throw a fit and he'll take her. I mean, her coach is Shea Adler, the old captain of the Assassins. That's fucking awesome, y'know?"

She rolled her eyes. She knew she should be impressed by her brother's statement, and she was, but her toe was still throbbing and the vivid image of her daughter waving her dildos in her face was still in her mind. So, needless to say, she didn't care that her daughter's hockey coach would be the amazing Shea Adler or that Rick was a complete dick.

"Yay."

"He's a legend, Luce."

6

"Yeah, I know. I'm in a bad mood."

He paused. "Wait, what? You have other moods?"

"Fuck off," she whispered as she walked by the couch where Angie was playing on her iPad.

"I heard that," Angie called to her, and Lucy let out a long breath. She was really trying not to cuss around Angie, but she was struggling a bit on that.

"Anyway, make sure she is there early so I can help her get ready."

"So, what time?"

"Four thirty."

"Ugh, Jayden! I have a consult at three. You're killing me," she moaned, closing her eyes. She knew she could get it done, but man, it was cutting it close. Especially since she had to go get Angie from the day care that was sucking her savings away.

"I would come get her, but I'll be rushing with Baylor's doctor's appointment."

Snapping her mouth shut, she closed her eyes as she covered them with her hand. She had forgotten that Baylor's appointment was tomorrow. "How's she doing?"

"Eh, day-to-day," Jayden said softly. "They are thinking another surgery."

She let out a long breath. Jayden's wife, Baylor, had been the first woman to draft into the NHL two years ago and she had been doing great. Well, that is, when she actually got to play. She had been hurt more than she got to play, and that was due to the fact that the men in the league didn't take it easy on her. Not that they should, but still, Baylor was having a hard time with it all. Because of that, Jayden was having a hard time. He was worried about her, as he should be. But he was the new captain of the Assassins, and Lucy worried he wouldn't be able to keep his position when he was so consumed with concern for Baylor. It sucked, but hopefully, they would figure it out. But even Lucy knew a third surgery to Baylor's knee wasn't good.

"Well, if you need anything, let me know."

"Yeah, 'cause you aren't jam-packed with shit," he shot back at her and she rolled her eyes.

"I'm trying to be supportive, asshole."

He laughed. "I know and I love you for it."

"I love you."

"Good, I'll see you tomorrow."

"Yeah, yeah, bye."

Hanging up the phone, she set it down and shook her head. The best thing would be for Baylor to just quit the NHL, but everyone knew she wouldn't do so willingly. Which was scary. Just more shit to worry about, she figured as she let out another long breath. Baylor was more headstrong than Lucy was, so Lucy wouldn't hold her breath on her leaving the NHL. They'd have to drag her out.

Picking up her folder for the MacKenzie job she was working on, she opened her laptop and got to work. It was her biggest job to date. A six-bedroom home that Jayden had gotten for her after he basically pimped her to all the guys on the Assassins. He was good like that, and she was excited, but MacKenzie's wife, Michelle, was an idiot. She wanted to decorate the house the way a teenager would. Pink, glitter, and leopard were her wishes, and while Lucy thought Michelle was on something, she still took the job. She would tone it down, but she'd give the client what she wanted.

Because she needed the money.

She wasn't struggling or anything, but she wanted to give Angie a good house. A big one with a huge yard and room for her play. She wanted to show Rick that she sure as hell didn't need him. Yeah, he rubbed it in her face that he had a new house, but that was because his mom had bought it for him. He still bragged, though, and she couldn't wait until the day she had everything she dreamed of. Because she had worked for it. To do that, though, she had to work and pay off her debt that she and Rick created during their short, hellish marriage. And because of that, she would put glitter on top of leopard if that meant she got paid. She just hoped that Michelle would like her ideas a little more. She had to keep her reputation, for God's sake, and glitter on top of leopard for two twenty-five-year-olds was not going to do that.

Maybe she could pass it off as a teenager's room on her webpage?

She didn't get too far into orders before her phone rang once more.

"Gah," she complained as she picked up her phone and saw it was her mother. Letting out an annoyed breath since she had so much to do, she knew she couldn't ignore her mom. Not because she didn't want to—she did—but because Autumn Sinclair would call back until she got ahold of her.

"Hey, Mom."

"Honey! Guess what?" her mother cried out.

"What?" she groaned, not matching her mother's excitement.

Her mother squealed, "River proposed! I'm getting married!"

Her heart stopped.

She knew she was supposed to smile. That she was supposed to be happy. Her mom was getting married! She was happy, and that's all Lucy wanted for her after the nasty divorce from her sperm donor of a father. But in some weird, misery-loves-company way, Lucy liked that she and her mom were both single and lonely. Well, that was until Coach came around, but she'd never thought her mom would get married again.

Before her.

God, she was pathetic!

And an asshole. She was an asshole.

Letting her head fall to the table as she held back a groan, she closed her eyes tightly.

Wow. Could this week get any worse?

"I love this weather. It's not cold but it's not hot, and you need a coat, y'know?"

Talk.

Fucking talk.

Move your mouth.

You haven't been laid in months.

Okay, years.

You need this!

She's willing!

Jesus, you're hopeless.

Looking away, Benji Paxton shook his head as the beautiful blonde eyed him with confusion lacing her blue eyes. She probably thought he was interested. Probably thought he wanted to go home with her. Hell, he needed to go home with her. It had been way too long and they were clicking. He was ignoring his friends just to talk to her, but something was holding him back.

She just wasn't his type.

She was too much like *her*.

Like Ava.

Shaking his head, he looked back at her. "Sorry, you're gorgeous, but I don't want to lead you on. I'm hanging with my friends, so yeah, I wish you the best. Sorry."

Of course, he was awkward about it. That was Benji, one big, awkward son of a bitch. The girl obviously meant no harm. She was nice and had a pretty face, but he couldn't do it. It just didn't seem right. Disrespectful almost to Ava's name.

When he heard his buddy, Vaughn Johansson, the newly acquired forward for the Nashville Assassins, the NHL team Benji played for, laugh, he held back an eye roll as he tried to smile at the girl. But he looked more like he was in pain.

Twisting her face in confusion, she held up her palms up at him. "Whoa, I just wanted to know where you got your jacket so I can get it for my husband. Didn't want to seem weird, started some small talk, but never mind," she said before getting up and walking away.

Oh.

"Macy's," he called to her retreating back, feeling every bit the idiot he was. Wow, he misread that to the extreme. But, really, what was he thinking? Girls don't pick up dudes in Chipotle. God, he was pathetic.

Sputtering with laughter, Vaughn leaned back in his chair as his big body shook with the hilarity of Benji's mistake.

"Shut it, asshole," Benji mumbled as he jerkily grabbed for his burrito. Well, wasn't he the mayor of idiot city? Taking a huge bite while Vaughn continued to cackle at him, Benji sat there thinking this was getting old. One would think that by now he would have this female game down. But then, how could he, when he hadn't had a real relationship since Ava died? A few little flings but nothing that was real. It was insane and something had to change; the only problem was he didn't know how to change it.

He didn't know how to get rid of the guilt.

And he was lonely.

Really fucking lonely.

"What made you think she was hitting on you?"

He shrugged. "I don't know. She had the eyes on her."

"Yeah, the eyes on your coat," Vaughn scoffed, his blue eyes blazing with amusement. "You're such a dork."

Making a face, Benji shook his head. "Why am I friends with you?"

Vaughn grinned widely, his false, white teeth shining in the light as he pointed to them. "Because you knocked all my teeth out when we were back in Jersey and you feel bad for it."

Benji thought that over. It hadn't been a good day when he shot from the blue line and Vaughn dropped down to block the puck. But the puck didn't hit the pads on his body. Nope, it hit the front of his mouth. He was right, Benji felt like shit for a while, but that wasn't why he was friends with him.

"Eh, no, that's not it."

"You heartless bastard," he cried, and Benji smiled as Vaughn's laughter filled the restaurant. When people started to stare at the large man who was laughing very hard, Benji looked down, his cheeks reddening. Vaughn was a big presence. At almost seven feet, it was easy to say he filled the room. He was just huge and scary and boisterous. He was very loud, and women loved him. Unlike Benji, Vaughn had no problems in the female department. But then, he hadn't lost a wife.

Just then, Jordie Thomas dropped down into the chair in front of him before picking up his burrito and taking a huge bite. Around the bite, he asked, "What'd I miss?"

Vaughn tilted his head toward Benji. "Benji making a complete ass of himself."

"Fuck off," he complained as Jordie laughed.

"Let me guess, a girl talked to him and he froze?"

Vaughn grinned. "No, he accused her of wanting him, and all she wanted to know was where he got his coat."

Jordie paused, looking over at Benji. He shrugged back. "You told me to be confident."

Jordie held his gaze, disbelief filling his brown eyes. Unlike when Benji had first met Jordie Thomas, when he was a recovering alcoholic who was twenty shades of fucked up, Jordie now had nothing but pure bliss in his eyes. He had a family, a beautiful wife, and an even more beautiful daughter. He was living the dream, still sober, and Benji was proud. It was hard being a recovering addict—he knew that firsthand—but Jordie kept beating the odds.

Benji totally took credit for it too.

If it weren't for Benji being Jordie's roommate on the road when the Assassins traveled to away games, Jordie could have faced temptation. He still did, but he never succumbed. That may be because he didn't want to let down his wife and daughter too, but hey, Benji liked to believe he was a big part of Jordie's sobriety.

Which was why Jordie was trying to help him with women.

Because, believe it or not, Benji was pathetic.

"I did, but shit, don't just assume every girl is coming on to you."

"She had the eyes!" Benji exclaimed in his defense.

"For the coat, which by the way, that is a snazzy coat," Vaughn commented, and Benji let out a long, annoyed breath. But yeah, it was a nice coat. A pea coat, to be exact.

"Thanks, but I really thought she wanted me."

When both of the guys shook their heads, Benji felt like a kid. Where the hell did his game go? He used to be smooth. Used to have all the girls chasing after him in school.

That is until Ava Donaldson moved to the little suburb in south Chicago where Benji had grown up.

She was gorgeous, long, flowing, blond hair and bright blue eyes. One look, that's all it took, and he was in love. It was that simple. They dated all through middle school, stayed together after she developed a body that had Benji in knots, and stuck it out through senior year. And when it was time for them to graduate, Ava found out she was pregnant. Big shock. His family was worried and so was he, but then he was okay with it. He knew he wanted Ava for the rest of his life; he wanted kids, he loved her, so he married her and they were happy.

But being a young rookie in the big leagues, he soon fell to the lure of drinking when on the road with his boys. It wasn't a big deal at first, but then it got worse. He had to drink all the time, and no matter how many times Ava tried to leave him, she never followed through. She stood beside him and loved him, even when he didn't deserve it. She cared for their daughter and for him, and he'd wanted to do right by her, he did.

But he never got the chance.

One bad decision was all it took to take her and his beautiful Leary from him.

Swallowing hard around the lump in his throat, the ache of loss burned in his chest as he sat in the middle of the burrito place. He had hit rock bottom after he lost them, he even lost his spot on the Rangers—but somehow, he found his strength. He cleaned up. But in a way, he knew he would never be happy again. How could he? He lost his loves, his everything. And while it had been twelve years since everything had happened, nothing could ever cure the ache in his heart from the loss of them.

He truly believed he didn't deserve to be happy and it was his fault they were gone. Yet, a part of him *wanted* to be happy. He wanted what Jordie had, but he wondered if maybe this was God's punishment. Sobered up, but never able to have that happiness ever again. He took for granted what he had, fell victim to the temptation, and now he was alone.

It was sort of depressing and really deep to be thinking about at Chipotle with his buddies.

"I think you want to get laid so bad, you're jumping the gun," Vaughn said, stealing his attention.

"I'm fine," Benji threw back at him. "I don't know what happened."

"Weirdo," he accused, shaking his head. "Maybe you should hire an escort or something. Someone to knock your socks off and get your jitters out."

Giving Vaughn a deadpan look, Benji shook his head. "I'm good. She just reminded me of Ava, and it fucked with my head or something."

His go-to excuse.

Saying that caused an eerie silence to fall over the table. Benji was honest, told his buddies the truth about his late wife and daughter. It was sad and it sucked, but he owned up to his mistakes.

"You do that a lot, though, bro," Jordie said slowly, and leave it to him to notice that. "And I get it, but, dude, you gotta stop using them as a crutch. You have to be happy."

He was right. Problem was, Benji didn't know how to do that.

It was scary, putting himself out there when, for so long, he had been alone. He didn't know how to love anyone; he wasn't even sure he could anymore. Maybe his heart had died with Ava and Leary. He wasn't sure, but man, he wished he could try again. That he could figure out how to be normal around the opposite sex. It was easy with his buddies' wives. Probably because the Assassins had the best wives in the league. All of them so sweet and inviting, but man, they meddled. All of them tried to hook him up with everyone they knew. He went out with whomever they fixed him up with, and every single time, he never got a call back. Even when he thought the date went great, they never called.

Maybe he was a bad date.

"Yeah, I don't know," Benji said slowly, feeling like a loser. "Maybe it won't ever happen, you know? Maybe I'm meant to be alone."

Vaughn grinned, his eyes flashing with laughter. "Which is fine. I mean, I love my single life, but, dude, you gotta get laid."

He was right. Benji craved a woman like he did the smell of the ice, but it just never worked out. He wasn't sure what he was doing wrong, or maybe he did.

"You gotta stop telling everyone your business. No one needs to know that you're a sober widower. I mean, it's on your eHarmony profile," Jordie accused and Benji shot him a confused look.

"You looked at my profile?"

What a joke that profile was anyway. He did it just to get Jordie and his wife, Kasey, off his back. Usually, the girls who contacted him on there only wanted his money. He didn't want that, for obvious reasons. Half the time, he didn't even go on the site. He was still paying for the subscription, though.

He should cancel that.

Vaughn laughed as Jordie shrugged. Running his finger along his beard to clean off the burrito lingering behind, he pinned Benji with a look. "I had to. Kasey said her friend wanted to go out with you until she read it. You basically tell your whole life story. You got baggage, dude, which is cool. A girl out there won't mind, but reel her in first and then unload the baggage. You can't do it on the first date."

"That's not fair to them, though. I want to be honest," he explained but they both weren't satisfied with his logic. He thought he was being fair. He didn't want someone getting involved with him and then finding out later that he was a sober guy who lost his family in a shitty car wreck he should have died in too.

"Whoa, what happened to just getting laid?" Vaughn gave them both a look and Jordie scoffed. "You don't need to be honest to get laid, bro. It's one night, not forever."

"He wants a relationship, dude," Jordie stressed, shaking his head. "But maybe you should just get some. Maybe it will help. Hell, I don't know. We've been trying to get you laid for a year and it isn't working."

Giving them both a dry look, Benji glanced down at his half-eaten burrito. "You guys are too concerned with my love life."

"Because you talk about it all the damn time," Vaughn accused and Benji scrunched his face up.

"I do not!"

"Okay, maybe not all the time. But, dude, I'm going out, getting some ass, and instead of getting some ass, you go back home to watch *Game of Thrones*. It's pathetic."

Giving him a dull look, Benji held his chin high. "Um, I've moved on to *Supernatural*, thank you."

"For fuck's sake, again?" Jordie balked and Benji looked back down.

"What? It's a good show."

"That won't get you laid!" Vaughn roared, causing everyone to look at their table. Benji knew they were right. He needed to get out of the house, go out and meet people, but TV was easy. No one could judge him at home. It was him and the TV. No one to pity him. It was easy…but it was lonely. Very lonely.

"BP, what do you want, dude?" Jordie asked then, bringing his gaze up to Benji's. "I mean, do you want to be with someone? Or are you cool with how life is going?"

He wasn't and he didn't have to answer for Jordie to know that. They had been friends for a long time now. They knew each other's darkest secrets—the perks of both being addicts. If there were perks… But, whatever, Jordie knew Benji.

He knew Benji wanted to be happy again.

"I'm saying this as your friend. Stop using Ava and Leary as your reason for not putting yourself out there. I'm not saying to forget them, you couldn't even if you tried, but you can't keep using them the way you do. I really don't think you realize how much you use them as a shield."

Looking away, Benji sucked in a breath and let it out. He did know.

"If you want to be happy, if you want what all of us have——"

"Not me, I don't have anyone 'cause I don't want them," Vaughn added and Jordie rolled his eyes.

"Anyway, then go get it, dude. You're a good dude, any girl would be lucky to have you."

"Wow, you sounded really gay there," Vaughn mocked, but Jordie ignored him, holding Benji's gaze.

"You know what I mean?"

And he did. It scared him, though.

Because, in the years since he laid Ava and Leary to rest, he hadn't found anyone who could spark even an ounce of the happiness they sparked inside of Benji.

But, if he was honest, he hadn't really been looking. He had gotten so used to feeling sorry for himself, he didn't know how to get what he wanted. On the ice, no problem, he fought to the point of exhaustion, but that was the player he was. He knew how to handle hockey, he knew how to win at that—but life, he kind of sucked at that. He had no fight. Probably because he had nothing to fight for.

God, he was pitiful.

And this wasn't the man he wanted to be. It was time to change.

"You're right."

"I know. It happens a lot. Ask my wife, she'll tell ya," Jordie said, flashing his pearly whites.

"You forget I know your wife very well, and she wouldn't say that at all," Benji teased back as his phone rang. Jordie laughed as Benji reached into his pocket, pulling his phone out. Looking at the screen, he saw it was the new captain of the Assassins, Jayden Sinclair. He liked Jayden, strong leader and cool dude. He was young, but the kid could lead like no one he had ever seen. They had formed a good friendship, especially now that they played on the same line together. He respected the guy.

"Hey, Cap," he answered as both Vaughn and Jordie started to eat the food that had been forgotten while they all discussed Benji's love life.

Or lack of one.

Whatever.

"BP, I need a favor." He sounded desperate.

Benji laughed. "Should I be scared?"

"Eh, that's debatable. And if, after this, you want to kill me, I fully understand."

"Oh, shit, what?" he asked, even though he knew he'd do it. That's the way the Assassins team worked. They helped each other. No matter what. Their boss, Elli Adler, was a prime example of that. She went above and beyond the role of owner of the Assassins. She was their friend, and they all followed her example.

"So I volunteered to help Adler out with his hockey team. But Baylor's appointment got pushed back, and now we have to meet with another specialist, and, well, I'm not gonna make it."

"Okay, I'll go," Benji said. He knew all about Adler's hockey team that he had retired to coach. He loved his kids and he wanted to coach them. Benji would do the same if he had a family. "No big deal."

"Thanks, man, really. But it's more than that." Again, he sounded very nervous, which kind of made Benji nervous.

"Okay?"

"My niece, Angie, is playing on the team. I'm supposed to meet my sister at four thirty to get Angie ready for the ice. I know you've never met her, and this is a lot to ask, but can you help her out—on and off the ice?"

"Yeah, no problem," he said without hesitation. Jayden had made it seem like way more than that.

"Okay, awesome, but one thing…"

"Yeah?" he asked, and why was Jayden so nervous?

"My sister can be a bitch, and she's gonna be pissed I'm not there. But I know if I tell her I can't be there, she won't take Angie, and Angie really wants to play. So I'm not gonna tell her, and if she attacks you since you're the messenger, I'm really fucking sorry. But, man, Angie is awesome and you'll love her, if that makes it any better. Did I mention the team is a bunch of seven- and eight-year-olds? Girls. They are girls. All girls. Are you sure?"

He said it all so quickly that Benji couldn't help but laugh.

"Dude, it's no big deal. I love kids, and I doubt your sister is that bad."

When Jayden didn't answer right away, the only noise coming from him one of hesitation, Benji would have been lying if he said he wasn't a little nervous, but also intrigued.

How bad could this chick be?

"Can I just apologize now?"

Hm. That bad?

That should make him not want to go, but Benji wasn't normal.

Instead, he was kind of excited.

Or a glutton for punishment.

Who knew?

"What's her name?"

"Lucy. She's tall, thin, green eyes, brown hair, and she has permanent resting bitch face. She'll look pained." Before Benji could ask why that was, Jayden went on. "Listen, gotta go. Thanks, bro, call me afterward."

"No problem." He hung up then, and as he leaned back in the chair, he found that he still wanted to know why Jayden's sister would look pained. He knew he shouldn't care. He hadn't even met the chick, but for some reason, he wanted to know.

What was up with that?

Chapter TWO

Why was Lucy in a group text with her brothers? She hated group texts, she did, but for some reason, she was in one with her brothers. As each chime of her phone sounded, it only made her realize how much she really hated the ongoing messages.

Jude: Is anyone else weirded out by the fact Mom is getting married again?

Jace: Hey, at least we won't be married to our sister. Can't say the same for Jayden.

Jayden: Fuck you, and it is weird. That's my wife's dad.

Jace: You might want to get used to calling her your sister-wife.

Jude: Ewwww, Jay is doing his sister! Haha

Jace: Maybe you guys can go on that TLC show? You know, make some money for your unfortunate situation.

Jayden: Get real, how old are we? And the only unfortunate (which by the way, I'm surprised you can spell that) situation is that I'm related to you losers.

Jace: Hey, I wents to skool.

Jayden: Yeah, we can tell.

Lucy: OMG! Leave each other alone and can we not be immature children about this? Just be happy for her and Jayden's stepdad?

She could have left off that last comment, and maybe that made her as immature as them, but if she was going to deal with this, she was going to do it the only way she knew how. Either with sass or making fun of someone. Because Lucy was far from happy about this, and she *was* weirded out by the fact her mother was getting married again. Though that was more because, let's be honest, she could be a jealous, unhappy bitch.

News of their mother's engagement had run through the family like wildfire. That was the problem with being such a close-knit family who were in each other's business all the time. They all acted very happy for their mom, and they were, but it was odd. Lucy and her siblings had only known their mom and dad together. Now that their sperm donor, cheating-ass father was out of the picture, it had been only a matter of time before their mom moved on.

It just seemed so soon.

Or maybe that was the jealousy speaking again.

It had been four years since Lucy had gotten divorced, and she hadn't even had a boyfriend. Mom, though, only two years after a nasty divorce, and she was back on the horse and getting married.

If she gets pregnant, I quit, she thought to herself as she parked the car, her phone going off like mad.

> *Jayden: Shut up! He's not my dad! Gross! And I am happy. Just weirded out.*
>
> *Jude: Yeah, what he said ^^ and technically, he's all of our stepdad.*
>
> *Jayden: Shut up, dude, you're making this worse.*
>
> *Jace: For real, but Lucy, sounds like someone is guilty cause they aren't happy for our sweet, amazing mother and our new, gag, dad.*
>
> *Jayden: Ugh, don't call him that.*
>
> *Jude: Coach, his name is Coach.*
>
> *Lucy: For fuck's sake, shut up, of course I am.*
>
> *Jace: Sure you are. Crazy mom got married before you and she divorced way after you.*
>
> *Lucy: Wow. Really? You used to be my favorite.*
>
> *Jude: We were all thinking it, and plus, you're the only one who hasn't made a congratulations Facebook post for Mom and Coach. Even Jayden did it, and soon his wife will be his sister.*
>
> *Jayden: I hate you guys.*
>
> *Lucy: Since I'm not a child like you assholes, I don't need to blast all over Facebook my happiness for my mother. Y'all know she loves me more, so fuck off and leave me alone.*

18

When she was answered by them laughing out loud at her, she shoved her phone in her purse before pushing her door open with more force than needed, but man, they just pissed her off. Stupid brothers.

"Dumbasses," she muttered as she popped the trunk while Angie bounced beside her.

"I get to be the flower girl, right, Momma?"

Sucking in a breath, Lucy smiled. "I'm sure you will be."

"Yay! Today is, like, the best ever. Grandma is getting married, and I'm playing hockey! Isn't it the best?"

Not really, but she wouldn't tell her baby that. "Yes, honey. Come on, we're kinda late, even though I don't see Jayden's car." Lucy looked around as they made their way into the ice rink, still not seeing her brother's big truck.

"I wish Jace and Jude were here. I like when I get to play with all three of them."

"I know, but Jace and Jude will be home for Christmas." Still looking for Jayden's truck, Lucy felt an uneasiness settle in her gut as she reached for the door handle. Maybe he parked in the back? Apparently, she was the only one worried about it because Angie was giggling with excitement. As they entered the building and went toward Rink B where they would be practicing, according to the email she received that morning, she kept looking for her brother. Thankfully, the texts had come to a stop. She loved her brothers, really, but they were exhausting.

When her purse vibrated, though, she closed her eyes, figuring she could answer it later. She needed to find Jayden, but she still didn't see him and that made her anxious. She may have grown up with the sport and loved it, but she sure as hell didn't know how to get Angie ready to hit the ice. Plus, Angie was looking forward to being with him on the ice.

Pulling her phone out, she turned her phone on to see it wasn't Jayden who had texted her, as she had hoped. It was Rick.

Fuck.

Ignoring the text since she was already on edge, she sent Jayden a quick message asking where he was. When she looked up, hoping to see him, she didn't. Instead, a very big and well-known man was coming toward her with a grin on his face. To say Shea Adler was a looker was an understatement. If he weren't a devoted husband and an amazing father, Lucy would climb that man like a tree and attach herself to him with no plans of letting go. Even with the years starting to be visible on his face, Shea was gorgeous. A fine wine that man was, and wine always made Lucy want to take off her clothes. God, she was going to hell. But Jesus, he had thick, dark hair, blue eyes that looked into your soul, and a smile that could stop a room.

Man, that Elli Adler was one blessed lady.

Lucky bitch.

"Hey, Lucy," he said, his Boston accent still very much present even after living in Tennessee for so long.

"Hey, Shea," she said with a dreamy smile.

Why couldn't she meet a Shea Adler type who would look into her eyes and make her feel like Ed Sheeran was singing in the background?

All she ever got was Rick the Dick.

Horror music played when he was around.

Directing his attention to Angie, his smile grew. "Angie! Girl, you ready? Posey and Shelli have been asking all day if you were coming."

Angie beamed. She loved the Adlers. Everyone loved the Adlers. They were just great people. "Yup, Coach Adler. I can't wait. I'm so excited! My uncle should be here to help me get ready." She was so excited, but Lucy didn't miss the same little fairy-tale look in her eyes that probably mirrored hers.

Shea was dreamy.

But when his face displayed confusion, the dreaminess Lucy felt disappeared and her eyes narrowed, the uneasiness back in full force.

Fucking Jayden.

"I thought he wasn't coming." He looked back and forth between Angie and Lucy as the annoyance started to bubble inside her chest.

Damn it.

"What?" Lucy breathed. "He told me he was meeting me." Pulling out her phone, she dialed his number, but it went straight to voice mail.

"Momma, I thought Jayden would be here."

"Hold on, baby," she said, a little panicky as she redialed his number.

Again, voice mail.

Instead of hanging up, though, she waited until the beep and muttered very quietly so Angie wouldn't hear her, "You shall die, Jayden Mitchell Sinclair. I don't know where you are. I don't care where you are. But when I find you, I will kill you."

Shea heard her though and smiled nervously at her. Kind of funny since he wasn't supposed to be scared of anything. "From what Elli said, something happened with Moore's doctor, so they are seeing a different one. But no worries, we've got Angie. A lot of guys came to help me today, so don't stress. It's cool."

"So Jayden isn't coming?" Angie asked, her eyes wide, which felt like daggers in Lucy's heart. Looking back at Shea, probably so she wouldn't scream, Lucy could see he was only trying to help. She got that, but of course, she stressed. Angie had enough disappointment in her life from her fucked-up dad; she didn't need this from her family. Lucy also didn't like asking for help from people who weren't her family. Shea had a team full of girls to worry about,

Angie wasn't his…unfortunately—she was only half kidding—and it was her responsibility to get her daughter ready.

Damn it.

Jayden was going to die.

"No, I'm good. I've got her. You've got a whole team. I got this," she said, flashing an overly fake grin. She was sure he didn't believe her by the way he eyed her, but thankfully, he smiled and nodded.

"Okay, if you need anything, let me know. Make sure you're on the ice by five, Angie."

She was nervous, Lucy could tell, but she smiled brightly as she looked up at him. "Yes, sir!" Angie said with a salute to him as she bounced on her heels. When he turned away, her grin was gone, and worry was back in her eyes. "Uncle Jayden really isn't coming?"

Typing very violently on her phone to Jayden that he was an asshole and that she hoped Baylor was okay because she was going to have to learn to live without her husband, she hit send and then tried to smile at Angie. "We got this."

"Mom! You do not."

"I do! I used to get your uncles ready for games."

She eyed her. "You did not."

"Okay, I didn't, but how hard can it be?" Lucy said with a shrug and Angie glared.

"Momma…" she whined and Lucy was going to kill Jayden. Or at least, make it to where he couldn't have kids. Opening the browser on her phone, she typed: *how do you put gear on a seven-year-old for a hockey game?*

Before the results could generate, damn faulty Internet in the rink, obviously, someone said, "Um, excuse me?"

She ignored it at first because who the hell would be talking to her as she waited for her phone to spit out the answer.

"Come on, Google. Don't fail me now," she muttered as she tapped her phone, Angie looking up at her, all kinds of nervous. *Damn it, Jayden.*

"Excuse me? Miss?"

Miss? What in the ever-loving fuck? Turning toward the very deep and very male voice, Lucy had to look up to meet a pair of gray eyes. Lucy was a tall woman, almost six feet, and still this guy towered over her. He was huge, big shoulders, and for a second, she was a little taken aback. He must have noticed that because he held his palms up, his eyes boring into hers.

Taking a step back, she eyed him. But then, he tried to smile and, God, it was so awkward, she found herself fighting her own smile. What the hell? Who was this guy? But soon, she was lost in his eyes. They were soft, his lips puffy, his face chiseled in all the right spots. His hair was shaved up the side but thicker at the top, while dark hair dusted his jaw and upper lip. He looked like a damn underwear model, yet something about his face didn't stun her the way, say, Shea's did. He was good-looking, hot even, but he was kind of awkward and she found that…adorable?

Hm.

As she eyed him, he did the same to her, his eyes drinking her in as silence stretched between them. She wasn't sure why she felt all girlie under his gaze, but she sure as hell didn't like it one bit. So finally, she asked, "Are you talking to me?"

Clearing his throat, he nodded. "Yeah, um, are you Lucy? Sinclair's sister?"

Tilting her head, she took in the familiar purple and black Assassins warm-ups and the hockey stick in his hands, along with a pair of skates. "Who's asking?" she asked, her eyes narrowing.

He smiled, his lips curving and his eyes lighting up a bit. "Okay. Hi, I'm Benji Paxton. I play with Jayden on the Assassins, and he asked me to come and help you with your daughter…Angie?"

Her gaze deepened into a scowl. So Jayden knew he wasn't going to be here and sent someone as a replacement. "That asshole sent you and didn't even tell me?"

He shrugged. "Um, I think so."

"And you think I'm gonna trust you with my kid?"

He looked unsure about it himself, yet the grin remained on his lips. He was really cute. "Yes?"

She glared. "How about no. I'm good."

His brows rose. "What?" he croaked out.

"I got it. I can do it."

"Momma!" Angie stressed, her eyes pleading.

Lucy tore her gaze from Benji Paxton's and looked at her daughter. "Baby, I Googled how to do it. We can do this," she said reassuringly, holding out her phone with a YouTube video on deck. "How hard could it be?"

But Angie was not convinced.

"You Googled it?" she cried out, and when Benji laughed, Lucy glared. She knew it wasn't his fault, but he wasn't needed. So he needed to go.

"You can leave."

That didn't seem to bother him any as he said, "Google can't help you, I can."

Angie looked hopeful, but Lucy wouldn't admit to needing help. Cutting a look to him, she held his gaze. "Do you doubt Google?"

His eyes were dancing with laughter as his lips curved. This time, it didn't seem forced, and hell, he was cute. Like a little bulldog puppy or something. "No, but I'm sure it doesn't have the experience I do. I've been playing hockey since I was three. I've won two Stanley Cups, and I play on the same line as your brother. So, I mean, word is I'm good, and I'm sure I know more about it than Google."

Glaring, she held his gaze, unfazed by his resume. "Was that supposed to impress me?"

His lips curved in a playful way that may or may not have had Lucy gasping for breath. Not that she'd ever tell him that. "Maybe. Did it work?"

"Nope, not even kinda," she said simply, turning back to Angie. "I trust Google. Not your uncle's replacement. We don't even know this guy."

"Yes, but he knows hockey, Mom. He won two Cups!"

"True, but I have Google and YouTube. I'm sure I've got this."

"Or we can just let him do it since Uncle Jayden trusted him to help us."

"Without telling me," Lucy added and Angie glared.

"Because he's scared of you!"

Lucy feigned hurt. "That's not true."

Angie just gave her a look, and Lucy shrugged as Benji said, "No, really, that's the rumor I heard. Heard you might try to hit me. Jayden apologized in advance."

Letting out a long breath, she closed her eyes. God, Jayden was overdramatic. She wasn't that bad. Glaring back up at Benji, which made her realize maybe she was *that bad*, she demanded, "Shh, you. And don't believe everything you hear."

He scoffed at that, and her glare deepened. The guy may be hot, but she decided she didn't care for him much. Fed up with all of this, she looked back to her daughter. "If you want the replacement to help you, I understand. But I think I got this."

She felt Benji looking at her, but she didn't meet his gaze as Angie shrugged. "I guess he can do it. He knows what he's doing."

Lucy wouldn't let that bother her. He was experienced, and all she had was Google. Plus, she was so angry at Jayden, there was no telling what Angie would go out there looking like. So she smiled sweetly and said, "Okay. Go get ready, and let's play hockey!"

Turning to Benji, she watched as Angie looked at him expectantly. But he was staring at Lucy. With a quirk in his lip, he said, "It was really nice meeting you. And don't worry, I'll take good care of her."

Yeah, she didn't like him one bit. Her eyes narrowed as his gray eyes seemed to twinkle. She hadn't been looked at like that in a while, and she honestly didn't understand it. This guy didn't even know her, yet he looked at her like they were friends. Maybe even more. She wasn't sure.

Strange…

"Yeah, okay, I'll make sure you don't walk right if you hurt her. I'll be watching from the stands," she said, leaning down and kissing Angie's temple. "Have fun, okay?" Angie smiled, but it didn't reach her eyes. She was nervous. "You okay, baby?"

"I wish Jayden was here," she whispered and Lucy bent down.

"I know, but I'm sure replacement guy—"

"Benji," he supplied, but there wasn't annoyance in his voice. Humor, though. He found her funny. Which was annoying as hell.

"*Benji*," she said slowly, enunciating each syllable just to be a bitch. He just laughed, a deep tenor that had her toes curling in the heels she wore. Clearing her throat, she said, "He will take good care of you."

When he crouched down beside her, Lucy stared at him in confusion as he cupped Angie's shoulder. Angie looked at him curiously, and Lucy glared. What was he doing?

"You know, I'm sure your uncle wouldn't have asked me to pitch in if he didn't think I would be great at helping you. I heard you're the best little hockey player in the world and that you're gonna show me some awesome moves," he said sweetly.

Hell, Rick didn't even talk to her like that and that dick was her dad.

Angie's cheeks reddened and Lucy smiled. "Yeah?"

"Yeah, so don't worry. I know I'm not your uncle, but I'm excited to hit the ice with you, and I'll do my best to help you out. I'm like your personal helper. I'm your trainer!" he said excitedly, and Lucy couldn't help it, she smiled a little. Just a little.

"You are?" Angie asked and Lucy was surprised how shy her daughter was being. She had been so excited about this, but now, it didn't seem that way.

"If you want to go home, we can, honey," Lucy said, but Angie shook her head.

"No, I want to play."

"Awesome, how about we go get ready real quick and hit the ice?" Benji asked softly, and Lucy glanced over at him, surprised. For a big dude, he was gentle. Which was nice. Standing back up, which meant he was towering over them, he held out his hand, and Angie took it without hesitation. That surprised Lucy. Angie wasn't one to trust so easily, but she seemed happy as she waved at Lucy while they walked toward the group of other little girls.

When Benji looked back at Lucy and he grinned, she narrowed her eyes at him. Yeah, he was good with kids, she'd give him that, but there was something else in his eyes. Almost like he thought he had won some underlying competition that she hadn't even realized she was in with him.

That bothered her.

Angie may trust him and Lucy's ovaries may think it was hot that he was good with her daughter, but she didn't trust him as far as she could throw him.

And with his size, it wouldn't be far.

So she'd watch Benji Paxton...and not because he had a hot ass in those Assassins sweats.

Good Lord, she needed to get laid.

Holy shit.

Sinclair's sister was fucking hot.

Looking back at her once more, he caught her watching him. When their eyes locked, he felt like he was really grinning. And not that awkward, fake, "I have no clue what I'm doing with my face" kind of grin, but a real one. It may have even reached his eyes. It was easy to do where she was concerned, it seemed, but she glared and then turned on those sexy nude heels before starting for the rink.

Well, then.

He watched her for a moment and saw her ass was encased in a snug black skirt that was so tight, he was sure she wasn't wearing any underwear. She was wearing a thick purple jacket, and her brown hair was up in a twist, a little tattoo peeking out of the neck of her jacket. He wanted to get closer, check it out, but then he wasn't sure he could stop himself from dropping his lips to that sexy, thin neck.

What in the hell?

What was wrong with him?

"Benji?"

Looking down at the miniature version of the spunky firecracker he just met, he smiled. "Sorry! Come on," he said, hoping that Angie didn't know he wanted to bang her mom. Wow, what? Good Lord, what was wrong with him?

Shaking his head free of his horndog thoughts, he brought Angie to where all the other little girls were getting ready. Parents were tying their kids' skates and pulling jerseys down over their heads. Stopping for a second, he watched everyone, and then the slow, fiery ache started to burn in his chest.

He was supposed to be doing this with his daughter.

Closing his eyes, he sucked in a deep breath and let the pain eat him alive. If he hadn't been an ungrateful jerk and had chosen his family over alcohol, then Ava and Leary would be here. They would have had this moment.

He would feel loved.

He would feel complete.

Fuck.

Opening his eyes because he could feel his little friend staring at him, he found that he was right. Angie was watching him, her eyes full of concern as she nodded to him. "You okay?"

"Yeah, sorry," he said roughly before kneeling down in front of her. She sat down as he opened her bag, pushing back his own tears. He really hadn't thought this through when he agreed to come help. He hadn't realized how hard this would be for him. That the pain of the loss of his child would shake him to the core like it was at the moment. It just wasn't fair. Why did addiction ruin lives? Why couldn't he have fought it? Damn it.

When he noticed she was still watching him, he cleared his throat free of emotion and tried to smile. "Sorry, having a moment."

"Are you sure you want to help me?"

He really smiled that time, reassuringly. "Yes, of course. I'm sorry. Just thinking about something."

"What?" she asked with all the curiosity of a child.

A child he didn't have anymore.

Swallowing hard around the lump in his throat, he said, "My daughter."

Angie smiled. "Aw, she doesn't play?"

"No, she doesn't," he said, his heart pounding in his chest. He'd like to think that she was in heaven. That there was a big rink in the clouds where she would play and she was happy with Ava. God, he hoped they were happy. "But, okay, let's do this."

Pushing thoughts of Leary away—not an easy feat—Benji reached for Angie's skates as she took off her jacket. He then started tying them up, and together they got her ready quickly. She was funny and animated, but he knew she was nervous. He'd hoped to ease those worries, but it was hard when he was battling his own demons in his head. He still tried, though, and he knew that meant something. That little Angie, his new friend, was important to him. Not sure why, but she was, and he was going to do right by the little girl.

He was the replacement and all.

Before putting on her helmet, Benji noticed her stick wasn't taped up. Reaching into his pocket for his roll of tape he had brought to retape his own stick, he grinned up at Angie. "All right, first things first—"

"You're the realest?"

His grin grew at her quick thinking, and he couldn't help but laugh. Nodding, he met her sweet, sassy gaze. She looked so much like her mother it was scary. They were two little twins, and of course, that made him curious about her father. Where was he? Why wasn't he here? Benji wouldn't have missed this for the world if he'd had the chance.

"All right, Iggy," he teased and she laughed happily, but then he paused. "How do you even know that song?"

She grinned. "My uncle Jace and me used to sing it all the time. He moved to Florida with my aunt Avery and my cousin Ashlyn. We miss them sooooooo much!"

"I bet."

"And then my uncle Jude and aunt Claire are in California and Vegas, but they have a house here and spent the whole summer here. I got to swim in their pool every day!"

"I bet that was a lot of fun."

"Oh my God, it was! You should come."

"It's a date next summer," he said with a wink and she grinned. "Okay, now your stick," he said, and she directed her attention to what he was doing as he taped it very carefully. It was a little too careful for a kid's stick, but he wanted it to be perfect. He wanted her to be confident, and if he was going to be Jayden's replacement, he was going to be the best damn replacement in the world.

He had to impress Angie…and maybe her mom too.

He wasn't sure why, though. That chick practically had signs hanging off her blinking brightly that she was more than unavailable. Yet something made him want to tear down the signs, take that face of hers in his hands, and kiss the stuffing out of her. She had the right lips, the bottom one bigger than the top, all cushiony looking, and those eyes… Man, he had never seen such green depths in his life. Her lashes were dark, her hair even darker, and she was gorgeous. She was like a cat. Angry, but he bet he could make her purr.

What in the…? God, he was a loser.

"Wow, that looks hard," Angie said, apprehension in her voice.

"Don't worry, sweetheart. We'll practice."

He hadn't meant to call her that, but thankfully, she beamed up at him as he tore the tape and then handed her the stick. "How's that feel?"

She stood up on her skates and tested the stick like a pro. Or better yet, like a little girl who was trained by three older, hockey-playing uncles. Benji knew all about the Sinclairs. Hell, he was sure everyone did. They had legacy written all over them—all strong, all fast, and all pretty badass. All drafted first, and it was the first time that had happened to three brothers. The NHL boasted about the three, and if they weren't so damn good, Benji would call bullshit. But they were good. Really good.

But still, it bothered him that Lucy Sinclair had been lost in all the hoopla of her brothers. He hadn't even known she existed until today.

Too bad.

He thought she should be the shining star.

"It's good," she said and Benji nodded at her form.

"Looks good, Sinclair."

"Hart."

His brows rose. Duh, Lucy must be married. "Sorry?"

"My last name is Hart. It's my dad's name."

He nodded. "Oh, my bad. Sorry about that."

"It's fine. I usually don't care. Everyone else is a Sinclair in my family, and my uncles call me 'Sinclair' because they hate my dad. But I told Mom I want my jersey to have my dad's name, so hopefully, he'll come to my games." She seemed unsure and that pissed Benji off.

"I'm sure he will."

She shrugged. "He doesn't want me to play. He thinks I should dance like my sister."

So Lucy wasn't married?

"Oh, you don't want to?" With his gaze on her as she pressed her stick into the ground, he slid his gloves on.

"Eh, I mean, I do because he takes me on his weekends. But I'd rather be playing hockey. Plus Heidi is so annoying and tells my dad I have to do it because I'm so tomboyish. But I'm not, she just doesn't like me much."

Okay, he was remarried, but was Lucy?

"Wow, that sounds like bullshi— Er, my bad," he pleaded and she grinned.

"Don't worry, Mom says bad words all the time and she apologizes. But I know she can't help it. I know I'm not supposed to say them, and that's all that matters. Yeah, I don't like dance, but I love hockey. I want to be like my uncles, or even my aunt Baylor. She's amazing."

"She is," he agreed before leaning over to whisper to her. "And also hockey is the best," he said with a wink and she grinned back at him.

"Absolutely!"

Standing up, he reached for his stick and then cocked his head toward the rink. "You ready, Hart?"

She pushed the cage of her helmet down and locked it in place. "I was born ready."

Determined little thing, he thought as he tapped her on the head. He liked her. Starting for the rink, he looked down but noticed she hadn't moved yet. Stopping, he looked back at her. "Hart?"

She smiled up at him through the cage. "Thanks for this. You're a great replacement."

Clipping the strap of his helmet to the other side, he nodded. "Thanks, I hope I do ya right."

"You are," she said as they started for the rink where Adler and most of the girls were already skating around. "Mom won't tell you that, though."

When he glanced over to where Lucy was watching, her phone resting on the tips of her fingers, he smiled. "No?"

"No, Jayden says she's mad all the time, and I guess she is to them. But she's awesome to me."

Benji grinned. "I don't think she's mad."

"Oh, she is, but I love her." When Angie waved wildly at Lucy, she smiled big, a real one that reached her eyes as she blew Angie a kiss and pumped her fist in the air, cheering her name. "She's basically the best mom ever."

"She seems like it."

Lucy's eyes cut to Benji's, her eyes narrowing as her lips went into a straight line. It was easy to tell that she didn't like him. For no reason at all, of course, except that Jayden set him up to be hated from the jump. But he didn't mind. He liked her, and her sassy mouth and resting bitch face wouldn't stop him. No, he'd change her mind. He'd get her to like him.

Wow. What?

As his foot hit the ice, he almost busted his ass and he braced himself with his stick as Angie laughed.

"It's ice, it's slippery," she teased and he grinned.

Smartass.

But instead of saying that, he found himself looking up to where Lucy sat.

Grinning.

A little kitten grin.

That shot hot desire straight into his soul.

Ooh-wee, she's trouble.

The kind of trouble he was starting to think he needed in his life.

Chapter THREE

"All right, ladies… Ladies," Shea hollered out.

But the girls didn't stop giggling or laughing as most of them fell, while the others did circles around them. It was like the Bad News Bears, well, except Angie. She stood beside Benji, her eyes on Shea and her stick hanging in her hand. She was determined, and he didn't know why, but a grin sat on his face. He liked that she was ready and focused. It really didn't matter, but in a way, it made him proud.

Shea hollered out some more, but it was easy to tell that he was taking it easy on the group of girls. Like Angie, though, his girls, Shelli and Posey, stood tall in front of their father, waiting for instruction. Shelli was built like Shea, big and tall, while Posey was on the chubbier side, a little shorter, but just as determined as her older sister.

"This is a fucking clusterfuck." Glancing over at Vaughn, Benji scoffed.

"Eh, it's the first day. Adler's feeling out the crowd."

It was easy to see the frustration on Shea's face and Benji almost laughed. The guy was used to leading a bunch of grown men who all had the same mindset as him. To win. Now he was dealing with a bunch of girls who did not have that mind-set. At. All.

"He's right. This is insane," Angie said up to him and Vaughn nodded.

"Exactly, cutie patootie. What's your name?"

"Not cutie patootie," she said with a bit of sass in her voice, reminding Benji of Lucy. "Angie Hart."

Holding his glove out for a fist bump, Angie did as he wanted and he said, "Nice to meet ya, Hart. I'm Johansson."

She only nodded before looking back up to where Shea was telling people to quiet down. Vaughn leaned in. "Sinclair's niece?"

"Yup."

"She's scary for being so little."

Benji laughed. "You should meet her mom."

As Benji cocked his head to where Lucy was sitting, Vaughn's mouth dropped. "Holy crap, it's Sinclair in a skirt with tits."

Benji rolled his eyes. "Whatever."

"No, really, that's Sinclair. Wow, those genes are strong. She's hot, though. Single?"

Benji cut him a look, nodding his head toward Angie, but Vaughn just shrugged. "I'm whispering,"

"And I can still hear you," Angie said then, looking up at him. "She's single, but believe me, you aren't her type."

Vaughn was taken aback, but Benji just laughed.

Finally, almost like he had just remembered he had a whistle, Shea blew into it and silence fell over the ice. "Ladies. Wow. First things first—"

"He's the realest," Benji and Angie said at the same time under their breath before meeting each other's gaze. When she grinned up at him, Benji paused, his heart hurting a bit.

He liked her.

A lot.

What a great kid.

"I'm your coach, Shea Adler. You can call me Coach Adler," Shea said, his voice booming through the rink. "I'm excited to be coaching you girls. Just a little bit about me, in case you don't know who I am—"

"Everyone knows who he is," Angie said then, and Benji nodded as Shea went on.

"I played in the NHL for a lotta years. I have four Stanley Cup rings, and I was very successful—"

"Why'd you leave, though? My daddy says you had a least ten more years in ya," Number Ten said, and a lot of the girls nodded, agreeing that their daddies had said the same.

Shea smiled, glancing over at his daughters. "I wanted to coach my kids, and I have this nagging pain in my shoulder, so it was time."

"You quit to coach a bunch of kids?" Number Thirty asked.

Shea nodded, his smile not faltering. "I always said I wanted to coach my kids when they wanted to play. Shelli and Posey said they were ready to play, so I retired."

Wow, that was some love right there. Benji had always been awestruck by Shea Adler. Since day one, the guy leaked awesomeness. He was a leader, and a damn honest man, but the love in his eyes for his daughters was breathtaking. He loved those girls—and his boys. He was just an all-around good man, and Benji respected his choice. Yeah, he wished like hell they hadn't lost him on the team so early, but Shea loved his kids and his wife, way more than the sport.

Which was a beautiful thing and Benji craved that kind of love.

Man, to be loved and to love someone more than he loved his stick and puck, he almost couldn't fathom it now. It seemed so foreign to him. Yeah, he'd had that love, for a little bit. But back then, he was so drunk he couldn't remember what it felt like—to be consumed by such a love. He wanted that again.

But how?

And did he even deserve it?

He wasn't sure, but as Shea spoke about his years and years in the league, Benji realized Shea did miss playing. Who wouldn't? It was the greatest sport ever. Benji loved hockey. It was his go-to, his identifier; he'd been playing since he was a baby. It was something he and his dad always did together, every day. Not so much now, since he hadn't spoken to his mom or dad in almost ten years, but he still had good memories of the long nights in the driveway, playing some stick and puck with his dad. Back when he spoke to his family. Back when they loved and supported him. Back when Silas was alive and begged to be their goalie.

He missed those times.

He missed his family.

Jesus, he thought, shaking his head and swallowing hard around the painful lump in his throat. His memories were flooding him like mad today, which wasn't unusual—he was lonely—but today was different. He may need to call Richie after practice. Just a quick check-in with his sponsor since he hadn't done it in the last three days. He was due.

"Thinking again?" Angie whispered up to him and he looked down at her, shrugging.

"Yeah, sorry."

"He's calling your name."

Benji looked up, meeting Shea's expectant gaze. "That's Coach Benji, who is off in his own world, and Coach Vaughn. I used to play with them on the Assassins."

Benji waved awkwardly as Vaughn rolled his eyes, waving too at his name.

"Coach Benji is here in replacement of Coach Jayden, so don't get too attached to him."

He heard Angie complain beside him, and he was two seconds from doing the same. He liked this and he hadn't even really gotten started; he'd need to talk to Shea. He felt right here. Like this was something he needed to do. He hadn't felt like that in a really long time, and that had to mean something.

After blowing his whistle once more, Shea broke everyone up into groups. Benji got group two, which included Angie. He had three drills he was supposed to run with the six little girls, and as they skated toward the other side of the rink, he thanked his lucky stars because he had all the kids who had played last year. They knew the drills, ran them like champs, well, except Angie.

"It's okay. You haven't done them before," he reassured her as she skated back, upset. He was starting to think he had misread her at the beginning. She might have been nervous instead of determined and focused. Each time, though, she watched the first three go to the blue line and back. He kept trying to reassure her, but more and more, he noticed her anxiety was getting worse. Until finally, when he blew the whistle, she stood there frozen as the other two girls raced around the cone, picking the puck up and going through the many little cones that were set up. So he blew the whistle again, but she didn't move.

Okay, then.

Lowering down into a squat, Benji met her worried gaze. Well, more like panicked. "Hart?"

"I keep messing up," she whispered, looking away.

He leaned down to meet her gaze again, seeing the tears gathering in her eyes. "It's okay. What's wrong?"

"I'm nervous."

"Why?"

"I don't want to mess up."

He smiled. "We all mess up, Angie. It's how we pick ourselves back up and try harder. Don't worry. You got this."

She swallowed hard, looking around as her teammates watched her. She looked to Lucy and he did the same, seeing that Lucy was standing now, her face full of worry. "I think I—"

But he shook his head. "You don't want to go home. I know you don't. You want to do this."

She met his gaze once more, a little more determination in her eyes. "I do."

"Then, go. Come on, we'll do it together."

"Together?"

"Yup, I bet you can't beat me," he said, standing and putting his stick down, ready to go.

Her lips curved as her eyes filled with excitement. "Yes, I can!"

His grin matched hers as he brought the whistle to his lips. "Let's go."

As he blew the whistle, she shot off, and he was behind her, running around the cones and sliding the puck around the little cones that were there for stick handling. Like he knew she would, she flew through the course, almost at the rate he did—he was maybe a few seconds in front of her. But when he finished, he faked a leg cramp and hit the ice, sliding to the finish as the little girls laughed and Angie rushed back, finishing with ease.

Turning, she pinned him with a look as he slowly got up, favoring his "cramped" leg. "My leg cramped. That's why you beat me."

"Sure," she said, her eyes bright with no anxiety to be seen. As he held his glove out, she tapped it and then nodded. "Thanks, Benji."

He tipped his chin to her and then blew the whistle once more, the next group going as Angie went to the back of the line. They were having a blast by the seventh time they did it, and Benji was convinced he had the best group of girls. As he watched the girls round the cones, his eyes diverted to where Angie's mom sat, her eyes on them intently. She held her face with one hand, the other holding her phone as she watched. She looked a little panicky, almost nervous and vulnerable.

He smiled, though, for her, but Lucy rolled her eyes and moved her gaze toward where Angie was about to go again. Man, she really didn't like him, but he was sure that wasn't his fault. He was a good enough guy, nice, and obviously awesome since Angie liked him. No, there was more to it. He didn't know the whole story—how could he? But man, he really wanted to.

He wanted to know her.

Which was crazy since he'd never wanted to know any woman but Ava. Though, something was different with Lucy. Maybe it was because she was so shut down. He wasn't sure, but he wanted to know her story. He suspected that her ex-husband was a douche and didn't treat them right. That had to be the reason why Angie was so nervous, almost too scared to do anything in case she failed. Or maybe Benji was way off. One thing was for sure, while she was with him, she was going to be reassured and she was going to be supported.

Because that sweet little girl had wiggled her way into his heart in the mere hour they had been together.

And for some reason, he wanted to be more than just the replacement for her uncle.

He wanted to be her friend.

That wasn't weird, right?

Crap.

Maybe it was.

But when Angie looked back at him for reassurance after killing it and beating the other girls back to the line, he figured, yeah, it may be weird to want to be friends with a seven-year-old girl, but he didn't care. This was supposed to have been his life now, but he'd lost his daughter and didn't get to have that chance. For so long, he had been lonely. Holed up in his house, all by himself, but being on this rink, surrounded by these mini-players and Angie, he felt right. Maybe this was his calling, following in Shea's footsteps. Coach a team one day, because he was having a blast.

And it was time for Benji to be happy.

If coaching a bunch of girls three times a week could do that, he was going to do it.

Practice was over before Benji knew it. They even had a little scrimmage at the end. Nothing crazy, but when Angie scored, you would have thought he had been the one to score. He was so excited and Angie ate it up. Lucy was in the stands, hollering her butt off too, but she didn't smile when he sent her a grin. She probably thought he was strange. Oh well, he probably was. For as much as he'd thought about her in the last two hours after just meeting her, he was starting to think he was an odd one.

Keeping the puck from Angie as the girls started to clear off the ice, Benji was laughing with Angie when Shea blew the whistle. "Come on, guys, they gotta clean the ice for the next group."

"Aww, man," Angie complained and Benji tapped her helmet.

"Don't worry. I'll get your mom to bring you early on Wednesday, and we'll do a little pickup before practice."

Her eyes lit up as her grin almost broke her face. "You're coming back!"

"Yeah, you're coming back?" Shea asked with a grin as they skated toward him.

"Yeah, when I can. We have a road trip coming up, so I might miss a lot more than I get to come."

Shea nodded. "I appreciate the help, of course."

Benji tapped gloves with him as he went off the ice to find Elli Adler kissing on her daughters. "Y'all did so good! I'm so proud. Boys, get off there!"

Benji grinned at where her three boys were jumping off the stands.

"They're boys, babe, let 'em be."

She shot him a look. "Oh, stay-at-home dad now, think you can handle broken bones?"

He cringed but still kept a grin on his face. "Hey, I've had my fair share. I can handle it."

Sending Benji a sideways glance, she rolled her eyes. "He'd cry."

"Hey!" Shea complained and Elli shared a laugh with Benji before patting his chest.

"Glad to see you out."

He grinned and shrugged. "It's good to be out."

"Angie, honey?" They all looked to where Lucy was standing, her eyes on Angie. "Ready?"

"Yeah, Mom. See ya, Coach. Come on, Benji," she said, pulling him along.

"Lucy, how are you?" Elli called to her and Lucy smiled, taking Angie's hand before coming toward them.

"Good, you?"

"Good, thanks. How's Baylor? I haven't gotten an update."

Lucy shook her head. "I haven't either. My brother is currently ignoring my calls."

Elli's brows rose and Shea laughed. "He didn't tell her he wasn't coming tonight. Sent Benji instead."

Elli tsked. "Brat, but hey, Benji is wonderful."

"Yeah, he is," Angie agreed and Benji's face warmed from the praise. But when he glanced to Lucy, she didn't seem convinced.

"Yeah, I might make it to where Jayden can't have children. Haven't decided." She said it so matter-of-factly, like it was as easy as swatting a fly.

Scary.

Elli and Shea grinned as Benji winced. "As long as he can skate and score, I don't care what you do to him."

Lucy grinned, pointing to Elli. "I got you, boss."

"Thanks, love, and I'm very excited about our appointment at the end of the week."

Shea looked confused. "Appointment?"

"She's gonna decorate our summer home in Florida."

Shea made a face. "God, how much is that gonna cost? We're poor now, Lucy. I don't play anymore."

Lucy laughed and, wow, what a sound. Watching as her face lit up and she shook her head, Benji found himself smiling too. Laughing looked so much better on that girl. She really should do that more. "Sure you are, Shea. Don't worry, y'all get the family discount."

"Thank God," he breathed and Elli smacked him.

"Anyway, let me know when you want to have a sleepover for the girls. Shelli and Posey have been asking for Angie to come over."

Wrapping her arm around Angie, Lucy nodded. "Will do. See y'all. Great practice, Shea."

Shea beamed. "Thanks! See ya Wednesday, Angie."

"Bye!"

When Angie started to pull Benji along, Lucy looked down at their hands and then to Angie. "Let go of the replacement, Angie."

"Mom! His name is Benji." Angie laughed and shook Benji's hand. "Plus, he's gotta ask you something."

Lucy's face twisted in confusion before looking up at Benji. Her eyes bored into his, and man… Was he breathless? Jesus, she was gorgeous. "Yeah?"

Confused, Benji looked at Angie. "I do?"

Still laughing, she rolled her eyes. "Yes! About Wednesday."

"Oh!" he laughed, tapping her head again, but when he looked up at Lucy, she was glaring at him. Man, Sinclair wasn't kidding about that resting bitch face…such a pretty girl, though. Hm. Well, it was about Angie, not her. "Yeah, I was wondering if you could bring her earlier Wednesday so we can get some pickup time in before everyone else hits the ice."

Lucy's brows came in, a little wrinkle appearing between her brows. "So you're, what, doing this full time now? Did you talk to Jayden?"

He shook his head. "No, not at all, but I had a great time tonight and decided to help out as much as I can."

Her face didn't change. "Don't you have to play?"

He shrugged. "Yeah, but I'll work it out. I might miss more than I can come, but I want to come when I can."

Still unsure, she held his gaze. "So you willingly want to do this when you have no child on the team? Or do you?"

Swallowing hard, he shook his head. "No child on the team, but I enjoy it."

"Hanging with a bunch of seven- through ten-year-olds?" she asked, deadpan. "I'm sure you have better things to do."

"Mom!" Angie complained. "You love hanging with me."

"'Cause you are my everything," Lucy said simply, her eyes never leaving Benji's. "I'm not trying to be rude—"

"No?"

She faltered a bit. "I'm just saying, seems like a guy like you would have something better to do."

Benji smiled. "Considering you don't know what a guy like me likes to do, I find your assessment of me a little unfair. But I'll tell ya a story—I'm boring and this was a lot of fun."

Lucy's eyes narrowed but she nodded slowly. "I'll see what I can do about Wednesday. I have a meeting that day, so getting her here at five is cutting it close."

"Can't Jayden bring me? I can play with both of them!"

Lucy cupped her face and smiled. "Ew, you're gross! All sweaty," she laughed. "But, yes, if your uncle ever answers my calls and he's alive, then we'll have him bring you."

"Well, if he can't, let me know and I'll come get her for you."

Why in the hell did he say that?

Lucy looked up, her eyes wide, and Angie grinned happily. "Cool! Mom, that works, right?"

Her look said, no, no it didn't. Benji knew that but he smiled just the same. "Not trying to sound like a creeper—"

"Eh, riding the line, buddy," she said more under her breath, but he heard her loud and clear. Who could blame her? Some strange dude asking to pick her daughter up? He'd punch a guy who said it, so he didn't blame her. He still felt a little dejected as he met her gaze, though, praying she saw he wasn't a creepy bad guy.

"But I can help out if need be."

Lucy only nodded, her eyes burning into his. He didn't think she thought he was a perv, but it was obvious she didn't trust him. Hell, he was sure she didn't trust anyone, which was sad and only made him believe he was right about the ex. As he held her gaze, her eyes staring into his, he swore he saw a little heat in her eyes. Then, maybe he was an idiot because just as quickly, she was nodding as she said, "Yeah, okay. Angie, say bye. Let's go."

Angie grinned up at him and held her fist out for him to bump. "Thanks for all the help. You really helped me out."

"Anytime," he said, bumping her fist. "I'll see you Wednesday."

"Cool," she cheered and then she looked up to Lucy. "Mom?"

"What?" As Angie jerked her head to Benji, he smiled as Lucy looked over at him confused. "What?"

"Don't you want to thank him?"

Lucy made a put out kind of face but quickly masked it with a winning, fake grin. "Thank you so much for helping my daughter on the ice. You are by far the coolest dude ever and not creepy at all."

Benji laughed. "Have you ever heard that you attract more bees with honey than vinegar?"

Holding his gaze, her lip quirked. "Good thing I don't like honey...or bees."

"Guess so," he agreed, her eyes darkening in color. "But either way, it was really nice to meet you. When I woke up this morning, I really didn't think I'd meet someone like you."

"One of a kind," she said with a wink, her lips quirking once more, almost like she was going to laugh. Instead, she waved. "See ya around."

"Look forward to it."

And he did.

She was sassy and she was suffering from resting bitch face, but maybe all she needed was someone to make her smile. Someone to make her laugh. As she walked away, she looked back, her eyes playful before replying to whatever Angie had said. All Benji could do was watch her walk. Her ass was killer and his palms itched to touch it. He wondered if she knew he was thinking of holding her ass because she glared before rolling her eyes.

When a hand came crashing down on his shoulder, he looked over to meet Vaughn's profile.

"She turned me down. Called me an idgit."

"Idgit?"

"Yeah, she's an angry one. Stay away from her," he said, shaking his head, but when he glanced back at Benji, he let his head fall back. "Shit, you like her?"

Benji shrugged. "She's different."

"Yeah, mean as a possum!"

"A possum?"

Vaughn's eyes widened. "Yeah, dude. Mean. Those things are mean. She's mean."

Shaking his head, Benji grinned. "No, she just acts mean to keep people away."

"Yeah, so stay away."

"Don't know if I can."

Letting out a long breath, Vaughn shook his head as Benji watched her untie Angie's skates. He wasn't sure if what he was saying was true, but a part of him really believed he wanted to know Lucy. Past the snark. Past the angry persona.

The real Lucy Sinclair.

"It won't end well," Vaughn warned.

Benji knew that.

So that meant one thing.

It couldn't end.

"Benji is so cool, Mom, like, really. He was so funny and kept, like, telling me I'm awesome and everything. Everyone loves him. He challenged all of us. And, come on, he plays in the NHL, Mom. He's, like, the best. But he let all of us win! He's so cool. Don't you think he's cool?"

"He's something," Lucy said under her breath as she pulled out of the parking spot and drove off. Something like hot and supernice. She couldn't help but watch the guy on the ice. He was huge! And he treated those little girls like they were in tutus with crowns on their heads. He was so attentive. So sweet and she didn't miss how he kept looking at her. She wasn't sure why, but it was nice.

When she actually allowed herself to enjoy it.

"That's wonderful, baby," she said to Angie and she beamed, continuing on about how wonderful Benji Paxton was.

But as much as Lucy wanted to listen and maybe even agree that Benji was supersweet with the kids, she couldn't shake the earlier text exchange with Rick.

Rick: Hey, I'm picking up Angie early Friday. I'll pick her up from school.
Lucy: I told you she has hockey on Fridays, that we'll be about 30 mins late to meet you at Walmart.
Rick: Okay, well that doesn't work. Heidi wants to take her to get her hair done.
Lucy: She doesn't need her hair done. I just had it cut the other day.
Rick: No, I mean like some kind of hairdo for the recital.
Lucy: What recital?
Rick: The one Saturday morning.
Lucy: You told me it was two weeks from now.
Rick: Did I?
Lucy: Yes. Whatever. Where do I get tickets?
Rick: They're sold out.
Rick: I thought you had already gotten them.
Lucy: Wow. Okay, so you didn't get me one, obviously. Whatever, Rick, I'll figure it out.
Rick: Yeah, okay, so I'll pick her up from school?
Lucy: No, you won't. You can get her at 7 at Walmart like we planned.
Rick: Are you serious?
Lucy: Yeah, I am.
Rick: You're so damn childish.

But Lucy ignored him.

She knew he did that on purpose, and she was done talking to him. She was so over him it wasn't even funny, and like always, he had ruined her whole night. Thankfully, she was able to call Jude's wife, Claire, who was one of the directors of the dance studio, and she took care of them. Even got tickets for her mom, River, Jayden, and Baylor. It was fucking avoidable, but then with Rick Hart, nothing was avoidable. He was an asshole, but she'd be damned if she was not going to be there for her baby at her fall recital. Angie didn't even like dance, but whatever.

If Rick wanted his reign as King of the Dicks to continue, that was cool, she'd deal.

As long as Angie was happy, that was all she cared about. The moment Angie wasn't, though, crazy Lucy was coming out.

"Don't you think Benji is, like, superawesome, Mom?"

Looking in the mirror, Lucy smiled. Benji probably thought she was thirty shades of crazy. She shouldn't have been so snarky with him, but she couldn't help it. Her life was one bad day after another lately, and dealing with Rick really fucked with her. It wasn't Benji's fault, though, and she'd apologize.

When she got around to it.

"He was nice."

"Right? So funny. Did you see him almost die when he got on the ice?"

Lucy snorted. "I did, I laughed."

"Me too! I laughed so hard and told him it was ice, that it's slippery. He gave me that look you do."

That's my smartass, Lucy thought with a grin as she turned onto the interstate. "I would have said the same thing."

"Right? I knew you would!"

Smiling, Lucy went into the other lane as silence fell on the car while she drove. As the car went from dark to darker from the street lights, Lucy realized she was dog tired and ready to hit the hay. It had been a long day, and she was still so angry with Jayden. She also didn't like how she felt about Benji. He was too nice, but then, he didn't give off that creeper vibe. Just a nice guy, which was odd. She didn't even think those guys existed. And the ones who did were married.

She almost thought Angie was asleep until she said, "Hey, Mom, I have to go to Dad's this weekend, don't I?"

Clearing her throat, Lucy nodded. "Yeah, baby."

"Ugh, I don't like going over there."

Her heart broke a bit as she met her baby's eyes. "I know, baby, but Dad wants to see you too."

Angie shrugged. "All he cares about are Heidi and Nina."

"Why would you say that?"

"'Cause he doesn't ever want to go to anything I like. It's only what they want."

"I'll talk to him," Lucy announced, because that was not fucking okay.

"No, don't. Y'all will just fight and I don't want that," Angie said sadly. "I just miss Grandma—and River."

Of course she did. They had been living with her mom since she left Rick. "We can go see them when I pick you up on Sunday, okay?"

Angie nodded, looking out the window. "What about Jude and Claire, and Jace and Avery and Ashlyn? I miss them too."

Another problem with having such a close-knit family, they all missed each other so much. "Well, we are going to Florida after Christmas and staying with Jace and Avery and baby Ashlyn. And Jude and Claire are coming for

Christmas and I think at the end of January, if Jude doesn't get invited to the All-Star Game."

"Which he probably will. He's, like, the best."

Lucy laughed. "Please don't tell him that."

Angie giggled. "Mom! You know it's true."

"Yeah, yeah," Lucy agreed with a smile and Angie grinned back at her just as her phone started ringing.

Jayden's ringtone.

"Ooooooh, he's in so much trouble," Angie sang as Lucy nodded in agreement, hitting answer on her steering wheel.

"Jayden Mitchell."

"Should I duck when I see you next?" he asked wryly.

"I would."

"Okay, listen, I'm sorry. I'm a coward, but I thought you wouldn't take her if I wasn't gonna be there."

She made a face. "Whatever. I'd take her no matter what. You don't need to apologize to me, you need to apologize to her. She was nervous. You know how she can get."

He made a sound of defeat and cleared his throat. "Angie, baby, I'm sorry."

"It's okay, Jay," she giggled. "Mommy was soooo mad!"

He chuckled. "I know. I'm a jerk. Do you forgive me?"

"Of course!"

"Lucy?"

"I am thinking of a long list of bad words that I could include with no, but Angie's in the car."

"Thank God," he breathed and Lucy smiled. "But really, I'm sorry."

"Whatever."

"I love youuuuu," he sang and Lucy smiled.

"I love you too, but I'm still mad."

"I know, I'm sorry. But please tell me you didn't hit my boy, BP?"

"BP?" Lucy asked confused.

"Benji Paxton? He showed, right?"

"Oh yeah! He was soooooooooooo awesome, Jayden! He's coming Wednesday too," Angie cheered and Jayden laughed.

"Cool dude, huh?"

"I don't know. Who volunteers to coach a bunch of girls? Seems a little unusual to me."

"He's a really great guy. I seriously only had to call, and he didn't even question me. Just said he'd be there," Jayden said, which didn't change Lucy's mind. She didn't like him. Or maybe, she didn't like that she thought he was hot. Or nice.

Man, she was fucked in the head.

"Can't he just be nice, Mom?" Angie asked and Lucy shrugged. She wouldn't allow herself to tell her daughter that no man was like that unless they were disgusting perverts.

"Or a child molester," she said under her breath, and Jayden sucked in a breath.

"Seriously, Luce?"

"What?" she asked innocently and Angie made a face. "It was a joke."

"What'd she say?" Angie asked.

"Nothing," they said at the same time.

"But a really, really cool dude. Supernice, and that's awesome that he wants to keep helping. He's kind of a hermit."

"A hermit?"

"Yeah, he doesn't get out much. He's quiet."

"No, he's not. He was superfunny," Angie complained and Jayden chuckled.

"Weirdoooo," Lucy sang and Angie glared.

"Mom!"

"Sorry," she said, rolling her eyes. Apparently everyone was a fan of Benji, but she was not and she needed a topic change. "So how's Baylor?"

Sucking in a breath, Jayden let it out slowly. "Not good. They are pretty sure she'll need another surgery, and even then, they aren't sure if she'll be fixed. She cried the whole way home. Coach is trying to convince her to retire from the NHL. That he can get her a job at Bellevue as a girls' coach or even a guys' coach."

Lucy shook her head, her heart dropping for her sister-in-law. Baylor's dad, who was marrying their mom, was the coach at Bellevue University. He had been saying he'd get her a job for the last year. No one wanted to see Baylor get hurt anymore. It was getting really scary. "Yeah, what are you thinking?"

He didn't answer right away, but when he did, the emotion was thick in his throat. "I don't know how many more times I can take watching my wife get hurt on the ice. I'm so worried about her that it's affecting my game."

Exactly, she thought as she cleared her throat. "You tell her that?"

"Not yet. She's sleeping right now. I'll talk to her in the morning."

"Okay, tell her that, though, Jay. Promise me."

He paused and she knew he didn't want to. Baylor was proud and didn't take well to not being the best, but it had gone too far. She was getting hurt more than she was playing. As awesome as it was that she was in the NHL, it just wasn't worth it. She was in constant pain and it was taking a toll on their relationship. They both knew that. "Yeah, I promise."

"Thanks," Lucy said softly.

"I'll text you if she doesn't kill me."

"I was gonna request that," Lucy laughed and he chuckled. He sounded so tired and that worried her. He was a fix-it kind of guy. Always worried about everyone else and not himself. He'd run himself into the ground before he would let anyone down. He was just a really all-around great guy like that. She did well helping raise him.

Clearing his throat, he said, "So, this weekend is the recital? Eleven?"

Her worry for her brother disappeared as white-hot anger came back. Stupid Rick. "Yup. Rick just decided to tell me today. Thankfully, our sister-in-law helps run that place."

"What are you talking about?" Angie asked.

"Your dance recital."

Meeting her gaze, Angie made a face. "I thought that was in two weeks."

Fucking douche.

Jayden muttered something along the same lines as Lucy shook her head. "Nope, this weekend."

"Hm. Okay," she said simply and Lucy rolled her eyes.

"Okay, well, we are almost home. Call me tomorrow. Get some sleep, Jay."

"I sound tired?"

"You do."

He laughed as Lucy smiled. "All right, love you guys."

"Love you," they both said and Lucy hung up as she pulled onto the street her apartment was on. Letting out a long breath, Lucy was pretty sure she could hear her bed calling her name. She wouldn't keep it waiting much longer. She was ready to fall face first into the happiness of her bed.

She parked and reached for her purse, but before she could get out, Angie wrapped her arms around Lucy's neck and kissed her cheek. "I love you, Mommy."

Relaxing as her lips curved, Lucy leaned into her daughter's head. "I love you too, honey. Did you have fun tonight?"

"I did. I love hockey so much and Coach Adler is so awesome and Benji was so much fun."

"Good, I'm glad."

"You should be nice to him."

"I am," Lucy said, looking over at her.

But Angie gave her a deadpan look. "You think he's weird."

She shrugged. "Doesn't mean I'm not nice."

"Mom, come on, just give him a chance. He's supercool. I think you'd love him."

Looking into her daughter's sweet green eyes, Lucy couldn't bring herself to tell her that she'd never love anyone again. How could she? Nope, she'd let her baby think that there were good, loving men out there, but Lucy knew the truth.

But she said, "I'll try."

"Don't try, do," Angie said, using her words against her. "He really is great. Really."

"Okay," she agreed and Angie must have been pleased with that answer because she kissed her on the cheek loudly before getting out of the car. As Lucy gathered her things, she pushed the door open and couldn't help but think about the fact that Benji made one hell of an impression on her sweet girl. That should mean something to her. Should impress her, but it didn't.

Not really.

Okay. Maybe a little.

But it didn't matter.

Because Benji Paxton wasn't the guy for her.

Hell, no man was.

Chapter FOUR

Leaning against the boards, Benji watched as the Stars rushed the puck into the Assassins' zone. Their offense was on fire, their passes were lethal, and that damn Seguin kid was a superstar. Within seconds and without anyone really noticing, he top-shelved it, hitting the top of the net over the head of Odder, the Assassins' goalie.

Goal.

Fuck.

Leaning back, Benji shook his head, taking a long pull of Gatorade. The Assassins needed more depth in their defense. Their defense was made of all kids, except for Benji, Sinclair, Karson King, and Jordie Thomas. Coach had paired Benji with Sinclair, and then King and Thomas were together, so the other line was kids from the AHL. They needed some power in the back because, even though they were stacked in the offense department and they had a great goalie, there had to be someone to help Odder out.

At least, he thought so.

Letting out a long breath, he looked up at the Jumbotron and saw they were one down with seven minutes left.

"Time to do work," he said with conviction to the guys around him, Vaughn on one side and Sinclair on the other.

"Yup," Vaughn agreed, basically bouncing on the bench.

"Let's do this," Sinclair said just as Coach called out their line, twenty seconds after the puck dropped. Going over the boards, he rushed to where the

46

puck was left for him behind the goal. As Benji's boys set up, Tate tapped his stick to the ice in hopes of riling up the boys. The crowd was loud; they loved their team and Benji loved them. Time to make them proud.

Carrying the puck out, Benji shot it up, hard, down the middle to where Erik Titov was waiting. But when he went to pass it to Vaughn, who was basically in the net with the Stars' goalie, one of the Stars blocked the pass. Passing it up to another player, he took it, racing down the middle and catching the Assassins on a two-on-one.

Benji was the one.

"Fucking hell," he yelled as Sinclair pushed hard to get back down. He wouldn't make it. The Stars player passed it to the other one, and he looked as if he was going to shoot. So Benji dropped down, stretching his body completely out in the hopes that, if he did pass it, Benji would block it. Praying to God above, he closed his eyes, hoping he didn't get hit in the mouth.

Dude did shoot, and it didn't hit Benji in the mouth.

But it hurt.

Right in the spot below his ribs where his pads weren't protecting.

Gasping for breath, he popped up just as Sinclair came in, taking the puck and passing it back up. Going straight for the bench, Benji tried to watch as their offense did work, but he missed when they scored the tying goal. The arena went nuts, as did the bench while Benji sat down, the pain still very much stinging in his chest. As Anderson skated, tapping his glove to everyone, he pointed to Benji.

"Wouldn't be tied if it wasn't for you, BP. Attaboy!" he called out with an extra tap on Benji's head.

He nodded, a grin pulling at his lips as the trainer came over to make sure he was okay. He told him he was, and he was sure of it. It would be a nasty bruise later, but for now, he had a game to win.

But even though the Assassins fought, the Stars scored two more times, winning the game.

Benji hated losing games. Probably more than he hated when someone died on *Game of Thrones*. Which was basically everyone, but whatever. He hated it. Especially when Coach ripped into them. He was loud, he was mad, and who could blame him? The defense let Odder down and Benji didn't like that. Every goal that was shot was something the defense should have blocked. It should have been easy for Odder, but when his own team was blocking him, how was he supposed to do his job?

They had some work to do.

Leaning back in his locker, Benji sucked in a breath and let it out before he gently eased his jersey off, wincing at the pain.

"Jesus, you got stung bad," Sinclair said from his left, and he nodded as he

touched the aching spot very lightly. The pain was red-hot.

"Fuck, it hurts."

"Nothing is broken, though?"

Benji shook his head. "I don't think so. We'll see tomorrow." Sinclair nodded as he leaned against his legs, pulling in a breath. "We need to work on the kids. The goals tonight shouldn't have been scored," Benji announced.

"Agreed. We'll take care of it tomorrow," Sinclair said, letting out a breath. "I mean, I get that I'm young like them too, but they were making careless mistakes."

"That's what I think."

"Oh, well, we'll get there."

"That's right," Benji agreed, continuing to take deep breaths to ease the pain.

"So, I know you're hurting and you can turn me down, but Baylor and I wanted to take you to dinner, if you're hungry."

Looking over at his captain, Benji smiled. Ordinarily, he'd turn him down. He wasn't much for going out after games. Usually, the guys went for drinks or to party after a win. Benji was more of a go home or to the hotel and chill kind of guy. That's just what he did, and he figured that was why Sinclair looked so wary when asking. But what he didn't know was that Benji hadn't stopped thinking about Sinclair's sister since Monday night.

It was getting bad. Like, he stalked her Facebook, her Instagram, and even her Twitter. He found that she really didn't post on Twitter, or even Facebook, but that girl's Instagram was loaded with pictures and videos of Angie. Some of Lucy too. One in particular that he couldn't get out of his head was her on the beach this past summer. She had a baby in her arms, her thin, sexy body curvy in every way possible, and the smile on her face was gorgeous. It made her ten times more beautiful than he already thought she was, and he still couldn't shake the image.

He wanted Lucy.

Bad.

So with a nod, he said, "I'd love to."

Sinclair's brows rose. "Really?"

Benji could only laugh as he untied his skates.

He really needed to get out more.

Maybe with Lucy.

Sitting across from Baylor and Jayden Sinclair at the little sushi bar they chose in downtown Nashville, it was easy for Benji to see they were made for each other. As much as she gave and he took, he threw right back at her. They argued over food choices, about where to lay her bum leg, and also what they were doing after dinner with him. Baylor wanted to go home and sleep, but some of the defense team had gone out to drink their sorrows away, and Sinclair wanted to go monitor. Benji kind of agreed with Baylor, but he knew that Jayden needed to go.

Not that it was any of his business, which is why he said nothing, only drank his water. Baylor took it in stride, though, and Benji was pretty sure their bickering was foreplay, which made things a little uncomfortable for him, but he was on a mission.

Lucy.

"Anyway," Jayden said after they ordered and he wrapped his arm around Baylor, pulling her into the crook of his arm. Or so Benji thought. But instead of resting his arm around his wife, Jayden pulled out a bag, handing it over to Benji. "This is a thank-you for helping me out Monday. Baylor picked it out, but I think you already have these."

Benji took the gift with a laugh. "You didn't have to get me anything. I don't mind. I loved it, plan on helping still."

Baylor beamed as Jayden scoffed. "Seriously? I heard those girls are nuts."

"They are." He grinned, opening the bag and finding at the bottom were a few *Game of Thrones* Funko Pops. He had two of them, but the other three he didn't, and it took everything out of him not to geek out in front of his friends. "Ah, awesome! I needed these. I've been looking. Where did you find 'em?"

Well, he tried to be cool.

Baylor giggled as she leaned on the table. "I was on a mission. Can't tell you my sources."

"You must. I have to go back for more," he begged and she laughed.

"The comic store downtown."

"Ah, I hadn't made it that way yet. Thank you, guys," he said with all his heart. "I really did need these."

"You're welcome, dude," Jayden said as Baylor leaned on him, her lips curved sweetly.

"It really means a lot to us that you were there for Angie. Jayden is such a rock for her now that Jude and Jace have moved, and we felt terrible. But apparently, you were awesome. She has been talking about you nonstop."

Benji grinned, his face reddening a bit as he laid the bag beside him. "She's an awesome girl."

"She is. The best ever, and I knew I could trust you. So thanks again," Jayden said with a nod. "And I'm so sorry if my sister was hateful to you. I know she kinda cut Vaughn down, so no telling what she said to you."

Before Benji could say anything, though, Baylor was talking. "Vaughn asked her to go home with him. I think that warrants her to call him what she did," she defended and Jayden shrugged.

"Yeah, I guess. But she's ice-cold to everyone, I swear. I don't even know how she is succeeding in her design business."

Ooh, he didn't know that… Or wait, yeah, he did. He remembered Elli saying something about coming to Florida for their house. "Like home design?"

Baylor nodded. "Yeah, she's amazing. She's done everyone's houses. She's about to do the Adlers' home in January. Jayden has basically made the whole team call her."

Benji made a face. "Not me."

"You have an apartment, that's why."

"No, I don't. I have a house."

Jayden's face showed confusion. "What? I thought you were staying over at the Hampton Places?"

Benji shook his head. "I moved this summer into my new house over by Anderson."

"Oh. Well, hire my sister!"

Benji laughed before saluting Jayden. "Yes, sir."

Laughter filled the table, but before anyone could say anything else, their food was delivered and they dug in. He liked Sinclair. He had been nervous when they were paired together. Benji was with Thomas, but Sinclair and King didn't click the way they did, and Coach moved Benji up. He was thankful, but when he first met the kid, he thought he was just that. A kid. But Sinclair was way more than that. Wise beyond his years. He was a good guy, and Benji was lucky to be playing with him.

Taking a bite of his sushi, Benji looked up as Jayden asked, "Was she bad? I've been dying to know, but then I'm worried you'll say she was horrible to you and I'll have to defend her and then we won't be friends."

Baylor snickered as Benji rolled his eyes playfully. "You sound like a teenage girl, Jay."

Laughing, he nodded. "I know, but she's hard, man. I love her. Like, with all my heart. We are all so close, my family and I. But Lucy and I have that temper, that undying kind of love for the people we love, so I know how she can be when she gets mad. Me not showing up or manning up like I should have, I'm sure, made her want to kill the first person in sight."

"Yeah, I'm surprised she hasn't killed him in his sleep yet," Baylor laughed, but then she paused, shaking her head. "No one hurts Angie and lives to tell the tale. I didn't even know he hadn't told her until I saw the death threats she was sending him."

Wow, Lucy had quite the reputation. Too bad he gave no shits about it. He was pretty sure the thick wall she had up was just that, a wall, and he was going to get over that thing. Why, he wasn't sure. Maybe it was her smile that had driven him to this madness, but he wanted the chance. He wanted to make her smile again.

"She wasn't that bad," he said softly, but they both didn't believe him.

"You don't have to lie. Was she really that bad?"

"Please tell me she didn't try to hit you," Jayden said, embarrassment all over his face, and Benji laughed.

Shaking his head, he shrugged. "She was snarky as shit, and she didn't trust me. Really, she wasn't bad, but then my main focus was making sure Angie was okay, you know? I think she appreciated that."

"Oh, I'm sure," Baylor said. "Angie is her world, and if you knew her backstory, it would make sense, you know? Her ex-husband is a piece of work."

"That's an understatement," Jayden said with a shake of his head. "But that's none of our business."

What? Yes, it is, Benji thought, but he didn't press. He could tell the loyalty between Jayden and his sister was unbreakable and he admired that. But yet, he wanted more. He wanted to know everything.

"Yeah," Baylor agreed. "I just want her to be happy."

Jayden nodded. "Yeah, but I really don't think it will ever happen. I've never seen her with anyone but Rick the Dick, and since they've been divorced for four years now, I'm starting to think my sister will never get with anyone else. She's gonna be one of those really angry old ladies who beat people with canes."

As they shared a laugh, Benji swallowed hard. Their laughter died down and Jayden slowly shook his head. He looked sad, but the anger was there. It was loud and clear that Jayden was not a fan of Rick the Dick.

"I just don't know. She worries me. She needs to be happy too," he said, more to Baylor than Benji, but there was no unhearing that. "I just don't know why she doesn't try, at least."

Clearing his throat, Benji leaned on the table. "Because it's easier to hide from the fear of rejection and pain than to put yourself out there and try." They both looked up at him and he shrugged. "But then the right person comes along and it makes you want to try. It makes you overcome the fear."

"Whoa, that's some deep shit, bro," Jayden said, his eyes widening.

Baylor's brows pulled together, a knowing look in her eyes. It sort of made him nervous. Did she know he was crushing on what was apparently an unattainable girl? "Sounds like you have some experience in that department."

Benji smiled. "Eh, a bit."

"Yeah, but you're different, BP. You're okay with being alone. I don't think Lucy is, and that's what makes her so mad."

Benji laughed. "No one is okay with being alone if they're honest. The

human race wants companionship—that's why God gave Adam, Eve."

Jayden nodded slowly. "My apologies."

"No big deal, but she'll come around. Don't worry. The right guy will come for her, as the right girl will come for me. God has a plan."

"He sure does," Baylor said, leaning into Jayden and he smiled.

"Yeah, he does," he said softly, kissing her nose. She smiled up at him and love was shining out of her pores. They reminded him a lot of him and Ava when they had first gotten together. Young, unadulterated love. What a beautiful thing.

When Jayden looked back over at him, he was breathless as he said, "But I pray that the guy He sends for her is ready for Hurricane Lucy."

When Baylor laughed in agreement, Benji knew their statements should have been a red flag. A clear sign that he needed to go the other way, that he wasn't even sort of prepared to take on Lucy. No matter what he felt, it didn't matter. She didn't want anyone.

But he didn't care.

And as much as he should be ready for Lucy…

She should be ready for him.

Wow, that sounded way more confident than Benji felt, but it felt right.

It felt true.

And for once, Benji was excited for the future.

"There's Benji!"

Angie full out ran toward him as Lucy followed behind, Angie's bag on her shoulder. Angie had been talking incessantly about meeting Benji early for some extra practice. Since she was leaving for her dad's in two days and she wasn't happy about it, Lucy figured she should try her best to get her to the rink. Thankfully, she was able to move a consult to later that night so they were able to come early. She was worried that Benji wouldn't be here, but apparently, he just assumed they'd be there. Or maybe he came just in case they could make it.

She wasn't sure how that made her feel.

As she watched Benji greet Angie, she couldn't help but notice that he was sort of hotter than he had been on Monday night. His hair was falling into his eyes in an unruly fashion, while his face was covered with coarse, dark hair. She was pretty sure he hadn't shaved, and if she was honest, she liked it. A lot. Like, a little too much…

Instead of the sweats he had on Monday, tonight he was wearing a girdle and socks, with a tight, Dri-FIT, long-sleeved shirt covering his torso. Every ripple of muscle on his chest was screaming at her, and for some reason, she felt like doing her laundry on his abs. Praise Jesus, his thick shoulders were almost screaming to have nails dug into them, and they did nothing but make it hard for Lucy to concentrate on the simple task of walking.

Her tripping was a sign of that.

Lord, he was gorgeous and, unfortunately, she had been thinking a lot about Mr. Benji Paxton.

More than she would like to admit.

She wasn't sure if it was because he was adorably dorky or if it was because he was so great with Angie, but she found her mind wandering to him more than it should have. She wanted to know if he was married, if he had kids. Angie had said he had a daughter, but when she Googled him—don't judge—she couldn't find anything about a wife and daughter. It was weird, and a part of her wondered if he was a deadbeat dad. That didn't seem right, though. He didn't seem like that kind of guy. But then, like he said, she had no clue what kind of guy he was. All she knew was her daughter loved him, and Lucy was sort of, in some crazy, weird way, attracted to him.

It was bizarre.

Or she was losing it.

Sucking in a breath, she came up just as Angie declared, "So I'm a little crazytown today, as my mom calls it. My day care forgot to give me my medicine this morning, so I might be a little crazy."

If waving her arms at the end didn't say crazy, Lucy wasn't sure what did. Her sweet baby had been diagnosed with ADHD two years before. Getting her medicated was a feat, but they overcame it, and now Angie was flourishing. In school and in life. She was just happier and, in turn, that made Lucy happy. It wasn't easy, though, especially when Rick blamed her for all of it. If it wasn't enough that she was already blaming herself—because obviously there was something she could have done to make sure her baby didn't have those problems—having her ex-husband throw at her that it was her fucked-up genes was just great.

It had been a tough couple of years, but they were good now. Rick didn't toss it in her face as much anymore, and Angie was great. Lucy was proud of her little nugget, and when she looked at Benji, she was happy to see he wasn't judging Angie, only smiling at her.

"It's cool. I love crazy!"

Angie beamed as Lucy smiled. "All right, Hans."

Benji looked confused, which made her question that he had a daughter. Anyone with a daughter had seen Disney's *Frozen* at least a million times. "Who's Hans?"

"From *Frozen!*" Angie said with a laugh and Benji chuckled. She then promptly started singing the "Love is an Open Door" song. Benji looked confused and Lucy just smiled. Man, Angie was a nut.

"I haven't seen that one yet."

"What!" she cried out and Lucy laughed. "Mommy, we have to watch it with Benji."

"Honey, I've seen that movie so many times, I don't think it would be fair to subject Benji to that. But we'll see. Okay?"

Benji looked over at her and smiled. What surprised her, and also made her a bit breathless, was that his smile filled his whole face. He was like a happy little puppy that had just been promised a treat.

She really needed to stop associating this man with a dog.

It wasn't nice.

But then, she never claimed to be a nice person.

His eyes were darker than a puppy's, though, and full of something. Something dirty, maybe. As he dragged his eyes from hers to her daughter, his face broke into a happy grin. "A movie night sounds awesome. I'll bring candy. But let's wait a bit. Gotta make sure your mom doesn't think I'm a weirdo."

Angie scoffed. "She already does."

"Angela!" Looking at Benji, her face beet red, Lucy shrugged. "Sorry?"

But he laughed. "No biggie. Maybe I can change that."

Whoa… Lucy's hands tightened on Angie's bag as she got lost in the depths of Benji's gray eyes, hot lust gathering between her thighs. If that wasn't suggestive, she didn't know what was. She'd been out of the game for a bit, but she knew when someone was hitting on her. And weird, puppy-dog cutie Benji Paxton just hit on her.

Felt pretty fucking nice, too.

"I'm so glad you guys came. I almost texted Jayden to make sure you guys could make it," Benji said then, his eyes still holding Lucy's.

Breathless, she nodded. "Yeah, Angie really wanted to come, so I moved some things around."

"She's the best," Angie said, her eyes full of love for her mom. "I'm so excited."

She was bouncing. Like, literally bouncing in place, and Lucy could only smile. "She is. Obviously."

"Me too. Why don't you go get ready? You know how to now, right?"

Angie nodded quickly. "Yeah, I've been practicing. I'm a little spotty on my stick tape, though, and getting my skates tight."

"I can help with that," he said with a smile.

Lucy swallowed hard, still very much reeling from two minutes ago. Apparently, she wasn't prepared to be hit on by this guy, which was odd. Usually, guys didn't affect her that dramatically. But the way he looked at her made her feel something, and Lucy didn't feel. So she was still trying to find her footing. But she was on a mission.

The other reason she made sure to move things around was not only to make Angie happy but also because she had to talk to him. After a long chat with Avery earlier that day about Benji, she decided she needed to apologize to him. She had been a bitch, and that wasn't fair. He was really good to Angie and she loved him already, so Lucy needed to man up and apologize for her actions. She wasn't sure why she felt the need to do so, but she did, and she was going to own up to her mistakes.

She knew what she needed to say to him, but the problem was saying it.

"Honey, why don't you go get ready so I can talk to Benji?"

Angie eyed her, and so did Benji. "You're gonna be nice, though?"

She gave her a frustrated look. "Really, Angie? Go get ready before I wear out that butt."

Angie's eyes widened before she glanced up at Benji. He shrugged. "I'd go."

"Yeah," she agreed, taking the bag from Lucy and then walking toward the bench to get ready. When she sat down, Lucy looked up to see Benji watching her.

"Um. Yeah, hi," she said with a wave because she didn't know what else to say or do. Why was she being so awkward with him? This wasn't Lucy. She was strong, she was smart, and guys didn't have any effect on her!

But when he grinned, she found everything she just thought was not true. Shit.

"Hey."

Ugh. Just that word had her skin breaking out in gooseflesh. What in the world? Swallowing hard, she said, "Thanks for not being put off or judgmental with the whole crazytown thing. I said it once, regretted it, but now, it's our normal."

He nodded. "No big deal. When was she diagnosed? ADD?"

"ADHD, two years ago."

"My brother had bad ADD when we were growing up, so I get it. No big deal. She's still the coolest kid I've ever met."

Lucy smiled. "She's great, but when she isn't medicated, she's too busy to feel her emotions so she may be a little scattered. That's why I worry like I do when she is medicated because she feels everything due to the fact she is so focused. That's why I probably came off as a psycho mom the other day. I was kinda panicking. But with Jayden not here to calm her and know her triggers, I was freaking out. But you did really great with her and I appreciate that."

Damn it, she was rambling. Telling him way more than he needed to know. But when he shrugged, like she wasn't rambling or crazy, her heart raced. "I don't think that's psycho at all. I think that makes you a great mom."

Looking away, Lucy tucked her hands into the pockets of her jacket and her heart stopped. "Er…thanks."

"It's the truth," he said, so simply that Lucy had to fight back the tears before looking back up at him. Angie and her family always reassured her that she was a good mom, but Rick wasn't kind and took every chance he could to knock her down. It was tiring, and she knew he was just a sick piece of shit, but still, it hurt. She had one job that really mattered in her life and that was caring for her daughter. Being the kind of woman her baby could look up to. To know that someone thought she was doing a good job… It just meant a lot.

Swallowing around the emotion in her throat, she smiled. Here went nothing. "So, anyway, I'm really sorry for the way I acted on Monday. Between the panicking about Jayden not being here, Angie's anxiety, and then just being tired—I'm tired a lot—I kind of lashed out at you, and I'm really sorry for that."

His face curved into a grin and he nodded. "That seemed really hard for you."

She laughed. "It was. I don't apologize much since I don't think I'm ever wrong, but I was wrong to treat you the way I did. So, I'm sorry."

His eyes were sparkling. How, she didn't know since they were dark like storm clouds. "Well, thank you. I'm glad we had this talk."

God, his eyes. They were really the windows to his soul. Did she just think that? She was insane. Looking away to keep it together, she agreed, "Me too."

Clearing his throat, he started. "I know I'm a little strange—"

"Just a bit," she said with a grin, looking back up at him. "But Angie and Jayden are good at reading people, so I'm gonna trust their opinion of you."

"But you won't trust me," he asked, his eyes challenging.

She scoffed. "I don't know you."

He moved his hands into his pockets, his eyes still holding hers as his lips curved. "So let's change that."

Her eyes narrowed. "Huh?"

"How about you let me take you out to dinner? Get to know each other. Angie said she's going to her dad's this weekend. So how about Saturday?"

Lucy's brows pulled together as her whole face scrunched up. "You're asking me out? On, like, a date?"

She hadn't realized her voice had escalated until Benji laughed. "Don't sound so surprised." She could only stare at him as one side of his mouth quirked up. "But yeah, I am."

Sputtering like a bumbling baboon, she couldn't keep her eyes from widening. She wasn't sure why she was so surprised. It was obvious he was feeling her and she was feeling him, but this was ludicrous. Why would he ask her out? "Why?" she squawked and he looked away, laughing.

"Because I want to. Because I think we'd have fun."

"Fun? You want to?" she said, repeating what he said, and his whole face smiled.

"Didn't know you had a part-time job as a parrot," he teased and she just gawked at him. Looking away, he chuckled nervously. "I'm not sure how to read you right now. Not sure if your surprise is good or bad. It's awkward and you're making me squirm, if that's what you wanted," he admitted, but all Lucy could do was stare at him.

He was so beautiful, but this couldn't happen. "You're my kid's coach."

He shrugged. "Eh, I mean, kinda. But not full time if that makes it better?"

"I don't know you."

"Yeah, which is why we'd go out."

"But—"

"Do you want to go out with me or not?" he asked simply and Lucy's eyes widened more, if that was even possible.

She hadn't expected him to be so direct, and while she thought it was hot, there was no way she could go out with him. She just couldn't.

"Um, I'm sorry," she said and his face changed. The smile dropped as he nodded slowly. "I just don't have time. I'm so busy and, yeah, no. I don't want this to be weird, but no, I can't go out with you."

He held her gaze. "Can't?"

"Yeah."

Taking a step toward her, his eyes bored into hers, his body radiating some serious heat as she got lost in those gray depths. "I don't take you for a 'can't' kind of girl."

"That's 'cause you don't know me," she breathed and he nodded.

"Which, again, is why we should get to know each other."

She shook her head, trying like hell not to lean into him. "I can't."

"But do you want to?"

She eyed him and, shit, she was gasping for breath. He smelled divine and those eyes, Jesus… But she knew she couldn't even try to date him. That would be disastrous. So she did what she did best. She lied. "No, I don't."

He didn't move, nor did his eyes change as he looked down at her. Silence passed between them, and as her eyes grazed down his face, the sharp planes of his nose, and the sweet color of his cheeks, never in the last seven years had she ever wanted to go up on her toes and kiss a man.

Well, there was Channing Tatum; she'd kiss him.

Or Justin Timberlake.

Or even, mmmm, Jared Padalecki…

But not some normal, dorky, puppy-dog looking dude!

What in the world had gotten into her, and why the hell did she feel he

could see right through her?

Especially when he moved toe-to-toe, his breath on her lips as he said, "You're not a very good liar, Ms. Sinclair."

"Ms.?" she asked breathlessly. Thankfully, she still had her brain…sorta. "I could be married."

"But you're not," he said simply, his voice so low, so deep, and…fuck, so sexy. "And that's cool. I'll get you to go out with me."

Then he winked.

She was pretty sure she came.

And without another word, tall, dark, adorable, sexy, puppy-dog guy walked away.

Like a fucking boss.

Where in the hell had that come from?

And why did she believe him?

There was no reason to, because Lucy knew she wouldn't be dating anyone. Probably never would. Or maybe when Angie was eighteen and she wouldn't ever have to deal with Rick again. But now, now she couldn't. It didn't make sense. She just didn't have time, and she sure as hell wasn't going to bring some dude around Angie whom she didn't trust.

But this was different.

Angie already loved Benji.

Which meant Lucy couldn't fuck that up. She may not trust the guy, but Angie did and she needed that. Especially since her father was a turd.

So she'd keep her distance.

No matter how hard it looked like that was going to be.

Chapter FIVE

Leaning on her desk, Lucy looked at the screen of her computer with no clue what she was doing.

She should be working. She had orders she needed to place for three different accounts. She had fourteen mock-ups to send to Elli Adler and seven to send to leopard-print couple. She also needed to call her mother back since she had been calling since eight that morning. She usually didn't ignore her mother—she loved her and loved speaking with her—but lately, she was exhausted with the whole wedding thing. It still all seemed so unreal to her.

Plus, Lucy was distracted.

Benji asked her out last night.

And she said no.

Her answer was driving her insane because she was starting to think she should have said yes. There wasn't a long line of men wanting to take her out. She hadn't been out in a very long time, and man, she needed some sex. Nice, hot, wall-banging sex. Benji was tall, and while he was a bit awkward, she was pretty sure he could deliver the wall-banging sex. It had to be the eyes that made her think that…mmm…

But no.

No.

It couldn't happen. She was busy, and he didn't look like the kind of guy who wanted to just screw around. She didn't have time for a relationship, and Angie—she couldn't do that to her. Bringing guys in and out, that was just not responsible. She wasn't that kind of a woman; she was smart and relationships led to heartache. The problem was, it wasn't only Lucy's heart that could be broken, and she couldn't do that to Angie. Wouldn't do that to her.

Rick already caused that girl enough grief, and she wouldn't add to it. Or really, she wouldn't give Rick the chance to give them both grief. He wouldn't take kindly to some guy coming around Angie. He had made that comment many times, and yeah, it was stupid of Lucy to worry about what he thought, but it did worry her. He was unpredictable, and she was okay with her life as it was. She didn't need a man. No, she would be the staple in Angie's life. She would be strong; she would be the best role model she could.

But was she being that without trying to love again? Angie was loved, over and beyond, but that was by family. Was Lucy not giving her the example of what marital love could be? All she had were the interactions between her and Rick—those were never good—but was she cheating her baby out of a family? But Angie had Rick and Heidi, if that was even an example. Who knew? Heidi was a dimwit, but shit. Was she fucking up? No, she was doing fine. Angie was happy, she was loved, everything was fine. God, why did she do this to herself?

What happened to just wanting hot, nasty sex from the guy?

Jesus, she was a mess.

Closing her eyes, she ran her other hand through her hair as her phone beeped and her assistant Rayne came over the speaker. "Lucy, do you have Angie this weekend?"

Looking at the phone, she closed her eyes again, holding back her moan. She really needed to hire another designer. "Nope."

"I have a guy on hold for a design on Saturday. He's leaving town on Sunday and wanted to get the ball rolling as soon as possible. He's offering to pay a rush fee if needed. When would be good? You have the whole morning blocked out, but then your mom called me and told me to block out your lunch and two hours after that."

"Jesus, why?"

"I don't know. Maybe you should call her back?"

Rolling her eyes, she shrugged. "I guess I should. Okay, so what, like, four? Would four work?"

"I'll ask, but you want to do anywhere between four and six? So I don't have to call you back?"

"Yeah, that's fine," she said with a sigh. "Does he sound rich?"

Rayne laughed. "He offered a rush fee and said he needs a design for his whole house. He just moved in and doesn't have time to make it adultish. He's funny."

That perked her interest. A whole house? "Is there a wife?"

"I didn't ask."

"Just wondering how much I'll actually be designing, or will I be trying to please a wife."

"Does it matter?"

Lucy scoffed. "Nope. Yeah, between four and six is fine."

"Party. I'll put it in the books."

"Fabulous, but make sure my Sunday is free."

"Yeah, I know," she said and then the phone went dead.

Lucy was curious about her new Saturday appointment, but instead of waiting for the info to come up on her calendar so she could stalk the guy, she decided she needed to call her mother.

So, obviously, she called Avery instead.

"Hey!" her sister-in-law said, sounds of sweet baby Ashlyn in the background.

"Hey, what're you doing? You busy being an awesome mom and songwriter?"

Avery laughed. "Actually, I just got done cleaning poop off my shorts. Ashlyn had an accident. Explosive one."

"Ew. Don't miss those days. Got time to chat?"

"Of course, missy is going down for a nap and then I gotta work some. My goal of selling to Ed Sheeran before the year is up is slowly but surely diminishing."

Smiling, Lucy leaned back in her chair. Avery had been writing a lot lately and selling like mad, but of course, the girl was wanting to sell to someone who really didn't buy. "He writes his own stuff, babe."

"Yeah, yeah, but I'm gonna get him, you watch. I've got four months to do just that."

"Chase those dreams!"

"You know it," Avery agreed and Lucy listened as she slowly shut the door. "So, have you talked to Baylor?"

"No, but I talked to Jayden and things aren't looking good."

"Yeah, she was telling me she thinks she's gonna retire before they tell her she won't be able to play anymore."

That broke Lucy's heart. "Man, that sucks. She wants it so bad."

"I know," Avery said sadly. "I hate it for her, but your mom is happy. You know how she worries."

"Yeah."

"And she wants them to have a baby."

Lucy scoffed. "Of course, she does. If she had her way, everyone would be pregnant."

"I think it's coming for Claire and Jude."

Lucy shook her head even though Avery couldn't see her. "No way, Claire is too busy. I think it will happen when her contract is fully up. She still has obligations and shit. Who wants to be pregnant around a bunch of burlesque dancers?"

Claire was a big shot burlesque dancer and choreographer in Vegas. That girl wasn't getting pregnant; neither was Baylor. It had surprised the hell out of everyone when Jace came home saying he and Avery were pregnant. They were both so young, but they were doing well. Way better than Lucy ever did when she was their age with Angie.

"True, I kinda want someone to get pregnant."

Lucy laughed. "Why?"

"So Mom will stop calling me! I love her, I do, but man, she calls me all day to check on Ashlyn."

Lucy smiled. Her mom could be very suffocating, and with her baby moving to Florida with his wife and baby… Yeah, she wasn't handling it well. "Yeah, sorry about that. I call a lot too. Do you want me to stop?"

"Please, never. It's just different with Mom 'cause she wants to know about Ashlyn and Jace, and then about me. And I'm like, Mom, we seriously do nothing but hang out on the beach and work."

"She misses you guys. We all do."

"I know. We miss you guys too," Avery said sadly, and Lucy crossed her legs, rocking back in her chair. "But Jace is soaring on the Panthers. They are doing so well."

"I know, I've been watching."

"I don't know how you do it, watching all the games. I sometimes forget to put Jace's on if we aren't there."

Lucy smiled as she shrugged. "Years of doing it. Guess I'm a pro."

"Guess so," she agreed, her voice happy. "How's Angie loving hockey? Jace said she was killing it, and we just love the pictures you guys sent."

"God, yes, she loves it. She's only gone twice, but she's awesome and enjoys it, so that's good."

"Yeah, Jace said something about a Benji? I thought Shea Adler was the coach?"

Why did butterflies go off in her gut at his name? Man, she needed to get that under control. "He's an assistant coach. He plays with Jayden on the Assassins."

"Oh! Okay, cool. She's taken to him, from what I heard."

"Yeah, I'm kind of nervous about her going to Rick's. I'm sure he's gonna have a lot to say."

"Fuck that dude. He'll be okay," Avery bit out. Rick didn't have any fans in the Sinclair family.

"Yeah, I just hate arguing with him."

"Jace told me about the recital."

"Bullshit."

"Yeah, oh well. Only eleven more years."

It was a bittersweet thing to think, but it was true. While she didn't want her baby to grow up, she sure as hell didn't want to deal with Rick anymore. "Yeah."

Silence fell between the two, and as it had been for the last twenty-four hours, Lucy's mind went to Benji. Would she defend him if Rick said anything? Or would she ignore Rick like she tried to do most of the time? Another reason why she couldn't ever even think of trying to date Benji—it would be cruel to subject him to the vile person Rick was. He'd run the other way. Yeah. It wouldn't work. She would be setting everyone up for failure.

"Whoa, silence isn't how you roll, Lucy. What's up?"

Lucy's lips curved as she looked up at the ceiling. "Angie's coach, Benji…he asked me out last night, and I've been thinking about it like crazy."

"Whattttt?" she yelled and Lucy laughed. "What did you say? Yes, right?"

"No," Lucy said, and she was surprised with how sad she sounded. "I probably should have. He's this big, awkward, sweet guy—God, he's so cute—and he's got to be in his thirties, so you know he isn't looking for a fling. I don't want to get involved, have it go south, and then Angie gets hurt, y'know?"

"Oh," Avery said, sounding just as sad as Lucy. "But you need to be happy too, Lucy. I've said this many times. Everyone has. Y'all are adults, and if he's as great as Angie says he is, I doubt he would let what happens between you two affect his relationship with her."

"Yeah, but I'm good. I'm happy."

Lucy paused, though, and she wasn't sure if Avery believed her. Hell, she wasn't sure she believed herself. Sometimes she felt like something was missing in her soul. A piece that Rick had taken and ruined. She wasn't saying that Benji was that piece, she didn't know the guy, but she'd be lying if she said she didn't want to at least see if he was. Which was a first. And that should mean something. But she knew at the point in her life she was in, a relationship just wouldn't work.

Clearing her throat, Lucy smiled as Avery struggled with her words. "I love you, you know that."

"I do."

"And I mean this with all the love in my soul, I do, Lucy, but you're happy with Angie, and that's the way it's supposed to be. But when she's gone, you're nowhere near happy. You are lonely and worry so much about her that it's affecting you. Jace tells me all the time that you used to be the person who had a grin on your face all the time. The only time I see you smile is when you hold Ashlyn or when you're talking to Angie—"

Offended, Lucy sat up. "That's not true, I smile all the time."

"But it doesn't reach your eyes. It doesn't seem real," Avery said slowly. "You're so bitter and angry, and you do so well shielding Angie from that, but sometimes I think maybe you don't want to be happy."

Swallowing hard, Lucy picked at a string on her twill pants. "I am happy."

"Lucy."

Just her name, and it said so much. Clearing her throat, Lucy shrugged. "I don't know."

"Did you want to say yes to him?"

"I did," she said simply. "But it just wouldn't work. My life is so busy, I don't have time, and it wouldn't be fair to him when the shitshow of Rick comes through."

"Why the hell does Rick matter?"

Closing her eyes, she fought back the tears. She didn't like thinking of Rick; she didn't like the power he held over her. But the memory of herself crouched in a corner, him above her with a belt, screaming at her, was something she still couldn't shake. She was gone with her baby as soon as she regained consciousness, her sperm-donor father drawing up divorce papers. But she knew what he was capable of. And that scared her. "He always said that if I ever tried to be with anyone, he'd ruin my life. That he didn't want any man around his daughter."

"Oh, Lucy, please don't tell me that's what's keeping you from being with someone?"

Lucy laughed a soulless laugh. "I'm not scared of him; I'm scared of what he could do. He can't touch me, and he won't—I know he won't—but he could hurt Angie trying to get to me, and I can't have that."

"So you are."

Lucy snapped her mouth shut and then shook her head. "For an eighteen-year-old, you're kinda smart, you know that?"

Avery laughed. "Hey, I'm nineteen! And yeah, I am. But I need you to let that go. You will protect Angie, and you know we all will too. But Luce, you need to be happy."

"Eh, it will come," she said simply, letting out a long breath. "Plus, I don't see men lining up at the door wanting to be with me."

"True, but there is one man," Avery added and Lucy glared. "Maybe give him a chance?"

Closing her eyes, she decided she wouldn't be calling Avery much anymore. The girl was too smart for her own good.

"I pissed you off?"

Lucy grinned, leaning on her desk. "I don't like when people point out what I'm trying to ignore."

"Oh. Well, then maybe we shouldn't talk?"

That had them both laughing. "I love you, Aves."

"Love you too. Now, call your mom. She needs you to go pick out wedding dresses with her."

"What? Are you serious?"

Avery giggled. "Yup. Have fun!"

Fucking hell.

"My name is Benji Paxton and I'm an alcoholic."

"Hello, Benji."

Benji looked around at the group of people who had gathered for his weekly AA meeting. Jordie sat to his left, a grin on his face while Benji sat there awkwardly, his hands dangling at his sides. Tucking them into his pockets, he cleared his throat as the group leader, Bethany, smiled happily at him.

"How are you feeling, Benji?"

"I feel good. Even after over eleven years of being sober, I'm still good."

The group clapped and Benji's lips quirked a bit. He had been coming to this group for the last two years. Jordie had joined it last year, and it was nice to share this with someone he trusted. When they were on the road, they always found a group and would go together. It was great, it really was. It was new to have a friend who could help support him as he did the same for that friend.

Bethany smiled. "Good. Do you have anything you want to share?"

Drawing in a long breath, he blew it out slowly.

"I was turned down last night," he said, and once he said it, he wasn't sure why he was sharing this. But then, he knew why. This group was his family. All of them had been over a year sober. Jordie was the youngest in the sober game, and people had come in and out, but the nine people who looked at him knew his deepest, darkest secrets. And he knew theirs.

Like how Phil was fighting day-by-day against his addiction. It had been really bad lately because his wife left him for another man. Joanna watched her mother blow her face off and still hadn't recovered. She said she had given up the powder, but Benji sometimes thought she was lying. Gabe was the oldest out of all of them, twenty-seven years sober, and he was so close to God, Benji was sure there was a seat right next to the big guy for him.

These were his people, and as they looked at him with worry in their eyes, he knew why he'd said something. "I've been helping coach hockey for a group of girls the last couple days, and they are great. I love it. I didn't realize how much I needed to do something like that until I was out there."

"Doesn't that hurt, though? Doesn't it remind you of Leary?" Ruby asked.

She had come to the group a few months before Jordie. She didn't share much, but she sure as hell listened. She had hit on him a few times, but he had to worry about his own sobriety; he didn't think he could worry about someone else's too.

"Yeah, it does. But in a way, it's therapeutic 'cause I feel like this is what I would have been doing now—with my own daughter."

"Good," Bethany said with a smile. "You need to get out Benji. Socialize."

He nodded. "I know, and I am. I went out to dinner with friends the other night, and well, I even asked a girl out."

"Oh, Benji, that's wonderful. Does she know the Lord?" Gabe asked and Benji smiled.

"I don't know yet. She turned me down." They all gasped, well, except Jordie, and Benji shrugged.

"How did that make you feel?" Bethany asked and he shrugged again, leaning on his knees.

"I didn't like it obviously 'cause I knew she wanted to," he said, and Jordie tapped his thigh.

"How'd you know? You don't talk well with women, nor can you read them right. So hearing this, I'm sorry, dude, but I'm holding back my laughter."

Benji smiled back at him and nodded. "She's different. I mean, right off the bat, I knew I wanted to know her. And the way she looks at me, it's just special, you know? But she shot me down, and I'm sure it's 'cause something is holding her back. Maybe her daughter."

"Her kid plays on the team?"

He nodded. "Yeah."

"I could understand her hesitation, then. I'm sure she worries that if things end badly with you two, then it would be awkward for her daughter," Bethany added, and Benji got that, he did, but that would never happen. He would never treat Angie any differently. He just wanted a chance. He still couldn't shake that look in Lucy's eyes. She wanted him, and he didn't know how to reassure her that, no matter what happened, he'd always do right by Angie. "I see it on your face, Benji. This is bothering you."

He shrugged. "It's just frustrating. I finally meet someone who makes me want to try, and she shoots me down."

Jordie scoffed beside him. "And you're gonna give up? That doesn't seem like you."

Benji looked over at him. "I just worry that maybe it's a sign, that I'm not supposed to be happy."

"No, son. God wants us all to love our life. He has a plan for you, son. Maybe it's not her, but then, maybe it is," Gabe said, his old eyes holding Benji's. "You just gotta pray on it."

"He's right," Jordie said. "But, dude, you are supposed to be happy, you know that. We've had this talk many times. You have to make your happiness. Surround yourself with people who do that. You've done it professionally, and if this girl seems different, then you can't give up."

Jordie made it seem so easy, but Benji knew it wasn't.

Not when the girl was Lucy.

He just didn't understand why she'd lied to him. Why she'd looked him in the eyes and said no. He could see it all over her sweet face. The way her lips parted, the way her body arched toward his. Her eyes were dark emeralds, and they narrowed like a cat that was being stroked to oblivion. She wanted him. Damn bad. And fuck, he wanted her.

But along with the lust in her eyes, he could see the hesitation. The hurt. Her backstory, the reason why hurt and hesitation were in her eyes wasn't for the fainthearted. He could see that and he hated it. He knew his story was one hell of one, but his was only his fault. He deserved his hurt. But someone had hurt her, and that didn't sit well with him. He didn't want anyone causing her pain, nor Angie. He cared for them.

Maybe he was crazy. He had only known them for a couple days, but not since Ava and Leary had he felt so overprotective of someone. After the car wreck, after losing his wife, daughter, and brother, and then his family because of it, he hadn't been able to feel anything. He went through life, building it back to somewhat normal. It wasn't easy, and it sucked being sober, but he was finally good in life. He had a good career, he had friends, but he yearned for love.

And then Lucy and Angie came along.

They were different.

They were special.

He just needed a chance.

And he was going to get it.

After the whistle blew, Angie raced across the ice, falling down on her stomach and then getting back up before skating back and redoing it with the rest of the team. Benji stood with Shea and Vaughn, watching as the girls did the drills, working hard. But something was off. He wasn't sure, but he thought that Angie was upset about something. He had tried to ask her, but she just shook her head, claiming nothing was wrong.

He knew that wasn't true, though.

"Hart seem okay to you guys?"

Vaughn shrugged, and Shea looked over at him. "I thought she was a little off. She doesn't seem as peppy, not like Wednesday when she was bouncing off the walls. I don't know, maybe this is her normal?"

Benji shook his head. "No, something is up."

"Okay, just keep an eye on her. I'll say something to Lucy about it," Shea decided, but once more Benji shook his head.

"No, I will."

Shea smiled and Vaughn laughed. "Someone's got a crush."

"Shut it, Johansson," Benji said as Adler blew the whistle and the girls stopped, gasping in deep breaths.

"Water break!" Adler roared across the ice and then looked to Vaughn. "You guys leave Sunday?"

He nodded. "Yeah. So we won't be here for the next week. The game next Saturday is at nine, right?"

"Yeah, you guys will make it?"

"Yeah, but do you have someone who can cover next week?" Benji asked, hopeful they would be good to the girls.

"Yeah, I'll call in some help. No biggie. Girls are going to miss you guys, though," Shea said as he started to skate toward the group. They followed along with him, and for once, Benji didn't want to go on the road. Usually, he didn't care, but he felt like he had things to do here.

Really, he didn't, but he wished he did.

When they reached the area where the girls were getting water by the benches, Benji saw that Angie was standing by herself, moving a puck back and forth. Before he could head over there, Shea's voice filled the rink.

"Coaches Vaughn and Benji are leaving us for some away games. So let's take a moment and wish them good luck on the road!"

All the girls clapped and cheered for them, a chant of "Go Assassins" beginning, and the guys grinned. The girls were a good group, and Benji was going to miss them. But when he looked over to Angie, she looked sad as she went back to playing with the puck. Skating over to where she was, he leaned against the boards and watched as she moved it in and out of her legs mindlessly, messing up, but he didn't think she cared. As the chants died down, Benji cleared his throat.

"Penny for your thoughts?"

She looked up, her little face twisting in confusion. She was sweaty, her cheeks red, but the frustration was in her eyes. He wasn't sure what a seven-year-old had to be frustrated about, but he sure as hell didn't think she needed to be. "What's that mean?"

He grinned. "Means 'what's up?'"

"Nothing," she said simply, shooting the puck against the boards with a little more aggression than needed.

He smiled. "Nothing, or you don't want to talk about it? Are you feeling okay?"

"Yeah, fine," she said and then let out a breath.

"Do you not want to talk to me?" he asked because—who was he? He was just her coach. "That's completely okay."

She looked up at him once more and then shook her head. "It's not that. It's just I'm worried about my mom."

His heart started to race as he came off the boards. "Is she okay?"

"Yeah, I just think she's mad because my dad is coming here to get me early."

"Early?"

She nodded. "Yeah, he should be here soon. I have to watch for when he comes."

"Oh," he said, and he wasn't sure why his heart dropped a bit. "Well, I'm sure she's not mad at you."

"No, I know," she said, letting out a long breath. "I just hate that she gets upset. She's always mad."

"I doubt that."

"Well, not at me, but at everything else. It just sucks. My dad is mean to her, and I tell him to be nice, but he just ignores me. He told her he wanted her to pull me from hockey, but Mom said no. So he screamed at her until she hung up— Oh, crap, he's here."

Benji looked in the direction Angie had turned. Sure enough, a man was standing there, looking out at the ice. He was average height, lanky, and maybe it was because Benji thought he was a bag of dicks, but he wasn't very good-looking. Lucy picked this dude to make a kid with? Praise God that Angie was a mini Lucy.

"I gotta go," Angie grumbled as she grabbed her water. "Have a good road trip. Sucks you're leaving."

"Yeah. Come on, I'll go with you. I need to talk to your mom anyway," he said as she started to skate away. "Adler, Angie's gotta go. I'll be back."

"Yeah, see you later, Hart. Have a good weekend."

She waved at Shea and then the rest of the team. "Bye, you too."

Benji opened the door for her, and she walked out. When he looked up, he saw Lucy walking toward them, her eyes full of annoyance. But still, she was so pretty.

Her long, brown hair was down, straight along her shoulders, but with a little curl at the end. She had it pinned to the side, out of her eyes, which were done up to enhance the color. The red dress she wore was tight across her breasts but flared out at her hips, her legs clad in dark tights and boots to her knees. She was wearing some kind of blanket looking thing that he had noticed was popular in fashion now, but that wasn't what had him gawking at her.

No, it was the red of her lips.

So shiny and so plump.

Lord Almighty.

But she wasn't looking at him, her gaze only on Angie. "Baby, your dad is here."

"I know," Angie grumbled, handing her mom her water and stick.

"Hey, Angie," the guy said, coming to them as Benji shut the door behind him. The guy looked up at Benji and his brows came together before dragging his gaze back to Angie. "Ready?"

"I gotta get my equipment off. Give me a minute," Angie said before walking over to where her bag was. Benji watched her for a moment, and when she looked up, he smiled.

"You good, Angie?"

She nodded, a little smile on her lips. "Yeah, thanks, Benji."

"Anytime," he said, watching as Lucy came over to help her. Sitting down, she helped her undress and Benji knew he should have gone back on the ice, but he wanted to make sure they were okay.

Plus, he didn't trust this guy at all.

"I need you to hurry up, honey. We gotta meet Heidi and Nina. We're already late," he called over to them, and Lucy looked up, irritation flying off her.

"We are," Lucy bit out, untying Angie's skates and sliding them off her feet.

"Well, if I didn't have to drive over here and you would have met me, we wouldn't have this problem," he snapped back at her and she looked up, glaring.

Whoo-wee, that girl was scary.

"And I told you that she has hockey Monday, Wednesday, and Friday, and games starting next week on Saturday. This is important to her."

"No, it's important to your family. She doesn't want this," he said, his voice rising. "You care more about making them happy than about what Angie wants."

"Excuse me?" Lucy roared, standing up. Her eyes cut to Benji's and she paused, her hands clenching at her sides.

"Mommy, don't fight," Angie said, slamming things into her bag before sliding her feet into her shoes. She then looked up to her father. "I do want to play, Dad. I love it. Mommy doesn't even have time to bring me, but she does. Stop being mean."

The guy glanced down at Angie, and Benji didn't like the way he looked at her. Like she was a nuisance and not the best damn thing in his pathetic life. "Whatever, we'll talk about this later. Let's go. Heidi's waiting."

Turning to Lucy, Angie wrapped her arms around her waist and hugged her tightly. Lucy's arms basically wrapped around the girl twice as she kissed her hard on the top of her head. It was almost too much to see. It was obvious Lucy didn't want to let her go, and when Benji looked away, his gaze met Rick's.

"Did you need something?"

Benji's eyes narrowed. "Not from you. Just want to make sure Angie was good, and I had to talk to her mom about the game next weekend."

Rick glared and then rolled his eyes before looking to Angie. "Let's go, Angie. You'll see her Sunday."

"I love you, Mommy," Benji heard Angie say, and honestly, he wasn't sure how Lucy did this. He would lose his fucking mind. Hell, he was and Angie wasn't even his.

"I love you too, baby. Have fun, okay? And I'll see you tomorrow at the recital. I can't wait," she said happily as she pulled back, cupping Angie's face. She was trying. She was trying so hard to be positive, it was killing her.

"What? You're coming?" Rick asked, and Lucy didn't even look at him.

"Of course, we wouldn't miss it for the world," she said and Angie grinned.

"We? The whole Sinclair clan, I'm guessing?" he seethed, and Lucy just smiled at Angie, her little dimples peeking out. It was his first time seeing them, and boy, what a sight.

"Yup, we can't wait."

Angie was beaming up at her mother, and when she wrapped her arms tightly around Lucy again, Benji swallowed hard. These two were something he had never seen before. Or maybe he had, but he was too drunk to remember. Which made him a bit sad.

Kissing her once more, Lucy patted her back. "I'll take your bag. Go on, I'll see you later."

"Okay, bye, Mommy," she said and then trudged to her father.

"Bye, baby, see you tomorrow," Lucy called as they walked toward the door. Once they were out of sight, her shoulders fell and she sucked in a deep breath. Benji didn't say anything, just watched as she slowly shook her head, swallowing hard. When she looked to him, she shrugged. "Sorry you had to see that."

Benji shook his head. "Don't apologize. You okay?"

"You'd think, after four years, that giving her to him would be easy, but it's not," she said. She looked so defeated. He wanted to wrap his arms around her and hold her in the hopes she'd feel better.

"Yeah, doesn't seem so."

Shaking her head, she picked up Angie's bag and then looked over at him. "Yeah, anyway, what did you need? Is it, like, my snack day or something?"

Benji smiled. "Oh, I don't know. I just wanted to make sure you guys were okay."

"You didn't need anything?"

"Nope," he said simply. "Just wanted to make sure you two were safe."

"Oh." She looked surprised by that. Her sweet eyes widened as her lip quirked a bit. She didn't smile, but at least she didn't glare.

"Yeah," he said, looking away and drawing in a breath. As much as he wanted to ask her out again, he knew that wouldn't be appropriate. She was upset and it wouldn't be fair of him to take advantage of that. So he'd wait. His moment would come. He'd just have to be patient. "Okay, well, be careful going home and have a good night."

"You too."

He went to turn, to hit the ice, but then he paused. Looking back at her, he saw she was turning, about to walk away, but he called to her, "Hey, Lucy."

Glancing over her shoulder, she met his gaze. "Yeah?"

"You look really pretty tonight."

As her lips curved and those dimples appeared, Benji found himself fighting for his next breath. Slowly, her cheeks reddened and then she was fully smiling at him. Yeah, that breath he was fighting for…?

He lost the fight.

"Thanks, Benji."

"Anytime. See ya."

"Bye," she said softly before turning to walk away. As he watched her walk, her ass swaying from side to side, he knew he couldn't give up.

Hell, he knew that from the start.

Now, he just had to get her to give him a chance.

Chapter SIX

"You know, just when I think I couldn't hate that son of a biscuit eater you chose to have a child with more, days like today happen, and I swear, I want to castrate the little bastard."

Lucy scoffed at her mother's proclamation as they walked into the dress shop after having a nice lunch with Jayden and Baylor. She guessed her mom had held it in while they ate with her brother and his wife. Things were already so stressful for Baylor with her surgery coming up that no one really wanted to talk about Rick. But it was evident everyone hated him.

"Jeez, Mom, tell me how you really feel."

Her mother shot her a look and Lucy realized she made that same face daily. She usually added a "What the fuck?" along with it, but her mother was too sweet for that. Unless Rick Hart had pissed her off.

And boy, had he.

Lucy hadn't expected him to do her any favors when it came to the recital. Hell, he hadn't even gotten her a ticket. But he also had not told her that she could have gotten a disc of pictures and a DVD, but that she had to pay for those two weeks in advance. She wasn't sure how she missed it on the days she took Angie to dance—she must have been working on something—but she had, so she didn't get to order. Even with a text to Claire, nothing could be done because everything was already paid for. But Rick had ordered, and when her mother asked him for a copy so that she could make a copy, he basically told her to go fuck herself.

Which Mom did not take kindly to, nor did River.

So, of course, when her mother stomped out of the lobby and River was very stern when he actually told Rick he could go fuck himself, Lucy was left with the aftermath. Which included Rick saying he didn't want Angie around River. Cold day in hell. River loved Angie, and he was about to be her step-grandfather, so Lucy decided Rick could suck it. Hell, she already had decided that. But if that wasn't enough to stress her out, Angie had whispered to her that she didn't want to dance anymore.

Fucking great.

It seemed like one thing after another, but she'd be damned if her daughter was going to be forced to do something she didn't want to. It could wait, though, until Lucy picked her up the following day. It had already been a morning of snide remarks and hellish death looks; Lucy couldn't handle a screaming match with that idiot. Especially when she had to go wedding dress shopping with her mother.

And not even for Lucy, but for her mom.

It was pathetic that she was jealous of her mother, but she was. Autumn hadn't let the divorce from Lucy's sperm-donor father or the cheating scandal ruin her. No, her mother took it in stride. She had her moment of mourning the loss of her almost thirty-year marriage, and then she was right back out there. It was kind of funny watching her crush on the boys' college hockey coach, and even funnier when she was the one to ask him out. It was cute and Lucy should be happy for her mother, but she envied her.

She wanted to be like her.

She wanted to be able to throw all caution to the wind. She wanted to give Benji a chance. It was insane, but it was all she could think about. That moment she said no when, really, she was screaming yes inside. It was so sad. She wanted to hope it would work between them because he was really proving to be a decent guy. He didn't have to stay at the rink yesterday and make sure she and Angie were fine. But he did. He also didn't have to say she looked pretty, but when he did, it meant the world. She may have spent some extra time getting ready because she knew she'd see him. For him to notice was just nice. So why couldn't she ask him out? Be the one to put it out there? Why couldn't she be like her idol?

Her mom.

Because their situations were so different, that was why. All her mother's children were grown, and once her husband was gone, he was gone. She didn't even speak to Lucy's dad. Hell, no one did anymore, not after the stunt he had pulled with Jace. Trying to buy him off so he wouldn't speak to any of them? Please, Jace was the baby. He needed them, and even if he didn't, he couldn't give up his momma. He was the biggest momma's boy in the world.

So really, Lucy couldn't even put them in the same category. She needed to be happy for the woman who had given her life and supported her no matter what. She was being an ungrateful, selfish brat and she needed to suck it up. And she also needed to let Benji go. Things would never work.

"I just hate him. I mean, how hard is it to let me get a picture to make a copy? I'll give it back! I've always been nice to that little brat, even when he doesn't deserve it. I'm done. No more Mrs. Nice Guy," her mother seethed, shaking her head as she moved each dress out of the way violently.

"Mom, those dresses did nothing to you."

She glared back at Lucy. "Shush. And also, don't they have a section for women who are older and getting married for a second time? I mean, jeez! I don't have the boobs for this."

Lucy giggled as her mother hung up a low-cut dress that had no back. She, in fact, did not have the boobs nor the back for that dress. Lucy did, though.

One day.

Lucy set her with a look. A bored one. "I mean, I don't even know why we're here. You two haven't even picked a date."

That made Autumn smile, which in return made Lucy breathless. It was a sight, seeing her mother smile. She was so happy now, so in love, and it meant the world to Lucy. Her mom was her best friend, and she wanted nothing more than for her to be blissful. River was really good to her mother and loved all her kids like his own. Hell, he stood up to her father many times in the past year they had been together. He was something, and she was glad he was with her mother. So really, she didn't know why she was so bitchy when it came to her mother getting married.

"We have set a date. Christmas."

Lucy's jaw dropped. "Christmas, next year?"

Autumn shook her head, her hands coming to her chest like some kind of Disney princess. "Nope, this one."

"Mom! That's in, like, two months."

"I know!" she squealed, doing a little jig. "All the boys will be home, there is a small break in hockey for Christmas, and it just feels right. It's gonna be so small, just us really, and Pastor Dwayne from our church. Nothing crazy or big, just nice and sweet. Us, our family, you know?"

Lucy's lips curved, tears gathering in her eyes. "Yeah, Mom, that sounds nice."

"Oh, it will be. Angie will be my little flower girl. You and the boys will give me away, and Baylor will stand up with River. It's gonna be a tearjerker, I'm sure."

Lucy was fighting back her own tears at the moment, so no telling what she'd do when they actually had the damn wedding. "I'm sure it will be."

75

"I'm excited."

"I am too," Lucy said, and she wasn't lying. For the first time since she found out, she was genuinely happy for her mom. Standing up, she went to her mom, leaning her head on hers. She sucked in a long breath as Autumn's hand came up to rest on her cheek.

"I love you, baby," her mother whispered and Lucy's eyes fell shut.

"I love you too, Mom." Clearing her throat free of emotion, she stood up and then clapped her hands together. "Now, let's find you a dress. Excuse me, do y'all have an older bride wedding dress section?" Lucy asked the dress consultant who had just come into the room.

"Oh, yes, ma'am. This way," she said cheerfully, and they followed her into the other room. "My name is Shawna, and I'll be helping you. I'm sorry to keep you waiting. My daughter is home sick, and I'm trying to talk my husband through it."

"Oh, you're fine. We were man-bashing my daughter's ex," Autumn said and Lucy rolled her eyes.

"Oh, my mom and I do the same. Thankfully, I only had kids with the second guy," Shawna laughed, bringing them into another room.

"Lucky. She didn't," Autumn added and Lucy gave her a look.

"Really, Mom?"

"What?" she asked innocently as Shawna laughed.

"It's fine. Okay, so what are we looking for?"

"I don't know." She eyed all the dress, and Lucy's throat was thick with emotion at the look on her mother's face. She was giddy, almost like this was her first marriage, her first love, and it was beautiful. "Baby, you think I can pull off a short dress?" she asked then, pointing to a gorgeous, tea length, off-white A-line dress that had a lace bodice and pearls all over it.

"I think you can," she said simply. "It's pretty."

"But what about my legs?"

Lucy shrugged. "What? They'll show?"

Autumn gave her a stern look. "No, I mean, do you think that's okay? It's a Christmas wedding," she said to Shawna and she nodded.

"You might be chilly. Do you want a poofy dress?"

Autumn laughed. "Oh, Jesus, no. I'm fifty-four!"

"What! I wouldn't think you were a day over thirty," Shawna said with a wink, and Autumn's laughter filled the shop. Lucy giggled as she leaned back against the puffy white couch, watching as Shawna went back and forth, showing them options, with Autumn having the final say. When they finally had four dresses picked out, Shawna took a very thrilled Autumn to the dressing room to start trying them on.

Letting out a long breath, Lucy picked up her phone and went into her group message with the boys.

Lucy: Mom is so happy.
Jace: You guys shopping? Avery said something about wedding dresses today.
Lucy: Yeah. It's supersweet.
Jayden: Good, she needs to be happy.
Jude: Yeah, for sure. Send us pictures.
Lucy: I will. They set a date.
Jude: When?
Lucy: Christmas.
Jayden: Cool.
Jude: Awesome.
Jace: Good, all of us will be there.
Jude: But man, that means you only have a couple more months before your wife is your sister, Jay.
Jace: Yeah, that sucks. Can you guys even do it then?
Lucy: I think that's incest.
Jayden: I hate you all. All of you.

Lucy laughed as she laid her phone down and watched as her mother came out in each dress. She didn't like the first three and neither did her mom, but when she came out in an A-line, princess V-neck, floor-length chiffon dress with beading along the bodice and cascading ruffles on the skirt, Lucy sat up straight, holding back the tears. The dress fit her mother perfectly. It fell along her curves and gave her such a sexy shape.

"Oh, Mommy, that's the one," she gasped, covering her mouth. Shawna nodded as Autumn looked in the mirror, holding back her own tears. Getting a birdcage veil that was made of the same chiffon, Shawna pulled Autumn's long, brown hair to the side and pinned it up, transforming Lucy's mother into a bride. Turning, her mom looked back at her and grinned.

"I think it's the one."

"It is," Lucy agreed, and then out of nowhere, Autumn squealed. Loudly. Making practically everyone in the shop jump, Lucy included. That had her laughing so hard, tears started to roll down her cheeks. Man, she was so happy for her mom. Getting up, she ran to her mother and held her tightly, the love for her and this moment overwhelming her.

She wanted this.

She wanted it so badly.

When Autumn pulled back, cupping Lucy's face, she beamed at her as she wiped her tears away. "You're next, my love."

Lucy scoffed, rolling her eyes. "Gotta raise Angie first."

But that made Autumn's smile drop and her eyes narrow. "What?"

She was confused as she held her mother's hazel gaze. "I need to raise Angie, and then I can worry about me."

"What in the world makes you think that?"

"I don't think it. I know it. I don't have time for a relationship," she said, but Autumn shook her head.

"The hell you don't. You make time. You can't just nurture that baby, Lucy Lane, you have to nurture you too."

"No, Angie is all that matters, Mom. One day, I'll worry about my needs."

But again, her mother was shaking her head. "Lucy Lane, no. I know you worry about that baby, I know you want to do right by her, but how can you when you aren't satisfied with where you are in life?"

Lucy's face scrunched up. Why did everyone think she was unhappy? "Mom, I'm good."

"Don't lie to me, girl," her mother snapped and Lucy's eyes widened.

"I'm not."

"You are so. You're moving through life, only worrying about Angie and her wishes, and forgetting all about you," she said. Her words had truth to them, but Lucy was fine. She really was. "When was the last time you went on a date?"

Lucy thought for a moment. She didn't remember. Fuck, she really didn't remember. Clearing her throat, she looked away and shrugged. "I don't know, a couple months ago."

"Liar."

"Okay, Mom, what's your point?" she asked, frustrated.

"Oh, I'm getting to it," she said then, her hands coming to lace with Lucy's. "Can you even tell me the last time you had sex?"

Lucy's face twisted in horror. "Jesus! I'm not telling you that."

"Lucy…"

"Mom!" she gasped, a laugh escaping her lips. "That's personal."

"Or is it because you can't remember?" she said, squeezing her hands. Yeah, Lucy was about to cry. Damn it. Her mother was right, she didn't remember. Somewhere in the last seven years, all that ever mattered—all that *still* mattered—was Angie. She was the first thing Lucy woke up thinking about, worrying about, and she was the last thing Lucy thought of at night. Nothing else mattered because Angie was it. Angie was her life, and there was nothing wrong with that. That's the way a mother was supposed to be.

"Angie is my only priority, Mom," she said, but it was more for herself than her mom. She believed her words, she did, but was she hiding behind them? She didn't know, but she suspected she was.

"See, and I think the same about you, Jude, Jayden, and Jace. You four are my life, but I've always made time for me. I had to, or you all would drive me insane," she said with a laugh and Lucy smiled. She had that right; the Sinclair kids were crazy. "But, baby, do you not see that in the last few years, you've become bitter?"

Lucy's brows rose. "No…"

"Yes, it started with Jude getting married, and then Jayden, and now Jace."

Had she? It wasn't a shock when Jude got married. She knew it was coming, but she always saw him as such a baby. When Jayden got married, he did it behind everyone's back, as did Jace, so both were shocks. But she was happy for them. Wasn't she? Yeah, she loved her sisters-in-law. No, she was happy for them.

"I see the way you act when I talk about marrying River. You hate it. You're jealous and, baby, green may be your color but not envy green. You don't have to feel like this. Any guy would be lucky to have you."

Crap. Why was everyone pointing out her faults lately?

"Don't you dare cry," she demanded and Lucy looked away.

"I just…" She paused, sucking in a breath. "I just don't know anymore. It scares me."

"Well, yeah, I'm sure it does. But, baby, don't you think a happy mommy would be better for Angie than a bitter mommy just trying to get by?"

"I don't need a man to make me happy," she shot back and Autumn nodded.

"Never said you did, but something needs to happen. Even if it's just a vacation of your own, you need to do some things that make *you* happy."

Lucy looked away and nodded. Her mom was right; she needed to do something, but what scared her was that her mind went right to Benji.

And she had no clue what the hell that meant.

Ugh, she was running late.

Of course, lunch, shopping, and talking about feelings with her mother always took a lot of time, but she hadn't realized it would only leave her with twenty minutes to get to her new client. She was hungry, and something smelled in her apartment. When she couldn't find the source of the smell, she started to panic because it smelled chemical. Like her fridge was about to explode or something. So she called the landlord, who promised someone would come over immediately.

After hanging up with him, she called Rayne. "Hey, send me the address for my five o'clock. It didn't populate in my calendar."

"Crap. Sorry, I forgot to transfer it for you," she said, and Lucy could hear the clicking in the background.

"No big deal, thanks."

"Have fun."

"Yeah," Lucy said with an empty laugh as she hung up and waited for the address to come through. God, she was exhausted. Her mother just drained her, physically and emotionally, and she had no desire to do this consult. Not even kind of, but she needed the money. Especially when she had three people coming in for interviews starting Friday for the second design position.

Finally, the address came through and Lucy hit it, the GPS coming up for her. Oh, good, it was only ten minutes from her apartment. Following the GPS while she sang along to some Sam Hunt, Lucy recapped her whole day thus far. It wasn't a day she'd like to remember, but then, it was. Seeing Angie on that stage, dancing with the grace of an elephant, was one of the sweetest things she had ever seen. She dreaded talking to Rick about pulling her from dance tomorrow, but she would. For Angie.

She thought about how happy her mom looked and how she wanted what her mom felt. She wasn't sure when she would feel like that, but a part of her considered doing what she said, maybe trying. She didn't need a man—she didn't. She was very independent, but maybe she could ask Benji if the offer of dinner was still on the table. She could get her mom to babysit, or maybe it could be on the weekend Rick had Angie.

She smiled at the possibility.

Yeah, she was going to do it.

When she pulled into the stately neighborhood where she knew houses were around a million a pop, her brows rose. The houses on this side of town were high-end and usually were brand-new. Why would someone want her to design here? Wait, was the GPS right? Pulling into the driveway it told her to pull into, she checked the address again and it was right. Looking up at the grayish-white stone home that looked like it belonged in the 1900s and not the 2010s, Lucy shrugged her shoulders.

Hm. It was spectacular and she was excited.

Her design skills were tingling.

Getting out of the car, she grabbed her bag from the back and then locked up before heading up the walkway. The house was gorgeous, with big windows and incredible stonework. The door was massive, and Lucy had always loved big doors. She wanted one on her house when she finally was able to buy. Reaching up, she used the old-fashioned doorknocker she was sure was just for looks. But she had to. It was too awesome not to use.

The door opened and the homeowner said, "Yes! You used the doorknocker. Awesome, right?"

But she missed all that.

Because standing in front of her was the man who had been starring in all her dirty daydreams.

Benji.

If Benji thought Lucy was hot in that red dress the night before, nothing could prepare him for the forest-green dress she wore as she stood in front of him on his porch. It hugged every single inch of her, stopping right at her calves. It clung to her breasts something insane, and he didn't even need a peek of them for his mouth to water. Nope. She was completely covered and still completely lethal. Her hair was cascading down her shoulders, a braid along the crown of her head tucked behind her ear. Her eyes were wide with surprise, and he assumed she hadn't known it would be him she was designing for.

He liked the O her mouth made, and he especially like the red lips she had.

"Benji?" she finally gasped and he grinned.

"The one and only. Wanna come in?"

"This is your house?"

He laughed. "Yup. Nice, right?"

"Uh, yeah," she said, her eyes still locked with his. "You called for me to design your house?"

"Yeah, Jayden told me I had to." That made her snap her mouth shut, her eyes narrowing a bit, and he thought he may have offended her. "I looked you up first and checked out their house and then some of the other guys, and I was impressed. I need someone because—don't judge me, okay?—my house is not adultish at all."

He was rambling, and his hands were shaking. Probably because she was standing on his porch. Looking at him. She was on his turf, and he should have the advantage. But he didn't feel as though he did. "Aren't you supposed to come in?"

She didn't move, her eyes looking away as she pulled in a breath. "Are you sure?"

He looked at her, confused. "Um, well, yeah. It's chilly out and I think your legs could get cold, so maybe you should come in. Just so you don't get hypothermia and die."

Her lips quirked into a grin as she looked up at him. "Was this a ploy to get me to go out with you?"

"I mean, that's actually a wonderful idea. And if I had that kind of game, I might have set up a dinner for you. But sadly, I didn't, and I really do need someone to decorate my house," he said with a grin and she smiled back. "So will you come in?"

"Okay," she said simply as she walked past him, her perfume making him dizzy. Jesus, what was that scent and could he bathe in it? "I really don't think you can un-adult this house. I mean, it's gorgeous."

"Right?" he said, shutting the door behind her. "I thought so too, but then I moved in, and, yeah…"

As she walked into the living room where a gamer chair and a mini-table for his drinks sat, he looked at her as her eyes widened. "I take back my previous statement. This is a bachelor pad. My brothers would kill for a TV like that."

Benji nodded as he closed the distance between him and his TV. "Most guys do. It's my pride and joy," he said, gently caressing his eighty-inch, LG baby.

"Wow," she said, looking around. "This place is bare."

"Yeah. My stuff's all still in boxes in the shed, but before I unpack any of it, I need help."

"I'd say so," she said, setting down her bag and getting her notepad.

"How'd Angie's recital go this morning?"

She looked up and smiled. "The girl is as graceful as a herd of buffalo."

He laughed. "Yeah, she skates hard. I couldn't see her as a dancer."

"Exactly," she said, exhaling a breath. "She wants to quit, which is gonna be hell when I tell her dad."

That made him pause. He wanted to offer to be there. He also wanted to offer to smash the dude's face in, but it wasn't his place, so he just nodded. Unsure what to say next.

Thankfully, she beat him to it. "Well, show me the rest of the house."

So he did. They walked through the kitchen, and she made little sounds of pleasure that shot straight to his groin. "This kitchen is immaculate," she gasped, running her fingers first along the marble countertops and then the white cabinets. "It's naked in here."

It would be nice if she were naked in there, but he couldn't say that. "Yeah, I don't know what to put in here."

"Oh, wow, it has a reading nook," she said, going into the little den that had a fireplace. "You could sit here and read while the fire burned."

"Good idea."

She looked up at him. "You read?"

"Yeah, I do," he admitted and she smiled. "I even have geeky reading glasses."

Her lips parted a bit and she looked dazed, but then she looked away quickly, taking a deep breath. "Onward, Paxton."

He took her upstairs, and as they walked around, he decided he loved having her in his house. It was easy to say she loved design, and while they walked from room to room, she was drawing and taking pictures. Her eyes widened when she saw something she liked. And when her brows touched, a little wrinkle appeared between them. It was sexy as shit.

Being in his bedroom with her was probably the hardest thing he had ever done. She walked around his bed three times, yes, he counted. And each time, he wanted to tackle her into it and kiss her until they both were breathless. When she bent down to measure something, all he could do was stand there, staring at her ass like a sixteen-year-old checking out his hot teacher. She was just so gorgeous.

"Do you have any ideas for what you want in here?" she asked, standing up and looking back at him. He cleared his throat, covering his groin with his hands to hide his massive hard-on. This girl was going to be the death of him.

"Nope, no clue. I don't know what looks good. I just want to seem like an adult, you know? I don't want a bachelor pad. I want a home."

She nodded slowly. "So I can get rid of the gamer chair?"

He scoffed. "Whoa, now, let's not get ahead of ourselves."

Grinning, she wrote something down and then shrugged. "Okay, isn't there one more room?"

He nodded and headed for the last room. He saved it for last because he wasn't sure how she would react to it. If she thought it was a bachelor pad before, she wasn't ready for what he was about to show her. Opening the door, he looked back at her as she entered, her eyes bigger than quarters. "I kind of want, like, a way to display them. I can't decide between cases or shelves. I don't know. What do you think?"

But she was speechless, her eyes wide as she took in all his action figures, Lego sets, and *Star Wars* collectibles. Like his prized lightsaber that he had gotten signed by Mark Hamill, who played Luke Skywalker in the original *Star Wars* movies.

"I think you have more toys than Angie does," she said, cutting him a look.

"Collectibles."

She pressed her lips together. "So you want me to design a room for your collectibles," she said, saying the last word very slowly. "I mean…wow."

He held her gaze, pretty sure she was teasing him. "Yeah, don't laugh at me!"

But she did. "I've never seen so many toy—collectibles," she said, correcting herself, and he shrugged.

"Hey, you know what they say about a man who collects," he said with an exaggerated wink.

"Yeah, he's a nerd."

"Ha. No, he's patient. It takes time to collect all this."

She didn't look convinced as she walked around the room. The heels of her black pumps clicked against the hardwood. Which, of course, made his mouth water. Those calves…man. "I've never done a collectible room," she said, more to herself. "Because usually adults don't have them."

"Because they aren't awesome," he said simply and she smiled.

"I didn't peg you for a nerdy kind of guy."

He looked over at her. "Well, if you would have gone to dinner with me, I would have told you."

Her eyes darkened as she nodded slowly. "I guess so."

He watched as she looked around, her eyes scrutinizing a lot of what he had. But then he thought maybe she was a closet nerd because she got excited when she looked at all his *Star Wars* figures. When she paused in the middle of the room, only inches from him, to mark something on her notepad, he rocked back on his heels, tucking his hands in his pockets just so he wouldn't touch her.

He wanted to brush her hair off her shoulder. Just to press his lips to her neck. He knew it would be soft. That she would smell like heaven.

Man, this was a bad idea.

He should have hired someone else, because having Lucy Sinclair in his house, looking as fucking sexy as she was, was going to make him combust.

"So what do you think?" he asked roughly, sucking in a breath.

"I think I can do some pretty awesome stuff in here, along with the rest of the house, but—" She paused, looking up at him. "It isn't going to be an overnight thing. I mean, I have a blank canvas and you have no clue what you want, so it's gonna take time to get it right, you know?"

Time. He had that. As long as he was spending it with her. "Sounds good to me. I'm not going anywhere. Well, I mean, I do have games, but we have email."

She nodded. "Okay, so let's head downstairs and—"

Her phone rang and her eyes widened. "Crap, sorry. I usually have it on silent, but when Angie is gone... And then there was this weird smell in my apartment... Hold on," she said quickly, answering her phone. Benji heard a man on the other end, and for a second he thought it was Rick, but then she shook her head. "You're kidding me. What?" she said, turning so her back was to Benji. "When can I go back? Tuesday at the latest! Can I come get some things? Jesus. Okay. No, I understand. No, I do, and I appreciate you working to get it all fixed. It's just an inconvenient— No, thank you. All right, keep me posted. Thanks."

Disconnecting the call, she let her arms fall to her sides, her notebook and phone hanging in her hands. She didn't say anything, just breathed in deeply, letting out her breaths in a whoosh.

"Lucy? Everything okay?"

She only shook her head, and he walked around her to look at her face. She was holding in her tears, her face flushed red as she sucked in another breath and let it out. "I swear, if I didn't have bad luck, I wouldn't have any."

"Is everything okay?"

She closed her eyes. "Can you, like, turn around or something? I need a moment, and I really don't want you to see me lose my fucking shit right now."

Panic was in her voice, which made him panic a bit. "Can I do something?"

She shook her head and her voice broke as she met his gaze. "I don't even know what you could do."

Holding her watery gaze, he knew what he could do.

He didn't even think, really, he just acted. Wrapping his arms around her, he pulled her to him, and it was like a fire had been set at his toes. Nothing but heat exploded between them as their bodies lined up, his arms holding her. She tensed, like he expected, as her nose pressed into his chest. But he just squeezed her tightly, resting his head on hers.

Sure of himself, he said roughly, "I think you need a hug."

She didn't move at first. She only stood there and he squeezed her, loving the feel of her in his arms. He had wanted this from the moment he saw her. When she dropped her phone and notebook, wrapping her arms around his waist, a grin curved Benji's lips as she slowly relaxed in his embrace. She smelled so good, felt like pure bliss in his arms, and he wanted to nuzzle his nose in her hair but wasn't sure how that would go. He was surprised he was able to hug her, but it was obvious she needed it.

When she let out a long breath, her heart pounding against his chest, he held his own breath, fully expecting her to pull away.

But she didn't.

Instead, she wrapped her arms tighter around him, nuzzling her nose into his chest and whispered, "Yeah, I think I do."

Chapter SEVEN

Oh, why did she hug him?

Why in the world did she let that happen?

Because, now…

Now, she didn't want to let go.

Every part of her body that touched his was seriously on fire. She had wanted this since the moment he asked her out. To touch him. To feel him against her. Even in her wildest dreams, nothing could touch the reality of him.

Benji.

He smelled like heaven. All rugged and manly, with a side of spice and sex. Mmm, he smelled fantastic, and Lord, he hugged like a dream. Like he was meant to hug and only hug. Nothing else. She'd seen him play hockey and he was great, but she was pretty sure the guy hugged better than he played. She had never been held so tightly, so protectively.

And she just felt safe.

Perfectly safe.

She didn't want him to stop, which was bad. She wasn't supposed to be this close to him. No, because deep inside her, the fear that something could come from this was screaming loud and clear. Maybe she was jumping the gun, but if he even made the simplest of moves on her, she was pretty sure she'd be naked in two seconds flat. Her whole body was aware of him. The way he breathed, so deep, so strong. The way his lips felt against her head, it was sweet, almost like she was a child who needed support and reassurance that everything was going to be okay.

And she needed that more than he'd ever realize.

God, how she needed this man's arms around her. Badly. After the call from the landlord that confirmed the odor she smelled was actually standing water behind the fridge, which led to the discovery of a burst water pipe and then all hell breaking loose, Lucy had found herself homeless. They weren't even sure if she could work in the building on Monday. Which meant she would be going to her mom's, and if she saw River's ass, she was going to lose it. She just couldn't catch a break. One thing after another, and it was really starting to weigh on her heart. And ugh, her mom had just picked out her wedding dress, which meant they were probably doing nasty things, and yeah, she didn't want to be the third wheel to that lovefest.

No, she wanted to stay right here.

In Benji's arms.

No matter how bad that was. No matter how much she knew she needed to let go and move away, she held him. Like a life preserver in rough waters. Because that's what her life was. Freakish, fucking monstrous waves of shit that kept hitting her right in the face. She almost started to cry, but then his arms held her tighter, almost like he knew. Knew she was about to lose her fucking shit.

Oh, Lucy, no. Keep your hands to yourself, she begged herself, but she couldn't. She just couldn't.

She needed him.

Moving her hands up his back, she snuggled closer against him as he inhaled deeply, his whole body moving with the breath he took. His hands tucked into her sides tighter, his fingers grazing the swells of her breasts. It was such a simple touch. No big deal, she doubted he even meant to do it. But shit, it felt good and everything went hot inside of her. Her whole body broke out in gooseflesh, totally aware of the sexy man who was holding her.

Hell, she had been aware of him since the moment she met him. If she was honest with herself, turned her fucking brain off, she'd realize that she'd wanted him more than her next breath since that moment too. But she wasn't sure she could. She didn't know how to give in to that need, and that was just sad. Because right now, she could do some pretty naughty things to this man. The only thing holding her back was the regret afterward. It would be a mistake.

Wouldn't it?

Closing her eyes, she moved her nose against his chest as his heart pounded against his ribs. She wasn't sure and that scared her. Everything was muddled. On one hand, she wanted him with the fierceness of a thousand armies. And on the other, she knew it wouldn't end well. He'd want more, or hell, she might want more. And then what? Shit, what was she doing? But she couldn't think

of that for long because the rhythm of his heartbeat was soothing, and all her worries, they…they just disappeared. It was insane, but damn it, she felt so damn good.

Safe.

It was such a beautiful feeling too, something she had never felt in her life. She used to think that Rick gave good hugs, that she was safe in his arms, but she'd been wrong. So fucking wrong. Not even hugging her father, when he was her world, or her brothers was like hugging Benji.

No, this was different.

And crap, she was turned on. So damned turned on. From a hug? Jesus, she was pitiful, but she couldn't deny how she felt. How he made her feel. She remembered Avery saying that moments with her brother—gag—would cause her to hear Ed Sheeran in her head, singing so beautifully to the moment she was in. Yeah, Ed was singing, loud and clear, and Lucy was swooning.

When Benji started to pull back, she whimpered. He paused, holding her closer if possible, chuckling against her hair. "Lucy, tell me what's wrong."

She couldn't. She didn't want to ruin this moment. She didn't want to cry about the shitstorm of her life right now. No, she just wanted to be held. To be protected by this man. That's all she wanted, and she felt she deserved it. She wanted to feel safe. Was that too much to ask?

"Let me help," he whispered, his lips brushing along her hair.

Closing her eyes, she sucked in a breath and figured she owed him at least an explanation for why she was clinging to him like he was the only solid thing in her life. Which was ludicrous. She was Lucy Fucking Sinclair, she didn't need any man… But right now, she needed Benji, which completely contradicted what she thought of herself. But it was becoming really exhausting being strong all the time.

Moving her nose up his chest, she opened her eyes, placing her chin in the middle of his chest as she looked up at him. Which was a bad idea. Because now, she was speechless. His lips were pressed together, only a little curve to them, worry in those gray eyes locked on hers. She had never looked into such intense eyes. Like she really could see his soul. It was tarnished, but still so beautiful.

And shit, she wanted to kiss him.

He must have felt her realization because he looked stunned, his eyes darkening as his mouth slowly parted. Swallowing hard, he held her gaze with his eyes and time stopped. She heard nothing as he moved his hand to cup her face. Just a simple motion, so sweet, his thumb tracing the line of her jaw. Slowly shaking his head, he quirked his lips and she was convinced he had never been sexier.

"I swear, I've never seen someone so beautiful as you in all my adult life."

Oh, God. Her pussy clenched as she gasped for breath. It wasn't like she hadn't been called beautiful before, but when Benji said it, it was real. Like he really hadn't ever seen anyone as lovely as she, and holy crap, it made her feel good. Special. She felt special. Crap. Crap. Triple crap.

"Really?" she croaked out, and instantly, she regretted it. Really? That was her answer? Where was her sassy demeanor? There was so much more she could have said there. Like, "Right back at you, stud." Jesus, was she Sandy Olsson? Stud? Who even thinks that? And crap, *Shut your brain off, Lucy! Now!*

While she was arguing with herself, Benji's gaze was on her intently, his thumb moving ever so slowly on her jaw, almost touching the side of her mouth as he drank her in. As she got lost in his eyes, the air around them crackled and popped and she couldn't move. She couldn't think. No, all she could do was look up into his beautiful face and drink him in. How his jaw was so thick, his eyes so dark, and Jesus, those lips. To feel them would be a blessing, she was convinced. And all she had to do was go up on her toes and she'd be there. Just one simple move.

"Lucy."

Just go up on your tippytoes. Kiss him. Jesus, Lucy, do it!

Yet, she didn't move. Only whispered, "Benji?"

He swallowed once more, his jaw clenching as his fingers threaded through her hair. His body was so taut, like he was trying so hard not to move. All she wanted to do was press her lips to his. But what if he didn't want it— Oh, who was she kidding? She could feel him. He wanted her.

"I want to kiss—"

Fuck it.

Before the words could leave his mouth, she went on her toes and then her mouth was moving against his.

And all hell broke loose.

He lifted her off the ground and whipped them around, pressing her into the wall with urgency. His body covered hers perfectly as their mouths moved together in an urgent caress. He felt so big, so strong, his lips so soft. It was everything she had ever dreamed of. *God, yes.* As she wrapped her legs around his hips, one of his hands held her ass while the other tousled her hair, his kisses becoming more demanding as his cock pressed into her soft center.

She wasn't going to make it.

When she opened her mouth, his tongue met hers as his hand slid down her body, his fingers biting into her hips. Arching into him, she moved her hands up his arms, then his neck, and into his hair. She wasn't sure how, but she deepened the kiss. His body felt so good, so hot against hers, and man, she wanted more. When his mouth tore from hers, his lips traced down her jaw, nibbling before going along her jaw to her ear, and she cried out. She didn't want to stop.

"I should stop?" It was a question, a stupid question she didn't answer. She only arched her body into his, wanting more. His hands moved up her body, grazing the sides of her breasts before sliding back down, taking ahold of her ass. When he pressed himself against her, the long, hot length of him caused her to whimper as he asked, "Shouldn't I?"

"No," she gasped and he smiled against her lips.

"No?"

"Fuck no, don't stop," she cried as his teeth sank into her bottom lip before their mouths met once more and her hands went up under his shirt, sliding along the ripples of muscles.

"Fuck," he moaned as her fingers dusted his ribs, and his skin broke out in gooseflesh. "I can't stop."

"Don't. Please don't," she moaned against his lips.

That must have been what he was waiting for because his kisses became more demanding and Lucy wasn't complaining. He kissed the way she thought he would.

Magically.

His lips were pillows for hers, and his hands, they were damned lethal. They felt her all over, and her body trembled beneath his as he quickly bunched her skirt at her waist, taking ahold of her bare ass cheeks. His fingers pressed into her as he arched against her, kissing her with what she was sure was everything he had. Had he wanted her the way she had wanted him? How long? How had he resisted her? Because she was surprised she had lasted this long.

When he lifted her farther, holding her up with his body, she cried against his mouth as his fingers moved between her legs, pressing his palm into her hot center.

"Oh, oh, God," she murmured and he answered with a growl against her lips. Moving her thong to the side, he slid his fingers inside of her and they both moaned.

"Oh, you're wet," he muttered against her lips as her eyes slowly rolled to the back of her head. As he moved his finger up and around her clit, she cried out, her whole body clenching. He met her gaze. His half-lidded eyes almost had her coming all over his hand as he asked, "Have you been this wet the whole time you've been here? Have you wanted me, Lucy? Tell me."

His demands only made her cry out more as his finger moved along her clit quickly and with efficiency. His hand was shaking, but it was getting the job done, and soon she was coming so hard, she saw lights behind her eyes as she cried out against his mouth, his name falling softly from her lips.

"God, yes," he moaned, pressing his thumb against her clit as her body shook with the aftershocks of her climax. Arching off the wall, her body vibrated, and when she heard the sound of him unbuckling his belt, she almost cried in relief.

Finally.

"Condom, shit, hold on—"

"Birth control," she muttered, holding him in place.

"Bed?"

"No. Here."

His lips curved against hers, his bare cock pressing into her center. God, he was big. A shiver ran through her body as she met his gaze, his lips moving against hers as he asked, "Here?"

"Right here," she demanded, taking ahold of him and directing him to her entrance. She had wanted wall-banging sex from him since she'd seen him in those Assassins sweat pants. Taking her by the back of her knee, he opened her more and then slowly thrust inside of her. One thrust, completely filling her to the hilt, and she was sure the neighbors heard her scream.

"Oh, oh, Benji," she gasped, holding on to him for dear life.

"Fuck, you're so tight," he practically whimpered, moving out very slowly and then just as slowly back in, both of them moaning as he disappeared inch by inch inside of her. Her whole body trembled, her pussy clenching him as her fingers bit into the back of his neck. As he moved out of her, his fingers bit into her knee as she slowly shook her head. Meeting her gaze, he smiled as his nose moved against hers, his thrusts becoming more demanding, more forceful. Each one took her breath away, her cries mixing with his moans as he pounded into her.

At one point, she forgot her name.

But when he took her behind her other knee, pressing her knees into the wall and proceeding to fuck her stupid, she was pretty sure she would never remember said name. Holding on to his shoulders, her nails digging into his skin, she watched him. Sweat was dripping down his neck, his shirt was wrinkled to hell, his hips were gorgeous, and fuck, he was beautiful. His jaw was clenched and she knew he was almost there. She could feel it.

But before he could come, he pulled out, dropping to his knees and burying his face between her legs.

"Oh fuck," she cried out, and she was surprised she wasn't scared she was going to hit the floor.

But he had her.

Boy, did he have her.

As he moved his tongue along her lips, she closed her eyes, arching off the wall as he sucked her clit into his mouth, and then blew on it. Crying out, she trembled as he flicked his tongue along her, her whole body going taut. His fingers bit into her knees as her fingers squeezed his shoulders, and she was sure he was going to be bruised tomorrow. She didn't think he cared, though, because he was ruthless, his tongue doing damage against her pussy. And when she came…

She came hard.

But she couldn't even bask in it before he was standing, lifting her up the wall and reentering her in one fell swoop.

"Oh, oh, oh," she panted as he started to pound into her, her body squeezing his as he pushed in to the hilt, filling her completely before doing it all over again. Over and over again, until a harsh yell left his lips and he stilled, arching into her before her name fell from his lips. He filled her as her body shook with her own orgasm, her pussy clenching him, milking him. Her eyes were shut, and as she pulled in deep breaths, she swore she had never felt this good in her life. That orgasm was due eight years ago, and still the blinding pulsation of it had her gasping for breath. Her whole body was on fire as he pressed his forehead to hers, his lips moving very slowly against hers while they both fought for air.

Good Lord, did that really just happen?

When she opened her eyes, he was watching her, his eyes dark. Yeah, she was pretty sure she was about to come again. And when he pushed against her, his pubic bone pressing into her swollen, pulsing pussy, to her surprise, she did. She came all over his dick, again. As she cried out, her body shaking, nothing but white-hot lust was in the gray depths watching her come, and boy, was it breathtaking. If she thought being hugged by him was heaven, she was wrong, so damn wrong. Because being fucked by Benji Paxton was out of this world.

And she wanted more.

Threading his hands in Lucy's hair, he opened his eyes, meeting her surprised gaze as her pussy squeezed him.

"Wow," he gasped and she grinned.

A real one. Dimples, bright eyes, the whole nine. Her face was red, her lips swollen, and her hair was a mess all falling in her face. But he thought she was the most beautiful creature known to man. And he'd made love to her. Hard.

"Wow is one way to put it," she whispered against his lips. She kissed him softly and then kissed the side of his mouth, a grin curving her lips. "Jeez, I just wanted a hug."

He chuckled, his nose moving along hers. "You started it."

"And you finished. I wasn't expecting that at all."

"Me either," he admitted softly before lifting her off the wall. Her legs wrapped around his waist as he stepped out of his jeans and headed toward his room. "But I'm nowhere near done."

He sat her on the edge of the bed. "No?" she asked as he moved her dress up and over her body, throwing it on the floor.

"Not even close to being done," he said roughly as she looked up at him, her hair a mess as her lips curved. The bra she wore didn't cover much since it was completely lace, and man, he was about to drool all over himself. "That's a nice bra."

She giggled before looking down at it, but when she went to look up at him, she paused at his cock. "And that's a nice cock."

She reached out, running her finger down the length of him and he shuddered. He wasn't going to make it through round two, he was convinced, if she kept touching him. As she ran the tip of her finger along the head of him, he covered her hand. He met her gaze, his cock pulsating so hard, he felt it in his ears.

"Keep your hands to yourself," he teased and she grinned.

"Ha, do you really mean that?"

"Fuck no, but I can't handle it." He chuckled as he leaned toward her, undoing her bra and pulling it down her arms, tracing kisses along the path the straps took down her right arm. Throwing the bra over his shoulder, he drank her in. Her breasts were like he thought they would be—gorgeous. Round, thick, and mouthwatering. He wanted to bury himself between them, but instead, he ran his tongue along her collarbone and down the valley between them before kissing each peak softly. Before he could take a nipple into his mouth, she reached for his shirt, pulling it up. He pulled back, helping her remove the shirt before throwing it on the floor with her bra and dress.

When she made a sound of pleasure, he had to fight back the grin. Her face was so cute, all flushed, and he wanted to kiss her. Damn bad. So he did, and when she smiled, he smiled too.

This was just right.

God, it felt so right.

Pulling back, he looked down at her as her fingers moved along his chest and abs. "Good Lord, for a guy who collects toys, you obviously don't miss gym time," she said, running her fingers along where his tattoo for Ava and Leary laid. She looked at it for a moment and then back up at him. He waited for her to ask, held his breath, wondering if he should tell her or do what the guys said. Hold that back, wait for the right moment. Hot and heavy sexy time didn't seem like the right moment. Might be a mood killer; he wasn't sure. He couldn't lie about them, wouldn't lie, but he didn't want to ruin this. This was awesome. Perfect, even.

Thankfully, though, she didn't ask. Instead, she brought him down on top of her, slowly lying back as their mouths met. He braced himself up, his mouth moving with hers as he fell between her legs, the warmth from her center teasing his growing cock. Moving his hands up, one went into her hair, and Lord, her hair was so soft. He had thought it would be, but feeling it in his hand was a whole other thing. It was flawless.

She was his kind of perfect.

Shaking, he cupped her breast, his thumb moving along her taut nipple as she arched up into his hand. Her mouth glided along his, their kisses burning hot and so consuming. As her hands came up onto his shoulders that were still aching from her nails, he pressed into her and she moaned against his lips. His mind went to mush. She was so responsive, so hot, and he was thanking his lucky stars he'd hugged her.

This was all from a hug.

It was one pretty fucking great hug.

Tearing his mouth from hers, he kissed down her jaw, her neck, his teeth scoring her skin and nibbling at her as she squirmed and whispered his name. She slid her fingers into his hair as he kissed down the center of her chest, licking each globe of her breasts before bringing a nipple between his lips. She cried out, her legs squeezing his waist as she moved herself along his cock. God, she was so wet, and it felt so good, but he wanted this to last.

He never wanted it to end.

He wanted to taste her again. Yeah, that's what he wanted. Or he wasn't going to last. Inching down her belly, he kissed her hip bone and then moved over to the other one as she trembled, her legs shaking. He kissed her other hip before opening her legs and snaking his tongue down the length of her lips.

"Yes, God, yes," she moaned, arching herself into him as his tongue found its way between her lips. Just the simple press of his tongue to her sweet clit had her thrashing and he almost laughed.

Good lord, where had she been all his life?

Holding her open, he dove in, flicking his tongue along her clit quickly as his other hand moved to her entrance, sliding two fingers inside of her and curling up into her. She cried out as he started to fuck her with his hand and tease her with his tongue. As he watched her, her hands came up onto her breasts, squeezing them as she gasped for breath, her moans getting louder and louder with every thrust of his hand.

Sucking her clit between his lips and then biting lightly, he almost came at the sight of her coming undone. Her whole body was flushed and she broke out in goose bumps as she screamed his name, struggling against his mouth. Closing his eyes, he sucked her harder. She begged him to stop, but he couldn't.

"I can't, Benji."

"You can," he demanded, still fucking her as she squeezed his fingers hard with her spectacular pussy.

When she laughed, he met her gaze and she shook her head. "No, really, I can't," she gasped, pushing his head away, and he paused, a grin pulling at his lips.

"Really?"

"What? I think you broke me," she said, still fighting for breath. Her eyes were dark and hard, beautiful. And as he lifted his mouth, he eyed her.

"I haven't even gotten started."

"Jesus take the wheel," she muttered as he covered her, pushing her thong down her legs. Rolling over onto her side, she kicked her panties off and then crawled on top of him. "Maybe I haven't gotten started?"

Benji bit into his lip as her hot, wet center descended on his swollen flesh. She leaned down, kissing him as his hands came up to hold her sweet ass. He moved her up and down on him, and she gasped against his lips and set him with a look. "I'm trying to seduce you."

He scoffed. "Baby, you seduced me the moment I saw you."

That surprised her, her little lips parting as she eyed him. "Oh, yeah?"

"Oh, fuck yeah," he agreed, rolling them over and pushing her leg up so he could enter her again.

"Hey, strong guy," she complained halfheartedly, but her complaints were a thing of a past when he entered her fully. "Never mind," she breathed, and he chuckled against her jaw as he pushed in and then pulled slowly back out. "As you were."

"Fuck, I can't handle you," he admitted against her jaw, pressing a kiss to it as he moved in and out of her.

"I was thinking the same thing," she gasped, her nails biting into the back of his arm. Arching into him, she squeezed his cock before crying out. "Please, don't stop."

"I couldn't if I tried," he moaned, before sitting up and bringing her with him. Sliding back on his haunches, he pounded up into her. Her breasts bounced against his chest, and yeah, he wasn't going to last. Her pussy was too good, too hot, and it held him like a dream as he moved up into her and back out. Holding her ass, he squeezed as her arms came around his neck, her mouth meeting his. And just like that, he was done.

Bucking into her, he cried against her lips. Her teeth sank into his lip as he moaned, filling her completely. She tightened around him, her body trembling against his as their hearts slammed into each other. Gasping for breath, she squeezed his neck, her nose pressing into his as their breaths became one and her lips grazed his.

Opening his eyes, he found hers still closed, her face flushed and ever so beautiful.

How was he supposed to let her leave this room?

When she opened her eyes, she blinked twice before a grin curved her lips and those dimples appeared in all their gorgeous glory. Licking her lips, and his, she wrapped him up tightly as his hands came around her.

In a hug.

"This all started with a hug," she whispered against his lips and he smiled. "Guess it should end with one."

"Who said anything about ending?"

Her eyes widened, and then she shrugged. "I assumed."

"You assumed wrong. I still have all night," he said, continuing not to move because he loved the feel of her.

She eyed him. "I pinned you completely wrong. I thought you were all shy and awkward."

His lips curved against hers. "I am, but it's different with you."

"Oh?"

"Yeah. Told you, you should have gone to dinner with me."

Her whole face smiled and she giggled. "Yeah, yeah. So, now what?"

"Sleep. I need sleep," he said then, falling over with her still in his arms.

Cuddling against him, she smiled. "A nap would be nice."

"Yup, because when we wake up, it's period three."

She rolled her eyes. "Hockey players."

He grinned against her hair and closed his eyes. "Shush, you. Get some rest."

"Don't tell me what to do," she demanded as she nuzzled her nose against his chin.

And as they fell asleep, Benji felt something he hadn't felt in a really long time.

Twelve years to be exact.

Whole.

He felt whole.

But she must have worn him out more than he realized, because when Benji woke up, he found not only was it daylight…

But Lucy was gone.

Chapter EIGHT

"Hello?"

"Avery."

"Lucy? What's wrong?"

Lucy leaned her forehead on the steering wheel of her car, sucking in a deep breath. She had one shoe on, no underwear, and she smelled like him—all glorious and sexy. But that didn't matter.

She had done the walk of shame.

Something she thought she would never do. Even as a teenager, she'd never done the walk of shame. Everyone she'd slept with was a boyfriend. But nope, now, in her twenties, she was doing the walk of shame. She was a mommy! Mommies didn't do walks of shame. It wasn't responsible, but nothing about last night was responsible.

The things they did.

The things she allowed.

Oh God, she had sex with a guy she had only known for a few days!

And after all was said and done, she'd had the best night's sleep of her life. Usually, she was restless, her mind going a billion miles an hour. But he had done her so well, relaxed her so much that when she closed her eyes, she didn't wake until seven.

And he was still beautifully asleep.

She could still see him. His chiseled jaw relaxed as he drew in deep breaths, his hair falling slightly over his closed eyes. His brown lashes touched his

cheeks, his plush lips parted ever so slightly, and Jesus… Did she miss him? Obviously not, because she hightailed it out of there faster than Angie moved when she hadn't had her medication. She had hustled moved so fast in her life, and because of that, she didn't give herself time to actually find her other shoe or panties.

God, she was a mess.

Squeezing her eyes shut, she considered just hanging up. Did she really want to share her indiscretions with her sister-in-law? What would it do? She wouldn't cry; she didn't regret it. She enjoyed every minute with him, but she was embarrassed. She hadn't wanted this to happen. She'd said it would be a bad idea. Yeah, she might have considered going out on a date with him. But that was it, a date! She basically jumped the dude. How was she supposed to face him? Ugh. It had been such a bad idea. She didn't have time for this.

"Damn it," Lucy muttered, shaking her head.

"What in the world? What is going on?"

"I slept with him," she said and then looked up at the Walmart in front of her. She was early. Rick wouldn't be there for another hour. But after going to the shop and her apartment, where she realized that she wouldn't be coming back for a while—Tuesday, her ass—she gathered what she could and stuffed it into her car. Hard feat when she was wearing a tight dress and no panties. There was no way to change in her apartment since they had torn down the wall between her room and the kitchen. She could have gone into the bathroom, but one of the workers was in there.

And apparently his breakfast did not agree with him.

So her week of hell was ending in a fiery heap, which was exactly how it started. But could she really consider last night part of her week of hell? Because it was on the opposite side of hell. No, it was perfect. So damn good and she wanted more, she did, but how? How in the world could that work? At first, she thought a date would be a good idea, but after being with him, no, a date would be a train wreck.

Because after one night.

One smile.

One press of his nose to hers.

She was fucking feeling something.

Damn it.

That was the issue with sex. It was a double-edged sword. One edge was great, "Woo-hoo, she loved sex. Giggity, giggity." But on the other edge, feelings could blossom. She'd wanted mindless, fun, happy, giggity sex, but she got more than that. She desired more. She wanted to know him. She wanted to never leave that bed, and that was what scared her so badly that she had to run. Never in her life had she had felt what she felt in Benji's arms, and she didn't understand it.

She didn't have time for it.

No, she had to raise Angie right. She had to deal with Rick, and bringing a man into that just wouldn't work. It couldn't. Rick would be such a fucking asshole, and that would have Benji running the other way. No one wanted to deal with stupid baby-daddy issues.

But Avery didn't know all that. Hell, she probably didn't need to know anything. Yet, Lucy whispered, "I slept with Benji."

Avery took in a sharp breath and then paused. "Okay. Why do you sound like you kicked a dog? I don't get it. I thought this is what you wanted."

Lucy shut her eyes once more, shaking her head. "I jumped him like a cat in heat, Avery. We went at it like rabbits and I ran. I left before he woke up."

"What? Why did you do that? And why so many animal references?"

"Focus, Avery," she complained and Avery laughed.

"I'm sorry, I just don't understand what is going on. You wanted to have sex, you had it, and it's okay that you ran. People do that all the time. It isn't like you guys are in a relationship. It was a one-night stand. So what?"

Why was she so callous about this? "You make it seem like not even a big deal!"

"It isn't!" Avery laughed. "People seriously do it all the time. Hell, I've done it."

Not something she wanted to know about her perfect angel sister-in-law who was married to her baby brother and had his child. "Avery Rose!"

She kept laughing. "That's how Jace and I got together."

Gag. "Oh, fuck. Shut up!"

Laughing, Avery cleared her throat. "It's not a big deal, really. Stop stressing."

"So you've done it with your daughter's coach, who is also your potential client?"

Avery paused at that. "Oh, also the dude who plays with your brother in the NHL. Okay, well, that does complicate things a bit."

"A bit!" Lucy screeched, shaking her head, and then wrapped her arms around her legs. "Avery, I'm sitting in my car, no panties, with one shoe on. I'm a mess. A water pipe busted in the wall of my apartment, and they have to tear down walls and fix shit. I'm homeless."

"Oh, Lucy—"

But Lucy stopped her. Why had she said all that? Shit. "No, you know what? It's no big deal. I'm gonna find some panties, pull them up, and then I'm gonna be okay. I'm always okay. I've got this."

"Lucy—"

"No, it's cool. I don't know why I called. I'm fine. Just a lot at once, and then Benji, yeah, he got under my skin. No big deal. I'll handle it with grace. I'll design his house and nothing will come of it. We are adults. People fuck all the time, no big deal. Maybe he'll pay me more," she said it as a joke, but even she didn't laugh. It wasn't funny. She wasn't a whore; that wasn't her. But last night she almost was, and she could feel Avery's sympathy coming off her in waves through the phone and against her face. But she didn't need that.

She was Lucy Fucking Sinclair, and she would handle this. She had it. She would stuff the stupid, crazy feelings back down, lock them up, and get on with her life. She didn't have time to complicate things further with Benji. She obviously needed his job because she had nowhere to live and could maybe lose the building for her shop. No, she had things to worry about, bigger things than stupid feelings.

Feelings that were completely and utterly insane to have.

It was one night.

Get your shit together, she thought as she shook her head. What, she slept with a guy for the first time in years, and all of a sudden, she liked him? That was insane. Stupid, even. God, she was a dumbass.

"Okay, no big deal. Don't freak. I'm good—"

"Did you ever think that maybe it's okay to be a little down sometimes? To reach out for help?" Avery asked, her voice a little hard. "You can't be strong all the time, and that's okay."

"Yes, I can, and I'm good. I promise. Little lapse of freak-out, no biggie. Don't worry, I'm good. I'll call you later. Rick just pulled up," she said, but it was a lie. Before Avery could call her on it, Lucy told her she loved her and hung up. Leaning back in her seat, she closed her eyes. Sometimes she was convinced she sucked at life. She was good with Angie, or at least, she tried to be, but everything else…? Yeah, she was a mess. It really wasn't fair. When was she going to catch a break?

As she watched the time, she didn't listen to anything on the radio. No, she was too busy replaying every single caress of Benji's hand. The sweep of his lips against her neck and jaw. The way he held her gaze and she felt beautiful. Safe. That was what she missed most and what was so hard to leave behind when she was carefully wiggling out of his hold.

The protection he gave her.

She wasn't sure what she needed protection from, but when she was in his arms, she felt like nothing could even come close to touching her. Nothing could stress her out. No, she was lost in those arms, the thickness of them. The warmth. She missed the warmth. It was just easy with him. She didn't have to try so hard. She was just herself, and he was into it.

Blah.

She also wanted to know more. Yeah, he was a great lay, best she had ever had—not that there was a long list to compare him to—but still, he was wonderful. So damn attentive, and those hands... Jesus. But, besides that, she wanted to know who he was. His house didn't give her anything to work with. It was so bare. Well, except that she knew he was a nerd who played video games and collected toys, but there weren't any pictures. Not even of him playing. It was weird, and she wanted to know more.

She wanted to know what the tattoo on his chest meant.

Laying right over his heart was a pair of angel wings with the words, "Your wings were ready, but my heart was not." She figured he had lost someone. Maybe his mom or dad or something. She wasn't sure, but she had this burning in her stomach from wanting to know. Though that would be such a bad idea. A date was completely off the table now. She had already slept with him. He'd had his face between her legs; what else could even come from a date?

Trouble, fucking trouble.

More stupid, dumb-ass feelings.

No, she needed to stay away from him. Far away.

She wasn't sure how that was going to work, but she'd figure it out. She would.

Or she'd probably end up in bed with him again.

It would go either way.

God, was she a whore?

Before she knew it, an hour had passed and she'd convinced herself she was the scum of the earth when Rick pulled up. Reaching for the tennis shoes she had grabbed out of her apartment, she put them on. She got out as Angie ran toward her, hugging her tightly.

"I missed you," she said against Lucy's stomach and she cringed. She should have showered. Did Angie smell him? *Ew, stop thinking that!*

"I missed you more, baby," she said, squeezing her tightly. "Tell your dad bye and then get in the car. I tried to leave you a spot, but it's tight."

Angie made a face, looking from the car to her. "Why is all our stuff in the car?"

"I'll tell you on the way to Grandma's," she said sadly before Rick came to a stop in front of her.

"Living out of your car? Not sure how that makes me feel. Maybe I should take her back with me."

Maybe you should go fuck yourself, is what she thought, but now wasn't the time for that. "She's fine," she said stiffly as Angie gave him a half hug.

"Bye, Dad."

"Bye, love bug," he said with a grin, but neither of them was impressed as Angie took her bag and got into the car. Looking to Lucy, he made a face. "You look like shit. Sleep in your car? Isn't that the dress you had on yesterday?"

Lucy rolled her eyes, exhaling a long breath. "Listen, two things. I don't want to fight with you, and I'm not going to. I'm going to say what I need to and then I'm getting in the car and leaving. I don't have time or patience for the whirlwind of dicks you like to throw at my face, okay?"

He scoffed at her, a condescending grin on his face. "I'm excited."

"Yeah," she said, letting out a breath.

"Wait, before you start running that mouth," he said, interrupting her. She glared. "Who's this Benji fucker? That's all Angie kept telling Nina about. Is he that coach? The one all up in my business?"

His name made her heart flutter. Swallowing hard, her face went red. Did Rick suspect she slept with him? Shit. No. That was silly. No one knew. Well, except Avery and Benji, but still. *Stop being crazy!* "Yeah, he's one of her coaches. He also plays on the Assassins with Jayden."

"Loser. Who wants to coach kids?"

Her eye twitched. Yes, she had thought the same thing, but Rick had no clue who Benji was. It surprised her but also worried her how easy it was to defend him. "Obviously, someone who likes kids."

"Or a pedophile."

Her body shook with anger all of a sudden. What the hell? "You don't know him. He's a good dude, really good with Angie," she spat back. But then she pressed her lips together.

Rick scoffed. "What, you fucking him like you fuck everyone else?"

She bit into her lip. *Hold it in, Lucy, hold it in. Do not point out that he is the cheating fucking bastard who broke up your marriage.* Sucking in a deep breath, she said, "Anyway, did Angie tell you she doesn't want to dance anymore?"

He crossed his arms over his chest. As he looked at her, like she always did, she wondered why in God's name she had chosen this fucker to have sex with. He wasn't who she'd thought he was. He wasn't as attractive as he used to be, and now she wanted to puke at just the thought of having put his dick in her mouth. Why couldn't Benji have been around then?

Ugh! Stop thinking of him.

"She said something, but I'm pretty sure you told her to say that."

She gave him a dubious look. The sass was there. She could have said something to be really shitty, but instead, she held his gaze. "Like I said, she doesn't want to do it."

"So you don't deny it?" he snapped and she glared.

"I told you I'm not fighting with you. I don't have it in me. Just please, don't force her to do it. She hates it. She has the grace of an elephant, and you know it!"

"Whatever. Nina is amazing at it. They are sisters," he said simply, his brown eyes dark and cutting.

"Half sisters. And Angie is not Nina," she bit out, her eyes blazing. *Angie was fucking better, damn it.* "Oh, and another thing. Angie said that when she's at your house, you favor Nina over her. I get it. You're with her twenty-four seven, you're married to her mother, but I can't have our daughter feeling like she doesn't matter when she's at your house. So can you please be a little cautious of that?"

That pissed him off, his chest puffing up as he took a step toward her. "She feels like that because you spoil her and I discipline her. I'm always the bad guy."

Because you're a dick. Sucking in a breath, she held his blazing gaze. "She is not spoiled, and I do discipline her. I'm just letting you know what she said."

"Yeah, and you probably coached her to do it. But you know what? You're right. I don't get enough time with her. Maybe we should change that."

That made her blood run cold. "We have a parenting plan."

"Which is shit. I get her every other weekend. I want more."

Calmly, which surprised her, she said, "You agreed to what we have."

"And maybe I want to change it. Maybe we should go week to week."

And just like that, Lucy flew off the handle. Hey, she tried.

"Oh, fuck no," she roared, her body starting to shake. "We aren't zoned for the same school. She loves where she is at. She's comfortable and they honor her 504 Plan perfectly. We can't shake up her world, Rick. She has to have consistency."

He glared. "This ADHD shit is a crutch you use to keep her all to yourself. She probably doesn't even have the damn ADHD. You're probably making it up."

"If you went to one fucking appointment with me, you'd know! But you didn't. I have no reason to lie. I have nothing to hide. I am a good fucking mother, and you know it."

"What the fuck ever, Lucy. It's your fault I don't have a relationship with my daughter."

Fucking douche.

Closing her eyes, she took a cleansing breath as she shook her head. She wanted to say she was too tired for this, but she'd had a great night's sleep and felt alert, so really, she just didn't have time to deal with stupid. It would go nowhere. He was a fucking idiot. "I'm not agreeing to an altered custody agreement, and if you want to fight me, get a lawyer."

"Maybe I will," he said sharply and she nodded.

"Okay, then," she said, turning and going to the car.

When she reached her car, her hand on the handle, he shouted, "You're a fucking worthless piece of shit, you know that? I just want more time with my kid. You're only hurting her."

She ignored him. Only because Angie was watching her. Damn it. Hopefully, she didn't hear much. Opening the door, Lucy got in quickly and shut the door with more force than needed. With a shaky hand, she started the car and looked into the rearview mirror, meeting Angie's gaze. "Hey, baby."

"Hi, Mommy."

"I missed you."

"I missed you too."

"Did you have fun with Nina?"

Angie smiled. "I did. We played all weekend."

"Good, no problems?"

"Nope, Dad yelled at me about dance, but I just ignored him."

Her heart sank. "So you told him you didn't want to dance?"

"Yeah, and he told me why can't I be like Nina? I told him I wasn't her and that was that."

Lucy nodded. "We'll get it taken care of. Don't worry."

"Okay," she said slowly. "Are you okay?"

"I'm fine, don't you worry." Lucy forced a smile.

"Then why are all our things in the car?"

Heaving a deep sigh, she backed out of the parking spot and started for her mother's. "Funny story."

But it wasn't funny.

Not even a chuckle.

No, it was a clusterfuck.

But even with all that, even with Rick's threats, there was a little curve to her lips.

A curve Benji had caused. But as soon as she realized it, she stopped.

Because the thing with Benji just would never work out.

It just wouldn't.

But when Lucy got to her mom's, it was not that hard *not* to smile.

Because her safe haven, her childhood home, well…most of it, was lying on the front lawn.

"What is going on?" Angie asked as they parked and Lucy shut the car off. "Did the house blow up?" Her voice was full of panic as Lucy threw the door open.

"Calm down, baby. I think they're fixing something," she said as Angie came beside her, pushing the door open and then taking Lucy's hand. "Mom?" Lucy called out, and seconds later, her mother, clad in her painting clothes, emerged, a mask on her face.

As she lifted her mask, her eyes were full of confusion. "Lucy? Baby, what are you doing here? You should have called. We are knee-deep in gutting the house. I don't want Angie to step on a nail. Honey bear, be careful, please."

Gutting? Just then, River appeared, waving happily at them. "Hey, girls! Angie, guess who's excited for your first game on Saturday?"

Angie grinned. "You?"

"Duh!" He laughed, and Lucy wanted to laugh, she did. River used to be so quiet, so to himself unless he was yelling at the boys on the ice, but now, he was animated. He was funny and he got along with Angie effortlessly. "What are you guys doing over? It's dangerous for Angie here, Lucy."

"I see that," Lucy said, on the verge of tears as he came down and stepped over the rubble. He reached for Angie, who went willingly to him. "What are you guys doing?"

"Did Autumn not tell you?" he asked, looking back at her mother as she came down the stairs, gobbling Angie up in her arms as she took her from him.

"I think I forgot to tell her. But I told Avery, probably because I call that girl twenty-four seven to make her talk to me."

"Mom, that's not okay," Lucy said, looking back at her. "Leave her alone. But really, what is going on here?"

"We are gutting the house. Gonna make our room into one huge bedroom with a sitting area, and then we are gonna add on a suite for when you kids come to visit and expand the kitchen. We are doing the gutting ourselves to save money. The contractors come in tomorrow," River said, looking all proud of himself. Any other day, she might have been proud of him too.

But not today.

"So my room is gone?" Lucy asked, her throat thick.

"Yeah, but you don't need it, baby. You have your own place, don't look so sad," she said, reaching out to pat Lucy's face, but she moved out of her reach. "Lucy Lane?"

But Lucy just shook her head. "Actually, I do need it. But, whatever, it's fine. Come on, baby," she said to Angie, turning to leave, but Autumn stopped her.

"Lucy, what's wrong?"

"Lucy, you've got us worried. Tell us," River demanded, and it was crazy how much he had become a father figure to her. That wasn't right, was it? At twenty-six, having a new father figure? But he was, and Lucy couldn't talk for fear she'd start crying. But where was she going to go? Could she expect her child to live in a hotel? That wasn't stable for her, and she had to give her stability. Damn it, this was worse than she thought. She thought she could come home. Crap on a cracker. What was she going to do?

"Our apartment is broke. A water pipe busted," Angie said, and her mother's eyes widened.

"What happened? Can you not stay there?" River asked and Lucy shook her head, explaining what was going on. When she finished, a tear ran down her face but she quickly wiped it.

"It's fine. I'll figure something out."

"No, you'll sleep here. We'll figure it out," Autumn said desperately.

"It isn't safe, Autumn, not for Angie," River said, shaking his head. "Well, hell, we need a plan, huh, girlie?"

"Yeah, because we're homeless," Angie said simply, and Lucy swallowed back more tears.

"We're fine, don't worry. I've got this."

But she didn't.

"Jayden! Call Jayden. He's leaving, so Baylor will be alone. She'd love to have you guys till the apartment is done," her mother yelled before pulling out her phone and calling him, despite Lucy's complaints.

"I can't just expect to—"

But Autumn ignored her, talking quickly to Jayden.

River looked over at her and smiled. "It's okay to have help every once in a while, Miss Do-it-All."

Lucy scoffed. "Hush, you."

He wrapped his arm around her, squeezing her into his chest. "Damn headstrong, just like my daughter."

"That's why I like her," Lucy said with a wink.

And that was a good thing because it looked like she'd be staying with her sister-in-law until her apartment was fixed. Leave it to her mom to solve everything in seconds. Plus, Jayden didn't mind. He urged her to come, even when Lucy said she'd get a hotel. She really didn't want to and she'd rather stay at Jayden's, but she didn't want to impose on anyone.

"You can't impose on family, Lucy. Get your ass in the car and come on. We have plenty of room," Jayden demanded.

And so they did. Of course, after her mom and River fussed over them, demanding to know updates as soon as she had them. She felt a little better, but not much. It was all such a clusterfuck. Once in the car on her way to Jayden and Baylor's, Angie was in the backseat, singing, oblivious to her mother's troubles while Lucy was having a mild panic attack. When her phone rang, she closed her eyes, praying it wasn't Rick or anyone else who was going to make this day an even more complete hell. Reaching for it, she saw it was Rayne.

"Hey, you never texted me yesterday about the Paxton job. Are you doing it?"

Lucy swallowed hard, feeling a flutter deep in her gut. "Not sure. Still in the works."

She had no clue what was going on with that. Couldn't exactly tell her assistant that she slept with him and things were up in the air. Didn't seem very professional. After telling her about the shop and to postpone the interviews with the designers who were coming in that week, she said she'd get back to her about Benji's account.

"Okay, do you have specs? Pictures, so I can get started on that?" Rayne asked and Lucy nodded.

"I'm driving to my brother's right now. We are staying with him until things are figured out. Let me get settled and get my laptop to upload the pictures from the downstairs—"

But she paused.

Her laptop and camera were in her bag.

In Benji's house.

Fuck.

Leaning against the counter, Benji crossed his arms over his chest. Before him sat one black pump, one naughty lace thong, and a bag full of designing stuff, all spread out on the island in his kitchen.

All belonging to his magician, also known as Lucy.

That girl and her disappearing act were impressive. Problem was she left a lot behind. Now he had to figure out how to get it back to her. He tried her business line, but they were closed on Sundays. He searched her bag for her cell phone number, nothing. He could drive to the shop since he knew she lived above it, but he didn't want to just show up. That was rude. So there was only one thing he could do, but he was stalling.

Because calling your linemate for his sister's number so that you could get her stuff back to her after a night of endless pleasure seemed a little tacky. Then again, maybe it didn't, but he still felt a little strange about it. He knew Jayden would ask questions and he wouldn't lie, but he also couldn't disrespect Lucy like that. So he was kind of stuck.

And looking at her things wasn't making it any better.

Man, why did she have to leave?

He'd had so many plans. He had wanted to wake up in the middle of the night and take her to oblivion at least ten more times. He wanted to make her breakfast; he wanted to plan to get together today. Maybe a movie or something, hockey with Angie, anything. He just wanted to see her before he left later that night. It pained him to know he wouldn't see her for the next five days, especially since he didn't get to do anything with her he'd wanted to.

Because she ran.

He should have known she would. That girl didn't ever do anything for herself, and of course, she would freak out about it. After last night, the way it felt… Man, it was like bombs going off all around them. He knew it would be—she was the sexiest thing he had seen in a long time, but he hadn't expected for it to feel so damn perfect.

As if he was only made to make love to her. That was a scary and fucking guilty-ass feeling. What about Ava? She was his soul mate, right? But then he slept with Lucy and it was just different. He couldn't explain it, but it was easy to say he felt like shit for it. He felt like he was betraying Ava. But was he? It had been twelve years. He had to move on. Didn't he?

Closing his eyes, he shook his head. He needed to return Lucy's things and then take a step back. No one feels shit like that after only one time, and he sure as hell didn't deserve to feel these emotions. But the thought of not having Lucy made him physically hurt inside. He was so tired of moving through life and not being happy. For so long, he had mourned Ava and Leary—and he would always love them, he would—but wouldn't they want him to be happy?

Fuck, who knows?

All he did know was that Lucy may have skipped out on him, but when she was there, in his arms, beneath him, he had been so fucking happy, he could have cried manly tears. He didn't know what that meant for him. Did he chase after her, demand she give him at least a minute of every one of her days? Or did he just hand her her things and walk away?

Why couldn't she have just stayed so they could have figured this out together?

He shook his head. He had known she was going to be trouble the moment he saw her, yet he still went after her. Still had to touch his lips to those red-hot lips of hers. Feel her body beneath his and hold her in his arms. He just had to. And now, now he was craving her like he used to crave alcohol. The only problem was his thirst for bitter liquid could never come close to the thirst he had for her at that moment. He was pretty sure no matter how much of Lucy he got, it would never be enough.

And while it scared him to no end to have those kinds of feelings again for someone who wasn't Ava, it also excited him.

It made him feel alive again.

Pulling his phone out of his pocket, he curled his toes against the tile of his kitchen floor as he hit Jayden's contact info.

Jayden answered right away. "Bro, what's up?"

"Hey, man," he said, grabbing his shirt into a fist at his ribs, his heart pounding against his chest. "Can you send me your sister's number? She was here yesterday for a consult on my house and left her bag. Something had happened or whatever, I don't know. She just rushed out of here without her bag."

Oh God, he was lying. He hated lying.

"Oh, hell. Yeah, her damn apartment flooded and they are starting work on it today. She's actually on her way here. She's gonna stay here till it's done."

Oh, no wonder she was so upset. "Oh, that blows. I couldn't get much out of her."

Except lots of moans. And sass. Yes, lots of sexy sass.

"Yeah, she's dealing with a lot right now. But, yeah, I can swing by and grab it for her. Or let her know."

He squeezed his eyes closed. "I'd really like to talk to her, set up another time, and get her the bag."

Jayden paused. "Okay, and usually, I wouldn't care, I'd give you the number. But my sister is insane, and if she didn't want you to have it—not saying she doesn't, but just in case—she'd kill me," he laughed and Benji smiled.

"I got you, man, and I get it, but I really need her number. Remember, you owe me," he said and he knew that made him a dick, but he was on a mission.

"Oh, low blow, dude! I can't."

"She won't mind," he said uncertainly, but he had to believe she wouldn't.

"Ha! You don't know my sister. She's psycho about who has her number. I don't even know her designer number, the one for her business cell phone, to give you."

"That one is in the bag with a dead battery, anyway," he said, and Jayden made a sound of irritation.

"Shit. Okay. Well, listen, she'll be here in a few. I can give her your number," he said and Benji rolled his eyes.

He wanted to laugh at the hilarity of the situation. "We sound like two fucking high schoolers, you know that?"

Jayden laughed. "We do. But seriously, I don't like poking the bear, aka my sister."

"Okay. I guess I'll come by and drop off the bag and talk to her about my… stuff," he decided, going to slide his tennis shoes on.

"Um, today? She's sorta, like, superpissy. I don't even want to be near her."

Benji laughed. "It's fine. I can handle her," he said confidently.

"Your funeral. Hey, can I get your gamer chair when you die?"

But he wasn't too sure of himself when he pulled into Jayden's driveway behind Lucy's car. Reaching for her bag, he got out of his truck and locked it up before heading for the front door. His heart was jackhammering against his chest and he thought about just leaving the bag and hightailing it out of there, but he stopped himself.

He wanted to see her.

He knocked on the door, and it opened a few seconds later and Angie grinned up at him. "Benji!"

"Hey, Hart, what's up?" he asked, fist-bumping her before she opened the door enough for him to come in.

"We're homeless. My grandma is gutting her house, so we're staying with my uncle and aunt till our apartment is fixed," she said happily as she shut the door and skipped up beside him. "What are you doing here? You homeless too?"

He laughed. "Nope, came to drop your mom's bag off. She left it at my house."

"Aw! She got to come play with you?"

Oh, kid. You have no idea.

Swallowing hard, he smiled. "She's gonna design my house."

"Supercool! My mom is the best, isn't she, Aunt Baylor?"

He looked to the left to see Baylor sitting in a chair, her leg propped up. "She is. Hey, Benji."

"Hey, didn't see you there. How are you feeling?"

"Okay, today. Thanks for asking," she said as Jayden came into the room, scooping Angie up and putting her on his shoulders.

"Hey, BP. Lucy's in the shower," Jayden said, but Angie smacked his head.

"She's been out like for twenty minutes. Mammaaaaaaaaaaaa," she yelled, and Benji met Jayden's sheepish gaze.

"Told you she was in a shitty mood," Jayden said simply and Benji grinned. "She told me to lie."

"It's fine. I'll be—" But he didn't get to finish his sentence because as she came out of the back room, Lucy's eyes met his and he was rendered speechless. Completely speechless. Her hair was wet, falling down her shoulders onto a white tee that was short in the front but long in the back, showing a bit of her belly. The same belly he had spent most of his time admiring last night. Her jeans were all but painted on and she had no shoes on. She looked exactly like what he imagined he would come back to after a long road trip.

She looked like home.

As his heart went wild, she moved her fingers through her hair, pulling it up into a wet bun. Looking over at Angie, she smiled. "Yeah, baby?"

"Benji is here. He has your bag."

Still not looking at him, she nodded. "Oh, wow, thanks for bringing that over. You didn't have to do that."

He willed her to look at him as she came toward him, reaching for it. But when she didn't look up, he held it tighter. "It's no problem. Wanted to check in with you."

She held the bag, pulled it once, and then pursed her lips. Letting out a sigh, she finally looked up. Just like that, everything stopped.

Did she feel that too?

Swallowing hard, he smiled as she blinked vacantly up at him. "Hey, Lucy."

"Hey," she said faintly, sucking in a big breath.

"Everything is in there," he said, his brows waggling at her, and her face deepened with color.

"Thanks," she said shyly, looking away as he let go of the bag. She set it on top of the couch and then crossed her arms. Looking around the room at her daughter, her brother, and his wife, she nodded as she cleared her throat. Not meeting his gaze, she tucked her hands into her pockets.

The silence made him nervous and everyone was staring at him, so he blurted out, "I tried to get your number from Jayden, but he told me you'd get mad."

She blinked at him. "He's dumb and was dropped on his head a million times as a baby," she said quickly and Jayden protested.

"I was not!"

"Yes, you were. I dropped you," she seethed back at him and Benji's eyes widened.

"You did not!"

"Ask Mom. Why do you think one eye is lazy?" she shot back and he glared.

"Don't listen to them, Benji. They are always like this," Baylor said with a laugh and Benji smiled.

"Yeah, she's always mean," Jayden spat at her and she glared.

"My grandma says that if they didn't fight, they wouldn't talk. But I heard Jayden whisper he loved my mom a lot, more than everyone else, to my aunt Baylor," Angie said sweetly, hugging Jayden tightly.

"I lied," he protested and Lucy growled at him before turning back to Benji. Her hands were shaking, and the nerves were coming off her in waves. Why was she nervous? Did she think he'd out them?

"Anyway, I'll get with you about your house later. I think Jayden told you about my current shop status. I should know more tomorrow, and I'll make sure my assistant gets back with you. So, yeah, bye. Thanks for stopping by and dropping that off. You shouldn't have."

Oh, so she was trying to blow him off?

"Jeez, Lucy, he can come in for a drink or something," Baylor teased and Lucy's eyes flashed with anger. "Or he can leave," she laughed and Jayden's brows rose.

Looking to Benji, he said, "What in the world? He's my friend, not yours. Wanna come in, bud? I'm getting them settled, but you can sit with Limpy over

there until I'm done."

"I just yelled an expletive at you in my head," Baylor said and he grinned.

"I do that a lot," Lucy muttered, and Benji laughed.

These people were crazy.

Grinning at only Lucy, he shook his head. "Actually, I need to talk to your sister."

Jayden's brow rose again as he looked around. "Oh, go ahead."

She paused, looking back at Jayden and then back to Benji, her eyes full of unease. "Why?"

His grin didn't falter, it actually grew. He swore he couldn't decide if she was hotter when she was coming on his face or when she was nervous like this. Clearing his throat, he said, "Well, I mean, I guess we can talk here. Totally up to you."

Her eyes widened and then she pushed him toward the door, pausing to put shoes on. "I'll be right back."

"Lucy?" Jayden asked and Baylor laughed.

"Shut up, Jayden," Lucy shot back before pushing Benji out.

"Are you leaving, Benji?" Angie called, and he paused as Lucy pushed.

"In a few," he said and her smile dropped.

"Are you leaving with Jayden?"

He nodded sadly. "Yeah, sunshine. But don't worry, I'll be there for your game, though. Wouldn't miss it for the world."

She grinned as she climbed off Jayden and ran to give him a hug. "Awesome. Kick some butt and score me a goal."

His throat was thick with emotion as he hugged her back. How had this little girl wiggled her way into his heart so fast? "Consider it done."

"Um, wow, I think I got replaced," Jayden said and Benji grinned at him. "I guess I'm chopped liver now."

Angie giggled as she ran back to Jayden, tackling him at the thighs, which caused him to fall onto the couch in a heap of laughter. Before Benji could even laugh or say anything, Lucy pushed him outside.

"I love when you put your hands on me," he teased as she shut the door behind them and then headed past him, down the stairs.

"Oh, Jesus. Hush and come on," she called back at him as he grinned.

So he followed.

Chapter NINE

Watching as her ass moved side to side in those sexy jeans, Benji was almost mesmerized before she stopped at the end of the driveway, right behind his truck. Looking back at the house and then to her, he scoffed. "I think we're far enough away. I doubt anyone will hear us," he said with an exaggerated wink.

"Oh, hush," she snapped, rolling her eyes and crossing her arms over her chest. "So what do you want to talk about?"

He grinned, matching her stance. "You're so cute when you don't want to talk about something."

Looking up at him, she glared. "I can go back inside."

"But you won't."

Her glare deepened. "Get to talkin', Paxton. I've had a shitty day."

"I heard," he said then, tucking his hands in his pockets. "How long will you be out of your apartment?"

She shook her head and let out a long breath, her shoulders sagging. "I don't know. They say Tuesday, but when I went there this morning, it looks so bad. Like the water was seeping through the ceiling of my shop. I don't know how it got so bad. I called right when I smelled something weird."

He nodded. "That blows."

"You have no idea. I love my brother and his wife, I do, but I hate imposing on people."

"Yeah," he said softly. "You know you're more than welcome to come stay at my house. I have room, and I won't even be there this week. Plus, you can work on it."

Her face scrunched up as she gave him a suspicious look. He wanted to regret asking her, but he didn't. He didn't mean it to get her back in his bed; he really did want to help her, and he understood not wanting to ask her brother for help. They were practically newlyweds. No one wanted to be under the same roof with that.

"I don't know you. Why would I move myself and my child in with you?"

He scoffed. "You had sex with me, though."

She balked. "Um… Yeah. So?"

"So you trust me. If you didn't trust me, you wouldn't let me between—"

"Jesus take the wheel!" she wailed, holding her hands up to stop him, which of course, he smirked at. "Maybe I just wanted sex. Maybe I'm a whore."

He gave her a dry look, shaking his head. "Even I know that's isn't true. You aren't like that."

"How do you know?"

He grinned, taking a step toward her. "Because even though I've only known you six days, I've seen the way you are with your daughter. You're a great mom. Great moms don't sleep with random men. They are responsible, they are smart, and it's okay, Lucy, you can admit you trust me."

That stunned her, but she recovered quickly. Scoffing, she said, "Please, you were there."

"Okay. Lucy, do you want another hug? You look like you need another one."

He moved toward her with his arms out, and she laughed as she pushed him away. "Stay away from me, you and those hugs."

"Dangerous, huh?"

"Yeah," she breathed, shaking her head.

"But, hey, it led to a great night," he said huskily, and her lip quirked as she looked away.

"Doesn't matter. It was a mistake," she said quietly.

He couldn't agree with her if he tried. Last night was not a mistake, but she already knew that. "It was?"

She looked up, her eyes wide and worried, distress all over her beautiful face. He may have been kidding before, but he really did want to hug her. "Benji, I'm so busy, especially now since I have to find a way to run my business out of my brother's house. I was supposed to hire a new designer this weekend, but that looks like it's going to shit and I'm a fucking mess. Really. Also, I have a kid—"

"I don't know what Angie has to do with us."

"Um, no man wants a chick with a kid or a baby daddy to deal with."

He snorted. "Your baby daddy is nothing to me."

"He's a dick. You don't want to deal with that or my kid."

"Again, he doesn't matter. As a real man, I don't care that you have a kid or a baby daddy. That baby daddy has no effect on me, and your child is an extension of you. Also, Angie is freaking awesome, just like you," he said with a wink, but she didn't look convinced.

"No one says that."

"Or you haven't met the right man," he said, pointing at her.

Exasperated, she threw her hands up. "When did you become a smooth-talker? You're supposed to be a huge dork."

He grinned. "I am, with a side of sex god and smooth-talker."

"Okay, just stop," she said, holding her hand up and he laughed. "Jesus, Benji. I mean, yeah, last night was *so* good, but let's be real," she said, talking with her hands until she shivered and had to wrap her arms around herself. It was chilly out, and he was sure she had been more concerned with getting him out the door than getting a coat. At least she'd put on shoes. "It would just be a waste of our time. We are in two different places in our lives, and right now, things are not easy for me."

He was listening, he was, but she was talking more for herself. Everything she said may be true, but Benji didn't care. He wanted to try. It was crazy, but he had to do this. Something inside him was begging him to do it.

Shaking out of his coat, he reached around her and put it on her. His body was so close to hers, and even though it was cold, she made him burn from the top of his head to the tip of his toes.

She tried to stop him. "I'm fine—"

But he ignored her, closing the jacket, and then pulling away slowly. Tucking his hands in the pockets of his jeans, he met her gaze. "Maybe it hasn't been easy because you don't let it. You do this thing, finding every single reason possible not to be happy. Isn't that exhausting?" When her eyes narrowed, he just grinned at her. "Aw, don't get mad. I'm just making an observation."

"An observation you can shove up your ass," she mumbled, but she didn't mean it. She was trying not to grin back at him.

"Always so snarky," he said, tapping her nose, which made her eyes widen. "What in the world?"

"What? You're cute."

She let out a frustrated breath. "Like I said, last night was awesome, I had a blast. But this, whatever you think it is, just isn't a good idea."

"I'm not asking for anything. Not yet, at least, and I don't think us getting to know each other and spending time together would be a waste of anyone's time, as long as we're having a good time."

She shook her head, sucking in a breath, and he smiled. "Benji…"

Taking ahold of her belt loop, he pulled her to him. He couldn't handle the distance anymore. He had to touch her. Coming to a halt against him, she looked up at him, surprised, as his hands slid underneath his coat to her back. She shivered against his touch and then relaxed. But as soon as she relaxed, she tensed up again, glancing back at the house. But he moved a hand and took hold of her chin, bringing her face up to look at him. "No one can see us."

"You don't know that."

"Hush, you," he demanded, and she snapped her lips shut, her eyes narrowing.

"Your hands are cold," she complained, moving closer to him.

"Someone has my coat," he said, moving his nose along hers. "Now, tell me something. Did you have fun last night?" Her grin fell, her green gaze blazing as she sucked in a breath. "Don't lie either," he admonished, and when her lips fought to curve, Benji's heart went wild. It was funny how life could change with just a flicker of a smile. Just a little bitty smile had Benji in knots.

Hell, this girl had had him in knots since the beginning.

"I did," she admitted, her hands coming up to rest against his chest.

"Okay, so we both have fun together, right?"

She nodded slowly, not liking that he was right. "Right."

"Okay, so let's get to know each other. And, if at any time, it gets to where either of us feels we are wasting each other's time, we'll stop. Okay?"

He was pretty sure that would never happen, but obviously he had to say something to keep this woman from running the other way.

Like he knew she would be, she was hesitant as she bit into her lip. "I don't know. I have so much baggage…and I just don't know."

She was preaching to the choir on that one, but it was time to no longer allow that baggage to hold him back from what he wanted. He wanted Lucy and she wanted him; he knew she did. So he just grinned, his hands coming behind her and reaching for her phone he had seen her tuck into her back pocket when they walked outside earlier. Her breath caught as he said, "Fine, let's start with just your number. Give me that, and we can talk. If you get bored with me, just let me know and we'll stop."

"You think I don't feel you taking my phone?" she asked as he dialed his number on it. "And that I don't know you are dialing your number so I have no choice in the matter?"

He gave her look as his phone sounded. "Oh, baby, don't act like you don't have a choice. You could've stopped me at any time," he said roughly against her cheek. He saved his contact info and then tucked her phone back into her pocket. Pulling back, he met her desire-filled gaze. "You just don't want to."

Her lips pursed and everything inside him went hot. "Maybe."

He held her gaze, watching her eyes darken as he held her tightly to him.

"Maybe you want another kiss?"

She pushed him away, her lips curving. "Not now. That's a bad idea."

He eyed her. "You sure? I'm going to be gone for a week."

"Okay...?" she laughed, rolling her eyes.

"Now, Lucy, I know it's going to be so hard remembering how I kiss. Maybe I should give you another taste?"

She rolled her eyes. "Dork, I'll survive."

"Will you?" he teased and she shook her head.

"I gotta go," she said as she went to walk past him, but he stopped her, his hand holding her at her hip.

"Because I think I need another taste of you to hold me over. Because, while I could never forget the feel of those lips on mine, I just want something to keep me going until I see you again."

"Bye, Benji," she breathed as she tried to walk away, but he took her by the hand, lacing his fingers with hers.

She looked at his hand holding hers and then back to him, her cheeks reddening as she held his gaze. Bringing her hand up to his mouth, he kissed it softly as she gasped, her lids dropping a bit into a sexy, kitten look. As his lips pressed to her knuckles, a dreamy look appeared in the depths of those green eyes and he smiled against her skin.

Moving his lips from her hand, he held her gaze, fully expecting her to pull away.

But she didn't move.

And neither did he.

With their fingers still laced together, he could see her eyes were dark. He was sure his were too from wanting her more than his next breath. He was pretty sure if she didn't give him a kiss, he was going to fall to his knees and beg. Pitiful, he knew, but he couldn't let her walk away. Not yet.

Letting out a long breath, she just looked at him, bewilderment in her eyes as she mumbled, "What the hell is it about you?"

And then she was moving. He was ready, taking her into his arms as their mouths met in a heated frenzy. Shit, he had missed her kisses. Her mouth. The feel of her. Jesus, it was almost too much to handle as his tongue moved with hers. Holding her close, he deepened the kiss as her fingers moved along the base of his neck, causing chills to run down his spine. His fingers dug into her back as she arched into him, moaning softly against his mouth.

But it was too much.

Way too much.

He pulled away because if he didn't, he was going to take her into the back of his truck and do the naughtiest things in the world to her. He was pretty sure the neighbors wouldn't appreciate that, or hell, Jayden. So he sucked in a deep breath, sliding his nose along her cheek. Begging himself to control his desire as her lips moved against his, he opened his eyes to find that her eyes were closed ever so sweetly.

"So beautiful. So fucking beautiful," he whispered against her lips and she grinned, leaning her forehead against his nose.

"I needed that," she admitted softly.

"Well, I'm your guy whenever you need to hear it," he whispered against her eyes. Closing his eyes, he took in her sexy smell as his grip on her tightened. "And just in case you forget, I'm a phone call away."

"Okay."

"And don't try to be all 'I don't want to call him 'cause it will make him think I want him' and not call me, okay?" he said, impersonating her. He was answered with laughter as she pulled back, looking at him. "I know you want me. It's cool, 'cause I want you. Okay?"

"I don't know what in the world you are talking about," she laughed and he grinned, loving the angelic sound that came out of her sweet mouth.

And because he couldn't handle it, he kissed said mouth once more, and then a second time for good measure before pulling away.

Tracing his cheekbone with her finger, she looked deep into his eyes. "This really shouldn't happen. That's why I ran."

"What's happening?" he asked. "I just wanted to kiss you."

She scoffed. "Sure, and kisses lead to sex, which leads to feelings, which leads to heartbreak."

He kissed her nose once more, his eyes searching hers. It was obvious that douche had hurt her, but Benji wasn't that guy and he wasn't going to do that. "Since I don't like heartache, let's skip that part."

She paused before slowly shaking her head. "It's not that easy."

"Before it wasn't, but maybe now it can be," he said with another wink that made her lips curve.

But as fast as they curved, they went back into a straight line as she looked away. "I don't know if I've got it in me to try. I've been hurt, Benji. I've got so much—"

Letting her go because he knew if he didn't now, he wasn't going to, he leaned toward her, kissing the side of her mouth before whispering against her lips, "Then I'll help you try."

As he pulled back, she watched him and then looked away. "You make it really hard to argue with you."

"Oh, thank God. I don't like fighting, but I love making up," he said with a wink, which made her giggle. Moving toward his truck, very slowly because he didn't want to leave, he smiled. "Good thing I have your number so we can see how much fighting and making up we'll do."

Her lips turned up as she shook her head, watching him. "You stole it and I'm still not sure how I feel about that."

He laughed. "Hey, what's the worst that can happen?"

Her eyes said it all.

She could fall for him.

While he really didn't see a problem with that, it was damn apparent it was a huge deal for her, and that worried him.

Was he, in fact, setting himself up for heartache?

He wasn't sure. But one thing was for sure.

He wasn't turning back.

What's the worst that can happen?

Really?

Easy!

Lucy could like him.

She could miss him.

She could fucking fall for him.

There was so much that could go wrong, but she'd be lying if she said she wasn't giddy walking back to the house, cuddled in Benji's jacket.

"Shit," she said, pulling out her phone to call him. When she went to her call list, the last number she had dialed was listed as "**My Sexy Dork**."

Seriously?

This guy.

She hit the number, and Benji answered, laughing. "That was quick. I was convinced you wouldn't text or call till Wednesday."

"Shut up. You forgot your jacket."

"Eh, keep it. Looks better on you."

She made a face. "It's huge on me."

"Yeah, but I like seeing you in it. I feel you should have to wear it all the time."

"You're insane," she laughed, reaching for the door.

"Yeah, but maybe it will inspire you to do something crazy and text me later. When you're lying in bed, naked—"

"I don't sleep naked," she said dryly, a grin pulling at her lips.

"No? Hm, you should. It would be hot."

"Noted."

"Okay, but text me tonight when you're wanting someone to wrap their arms around you. Just a hug, of course."

"Of course."

"But then, maybe when you want someone between your—"

"Goodbye, Benji," she said, hanging up to his laughter.

Sucking in a deep breath, she closed her eyes.

Be still, heart.

And behave, vagina.

But, good Lord, that man was a big ball of hotness and he drove her absolutely senseless. She would never let anyone talk to her like that, but when he did it, it was playful, silly. He was a dork. A big sexy one, but he had her number, which meant he'd call her or text her and then she'd have to talk to him, and then… Shit, were they dating?

No.

No…

"Fuck," she complained as she pushed the door open and went inside. She found the living room was empty, that was until Baylor came limping through, a plate in her hand. Lucy went to her, taking it despite her protest.

"Just go sit down," Lucy said with more force, and Baylor took notice.

"Jesus, for someone who just got the stuffing kissed out of her, you'd think you would be a little nicer," she teased in a whisper as she sat down.

Lucy glared and almost threw the plate at her. "I want to throw this at you."

"Yeah, I know," she said, taking it and winking. "But I'm hurt. You can't."

Lucy rolled her eyes and then fell into the other chair beside her. Slouching down in it, she glared over at her sister-in-law. "You saw it all?"

Baylor scoffed as she grinned around the bite of sandwich she had just taken. "You mean Benji almost doing you against his truck? Yeah, I saw it, and I put two and two together."

"Hellfire," she cried out, covering her face with her hands as her cheeks turned deep red.

"I didn't think it was like you to leave a whole bag over there, but if you were doing a walk of shame, you just might."

Peeking through her hands at her grinning sister-in-law, she said, "Have I told you lately I don't like you?"

Baylor feigned hurt. "Me? I thought I was your favorite."

Lucy covered her face back up and then shook her head. "What am I doing?"

She said it more to herself, but Baylor took it upon herself to answer. "I think you should go with it. He had those sex eyes and it was kind of hot. Usually, I look at him like he's kinda goofy, but with those sex eyes… Rawr."

Sliding her hands down her face, she set Baylor with a look. "Please don't ever say that about him again."

Baylor giggled as she shrugged. "Aw, how sweet, you're jealous."

Lucy glared because there was no way in hell she would give that sentence life. Ignoring it because it was silly to even think about it, she said, "I'm a mom."

Baylor shrugged. "Yeah, who needs a hot dude to spice up her life. I say go for it."

Closing her eyes, she let out a long breath. "Where are Jayden and Angie?"

Baylor took another bite. "Upstairs."

"Okay," she said, standing up. "I hope you choke on that sandwich."

Baylor sputtered with laughter, and Lucy grinned back at her as she headed for the stairs. "They didn't see anything," she called back at her and Lucy's grin disappeared.

Should she tell them?

Tell them what?

They weren't even, really, kind of dating.

Like, kind of. But not really.

She did sleep with him, though, and he did hang out with Angie, but that didn't matter. It was nothing. Nothing to even speak about.

Yeah, she'd wait.

For what, she wasn't sure, because this was going nowhere.

He probably wouldn't even call her.

Or text her.

Yeah, he was just being nice.

…or she was a big idiot.

It was a toss-up.

"Hey, Coach!"

Shea Adler turned around just as Lucy and Angie made their way to him. With a big grin on his face, he waved happily. "Hey, Hart. How's it going?"

Looking exhausted, which was a complete sham since the girl slept more than Lucy did, she slapped her leg. "Well, funny story."

Jesus.

Angie had told everyone she saw they were homeless, and no matter how many times Lucy told her to stop, she still proceeded to tell the world. Lucy had just finished writing a very lengthy email to Angie's teacher, guaranteeing her that they were not, in fact, homeless.

"So our apartment got flooded and they are tearing it up. They called Mom and told her we couldn't go back for a while. It's a mess. I would say we're homeless, but I don't want to lose my iPad and Mom has already threatened me with that if I tell one more person we're homeless. So we're not homeless, but we don't have a home."

This kid.

Letting out a long breath, Lucy ran her fingers through her hair before meeting Shea's stunned gaze. "Wow, okay."

Lucy shrugged. "Ladies and gentlemen, Angela Lynn Hart."

Shea laughed as he bumped fists with her and smiled over at Lucy. "You guys are good, though, right? We have a house y'all can stay at, but it's an hour from here."

She appreciated his worry. He was such a good guy, and she knew what house he was speaking of. It was Elli's old house. A lot of people had rented it from her, but like he said, it was an hour from here, and that wouldn't cut it for her. "Yeah, we are staying with Jayden until we get things figured out. They aren't sure if the building is even safe anymore. There was way more damage when they got farther into it. We've had to move my office into my brother's den while he's gone. So I've got until Friday to figure out what I'm going to do. It's a mess."

"Man, that blows. Let me know if you need anything, okay? I can help, Elli will help too, you know that. Even if it's just to keep Angie. She can come hang with us."

Lucy smiled. "Thanks, Shea. Really, that means a lot. I've got this, though."

Shea nodded. "Oh, I know. Just wanted to let you know we're here for you," he said with a grin before turning to Angie. "Ready to hit the ice?"

"Yes, sir!" she cheered before taking her bag from Lucy. She said a quick bye, and as Lucy was walking away, she heard Angie telling Shea about quitting dance, which made Lucy roll her eyes.

Angie was telling everyone, and because of that, Lucy knew she had to have everything figured out before Angie went back to her dad's. She wasn't sure if Angie would tell him about their housing issues, but to be sure, she wanted to have a plan. No reason to give him anything he could use to get custody of Angie. Things were good the way they had it, and she wasn't using Angie's diagnosis as any kind of excuse. She needed consistency and she needed stability. Rick was not that. He never had been. So what made him think he was now? It made no sense. But thankfully, they were staying with family, so that was normal for Angie. But she worried what would happen when they needed to move.

If they had to move.

Shit, she didn't know.

Such a mess. That was her life, though, a jumble of mess.

Going up the bleachers, Lucy sat in what she had decided was her normal spot and leaned back, waiting for Angie to take the ice. Going through some emails, she answered back her vendors, set up appointments for the following day, and looked through some possible offices that Rayne had sent her. But she didn't want to move. She wanted to stay where she was. It was so perfect for her. Home on top, office on bottom. It worked.

But nothing ever seemed to work for her for long.

Letting out a sad sigh, she noticed that each office was way out of her price range. She knew if she picked one of them, there would be no way she could hire another designer. What a clusterfuck. Maybe she could set up an office in her warehouse? But as soon as she thought it, she knew she couldn't. It wasn't an office setting, and it was cold in there during the winter and hot as hell in the summer. No, that wouldn't work.

Damn it.

When the girls hit the ice, Lucy smiled as Angie did her usual laps. She wondered if Angie missed Benji because she looked a little sad as she made her laps. When she came to a stop, she looked up at Lucy and shrugged. Lucy could tell she was a little unsure of herself, so she held up two thumbs and Angie smiled at that as Shea gave direction. At least she had Shea. He was good to her.

But even Lucy missed seeing Benji out there.

When her phone sounded, she looked down to see a text from the very man she was thinking about. Well, she thought about him all the time, but no one needed to know that.

Benji: I know what you're thinking.

Her brow rose as she typed him back. To her surprise, and proving her to be an idiot, he had texted her last night. It was only a "Good night, beautiful" text, but still, he took the time. And it was easy to say that Lucy slept with a grin on her face. It also made her think maybe she should give this relationship a try. She was still on the fence about the whole thing.

Lucy: What?
Benji: You're wishing I was out there with Angie.
Lucy: I am not.
Benji: Didn't I tell you about that lying stuff? I can see right through you, woman.
Lucy: Whatever. You don't even know me.
Benji: Okay…
Lucy: And I haven't even thought of you. Not once.
Benji: Is your nose growing?

Lucy laughed out loud and quickly covered it as she shook her head. He was crazy, or so she thought, because then her FaceTime started to ring.

It was him.

He was nuts!

Answering it, her face was puzzled as she said, "Hello?"

"Hello, it's me," he sang like Adele did in her song, which made Lucy sputter with laughter.

"Oh my God, dork," she giggled and he smiled. He was in a locker room or something, his jersey hanging above his head. Her smile dropped and her eyes went wide. "Are you in the locker room with my brother?" she screeched and he laughed.

"No, I'm in here alone. Everyone is in the hall playing soccer. Plus, I have my earbuds in. No one can hear you, so please proceed to tell me what you want to do to me naked."

She closed her eyes, laughter bubbling from the base of her throat. When she noticed one of the moms looking at her, an offended look on her face, Lucy's face burned as she dug her earbuds out of her purse and put them in. "I did not have mine in, and another mother just heard you," she said into the phone, which made him laugh.

"Oh, well. She probably doesn't get laid or she's jealous of how hot you are," he said simply and she rolled her eyes.

"Stop sucking up to me and tell me what you want," she demanded and he grinned.

It took her breath away.

He was a little sweaty and his hair was pushed to the side, obviously by his hands. He wasn't wearing a shirt, and his jaw was covered in hair. He hadn't shaved, and she decided she liked him a little hairy. Yesterday, he was clean-shaven and he was adorable, but he looked sexier with a five-o'clock shadow.

"Well, if you must know, I still want you."

Shaking her head, her face burning, she had a hard time not grinning. "Stop."

"Fine, show me the ice. How's Angie doing?"

Her heart grew in her chest as she hit the button to turn the camera so he could see the ice. She watched his face as he looked closer at the phone, finding Angie and then nodding as she ran the drills. "She looks good. Was she okay? Not nervous?"

Really? How was she supposed to be hard and cold around this dude?

"Eh, when she went on and did her laps, I could tell she missed you."

"Yeah, I wish I was there. I was thinking about her all day, worried how she would do. Who's out there with Adler?"

"I don't know who they are, but he introduced them as his buddies."

He looked closer. "Oh, I think they played with him his rookie season. I'm not sure. I trust Adler with my life, so I'm sure she's in good hands."

"Yeah, he offered me Elli's house."

"Put me on you," he said and she did what he asked. "There you are," he said, his eyes dark. "I think you get more beautiful by the second. Ooh, and today we get a peek of boobs. Why didn't you wear that shirt last week?"

Covering her chest, she laughed as she looked away. "Stop, you're making me blush."

"Good, I like that color, along with the dimples. They're my favorite."

"Are you done?" she demanded and he shrugged.

"I can be, for now. But you're fair game, Lucy Sinclair." She looked at the screen, and when she saw herself in the little box at the top, she almost didn't recognize who that person was. She looked different.

Happy.

Wow.

"So, Adler's house is way out of the way. Like an hour. Could you pull that?"

She shook her head. "No, that's why I said no."

"Oh, okay. So what's going on? Do you have an ETA?"

"No, he said it wouldn't be Tuesday for sure. The more they got into it, the more problems they've found. My landlord's daughter told me she thinks I should start looking for something else. That they might have to give me my money back for the month and my deposit. It's a mess."

"Shit, that sucks, babe. I'm sorry. Can I help?"

She smiled, shrugging. "Thanks, but not really. I've just got to find a place to live and an office building. Has to be by Angie's school, not out of my price range, and will allow me to grow in it."

He slowly nodded, watching her. "The offer still stands for my place."

"Benji, be real. We've known each other a week."

His face lit up. "Aw, it has been a whole week. I'll send you some chocolates."

Giggling, she rolled her eyes as she leaned back. "I'll be okay. I always am."

"No doubt. I can tell that about you."

She looked away as she swallowed hard. She didn't like to admit weakness—it wasn't her. But for some reason, he made it a little less shitty to make such a confession. "Just sucks. I could really use a hug today."

His bottom lip puckered out, and just like that, a grin covered her lips. "Would a virtual hug work? I'll even tongue the phone."

Sputtering with laughter, she shook her head. "Not the same."

"I know, but I got you Saturday."

She let out a sigh and said, "So far away."

Crap. Did she say that? Why did she say that? Crap!

"Yeah," he said slowly, a little bit of sadness in his eyes as he moved his hands through his hair. She didn't know why he looked sad; she meant nothing to him, just some chick he slept with. But the look in his eyes said something entirely different and that was crazy. They'd just met. They were just friends. Sort of dating.

Ugh, she was stupid.

"But, hey," he said, pulling her back to their conversation. "You know what I just thought of? I have an office building."

Her brow quirked in confusion. "What? No, you don't."

"No, I do. Behind my house, there is like an in-law guesthouse that they had turned into an office. The people before me ran a carpet business out of it. You could use it if you want."

"An in-law guesthouse?"

"Yeah, it's a good size. You could easily put five people working comfortably in there. Go by the house and look. I have an extra key under the rock by the third bush on the side, where I parked my truck."

She paused, giving him an incredulous look. "Benji, you shouldn't tell people that when you've just met them."

He shot her back the same look. "We've known each other a week, I slept with you the other night, and plus, you're designing my house. You aren't a stranger." She rolled her eyes and he scoffed. "Shut it, just go check it out. See if it's something that can work."

"I don't know," she said slowly. "I mean, we're cool now, but what if we aren't later?"

He shrugged. "We'll have a contract if that makes you feel better, and I'll even take your money if you want. But what I do with it is my business."

Her brows came together, her lips curving in confusion. "What the hell does that mean?"

"None of your business, just saying."

She eyed him and then shook her head. "Let me think about it."

"Fine, but while you're at it," he said and she brought her attention back to him, "make sure you think of me."

Chuckling, she held his gaze. "Why would I do that?"

"'Cause I give good hugs."

He sure as hell did.

And she was craving him like mad. Her lips curved as she leaned on her hand, looking at him. The tattoo on his chest was screaming at her, and man, she wanted to know, but it didn't seem like the right time to ask. No, she'd want to do it face-to-face when they were alone. She had no clue when that would be, but maybe...

"What are you thinking about so hard?" he asked, his eyes on her.

She shrugged. "Do you wanna go on a date with me?"

He was taken aback and then he laughed. "I actually asked you out, I think, Wednesday, and you turned me down."

She grimaced and she nodded. "I did, but if we are still talking in say, two weeks, do you think you could meet me somewhere to eat and hang out?"

126

He shook his head and her heart fell. He was rejecting her? "No, I can't. Because after two weeks of us talking and getting to know each other, I'll come to where you're living. I'll knock on the door, and when you answer it, I'll be holding a single rose and I'll tell you how beautiful you look. Then I'll drive you to dinner and a movie, or dancing, or whatever you want. I'll then take you back to my house for a long night of you know what," he said, waggling his brows and making her giggle, "and then, I'll kiss you goodnight. But I will not meet you somewhere, Lucy. You are way too special for that, and we aren't fuck buddies."

No one had ever spoken to her like that.

Breathless, she held his gaze. "We aren't?"

"Fuck, no. I'm thirty-two, I don't have time for that. If I'm talking to you, being a complete and utter dork, showing who I really am, it's because I see something in you. Something extraordinary. Something I haven't seen in a very long time."

Blinking twice, she looked down and sucked in a deep breath. "No clue what to say to that."

"Don't say anything. Just look at me, show me those dimples, and tell me to have a good game."

Looking up, she gave him what he wanted, her grin so big she even felt her dimples cutting into her skin. When he smiled back, his eyes bright, she said, "Have a great game. Maybe text me afterward?"

"That was the plan," he said simply and her heart fluttered. "I was going to try to score you a goal too."

"I thought you were scoring one for Angie."

He scoffed. "Do you know who I am? I'm the leading scoring defenseman of the league."

She bubbled with laughter. "You are not!"

"Of the Assassins?"

"Nope," she said simply and he laughed.

"Okay, I'm not. But maybe tonight, I will be. I feel I got some good luck from our virtual hug," he said confidently with the cutest grin ever. It actually made her heart skip a beat. Like a freaking teenager's. What was this dude doing to her? He was making her go soft is what he was doing.

"Well, either way, I'll be watching."

He feigned worry. "Shit. I better play good then, huh?"

"You always do."

He eyed her, his lips curving. "Someone has been stalking me?"

"Just a bit."

"Good. I like that."

"I bet you do, weirdo."

"Ha, you're the one who likes me," he accused and she looked away, laughing.

Looking back at the screen, she pressed her lips together. "Who said that?"

"I did, now don't ruin my dreams. I gotta go score two goals, gotta get my head into the game," he said, and she sputtered with laughter but didn't let it out fully.

"Fine, you go be awesome."

"That's the plan, Stan. I'll text you later."

"Okay."

"Okay," he said slowly. "Bye."

"Bye," she said as her heart went crazy in her chest before she hit end.

And when her phone went blank, she missed him.

Oh boy, she was in trouble.

Chapter TEN

Benji wasn't one to go out, but when the Assassins landed in Wisconsin, most of the guys wanted to go down to the hotel bar and Benji agreed. He wasn't sure why—maybe it was because Lucy was already asleep and he couldn't text her, or maybe he just didn't want to be alone in his room. But as he sat around with most of the guys as they cut up and razzed each other, he suddenly wished he hadn't stayed locked up so much before.

These guys were actually really funny.

"I am not kidding, Phillipe is the next all-star goalie. He's almost two and the kid can block anything. I try! I shoot at him all the time," Tate Odder, their goalie, said, all seriousness in his eyes. "Audrey, she believes too."

Lucas Brooks laughed but nodded. "No shit, I watch the kid too. He's amazing for being so little. Well, young, I mean. The kid is a mini-giant."

Everyone laughed at that as Tate nodded. "True! Aiden and Asher are always trying to score on him. They cannot!"

"Of course they can't. They take after their dad," Erik Titov joked as Phillip Anderson laughed from his gut.

"Yeah, isn't it time for you to retire yet, Brooks?"

Lucas glared, leaning on the table. "I can outskate, outshoot, and whoop all your asses. Shut it and don't start with me, Anderson. I'll call your little son-in-law to take you out when we get to LA."

Phillip scoffed. "I'm not scared of that little shit. No offense, Sinclair."

Jayden laughed. "Hey, he is a little shit," he joked. "But don't act like you don't love the dude. We all know you do."

The look on Phillip's face said otherwise as Erik teased, "Isn't Claire pregnant yet?"

"The fuck? I will kill you!" Phillip said, reaching across the table for Erik, and everyone just laughed. It was apparently an ongoing joke about Claire, Phillip's niece, who was basically his daughter. They'd had one rough start, but the girl, who was married to Sinclair's brother, Jude, was doing well for herself. Phillip was really proud of her, minus her husband choice. Apparently, Jude was annoying. Surprising, with how awesome Jayden was.

"My mom is begging for a new grandbaby already. And since I know Bay and I aren't getting pregnant, I feel sorry for her 'cause I don't think they're gonna come through for her either," Jayden said and Phillip's eyes narrowed.

"They don't need any kids. They are kids."

Everyone nodded but Jayden. He just smiled. "You just don't want to be a grandpa."

"Of course, I don't. I just became a father for the second time. Third, if you count Claire, which I do."

Jordie laughed as Karson leaned against the table, a grin on his face. "Speaking of new fathers, got some news."

"You're pregnant?" Vaughn asked. "I thought you were getting fat."

Everyone horselaughed as Karson glared. "I am not."

"Eh, your ass is getting bigger," Phillip decided, but Karson just rolled his eyes.

"Anyway, we just found out that Lacey's pregnant, asshole."

That started a round of cheers from the veterans around the table, while the rookies all looked as if life was ending. Benji, though, he was happy for his friend. Lacey, his wife, had some trouble with postpartum depression after she had their first daughter, Mena. But she had been doing great from what Karson had said. A new baby was awesome, and while Benji was a little jealous of his friend, he slapped him on the back. "Congratulations!"

Karson grinned. "We are excited. Nervous, because of all the issues after Mena was born, but at least, this time, we know what to do."

"She'll be fine. Lacey is the strongest chick I know. Don't tell your sister I said that," Jordie laughed and Karson grinned. But Jordie was right, Lacey was one strong chick. With beating cancer and then living her dreams by making lingerie for breast cancer survivors, Benji wasn't the only one that looked up to her. But Kacey, Jordie's wife and Karson's sister…that woman was scary strong. She kicked their asses as the Assassins' strengthening coach and owned her own gym, one that Benji had no desire to go into. She'd made Benji cry at least twice. So, yeah, he gave her a wide berth when it came to fitness.

"Yeah," Karson agreed, and then he sent Lucas a grin. "Heard Fallon is going for baby number five, trying to tie with the Adlers."

Lucas's face went white. "Who the hell told you that?"

"Heard it through the grapevine," Karson laughed and everyone snickered at Lucas's alarmed expression.

"Dude, no. I'm getting my shit cut. I can't do any more. Have you met Emery? That baby is her mother made over. And I'm sorry, I love my wife, I do, but she's insane. I can't do her pregnant again. She's so damn *hangry*."

Tate laughed. "It's probably 'cause Aiden took all the awesome genes."

Lucas let out a long breath. "That kid. I'm gonna strangle him. He has a girlfriend. A fucking girlfriend. Do you all remember what your first girlfriend was like at sixteen?"

The guys snickered as Benji grinned. He had done a whole lot of nasty things at sixteen, which made him cringe for his buddy.

"Do you know what it's like to have the sex talk with your kid? Oh no, because I'm the only one here with a teenager."

That got him a round of old guy cracks that he did not appreciate, but Benji thought it was funny. "Man, it's not right without Adler not being here," Tate said and everyone nodded. It was weird. He had been the most adult out of all of them and had such a big presence.

"Yeah, he was our old man. Now we have to settle for Brooks," Vaughn said sadly and Lucas glared.

"Fuck off. But yeah, it does suck without him."

"Yeah, someone should tell him to come back," Karson said with a nod.

"He's happy," Benji said, leaning on the table. "He loves coaching the girls' hockey team, and he's really good at it. I heard he's got a stacked team for the boys."

"Oh, yeah, especially with how good Owen and Evan are," Jordie said with a nod, speaking of Shea's boys. "Who's all going to the games this weekend?"

The ones closest to Shea raised their hands as Benji said, "I'll be there for the girls, but I'm not sure about the boys."

"Yeah, me too. I think Lacey has a doctor's appointment that day," Karson said, and Jordie looked over at his brother-in-law.

"Need us to watch Mena?"

"Yeah, if you don't mind."

That was one of the biggest things that Benji loved about the Assassins. Everyone was family. No matter if there was blood involved, though most of it was blood, since everyone was married to someone's sister. Or someone's niece was married to someone's brother. That always made Benji laugh. The Phillip/Jude feud was just hilarious. But other than that, the team was one big family, and Benji appreciated that. He needed that, but he wanted what they all had. He was too old to be like the rookies, fucking around and partying. Plus, he didn't drink. But sometimes he didn't fit in with the older guys because he wasn't married and didn't have children. Which was another reason he stayed in his room a lot. He just felt left out, but as he sat there, joking with his friends, talking about their families, he was actually upset he hadn't allowed himself to enjoy this before.

When Jordie took him by his shoulder, shaking him, Benji laughed. "Dude, it's good having you here!"

Benji grinned as a lot of the other guys nodded in agreement. He had gotten so used to not putting himself in a position where his sobriety could be tested that he had become a recluse. But to his surprise, as his friends drank and hung out, he didn't even care to drink. His glass of pop was good for him. He watched Jordie, worried about his friend, but Jordie was good too. Being with Kacey and having Ella really woke that dude up.

Benji was jealous of that.

Meeting Jordie's gaze, he shrugged. "I don't know why I didn't come down sooner."

"'Cause you're a loner," Vaughn laughed and everyone joined in.

"Leave him alone. I don't blame him for liking *Game of Thrones* more than us," Jordie added and Benji laughed.

"I don't know, I think he's acting different," Karson said and Lucas nodded.

"Yeah, something is up. I just can't decide what it could be."

Lucy.

It was all Lucy.

Or at least, he thought so. He had never felt happier in the last twelve years than he did now. When he wasn't playing or practicing, he and Lucy were texting or FaceTiming. She was adorable and funny, and he could tell she was hesitant. But, he knew she was slowly getting comfortable with him. She had been so stressed lately, and he hated that. He wanted to fix it, but she wouldn't let him. She was independent, and that was one of the things he liked so much about her.

She didn't need anyone.

But the fact that she wanted him somehow meant more.

"Wait, are you dating someone? You getting laid, bro?" Vaughn razzed as he came up behind Benji, shaking him by his shoulders as everyone cut up. "Did our little boy finally lose his virginity?"

That rewarded him with a round of guffaws since everyone knew Benji wasn't really good with the ladies. Well, he used to not be good with the ladies. Now, he was good. Real good—with one lady. But before, being on a team with thirty guys, it was unheard of that one of them wasn't getting laid. And of course, all of them had advice. It ranged from hiring a hooker to sleeping with one of their relatives. Everyone had a single sister or cousin or mother. The last always made him cringe. But Benji didn't have to worry about that anymore. He was talking to the queen of women and it felt good. Real fucking good. Still, though, the guilt was there, but he was trying to get over that. He had to get over that. Or it could have the potential to ruin a damn good thing.

And that couldn't happen.

No. Lucy and Angie were special, and he refused to hurt them.

He couldn't.

"Aw, look, our little boy is blushing," someone said. He thought it was Vaughn, and he just rolled his eyes.

"Oh, shut it," he laughed, but they didn't, razzing him to the extreme. But Benji just laughed them off.

He enjoyed it.

He felt like one of them.

It was well past his bedtime, but he was still downstairs with the boys when his phone vibrated in his pocket. Surprised and a little confused, he pulled his phone out to see it was from Lucy. A little grin sat on his lips as he hit her message.

Lucy: *You awake?*
Benji: *Yes, surprisingly. I'm down at the bar with the guys. Hanging out.*
Lucy: *Oh. Well, call me in the morning.*
Lucy: *Sorry to bug ya.*
Benji: *Please. I've been thinking about you and you never bug me. What's up?*
Lucy: *⊠ Been thinking about me, huh?*
Benji: *Yeah, it happens a lot.*
Lucy: *Well. What about?*
Benji: *It would take me an hour to text you everything I think about, so how about I call you when I get back up to the room?*
Lucy: *Boo. I'm about to go to bed. Angie is sleeping with me tonight. She doesn't like the other room.*
Benji: *She okay?*
Lucy: *Yeah, something about the closet. It does look sketchy, but Jayden said he'll fix it when he gets home.*
Benji: *Okay, well then, can I call you in the morning?*
Lucy: *Yeah, I'd like that.*
Benji: *Me too.*
Benji: *Goodnight, gorgeous.*
Lucy: *Night <3*

"Aw, are you texting her? Who is she?" Vaughn joked and Benji hid his phone as everyone laughed.

"Get away from me," Benji laughed, tucking his phone into his pocket and rolling his eyes. When Jayden got up to go to the bar to order some food, Benji watched him and wondered if he should follow him. He had wanted to talk to him since they left for the trip, but he hadn't had the right moment. Or had the balls to do it. He respected Jayden and knew how much Lucy meant to him. He kind of wanted to be the one to tell him. Man-to-man. But he didn't want to piss Lucy off by saying something to Jayden. He just didn't feel right about not saying anything, though. They were kind of in a relationship, weren't they? He wasn't sure—that was probably something he should verify with Lucy—but he still felt like he was hiding something and he didn't like that.

Getting up, he moved past Vaughn as he told a story of himself and a set of triplets. It was a very interesting story, but Benji wanted to talk to Jayden. Plus, he had heard it three times. It was one of Vaughn's highlights.

Moving across the bar, a girl stopped him.

"Hey, aren't you Benji Paxton?"

He paused, looking around, confused. "Me?"

"Yeah," she giggled, her friends looking at him like a piece of meat.

What in the hell?

"Um, yeah, that's me."

"I didn't know you wore glasses—very Clark Kent," she said. Any other day, he would have said she was hot, especially with her Clark Kent reference, but she wasn't Lucy.

"Yeah, I can't see without my contacts," he said, and then he tapped the table. "Sorry, but I'm meeting my buddy. You ladies have a nice night."

He went to walk away, but the blonde said, "Maybe with you?"

He looked back, his eyes wide, and then he chuckled.

Figured. He started to talk to someone, and now he was apparently attractive to women.

Whatever.

Waving at her, of course, in the most awkward way possible, he went to the bar where Jayden was. He'd seen the whole thing and was laughing.

"Dude, she wanted the D. Shit. I just sound like my little brother."

Benji scoffed. "Yeah, no."

"No? She was basically humping your leg with her eyes," Jayden commented, shaking his head as the bartender placed a plate of wings in front of him.

Taking one, he put it in his mouth as Benji said, "Actually, I'm good. Which is why I wanted to talk to you."

Chewing, Jayden's face scrunched up. "Talk? About what?"

"Um," Benji said, leaning on the bar as a grin pulled at his lips. "Your sister."

Jayden stopped eating. "My sister? Lucy?"

He nodded, facing his friend. "Yeah, er, well, I'm kinda into her."

Jayden's face took on a look of horror as his head tilted to the side. "Lucy? My sister? You're into her? Wait, am I drunk? Is this real life?"

Benji scoffed. "You haven't even had a drink tonight."

"Yeah, but surely I'm hearing you wrong. My sister, Lucy? Angry brunette who could start a fight in an empty room?"

He nodded, a grin pulling at his lips. "Yeah, but she isn't that bad."

Jayden didn't agree, his eyes still wide. "Are you sure? She doesn't like guys. I think she might be a lesbian. Who wouldn't be after Rick?"

"No, no, she's not," Benji laughed which made Jayden's brows come together. "We're actually talking."

"*Talking?*"

Benji met his gaze. "Yeah."

When Jayden didn't say anything, Benji looked away and sighed. "Listen, I respect you, dude, and I know she means the world to you. We aren't together or anything yet—"

"Yet? So you've already decided this is going somewhere?"

Benji scoffed. "Dude, I'm thirty-two years old. I lost my family twelve years ago. I don't have time to just fuck around. I want to be happy."

Jayden sucked in a deep breath. "Man, I hear you and I respect you, you know that. But my sister is tough. She's been burned bad."

"I know, but I just wanted to make sure that you know I won't burn her. I won't hurt her."

Jayden nodded slowly. "I wasn't even worried about that. Really. But she could hurt you." Benji paused as Jayden's eyes searched his. "I haven't seen her with anyone since she and Rick divorced, and it worries me. I want my sister to be happy."

"Me too," Benji said. "I'm not one of those guys who—"

"Dude, you don't have to sell me on you. You're one of the most stand-up and honest people I've ever met. My sister deserves the best. I know, as her brother, I'm supposed to be like, no one is good enough for my sister. But, really, you are. Seriously."

Benji's heart warmed as the emotion choked him. He'd never thought he was much of a man. He tried hard to be honest and good to the people he knew, but to hear that from Lucy's brother meant the world to him. Maybe he was doing something right. Meeting Jayden's gaze, he nodded. "I would be the luckiest man on earth if I was loved by Lucy and Angie. But like I said, it's new, only a week, but I wanted to be honest with you."

"And I appreciate that, I do. Though, remember, Lucy is harsh. But the fact she's even talking to you and you feel like this could go somewhere means

something and, dude, that's awesome. I miss her smile."

That was clear and it made Benji's heart hurt. What did that jackass do to her? It wasn't Jayden's place to tell him, and he didn't want to hear it from him, but he needed to know. When Jayden looked back at him, he didn't smile as he asked, "Does she know about Leary and Ava?"

Benji swallowed hard as he shook his head. "Not yet. I'm waiting for the right time to tell her."

"And I assume she hasn't told you about Rick the dick?"

Benji shook his head. "No, but I've met the dude and wanted to punch him in the face."

"Yeah, he has that effect on people," he laughed and then shook his head. "Well, I'm rooting for you two. I hope it works out. Just know it won't be easy. Nothing is easy with Lucy."

"Funny, she said the same thing."

"Yeah, 'cause she makes it hard as hell," he said, exhaling a breath. "She's headstrong, very do-it-herself. I mean, you know about the shop and shit?" Benji nodded and Jayden threw up his hands. "I told her, stay with us till you get things figured out. She wants to rent a hotel when I get home Friday. She's fucking insane."

"A hotel?" he asked and Jayden shook his head.

"Yeah, she's driving me up the wall. I almost want to rent her an apartment just so I know she's good, but she would kill me."

"Yeah, she doesn't take handouts well."

Jayden scoffed. Hard. "Dude, you have no idea. She's got everyone so stressed out because she's so stressed. I'm about to glue her ass to my house."

Benji smiled. "I offered my house, but apparently, that's weird."

Jayden laughed. "Yeah, it is."

Benji grinned. "Well, I just want them to be safe."

Jayden cupped his shoulder. "I know, dude, but somehow, she's always okay. It's crazy, but she is always good. She's just like that."

"Yeah, well, it's time for her to be better than good," Benji said and Jayden smiled.

"Man, I hope you stick around."

He laughed as he met his friend's gaze. "I'm not going anywhere."

And he wasn't.

"Good morning, beautiful."

Lucy's face burned as her lips curved while she pulled out of the school parking lot after dropping Angie off. From where her phone sat on her dashboard, Benji watched as she turned onto the main street. She had said she would call him, but when he ignored her call to FaceTime her, she decided she liked that more. She liked seeing his face, especially when he was all tired and sleepy. She also very much liked when he called her beautiful. Particularly when she felt like she looked like dog shit. But under Benji's gaze, she felt like a princess.

It was really fucking stupid, childish almost, but she sort of, maybe, liked it.

"Morning. Late night? You look tired."

He smiled. "Yeah, I didn't get back to the room until two. Those dudes are crazy. We have to be at the rink for morning skate in an hour. I'm dead."

"Aw, does that mean I won't get my goal tonight? I mean, you got Angie one. Where is mine?" she teased and he laughed.

"I'm getting there, I can feel it."

"Well, you have one more night," she reminded him as she turned onto the interstate. She was heading to Rayne's house to pick her up to run some errands.

"Yeah, I know. But the question is, if I don't come through, will I still get a kiss tomorrow when I see you?"

She met his gaze for a moment as she chewed her lip before looking back to the road. "Benji, my family will all be there and so will Angie. I don't know."

"We can sneak off like kids."

"'Cause no one would suspect anything," she said sarcastically and he smiled.

"I want to kiss you, and I'm going to."

She sucked in a breath, her belly going crazy with butterflies. "I don't know."

"You'll see."

Her lips curved. "Well, one thing is for sure—I'm excited to see you. Like, the real you."

"Yeah, Ms. Change the Subject," he accused and she grinned.

"I'm not changing anything. We were done."

"Okay, I wasn't."

"Oh?" she asked, turning off the interstate.

"Yeah," he said and she watched as he sat up, his bare chest coming on the screen as he repositioned the phone. "Never mind."

"Never mind?"

He shrugged. "Yeah, nothing. What are you doing?"

It wasn't nothing, and she didn't like that. Glaring, she snapped, "No, what? Why aren't we done? You got something to say?"

He shook his head. "Nothing, I'm just tired."

"Ha, and you say I lie a lot," she accused as she pulled onto Rayne's street.

"Don't hold back, Benji. If you've got something to say, please say it."

"You're being snarky, missy."

"Because you're holding back," she said simply as she pulled into Rayne's driveway. "What? Are you mad that I won't kiss you in front of my kid?"

"Lucy, I didn't say that, and I don't want to fight with you—"

Frustrated, she let out an angry sigh. But she knew it wasn't all his fault. Before she'd dropped Angie, she'd gotten the call that she would be getting a refund on her apartment and shop because they weren't sure they'd have the money to fix it. The damage was more extensive than they'd thought, and the landlord's daughter was scared Lucy would sue. She wouldn't. They were good people and honest, but it fucking sucked. She was pissed, she was annoyed, and she sure as hell didn't like how much she missed Benji.

Glaring at him, she snapped, "I told you this wouldn't work. I have a kid—"

"Jesus, woman, shut up," he said sternly and she glared, but her lips slammed shut.

What the hell?

"Don't tell me to shut up," she snapped and he glared back.

"No, why are you so pissy? What happened?"

"Nothing."

"Lucy."

"Fuck, fine. I got word that I can't go back to my shop or my apartment."

His shoulders fell. "I'm sorry. I know how much you loved it there."

"Yeah, it's whatever. I'll be fine."

He shook his head. "Yeah, but don't snap at me."

She shrugged. "Sorry."

He held her gaze. "All I was saying was that I fucking miss you, Lucy, and the first thing I want to do when I see you is wrap you in my arms and kiss you stupid. But I get it. We aren't even together and it's wrong of me to want that, especially with Angie being there. You're right, it's just hard. I get that you're upset and I'm sorry, but stop throwing Angie in my face. I know you have a kid, and I adore your kid. So, yeah, I'll respect your boundaries. Just know it's fucking hard, but I'll respect them."

Why was he so great? And why was it becoming really difficult to keep her heart locked up? She swallowed hard as she looked down at her lap. If she was honest, what he said was what she wanted. She missed him so damn much, which was just dumb and irrational on her part. Like he said, they weren't together. They were just talking. But that night together, wrapped in his arms as he bestowed those kisses on her had spoiled her. The fact he called her beautiful any chance he got had also fueled her need to see him in person, but that was insane. And the way he was with her when she was being a fucking bitch was award-winning. But they were just talking.

Weren't they?

Letting out a long breath, she looked back at the phone to find him watching her. "We've only been talking a week, Benji—"

"It feels like years," he said then and her lips quirked.

Because it did.

Their conversations were awesome, and she was having so much fun talking to him. They liked so many of the same things, and while he was a big nerd, she was starting to think she might be one too. She loved all the same movies, she loved hockey, and she loved crossword puzzles. Like him. They just clicked, but something was still holding her back.

And it scared her.

She finally found someone she liked and who got her. She could complain about the shop, her job, anything, and he would listen. She didn't talk about Rick because she just didn't like to talk about him, but she was sure Benji would listen. The big thing was Angie, though.

"I just worry about Angie. I don't want to bring anyone around her and have her get her heart broken. There is only so much Ben & Jerry's, and I'm not fighting my kid for it."

Benji smiled, moving his hand through his hair, pushing it to the side. "Let's get one thing straight. No matter what happens between you and me, I will always care about that little girl. I can promise you that. She and I were friends before you and me."

Lucy rolled her eyes. "I know, but it's just different. I'm guessing you haven't dated anyone with a kid before which is why you don't really get it."

Something flashed in his eyes and he shrugged. "I get it, Lucy, I do."

"So you've dated someone with a kid?"

But he shook his head, his lips pressing together. "Not really, but then I really don't date."

"Oh?"

"Yeah, I've tried, but no one has really stuck."

This was the first time they had really talked about their pasts. Well, his past. Her past pretty much involved Rick and only Rick. Biting her lip, she looked up and shrugged. "I haven't been with anyone since Rick."

"Yeah, so we are both trying to navigate through this. It has to mean something that neither of us has found anyone who matters until now."

She grinned. "Who said you matter?" she teased and he grinned.

"You know I do."

"Maybe."

He rolled his eyes. "The thing is, I don't want to do any navigating with anyone but you, and I will respect what you want. I will. Just stop throwing that kid card up at me and stop saying this won't work. Give it a chance."

She swallowed hard as she moved her hands down the front of her skirt. "What is this?" she asked, and as soon as she said it, she wondered why it mattered. Why did it need to be labeled?

Looking up at him, she was breathless as his lips curved. "Something spectacular. Just give it a chance, okay?"

Lucy smiled as she nodded. "Okay."

"Good," he said, letting out a long breath. "We good?"

She met his gaze and couldn't help but grin. He looked so delicious and sexy, and while it bothered her that he had a way with her, she actually appreciated it. It felt good that he respected her but was quick to put her in her place. Lord knows she was a little bit of a bitch. Okay, maybe a lot of one, but with him, it was different. She didn't feel as bitchy.

"Yeah, and I'm thinking that, next week, when we go on our date, I want you to take me back to your house."

His eyes widened. "For what?"

She giggled. "You know what."

"The sex?" he said so seriously, his face made of stone, and Lucy couldn't handle it.

He was a nut.

Giggling uncontrollably, she leaned back, her stomach hurting as he watched her with a grin. Catching her breath, she sputtered with laughter. "Yes, Benji, the sex."

He nodded, a smug look on his face. "I like the way you think, Sinclair."

"Well, be ready because I'd take you now if I could," she admitted, her body catching on fire for his. It had been six days too long, and while it should worry her that she was craving him like a smoker craved a cigarette, she couldn't help it.

She wanted Benji Paxton.

Bad.

As his eyes darkened, a sexy little grin graced his lips. "Oh, sweetheart, you have no idea how much I want you," he said roughly. "It's so hard being on the other end of this phone, gazing into those eyes and staring at those sexy lips. I just want to feel you."

"Me too," she admitted, breathless. "God, stop. I've got errands to run. Can't do it all hot and bothered."

He scoffed. "If I can play hockey all hot and bothered, you can do errands."

She giggled at that. "Oh, that reminds me why I called," she said and his grin dropped.

"Aw, man, we aren't gonna talk about the sex anymore?"

"Focus, Paxton," she laughed and his eyes brightened. "I'm gonna run by your house and check out the in-law spot, if that's still okay."

"Yeah, of course. You can also go inside and stay there until I get there," he said with a waggle of his brows and she rolled her eyes.

"Anyway—"

"No, you know what I need you to do?"

"I'm afraid to ask," she said as the front door opened and Rayne threw her hands up. "Shit, hurry, Rayne's coming."

"Who's Rayne?"

"My assistant."

"Oh, okay, well, do me a favor?"

"Benji, I will not be naked in your bed when you get home," she said dryly and he laughed.

"So unfair. So selfish," he accused playfully and she grinned. "No, after we hang up, listen to the song 'Kiss Me Thru the Phone.'"

"By Soulja Boy?"

"Yeah."

"Are you a closet rapper?"

"You know it," he said, moving his thumb along his lips like he was cool.

"Dork."

"Hush, do it."

Exhaling a breath as Rayne opened the door to get in, she agreed, "Okay."

"And if you want to be naked in my bed when I get home tonight, you know where the key is. I should get in at three."

"Don't hold your breath," she said, ignoring Rayne's shocked expression. "I gotta go."

"Why, don't want Rayne to hear us talking about banging each other all night long?"

"Good Lord, bye," she said, hitting end as her face burned.

"Well, goodness, who did that sexy voice belong to?" Rayne asked as Lucy grabbed her phone.

"No one," she answered simply, clicking on her Spotify to find the song. She remembered it, but she wanted to listen to it again. Before she could click on it, though, a text message came through.

Benji: I miss you, call me later?

Her heart fluttered as she typed back quickly.

Lucy: I will. Sorry for hanging up on you.
Benji: No, you're not, but that's fine. You can make it up to me by being butt-ass naked when I get home.
Lucy: Bye, Benji.
Benji: Bye, sweetheart.

Laying her phone in her lap after hitting play, she looked over at Rayne. "Let's go."

"Wow, you're smiling, like, so hard. It's so cute!" she cheered and Lucy rolled her eyes.

"Shut up," she said, pulling out of the driveway.

"I can take a hint, but it's nice," she sang, but Lucy ignored her, hitting play and heading toward Benji's house. It was nice, it felt good, but she wasn't ready to talk about Benji like that. Not until she was sure. In the back of her mind, she knew she was sure; this had the potential to work. But she didn't want to get ahead of herself. No reason to get excited about something that would probably fail.

Nothing ever worked out for her. Why would this?

As the song played, her smile didn't drop. It was silly and crazy, but the song fit them. It was disgustingly cute. When the song was over, though, Rayne and Lucy talked about some clients and how everyone was really understanding about her current situation.

"I mean, the work isn't suffering. We are still kicking ass," Lucy said and Rayne nodded.

"Yeah, which everyone sees. But those applicants really want to be interviewed."

"Yeah, I know. Let's get a place first," she said simply, turning onto Benji's street.

Rayne made a face before looking over at Lucy. "I thought we were checking out a potential office building."

"We are."

"Um, this is a neighborhood. Wait, this is Benji Paxton's road."

The downside to having a good assistant was that she forgot nothing. Nodding, Lucy pulled into the driveway and shut the car off. "Yeah, he has an in-law suite that he thinks can work as an office for us. And I was thinking, since I'm designing this whole house, it could work. I can use his house as a model. Not sure on the latter, haven't asked him, but yeah, that's my plan. Let's check it out."

Rayne didn't move, though, her lips curving. "So you guys talked about something more than his design? Because how would he know we need an office space?"

Lucy made a face. "Everyone knows, Rayne, come on."

"No, you like him! Your face is red. Was he the one on the phone? Is he your boyfriend? Finally!" Ignoring her, Lucy got out of the car and went to the bush to get the key. "He told you where the secret key is? Wow, is this more serious than I thought?"

"Hush," Lucy demanded as she headed behind the house. Then her eyes widened. The backyard was huge, with an in-ground pool and a pool house. And then in the very back was the guesthouse. "Man, it's bigger than I assumed."

"That's not a suite. That's a minimansion," Rayne said as they walked down the walkway to it. "It's cute. Like a mini version of the house."

"Yeah," Lucy agreed as they reached the guesthouse, or minimansion like Rayne had said. The brick was white like the rest of the house, it had big windows, and she was pretty sure it was bigger than her old shop.

"I think it's great. He sounded really nice on the phone," Rayne said as she unlocked the door. "And it's obvious he likes you if he is offering his guesthouse to you."

"I'll be paying him," she said as she pushed the door open. Her eyes widened at the size of the suite. Benji wasn't playing; it was huge and no wonder he thought it could work. He was right.

"That's probably 'cause he knows it's the only way you'll agree to take his help."

Lucy turned to her. She may be right, but Lucy didn't want to hear that. "Do you like your job?"

Rayne giggled, her brown eyes flashing with humor. "You wouldn't fire me. You need me. This is a great space."

And it was. It was a big, open floor plan with a little cooking area, one main room, another room with a door, and a bathroom. The in-law who got to stay here was one spoiled in-law, in her opinion. Looking around, Lucy bit the inside of her lip.

Shit, this could really work, and it was cute.

But should she do it? She hadn't known Benji long, but she knew he wouldn't screw her. He also said they could do a contact, which was good. She'd want one, but was this mixing business with pleasure ? What the hell was she thinking? She was sleeping with him and he was her client. She had already crossed that line.

She was so damned professional.

Not.

"What do you think?" she said to Rayne, but when she glanced at Rayne, she was taking pictures with her phone.

"Oh, I was taking pictures so I can figure out how to put my desk."

Lucy gave her a dry look. "I haven't decided yet."

"You haven't?" she asked, a deadpan expression on her face. "You know this is the right fit for us. It's great. Parking might be an issue, but maybe we can put in a bigger driveway?"

Lucy looked away and then looked at her phone. "I'll be right back."

"Okay, I'll take pictures for you to design later," Rayne said, so confidently that it made Lucy roll her eyes.

But she did love the place.

Walking outside, she dialed Benji's number.

"So what do you think?"

She smiled. "I kinda love it."

"Kinda?"

"I'm just nervous to commit."

"Sounds like you," he teased and she pursed her lips, glaring at the bushes. "How much do you want a month?"

"How much can you afford?"

"My rent at my other place was fifteen hundred, but that included the upstairs apartment."

He made a clicking noise as he thought, and then said, "Okay, so what, like, six hundred?"

She gasped. "Six hundred? That's too low!"

"No way, I'm only worried about covering my utilities."

"That's with utilities? Are you crazy?"

He scoffed. "About you? Yeah."

"Benji," she sighed as her heart went wild in her chest. "Focus."

"Fine. Six hundred is my final price, take it or leave it."

She hesitated. "How do you feel about expanding the driveway? I'll pay for that, of course."

"There is a driveway on the other side that they used for their business," he said, and she looked up to see that, in fact, connected to the little walkway was a long driveway. She hadn't noticed it, probably because she came from the other way and hadn't had to go that far.

"Oh."

"Yeah, so it's pretty much set up," he said simply. "You could move in tomorrow and you'll be fine."

"What's the deposit?"

"Good Lord, Lucy. Are you looking for something to make you not do this?" She paused as he laughed. "Just say yes and be good, babe."

"I just don't know if I want to mix business with pleasure. It makes me nervous."

"Um, we slept with each other a week ago and I still want you to design my house, so we're past that," he said and she closed her eyes. "And I still very much want to sleep with you again."

Ignoring the last sentence, she bit into her lip. "I thought that too."

"Yeah, I just want to help out any way I can. Let me, please?"

She looked around, her gut telling her this was good as she tapped her foot. She'd be stupid not to take it. It was perfect for her. Almost like it was made for her. "And I can paint and design it any way I want?"

"Yeah, do whatever you want. I don't need it. I had no clue what I was going to do with it, anyway. "

She sucked in a deep breath. "Can you get a contract drawn up?"

"I already did," he said, clearing his throat at her intake of breath. "I'll have my lawyer get with you, and we can get the ball rolling. But like I said, you can move in this weekend if you want."

God, why was this so hard for her? Why couldn't she just accept what he had done and be good with it? She had never been good at accepting help, and now was no different.

"Are you sure?"

He scoffed and she could hear the smile in his voice. "Knowing that you are working behind my house daily? Yeah, I'm sure. At least this way I know you'll be safe and you'll be good."

Geez, he was sweet. "But being so close, I might need you for some lifting," she teased and he chuckled.

"If lifting you against the wall as I pound into you is one of these 'lifting' requests, then, sweetheart, sign me up," he said, his voice dropping a few octaves.

"You dirty, dirty man," she accused breathlessly as she looked up at the sky. His laughter ran down her spine as she shook her head.

What in the hell was she doing?

She was doing what she had to. This could blow up in her face, but then, maybe it could work. She had to get the ball rolling. She had to get her business back up so she could find a permanent place to stay for her and Angie. So even though she wasn't sure if it was a good idea, she had to follow her gut. And it was telling her to say yes.

"Okay, have your lawyer get with me."

"Will do, but is it okay if I give him your number?"

She rolled her eyes. "Yes, dork. What am I going to do with you?"

"I have a few ideas," he suggested, his voice so low and rough she felt it between her legs.

"I'm sure. Okay, let me let you go."

"Do I have to?"

"Yes, gosh, you drive me crazy."

"Good, crazy is good," he decided and she smiled.

Biting the inside of her cheek, she sucked in a breath. "Thanks, Benji."

"Always, babe. Anything you need, I got you."

And for the first time since her divorce, Lucy trusted someone.

She trusted Benji.

She just hoped it didn't blow up in her face like everything else always did.

Chapter ELEVEN

It was one o'clock in the morning when Jayden came through the back door, his brow rising when he saw Lucy at the kitchen table, working.

Matching her brother's expression, she said, "Hey, you're home early."

"Yeah, we took off earlier than we thought. I think everyone was ready to be home," he said, dropping his suitcase by the table and then leaning over to kiss her head. "How'd you know when I was coming home?"

She paused. "Baylor told me," she lied and he smirked as he grabbed a bottle of water from the fridge.

"Sure."

"Sure? What's that mean?"

He shook his head. "Nothing at all."

Oh, he was such a liar, but she ignored that, clearing her throat. "Well, I don't know what you're insinuating, but you can shut it."

Okay, she tried to ignore it.

He chuckled. "What would I need to insinuate, Lucy? Got something to tell me?"

She glared. "Nothing at all, why?"

His gaze was knowing as he grinned. "Oh, just making sure. You look like you want to share something."

"Shut up."

He scoffed as he leaned against the doorjamb. "Why are you working so late?"

"'Cause it's what I do. Gotta make money to find Angie and me a good place to live."

He nodded. "So, it's final, you can't go back to your shop?"

She exhaled sadly. A part of her had thought maybe, just maybe, she would be able to go back. But nope, that wasn't her luck. "Yeah, they cut me my checks today, and I'm gonna store my crap in my warehouse until I find something."

"Shit, I'm sorry, Luce," he said and she shrugged.

"Eh, that's my life," she said with a soulless laugh. "But I did find an office today."

"Oh, yeah?"

"Yup," she said, clearing her throat. "It's actually your friend Benji's little guesthouse in the back. He's gonna let me rent it."

He nodded, a small grin on his lips. "Good dude, Paxton is."

"Yeah, he is," she agreed, looking away as her phone vibrated.

"You know he's single," Jayden said, pushing off the wall.

She swallowed hard as she reached for her phone to see the text was from the guy they were speaking of. "Yeah?"

"Yeah, you two would be good together."

Her brows came together. "How do you know who I would be good with? Don't you need to shower? Jesus. Leave me alone."

Jayden laughed as he walked away and she clicked Benji's text. "Yeah, yeah."

Letting out a long breath, she read his message, her lips curving.

Benji: Completely and utterly disappointed.

Looking to confirm that Jayden was climbing the stairs, she went back to her phone.

Lucy: Why is that? Are you home?
Benji: Yeah, and my bed is empty. Bullshit.
Lucy: lol. Sorry. Told ya it would be.
Benji: I was hoping you were playing with my mind.
Lucy: Nope.
Benji: Then why are you awake?
Lucy: Working.
Benji: You work too much.
Lucy: Got a daughter to care for.
Benji: True. Has anyone told you you're a great mom today?

Lucy couldn't smile any bigger if she tried. Her heart, man, it was going crazy, and her stomach, those butterflies were having a dance party.

Lucy: No, they haven't.
Benji: Well, let me be the one to say it. Because you are a great mom, Lucy Sinclair.
Lucy: Thanks <3
Lucy: Are you about to go to bed?
Benji: I mean, I don't have to if you want to come over.
Lucy: I can't. Angie is in bed.
Benji: I know, but hey, can't blame me for trying.

She couldn't and she was a little upset with herself that she really wanted to go over. She just missed him and wanted to see him, but that was so irresponsible. Angie was asleep and she couldn't leave her. But Jayden and Baylor were there… No, they wanted to have naughty time and enjoy each other. Jayden had just gotten home.

No, just get it out of your head. Work, Lucy.

When a text came through from Benji with a link to YouTube, her brow quirked as his next message followed.

Benji: I'm being ruthless I know, but this is me right now.

Hitting the link, Sam Hunt's "Come Over" started playing.
Oh, he was dirty.
This was her jam.
She knew it by heart, and as the music played, Sam's gorgeous voice hitting her straight in the gut, she wrote Benji back.

Lucy: You're playing dirty, Paxton.
Benji: Yeah. Sorry. I'm dying here. I miss you so fucking much.

And she missed him, but no, she couldn't.

Lucy: I can't leave Angie.
Benji: I know. I just want you to suffer with me.

She scoffed at that.

Lucy: I was suffering before the damn video. Jerk. Now I'm dying.
Benji: Good. Wanna meet me behind the bleachers tomorrow?

God, he made her giddy. Grinning so hard, she shook her head.

Lucy: *Maybe.*
Benji: *Yes?*
Lucy: *Yes.*

Letting out a long breath, she smiled as she leaned back in her chair. What was she doing? Really, what in the hell was she doing with him? She was having way too much fun with him. He made her laugh, he made her smile, and shit, he made her feel things. Good things. Slowly he was knocking down her walls—but with the utmost respect. It was amazing and special. But man, it scared her to the core because people like him didn't work out for her. But then how could she say that when she had never really tried?

And why was she trying now?

She knew the answer right away.

Because he was different.

And she wanted to see him.

So damn bad.

When Jayden came back down the stairs, his sweats hanging loosely at his waist and, of course, no shirt—the guy had never worn clothes when they were younger—he flashed her a grin as he fell into his chair.

Confused, she said, "I thought you were going to be with your wife."

He turned on the TV. "No, I'm too wound up to sleep."

"Hence, why you go to bed with your wife," she said slowly because, Lord knew, if she could get in bed with Benji, they would not be sleeping.

Jayden chuckled as he shook his head. "Nope, Baylor is passed out. And you don't wake her when she's sleeping."

"Such a good husband, you are."

"Yeah, I thought so," he said with a laugh before leaning back in his chair.

"So you're not going to bed?" she asked and then paused. *What was she doing?*

"Nope, I'll be up for a while," he said, looking back at her. "Why? Got somewhere to go?"

She made a face and shook her head. "No, why would I?"

"Oh, I don't know. I know I'm not the only one who just got home."

She glared. "Are you insinuating something again?"

He feigned surprise. "Me? Never. Just saying, if you wanted to leave and go see said person we are apparently not mentioning exists, I'll keep an ear out for Angie."

Her glare deepened. "I'm a responsible parent. I'm not gonna leave my kid so I can go get some ass, hypothetically speaking, of course. I have no ass to get, obviously."

He shrugged, a carefree grin on his face. "Of course, but hypothetically speaking, even moms need to get some. Maybe then they wouldn't bite people's heads off for suggesting said act?"

"Hypothetically speaking, this is true. But I'm not one of those moms. Hypothetically."

"You? Bite people's heads off? Oh no, never. I wouldn't suggest it," he said with a grin and she wanted to slap him.

"I don't like you."

Turning in his chair to look at her, he grinned. "Well, I love you, and I think you should go see the person who shall not be named," he said, and then he chuckled. "Tell him I said that. He'll get a kick out of it."

He would, but her face was stone as she shrugged.

And that also meant he knew about Benji.

Shit.

Rolling her eyes, she looked down at her computer. "I have no clue what you're talking about."

But she didn't miss the defeat in his voice as he muttered, "Oh. Well, then tomorrow should be a blast with your ex and your non-sexed self."

Ugh, she did have to see Rick tomorrow. If he showed.

Shit. Tomorrow was going to suck, minus seeing her baby rock out on the ice.

And Benji. She'd see Benji at the game.

But she wanted to see him now.

Sucking in a breath, she looked at the clock on her computer and then back at Jayden. She really wanted to go, but was that right? Should she leave her child to go get some ass? It sounded so bad when she thought of it like that. She didn't know what to do.

"Lucy, I can hear you thinking all the way over here. Angie is fine. Go."

She swallowed hard, and, fuck it, she was going. "I mean, I guess I could go to the store."

"Yeah, 'cause there is so much you need at two in the morning."

She stood, reaching for her keys. "I do need stuff for snacks tomorrow."

"I saw the oranges in the fridge," he pointed out.

"Oh, yeah, but I mean for us," she said, reaching for Benji's coat.

"True, true. Have fun picking out Skittles," he said with a wink and she glared.

"I'm seriously going to Walmart," she said, trying to save face, but Jayden saw right through her.

"Yeah, of course. Good thing they're twenty-four hours, huh?" She felt her lips turn up and her dimples cut into her skin as Jayden grinned. "Have fun. Tell Benji I said he's welcome."

Reaching for the door, she looked over her shoulder at him. "I have no clue what you're talking about."

But even she couldn't hold in her laughter as she shut the door and hightailed it to the car.

Once in the car, though, she had second thoughts.

She should go.

Should she stay?

She really wanted to go.

But…

You need to do some things that make you happy. Her mom's voice rang loud and clear in her head, and she was right. Putting the car in reverse, she pulled out of the driveway and headed for Benji's. She considered calling him, telling him she was coming, but then, she kind of wanted to surprise him.

But what if he had someone there? She couldn't come, so he got a replacement?

Stop, he isn't Rick.

Swallowing that absurd thought, she drove faster to Benji's, nearly bouncing in her seat. She was doing this. She was going to freaking do this.

Stopping at a stoplight, she grabbed her phone, texting him.

> *Lucy: Are you asleep?*
> *Benji: No, I unfortunately slept on the plane thinking I was coming home to hot, naked butt.*
> *Lucy: That sucks.*
> *Benji: You have no clue. So if I suck at kissing tomorrow, we can blame you.*
> *Lucy: Me?*
> *Benji: You.*
> *Lucy: Rude.*

When he sent an emoji smile that had his tongue sticking out, she giggled. When the light turned green, she set her phone down as she hit the gas, taking off in a frenzy. She was ready to see him. Now. Turning into his community, she sang to Sam Hunt, loud and with no cares. She was so excited, so damn happy, and she felt good. A little guilty, but then Jayden was Angie's family, she was fine. Lucy was doing this for herself. She needed this.

She missed him.

When she turned onto his road, she could see his house and a grin appeared on her face as she slowed to pull into his driveway.

But then she noticed a pair of blue lights flashing on his white house.

Looking behind her, she saw they belonged to a cop car.

That had his spotlight on her car.

"Driver, stay in the car."

Stunned, she muttered, "You've got to be fucking kidding me."

But this was Lucy's life.

A fucking mess.

When blue lights started to flash in his window, Benji turned in his chair to see that there was, in fact, a cop car in front of his house.

At two in the morning.

Probably some dumbass drinking and driving.

"Idiot," he said, getting out of his chair to shut his blinds since the lights were distracting as he tried to watch Netflix. He really didn't think Lucy would be there, but a part of him hoped she would be. Because of that, he was annoyed, and this was not helping. As he reached for the cord to the blinds, he looked out to not only see the cop car, but also a car that looked very much like Lucy's.

In his driveway.

"What the hell?" he said, moving to the front door and opening it. As he stepped out onto the porch, the cop turned, and sure enough, Lucy was sitting in the car, looking at him with a sheepish expression on her face.

"Sir, return to your house. Nothing to see here."

Benji scoffed. "You're in my driveway. Obviously, there is something to see," he said, coming down from the porch.

"Sir, please stop where you are. I'll be done in just a minute," the cop demanded and Benji paused, Lucy slowly shaking her head. Even in the dark, he could see her face was beet red. "Ms. Sinclair, why are you driving over here so late at night? Have you been drinking?"

"No," she said, frustrated. "My, er, friend, just got home from a trip, and I came to see him."

The cop looked back at Benji, and he waved. "Hi. I'm the friend."

Turning his back to Benji, he said, "Now, ma'am, you were speeding through a residential neighborhood."

"I know, and I'm sorry. I was excited to see him and wasn't paying attention. Please, don't give me a ticket. I get one more ticket and my license gets suspended and I have a kid, and ugh, I should have never left the house."

"I agree, ma'am," the cop said sternly, looking at her paperwork. "But give me a minute. Let me make sure you don't have any flags on your record."

As he walked away, he looked back at Benji. "Stay where you are."

"Yes, sir," he said as he sputtered with laughter, which did not please the cop at all. When the cop got in his car, Benji shook his head, meeting Lucy's gaze.

"Really?"

"Surprise?" she said with a shrug and he laughed.

"Only you."

"I know. It's so bad," she said before letting out a long breath. "I just wanted to see you."

"Hey, I'm not complaining, and if you get a ticket, I'll pay it," he said with his hands up in the air and she grinned.

"Shut up," she said as the cop got out of the car and came toward her.

"Ma'am, are you related to Jayden Sinclair?"

Lucy's face changed, dimples beaming as she cheered internally. "Yes, sir, I am. That's my little brother, and I love him more than anything and he loves me. I'm his favorite."

Benji snorted with laughter as the cop nodded. "You're in luck. He's my favorite player on the Assassins."

"Really? He's one of mine too, but my other favorite is Benji Paxton. He's standing behind you."

The cop paused and then turned to look at Benji. "Really?"

Benji nodded. "Yup. How you doing? Can I move?"

The cop smiled as he came over, shaking Benji's hand. "Yeah, wow, it's really cool to meet you. Great playing in Minnesota. I watched it in my car tonight."

Benji grinned. "Awesome. Thanks, man," he said, slapping the cop on the shoulder and taking in his name. "Listen, Edwards, call up the box office and there'll be some seats for you come Monday, all right?"

Officer Edwards beamed. "Yeah, thanks, man!"

"No problem. I truly believe in supporting our first responders. I appreciate you keeping the streets safe from thug speeders like my girlfriend."

Lucy glared and Edwards laughed. "Eh, she wasn't so bad."

"I don't know, maybe you should arrest her to be sure. I can frisk her for you," he teased, and he was sure he was tiptoeing the line between getting laid and getting killed once she was inside. As he wanted, Edwards laughed and shook his head.

"Nah, she's good. You guys have a good night. Go Assassins!"

"Thanks, buddy," Benji said as he walked to the car to open the door for Lucy. After rolling the window up, she stepped out, glaring at him. "Hello, Speedy."

"I should go home," she said, but she wasn't going anywhere. Shutting the door, he reached for her, pulling her to him.

"You're not going anywhere, you sexy delinquent," he whispered against her lips before crashing his mouth to hers. Gasping against his mouth, she slid her hands up onto the back of his neck as he hugged her tighter to him, moving his tongue into her mouth.

God, he had missed her.

As she melted against him, their kisses became more urgent. He knew if he didn't stop while he was ahead, they were going to get arrested for indecent exposure. So reluctantly, he pulled away, kissing her nose.

"Come on, my smooth criminal. Let's take this inside."

Rolling her eyes, she smacked his arm as he pulled her down the walkway. "Shut up!"

"Oh, give me a second and you'll be yelling something else," he promised and she took in a sharp breath as he helped her up the steps. Once inside, he slammed the door shut, pressing her body into it as he caught her mouth with his. Arching into him, she wrapped her arms around his neck, her leg coming up to hook along his hip.

Pulling away, he kissed her jaw as she lengthened her neck, gasping his name. He wanted to take her right there, right then, but first, he found himself asking, "Angie okay?"

"Yeah, Jayden is with her."

"You told Jayden?" he asked, surprised, between kisses.

"No, somehow he suspected. Any idea how?"

He paused, moving his nose along her jaw. "I'm gonna lie and say no, okay?" he said, pulling back to look at her. Her eyes were dark as stone, full of lust, and fuck, she was beautiful. "Only because I don't want to fight with you right now."

Shaking her head, her eyes narrowed. "You told him?"

"Shh, kiss me," he demanded, taking her mouth with his, and she didn't protest or stop. Instead, she wrapped her legs around his middle, her mouth meshing with his in a sexy frenzy. She was just as hot as he remembered, if not hotter, and he swore there would never be enough time to truly get his fill of this gorgeous woman. But he was going to try. He was going to try until he couldn't try anymore.

Lifting her away from the door, he tore his mouth from hers so he could see where he was going. She dropped the jacket she wore, and he stepped over it, heading for the stairs. She held on to him, her lips trailing along his jaw, and then his neck as he climbed the steps to his bedroom. Once there, he laid her down, covering her body with his as he pulled at the T-shirt she wore. Lifting it over her head, he kissed down her breasts, which were held by a very sexy white lace bra.

"Jesus, you're so hot," he murmured against her skin, dipping his hand into her sweats, cupping her pussy. Arching into his hand, she cried out, her body vibrating underneath his. "God, I've missed you."

"Less talk, more do," she demanded, and he chuckled against her goose-bumped skin.

"Maybe I want to talk about my feelings?" he said, pulling up and looking down at her flushed face.

"Feelings?" she asked, out of breath, arching more into his hand.

"Yeah."

"Well, here's one: horny. I'm feeling fucking horny, and if you don't fuck me, I'm gonna get myself off and go home."

His brow quirked. "I mean, I might be down with that. Except for the going home part. But watching you get yourself off could be very satisfying for me."

Her eyes narrowed and he grinned. "Don't try me, Paxton."

"Oh, baby, I'm not trying. I'm actually about to beg. Here, let me take your pants off for you," he breathed, pulling down her sweats and thong, throwing them to the ground. Drinking her in, he bit into his lip, shaking his head. Her body was beautiful, all flushed, and her pussy was so pretty, her lips shining with her arousal. He wanted to drop his lips to her, suck her into his mouth, but he liked her idea better. Swallowing hard, he looked back up at her face and then nodded. "Please, don't let me stop you."

She eyed him, her breathing heavy as she held his gaze. The challenge was in her eyes, and he wasn't sure if it was her hotness or her never-back-down stare that had his body taut. Her eyes were so dark, so gorgeous, and fuck, he wasn't sure he could handle this. Moving her tongue along her bottom lip, she closed her eyes a little and his breath caught.

Yup, he was a goner.

"Are you serious?" she gasped, her hands slowly going down her belly, stopping right at her beautiful, plump pussy. "You want me to?"

He could only nod as she traced the outline of her lips with her forefingers. Swallowing hard, he watched as she moved her fingers up to his mouth. "I need some wetness, please."

"Baby, that pussy is good and wet, I can promise you that," he somehow managed to get out and she shrugged.

"Maybe I just want your mouth on me?"

Fuck, where had this sex kitten come from? Taking her fingers into his mouth, he locked his gaze on hers. He swirled his tongue around her fingers, flicking his tongue at the tips, causing her breath to hitch as she watched him. After pulling them from his mouth, she moved them between her swollen lips and into her delectable center. Breathless, he watched as she moved them along her clit, inside of her and out, her eyes never leaving him. A shiver ran down his spine and his cock; it was rock hard, begging to come out.

He almost brought it out, but he couldn't move. But then, licking her lips, she reached out with her other hand, moving her fingers along the bulge in his sweats, still pleasuring herself. Closing his eyes, he arched into her hand, unsure if he could handle much more. She kept him on the edge, and he was really about to embarrass himself. Or so he thought.

Suddenly, her hand was in his pants, pulling his cock out into her soft, cold palm. He cried out from the sensation, and she grinned before sitting up and moving to him, taking the tip of him in her mouth.

"Oh fuck," he hissed, his hand coming up into her hair. It was in a ponytail, so he quickly undid it, her hair spilling onto her shoulders only for a second before he balled it up in his hands, squeezing as she took him into her hot fucking mouth. "Mmm, yeah, baby," he urged her as she sucked him in, all the way to the back of her throat, and then back out.

He couldn't handle it. She was pleasing him and herself, and he wasn't sure what to watch, what to do, for that matter. So he just felt, his eyes falling shut as she continued to wreak havoc on his body. When she gasped, crying out against his cock, he sucked in a breath as she came, her body jerking forward, his cock going farther down her throat and causing her to gag. Backing up, she glanced up at him, desire swirling in those green depths, and he knew he couldn't come like this.

No, he had to be inside her.

Moving out of her mouth, he went to lay her down, but she pushed him back against the pillows, reaching for his pants and pushing them fully down his legs and onto the floor. A cute little grin sat on her lips as she undid her bra, and he threw off his shirt before she climbed into his lap, her wet center sliding against his engorged, sensitive flesh. He hissed out a breath, and their mouths joined as she rocked against him, making him completely and utterly crazy.

Still kissing him, she went up on her knees before reaching for him and directing him inside her. To his oblivion. She lowered onto him, their moans filling the room as their eyes met and the world stopped. Reaching up, he cupped her face, and everything inside him was on fire. This woman. Fuck, this gorgeous fucking woman. Leaning his head to hers, he whispered, "I'm so glad you came and almost got arrested."

She grinned against his lips, her nose brushing his as she clenched herself around him. "I would do it again if this is what waited for me."

His eyes searched hers, and he wondered if she was feeling what he was. Hell, what was he feeling? But before he could even figure that out, she was moving up and down on his cock, sending him into another universe, slowly and almost painfully. Holding her ass, he wanted to go deeper. He wanted to feel her all over him, but she was drawing out each movement, blowing his mind and making him crazy all at once.

"Faster," he said, smacking her ass, which she glared at.

"Shh, this is a good speed. It's nice," she said slowly, undulating on top of him.

"I want more."

"More?"

"Yes, fuck," he said, sliding his arms beneath her legs and lifting her as he went up on his knees. "Faster," he said more forcefully before jackhammering up into her, her body slapping against his. Crying out, she hung on as he went deeper and deeper, her whole body clenching around his.

"Yes, yes, yes, yes," she panted, her body jerking against his, her pussy squeezing his with another release. Closing his eyes, he nuzzled his nose into her neck as his body jerked. Then he was arching up into her, his body stilling with his own orgasm. It shook him to the core.

The fucking core.

As she gasped for breath, her body squeezed his while he pulsated inside of her, his body shaking from the aftershocks of one hell of an orgasm.

God, he had never come so hard in his life.

Never.

Whoa.

Panting, he held her like that for a long time as she drew in deep breaths. Kissing her neck, her jaw, and then the side of her mouth, he opened his eyes to find her smiling at him.

"Faster, huh?"

He nodded. "Yeah, faster."

Wrapping her arms around his neck tighter, she kissed him again, her lips lingering against his as they both pulled in air. Laying them down slowly, he pulled out of her and moved his thumb slowly along her face.

"I think we should do this every time I come home late," he suggested and she giggled, the most heavenly sound, as she pressed her chest to his, her heart still beating out of control.

"I bet you do," she said, sleepily. "God, you wear me out."

"Glad I'm not the only one," he said, exhaling a long breath. "Round two will commence in a jiffy."

She bubbled with laughter. "A jiffy?"

"Yeah, shh. Rest your eyes, but do not go to sleep," he demanded, setting her with a look. "We both remember what happened last time," he teased and she smacked his arm, a sheepish grin on her face.

"I'm not going to leave yet. But I do need to go before Angie wakes up."

"Yeah, of course."

He moved his hand along her back and then down the curve of her ass. She shook with a shiver before looking up at him. Gliding her fingers along his jaw and the coarse hair, she whispered, "I like being with you, Benji."

Turning his head to her, he smiled. "Like? Shit, sweetheart. I *love* being with you. Highlight of my day—hell, my year."

Her eyes widened a little bit and then her sweet lips curved as she nuzzled against him. "Well, then."

"Just saying."

"So I guess you like me."

"*Like?* Yeah, I guess." She shook against him with a giggle. "Do you like me?"

"Nerd. Yes. Or I wouldn't be here."

"Just making sure," he said simply as her nose moved along his shoulder. "You can be hard to read through all the sass and excuse after excuse."

"I'm gonna stab you."

"And threats. Lots of threats."

She giggled. "If it's so bad…"

"Please, you're a teddy bear," he scoffed. "A prickly one, but a teddy bear."

"You're insane."

"I know."

She didn't say anything for a moment and then she looked up at him, digging her chin into his shoulder. "You told Jayden about us?"

He smiled in the hopes it would defuse some of her anger. "I wanted to make sure it was okay for me to proceed with you."

She eyed him. "And if he would have said no?"

"I would have lost a really good friend," he said automatically. "'Cause I'm not ending this with you. Whatever this is."

Her lips quirked as she looked at his neck, drawing in a breath through her nose. "You told the cop I'm your girlfriend."

"And you said I was your friend," he reminded her and she looked up at him.

"I don't know if I'm ready to admit you're my boyfriend."

He'd figured that, so he shrugged. "Labels are overrated, anyway—"

"But I want to try," she admitted and his face broke into a grin. "It's insanely early and it's probably dumb. But I agree, we aren't fuck buddies. You mean more than that, but we really haven't dug into who we are. And it worries me that you might not want to be my boyfriend when you see all of me."

He eyed her. "I mean, the same could go for me, babe. So, we can jump in or we can keep skirting the edges."

She looked away, chewing her lip. "What do you want to do?" she asked then and he reached for her, tipping her face up to his.

"I want to be with you. Everything else will fall into place."

Her eyes lit up as she leaned into his hand. "That sounds like a plan."

"I thought so," he said with a nod. He felt good about where they were. He wanted more, but he understood she had to be comfortable too. He didn't want to rush them, he didn't want to burn them out, he wanted this to last.

Kissing her forehead, he nuzzled against her as she whispered, "If I close my eyes, I'll fall asleep."

He nodded, his lips dragging against her forehead. "Well, then, we need something else to do."

"The sex?"

He scoffed. "Not yet."

She looked up at him just as he looked down at her, and they both smiled. "Bath?"

Her eyes lit up. "Bath!"

Chapter TWELVE

Of course, Benji's gorgeous house would have an even more gorgeous bathroom. Everything was very modern, two vanities that were probably the size of her whole bathroom back at her old apartment. It was crazy and amazing, and she never wanted to leave. The shower was completely glass, with three different showerheads and even a place for someone to sit. It was really nice. But that wasn't the best part. No, it was the huge garden tub that would probably fit the whole Assassins team in it. All this for one man—it was such a depressing thought.

"Why did you buy this big ol' house for just you?" she asked as she lowered deeper into the hot water, the spa going, the jets hitting her in the ribs. It felt so good. Even with all the room in the tub, she sat between Benji's legs, her back to his chest as his hands slid up and down her thighs.

"Well, not only did I love the way it looked, but I also wanted a big house so I could fill it with a family one day."

She smiled. "I'm pretty sure there aren't many men like you," she said, cuddling closer into him. A bath had been a good idea and she wished she didn't have to leave, but she only had three more hours until she had to head home. She had even set her alarm just to make sure.

"We are a rare breed," he teased against her ear and she giggled, squirming against his lips. "Women need to pay attention to the dorky, geeky guys."

"Guess so, but I wouldn't put you in that category."

"No?"

"No, you're too hot."

He smiled. "Oh, yeah?"

"Yeah, after I decided you weren't a child molester, I thought you were hot."

He paused, a little disbelief in his voice as he asked, "You thought I was a child molester?"

"Hey, I was mad. All men were either pedophiles or assholes."

"Man, damn that Jayden," he muttered, kissing her jaw. "But, hey, look at you now. I think you knew all along I was okay."

"Yeah, okay, I guess," she teased, and when his fingers bit into her thighs as he nibbled on her neck, it caused her to giggle. "I was a bitch. I'm sorry."

"Another apology. Wow."

"Shh, take it and run," she said and he kissed her hard on the cheek.

Holding her close, he kissed her neck and then her jaw once more. "I don't want you to leave."

"Me either," she whispered. "This is nice, and this kind of stuff doesn't really happen for me."

"Because you don't let it and no one ever wants to try to fight you for you."

Her lips tilted. "So you wanted to fight me for me?"

"Um, yeah, and I still will," he declared, his arms coming around her belly, hugging her from behind. "As long as you want me to."

"No one fights for me. I do the fighting."

He smiled against her cheek. "Well, how about you fight for what you need to fight for, and I'll fight for you."

"I don't understand."

"I don't either, I just want to be there for you," he said honestly and she smiled, her body trembling with happiness.

"Sounds good to me."

"Good," he decided, kissing her once more, his hands moving along her stomach. Silently, they relaxed, the water so warm and soothing against her skin. Her eyes fell shut as she cuddled against Benji's thick, gorgeous body. He was covered in bruises, but it wasn't a surprise to her. He was a hockey player, a defenseman who blocked a lot of shots. They were kind of sexy. "I have a question."

Opening her eyes, she said, "Okay?"

"There is a tattoo on the back of your neck. Explain."

She smiled as he moved her hair off her neck, running his fingers along the ink. "It's for my family," she said softly, moving her hands up his thighs. "We all have Sinclair written somewhere on us, I added the peonies to mine along with Angie's name."

"It's beautiful."

"Thanks," she said and then she sucked in a deep breath.

She needed to ask about his tattoo, but before she could, he said, "Another question."

"Inquisitive today," she teased and he chuckled against her ear.

"Yeah, so River Moore, Baylor's dad, is not your real dad. But he's marrying your mom, right?"

Lucy nodded. "Aw, you listen when I bitch."

"You do it a lot, so yeah," he teased and she elbowed him in the gut, not hard but he faked hurt anyway. "Meanie." He didn't mean it as he chuckled against her cheek. "Anyway, before you beat me up, where is your real dad? Do you know him?"

She paused and leaned her head into his. "Yeah, my mom and dad got divorced about three years ago, give or take."

"Oh, you never speak of him."

"'Cause I hate him," she said simply. "He broke our happy home. My family is so close, all of us. I mean, Jude shits glitter. Everyone knows in seconds, we're that close."

He laughed. "Yeah, I can tell."

"Yeah, well, even though my dad was kind of tough on us, he was our dad and we loved him. But come to find out, he had another life with another woman. Broke my mom's heart, broke all our hearts. Over the years, he's just kept on being shitty. Like, he's never apologized to any of us, and he just keeps causing issues."

"Wow. That's sad."

"Oh, you have no clue. He almost physically fought my three brothers. He stalled on the divorce and cut my mom off financially when she was stay-at-home mom, so she had to go back to work. He refused to let the boys get access to their trust funds to help our mom. Then he tried to buy Jayden back, but Jayden hates him the most, so there was no help there. But Jace, he just wants to be loved, you know? He wants his whole family together, and my dad tried to buy him to keep him from all of us because Jace was in a bind with his wife and they were pregnant. It was a mess." She inhaled deeply. "Wow, I really went off there. Sorry. Gosh."

What in the hell? She never did that. Never talked about her dad.

All of a sudden, she had diarrhea of the mouth.

This guy... Man...

"No, I want to know. I'm sorry that happened, baby. That blows."

"Yeah, he's a dick, which is why I don't talk about him. It just sucks 'cause Angie loves him so much, and he's always been good to her. But I can't do it. Sometimes I feel like such a piece of shit for not allowing him time with her, but I'm still so mad at him."

"Has he tried to see her?"

"Once or twice, but I can't, and I know that makes me a shitty person."

But Benji shook his head. "You know what's best for your daughter. You're her mother, Lucy. You have to trust your gut."

"Yeah, exactly," she said, turning to look at him. "Like, what if he tries to buy her off? She's young and impressionable, and fucking Rick already does enough of that. So, no, I can't do it."

"And you shouldn't have to. Come here, it's okay," he said, cuddling her in his arms. "You need a hug, you're all riled up. Sorry I asked," he murmured against her cheek.

"No, it's fine. He just bugs me."

"Understandable."

For a moment, she thought she'd said too much, but then, wasn't that what a relationship was? Talking about stuff you didn't like? And Benji did it wonderfully. He listened like he always did and it was nice. Really nice. Leaning into him, she closed her eyes, feeling completely content. Something she hadn't felt a lot unless she was with him. That should be a blinking sign in her face that he was becoming more, but she had her blinders on because she liked the way he felt. Was that such a bad thing?

When it was just them, alone, with nothing from the outside world in the way, she was good. Walls down, she was happy. It was the thought of everyone knowing that she liked him, Angie knowing, and ultimately Rick, that had her sick to her stomach. Angie would handle it like she did everything else—head on, fast, and with zero cares—unless Lucy was upset and then she would be upset. Lucy couldn't have that. She couldn't stress her baby out. Her family would get too excited way too quickly. Knowing her mother, she'd want to have a double wedding, and Lucy could handle that, but she couldn't handle Rick. Knowing her luck, he'd run Benji off, and in the end, break Lucy's heart all over again.

And Angie's.

And she could never let that happen.

But in his tub, Benji's arms around her, nothing could touch them.

No. She was good, real good.

"All I need is a glass of wine, maybe some chocolate-covered strawberries," she said with a giggle, and he chuckled against the back of her head. "Do you have any wine? We should pop open a bottle, drink it like queens and kings."

He chuckled against her ear, kissing the spot below it. "No, I don't."

"That's a travesty. We'll need to get some for next time."

He didn't say anything right away, but then he cleared his throat. "About that…"

She opened her eyes, leaning over so she could look up at him. "What? No next time?"

He scoffed. "Oh, Lucy, if I had my way, this water would stay hot and we wouldn't leave. But it's not that."

"Then what?"

He paused and sucked in a deep breath before meeting her gaze. He was unsure, something was holding him back, and that made her concerned.

But nothing prepared her for what he said next.

"I'm an alcoholic."

Whoa. What?

Her face must have given her away before he looked away. "I've been sober for twelve years, though."

"Oh. Okay, wow, yeah. No, it's fine. I just… I'm gonna shut up," she said quickly and he smiled. "Sorry, I wasn't expecting that."

"No, it's cool," he said simply, nuzzling his nose against her neck, apparently done talking about it.

But she was not.

"You feel so good," he whispered, kissing her neck, and she almost let him move on.

Almost.

"Okay, Mr. Change the Subject, I kinda wanna go back a bit," she said, moving so she could see his face.

Repositioning her legs over his so she was almost straddling him, he cleared his throat. "Using my words against me."

"Yeah," she said, eyeing him. "Like, I need more there. Not that it changes anything, but I kind of need to know."

He looked down at the water, taking a deep breath. "No, I know."

He wouldn't look at her, and his shoulders fell. Shit, she was messing this all up. "I'm not looking at you differently, I promise." He gave her a look, and she stressed, "I'm not!"

"You are."

"No! It's just crazy. You don't seem the type to do that."

"I was a different person then," he said simply and she shook her head.

"I'm sorry I can't wrap my head around it. You seem like such a stand-up guy."

"But I wasn't back in the day, I was shit," he said, his voice breaking a bit. She reached for him, holding his hands.

"Whoa, I don't want to upset you. You don't owe me anything; you don't have to tell me anything that is uncomfortable," she said quickly. She was surprised how upset she got for him. She didn't want to hurt him, she didn't want him to relieve a shitty past, she didn't like the look on his face. The look of pure defeat and regret. She couldn't handle that. No, this wasn't her Benji.

Her Benji.

Okay. She'd come back to that.

Looking at their hands, he sucked in a deep breath. "No, it's a part of who I am now. I want you to know because you worry about me not liking part of your past. Well, there is a damn good chance you won't like mine."

Her heart sank as she watched him—the way his jaw was taut, the way he wouldn't look her in the eye. This wasn't how he was. Yeah, it had only been a week with him, but Benji was all about eye contact.

Shit, she was scared. "Okay."

Moving his tongue along his lip, he swallowed hard. "I got swept up in the rookie life. I was with a young team, and they liked to party. I had grown up drinking with my family. Started young, really." As he took another bracing breath in, his nerves vibrated Lucy's soul and made her anxious.

Her nerves getting the better of her, she started talking. "Everyone drank early, at least, my family did. My mom and dad, as soon as each of us turned sixteen, made us drink with them. They'd get us trashed to where we would wake up, sick as dogs. It worked on me as a deterrent—I wasn't much of a drinker. But it had the reverse effect on the boys, and they can still drink. I'm rambling. Why am I nervous? Okay, I'm shutting up."

She snapped her mouth closed, and he smiled. Leaning to her, he pressed his lips to hers. "I really like when you ramble."

She smiled sheepishly. "You're making me nervous 'cause you're so nervous."

He shrugged. "Sorry, I really don't like talking about it, but I want you to know." She didn't know what to say, so she just kept locked in his gaze as he cleared his throat. "But yeah, I came from a drinking family, lots of functioning alcoholics. Then I was drafted early, hit the NHL quick, and everything went downhill. I was a nasty drunk and I hurt a lot of people, almost lost my career, I, ugh—" He paused, letting out a long breath and shaking his head. Her heart was breaking.

Wow, she really cared for this guy.

Because one look in his grief-stricken gaze and she wanted to fix it. She wanted to make everything better. She wanted the grin, the teasing—she wanted her Benji back.

Not this nervous ball of regret.

"It's okay, Benji, really. You aren't that person anymore. I seriously didn't ever think you could have done anything like that. You're so upstanding, so great. Really," she said, cupping his face and flashing him a small smile. "You beat it. You're clean. How many people can actually say they did that? Not many, but you can, and I'm so proud of you." He leaned into her hand and stared into her eyes, his eyes searching hers as he took in gulps of air. "God, smile, Benji. You're killing me."

His lips curved, but it didn't meet his eyes. It was almost like he was struggling with something. Like he was holding something back, and she didn't know why. It was crazy how easy it had become to read him in such a short amount of time. But she could, and he was killing her.

As he reached for her hand, lacing her fingers with his, he brought the back of her hand to his lips and kissed it softly. When he looked back into her eyes, something shifted between them as her heart ached for him. She wasn't sure what it was, but she knew she cared about him enough to want to fix him.

To make him smile.

How did he do this to her? How did he become so important so quickly? Maybe she should take a step back. Maybe this was moving too fast. But it felt right.

So fucking right.

"I never thought I could ever feel like this again. Happy." His voice was so stricken that her eyes welled up with tears.

"Me either. But please stop looking like I'm about to bust a move out of here."

He scoffed. "You're not?"

"No!" she screeched, her lips curving. "You're an alcoholic—you admit that and you didn't hide it. You were honest and I appreciate that. I'm so proud of you. Why would I run?" Looking away, he slowly shook his head and her heart sank. "What is it, Benji?"

"Maybe it's too early to go so deep?" he asked as he glanced up at her.

She sucked in a breath. "I mean, we haven't gone on our first official date, but we've bumped uglies a few times and—"

"Bumped uglies?"

She made a face, unsure why she phrased it like that. Damn those younger brothers of hers and their crass language. "I'm freaking out here. But I will listen if you want to talk. If you don't, then I'll try to let it go. I'm not guaranteeing I can since I'm a nosy thing, but I'll try."

His lips curved as he took her by the back of her head, bringing her face to his, kissing her forehead. "You're so adorable, you know?"

"I think my brothers say I'm insane."

"That too," he agreed, kissing her once more, taking her hand in his as she smiled. "I want to tell you, I do. But maybe right now isn't the time."

"Tell me what?"

"Why I cleaned up," he said simply as she pulled back, meeting his eyes.

Holding his gaze, she nodded. "Does it have to do with this?"

She pointed to his chest and he looked down, nodding slowly. "Yeah."

Chewing on her lip, she wanted to know. God, she wanted to know, but…

"Why wouldn't now be the right time?"

He shook his head. "'Cause we've only been talking a week, and I don't want to ruin our good time. The good thing that is coming from this."

She understood what he was saying, and he was right. They were having a great night, lots of sharing and fun, but she needed to know.

Looking up, she met his remorseful gaze, and despite the heavy feeling in her gut, she whispered, "Tell me."

She just hoped her gut wasn't right—that this wouldn't end them.

Benji wasn't sure how this was going to go.

She was breathing deeply, apprehension radiating from her, and she almost looked like she was seeing him in a different light already. Which was not what he wanted, but maybe that's how it was going to be. Either way, he had to be honest.

"Benji?" she asked, probably because he was trying to choose his words and was just sitting there, the only sounds their breaths and the jets of the tub. This wasn't supposed to happen yet. They were supposed to have fun, tub sex, cuddle, and be together, but of course, he had to be truthful. He couldn't hide what he did; she meant more to him than for her to find out some shitty way later.

When she took his hand, she squeezed it. "Don't mistake my freaking out as anything more than that. I'm freaking out because I'm worried about you. I'm worried that you're scared this could end what we have."

"You're right," he admitted, looking up at her. "I tell people and they run the other way."

Her eyes widened but she didn't let his hand go. "Jesus, what the hell happened?"

Taking in a long breath, he looked at their hands as one and prayed to the God he loved and believed in that she wouldn't run. She couldn't. He couldn't handle it. She meant way too much to him, and it would be almost cruel to take her away now. But then, maybe that was his punishment—wave the woman, the life he wanted in front of his face, and then snatch it out of his grip.

God, he was so fucking scared.

"When I was a kid, I met Ava Donaldson," he said, his lips turning up at her name. "She was this gorgeous blonde who stole my breath and made me feel things I had never felt before. We got pregnant as teenagers, and I married her two days after we graduated high school. We were both newly eighteen, with a baby, but I loved her more than anything in this world. And I loved our baby, Leary," he said softly, and Lucy's eyes widened as she watched him.

"Wait, you're married?"

He shook his head. "No, not anymore."

Her face was full of misunderstanding as she held his gaze. "You've never spoken of them."

"Yeah, because I'm ashamed."

Her brows rose. "Oh."

"Yeah, so…" he said, clearing the emotion from his throat. "I got drafted quick, promised her I would give her the life she wanted, and I did, moneywise, but I wasn't there for her. I was running with my boys, drinking, having fun. I never cheated on her—that's one thing I can be proud of, I never ever broke her heart that way—but I did break her heart with the drinking."

"Oh, Benji," she whispered, holding his hands with both of hers.

"She threatened to leave me so many times. I somehow convinced her not to, throwing out that Leary didn't need to grow up without a father, in a broken home. She came from one and I used that to keep her. I wish I had let her go, though. Maybe things would have ended differently," he said, the guilt eating him alive. He had never admitted that part to anyone. Not even to the group, but for some reason, he told Lucy. Because it was true. Man, how he wished he would have let Ava leave him. "I needed her. I loved her, and I promised and promised that I would change. I never did, though."

Clearing his throat, he looked up, seeing that she was watching him, uneasiness all over her sweet face. It killed him; he didn't want her to worry about him. To feel sorry for him. He did this all himself. He broke Ava's heart. It was his fault, his burden, not Lucy's. He shouldn't have said anything, but when she lifted their hands out of the water, kissing his knuckles, her eyes urged him on and he couldn't hold back.

He owed it to Ava and to Leary, to be honest.

"What happened then?"

"I talked her into a trip home, to Chicago, where we were both from. She didn't like going home—she didn't like my family much. Well, my brother, she didn't mind, but my mom told everyone she was the whore who ruined my life," he said and Lucy scoffed.

"Rick's mom still says that about me," she said with a shake of her head.

"Yeah, well, Ava didn't take kindly to it and never wanted to go home. But I convinced her to because my family was having a family reunion and I wanted to go. My family knew about my drinking problem, but they were all drunks, so they fed into it," he said, complete disgust in his voice. "I got fucking trashed. Crazy drunk, drunkest I've ever been. I remember Ava saying we needed to go because Leary was tired. I couldn't drive, and Ava didn't know how to get back to the hotel. This was before there was GPS on our phones," he said, and she nodded as his throat closed with emotion. "I got in the backseat, with Leary in her car seat, and she said, 'Daddy, hold my hand.' She was so cute," he said, his voice breaking, and he had to look away, his eyes filling with tears. He could still hear her voice. The sweet lisp of her little voice, still trying to get her words right. She knew "Daddy," though. She had that one down, and man, he loved that baby. He loved her more than he could love himself.

He still loved them.

Always would.

Clearing his throat, begging himself not to break down in front of Lucy, he went on. "My younger brother Silas offered to drive us back, so he got into the driver's seat. By the time we took off, I was passed out, my hand in Leary's. But when I woke up, I was in the hospital and they explained to me that I was the only one who survived a crash with a semi."

Lucy's hands dropped his, covering her mouth as her eyes filled with tears. He had to look away again, swallowing hard. "Leary and Silas died on impact, they were hit first. But Ava wasn't so lucky. A piece of glass slashed her throat and she bled out slowly, and I did nothing. I was passed out drunk, and I still hate that I couldn't save her. That I was so fucked up, I couldn't be there for my wife. Once again."

Shaking his head, the tears threatened to fall as his jaw clenched and he was unable to look at Lucy. "I buried my brother on a Tuesday, my wife and my daughter on a Wednesday. All closed caskets because they were all so fucked up, and all I had was a stupid fucking broken arm."

"Benji, oh my goodness, Benji," she cried, her voice full of sorrow as she crawled into his lap, wrapping her arms around his neck.

He wasn't done, though. Tightening his arms around her, he pressed his head into her shoulder as his own shoulders started to shake, and he whispered in a tear-filled voice, "I lived, while they didn't. My family, her family, all hate me. I haven't really talked to them since the day of the funeral. I was alone, empty inside. So it's easy to say I went off the deep end." As he sucked in a breath, those months of hopeless bewilderment flashed through his mind. "I drank until I couldn't drink anymore. I got into fights. I fucked anything with tits. I was a poor excuse for a person. And one night, after a nasty fight in a bar, they threw me out the back, my face hitting the curb. God, it sucked. I rolled over, and when I sat up and I looked around, I saw this mirror. The person looking back at me, I didn't even know. I was disgusting. I didn't even remember the last time I'd showered. I wanted to die. There was even a piece of glass lying there, and I almost just ended it, I did. But then she was there, in the mirror. Ava. She was disgusted—who could blame her? She just shook her head, saying this wasn't the man she loved, and she was right. I wasn't that fresh-faced teenager; that kid was gone. All that was left was shit."

Swallowing hard, he closed his eyes. "I promised her I would change, and she said, I've heard that before. But this time was different. Somehow I got up,

I went to the closest church, and I prayed. I prayed so fucking hard, it hurt. I asked for forgiveness, not only from the Lord, but from Ava, Leary, and Silas. When I opened my eyes, I knew what I had to do. I took a cab to the nearest rehab center and I checked myself in."

Pulling back, she looked at him, tears streaming down her face as he spoke the words that choked him on the way out. "Never touched another drink another day in my life. Never wanted it. Never wanted to disrespect their names, since I had already taken their lives."

"You didn't take their lives, Benji. It wasn't your fault," she tried, but he shook his head. He had heard that plenty of times.

"If I hadn't been drunk, I could have driven my family home. My seventeen-year-old brother wouldn't have had to drive on the interstate where he wasn't comfortable. It's my fault they are dead and I've coped with it, but I turned into a hermit because I blame myself so bad. I always knew that someone would come along and wake me up, make me happy again. And I don't want to scare you, Lucy, I don't, but I believe that person is you." Her eyes widened and, shit, why did he say that? Before he knew what he was doing, he was stammering out words. "Wow, okay, sorry. I just got carried away there. Please—"

"Don't apologize," she demanded, holding his face. "But you listen to me right now."

He met her gaze. Her eyes were full of tears, her mouth parted, her nose red from her crying.

For him.

For Ava and Leary.

"First, please tell me that you like me for me and not because Angie and I remind you of Leary and Ava." Her eyes were wild, and fear settled deep in his chest as he quickly shook his head, his eyes widening.

"God, no, not at all. It's been twelve years since I lost them. I promise, I was attracted to you for you. I saw *you* first. I saw your eyes, Lucy. It was you, not you guys as a package—that's just a bonus. I promise. I can't replace what I lost, I know that, but I want to be happy. I want to love my life."

"Then you can't fucking blame yourself, Benji," she said, her hands tightening on his face. "This fucking sucks, and I hate that you have suffered this kind of loss. I do. It hurts my soul. No one should have to go through that, but, Benji, it is not your fault. Yes, you were a drunk, you fucked up, but you did not kill them. Yeah, shoulda-coulda-woulda, but *you* have to stop blaming yourself or you will never move on. Believe me, I know. Totally different situation, but you can't blame yourself."

He swallowed thickly. "I know, but it's hard."

"And I don't doubt that. I can't imagine. But you will never be happy until you are at peace with what happened."

"I'm happy with you," he whispered, holding her gaze, and her face contorted in pain.

"But are you using me to mask that pain?"

His brows came together, his lips twisting in confusion. "No, not at all. I blame myself," he said, and her eyes pleaded with his, needing to know that he wasn't bullshitting her. "But I've coped. I accepted that I can't change what happened. I understand that it was out of my control. I still believe I should have done something different, but I want to move on. I want to be happy. I'm so tired of being lonely and sad. I've been trying to find someone, but no one has stuck, Lucy. Then you came along. And you make me feel things I've never felt in my whole adult life."

Her eyes searched his, and she bit into her lip before nodding slowly. "I just worry that we'll get too far into this, and then you won't be able to feel what you need to feel for me."

He knew what she was saying and he understood, but what she didn't know was that he was already falling in love with her. He couldn't tell her that, she wasn't ready, but he had to reassure her that he was good.

"Losing them, my family, sucked. No other words can adequately describe it. Being alone, dating people and not clicking with them, blows. If finding you had happened a year or two ago, I could completely understand your worry, and you are completely right to have it. But Lucy, I've known you for two weeks, and in these two weeks, I've never been so damn happy in my life. I get excited to wake up, to talk to you, I love helping Angie on the ice, and seeing you does things to my heart. So please don't worry about me not being into this. Us. I am *so* into us."

Her lip wobbled and she closed her eyes. Opening them again, she held his gaze as she sucked in a deep breath. Then, with all the strength in the world, she said, "I don't trust people. Ever. The grown men I loved, trusted, needed, depended on, both fucked me over. Badly. And I haven't recovered from it. Then you came along… And I trust you, Benji. So I'm going to say, okay, I'm going to believe you and I'm gonna trust that you have my best interests in mind. But I swear to God, you fuck me, you break my heart, I will skin you alive."

He couldn't help it, he grinned as he leaned his forehead to hers. "I don't make promises lightly, Lucy, not since Ava, as you can understand. But I promise I will not hurt you. I promised your brother that, and I have no problem promising the same to you."

Her lip wobbled again. "You did?"

"I did."

Wrapping her arms around him, she hugged him tightly and his eyes drifted shut. Holding her as she straddled his lap, he kissed her temple and

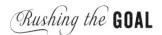

then her cheek as she clung to him.

"I'm sorry about your family," she whispered, her lips moving against his jaw.

Swallowing hard, he kissed her cheek once more. "Thank you."

They clung to each other. He was holding her for support, for love, and he hoped she was doing the same. She didn't say anything for a long time, almost until the water started to chill a bit, and then she whispered, "I feel good about this. That we talked about all this."

And his heart just blew up in his chest. "Me too, Lucy. Me too."

As he held her, her heart pounding into his, he was pretty sure he had just fallen in love with her.

Chapter THIRTEEN

Lucy was running on coffee.

Only coffee.

Because she hadn't walked into Jayden's house until eight in the morning, four minutes before Angie woke up. And, of course, there was no time for a nap. Nope, Angie was up, ready to go, already fully dressed in her equipment before Lucy even sat down on her bed.

No rest for the wicked, she guessed. And last night, she was *wicked*.

Oh, the things she did with Benji… Great freaking sex, never-ending orgasms, and tub sex. God, she loved tub sex. While Lucy wanted just an hour—one hour of sleep, that's all—she didn't regret one thing about going to Benji's. Not the run-in with the cops, not the endless amounts of orgasms, and definitely not when he opened up to her. No, last night was amazing, perfect even, and she still felt it way deep in her soul.

One thing was for sure, she would never forget the look of pure loss on Benji's face. Or how his body shook with sobs as he talked about his wife and daughter. It was hard to hear, and it gutted her as if she had lost two people she had loved. But at the same time, it was beautiful. He loved them—hell, she was sure he still loved them—and he felt horrible for his mistakes. She appreciated his honesty and the fact he wanted to move on. She felt like he trusted her, cared enough about her to share that side of him. He might never know how much that meant to her. How much he touched her heart last night.

And one day, well into the future, she hoped he could love her and Angie like he did his wife and daughter.

The thought scared the living bejesus out of her, of course. She hadn't had that hope in her heart since Rick, but it was true. For so long, she couldn't trust men, minus her brothers. Rick ruined her, and then her dad broke her heart—the two men she had loved and looked to for guidance. For the last four years, she had been doing it on her own, navigating life, and then she met him.

Benji.

When he said he would fight her for her, the walls around her heart crumbled, and it just felt right. He felt right. So damn right. No one had ever said that to her, and he was saying it. After only knowing her two weeks. Shit, it was all going so damn fast, and she almost felt like she was getting whiplash. Was it too good to be true? Could this really be happening? And really, why couldn't she have met him sooner? Or maybe this was good timing because they were both ready?

She was ready.

Right?

Yes.

But fuck, above all, what was he going to say when he had to really deal with Rick? Learn of his betrayal and be able to do nothing about it, because Benji couldn't take him out. No, that would be bad. But she felt in her heart that he would try. It scared her to the core. She wasn't sure what the future held, but today… She just hoped today went okay.

For Angie.

"Mommy, were you working last night?" Lucy looked up in the rearview mirror, her little hockey player looking back at her. Helmet and stick were both in place as Angie held her gaze, and panic filled Lucy's gut. "I woke up and you weren't in bed. But Jayden walked in, like, right as I woke up and asked me if I was okay. I said yeah, and then I went back to sleep."

"Um, yes," Lucy replied and felt like the lowest scum on earth. She had just lied. To her baby. Because she was out doing her coach. Why did she keep thinking things like that?

"You work all the time. When do you sleep?"

Lucy smiled; she hadn't really cared about sleep last night. But now…now, she was realizing she was way too old for such late nights. "I get it in. I'm just trying to get everything taken care of."

"So we aren't homeless."

"Angela Lynn."

"Oops, sorry. You know what I mean."

"Yes, and yes," she answered before clearing her throat. "But hey, good news, I have a new office."

"Woo-hoo!" Angie said, throwing her hands up and doing a little shimmy in her booster seat. "Is it nice?"

"Yeah, um…" She paused. She didn't have to say her next sentence, but she wanted to. "It's actually in Coach Benji's backyard."

"No way! Can I go hang out with him when I'm not in school?"

Lucy smiled. "I don't know. We'll see."

"He's so freaking cool. It's so nice he is letting you use it."

"I'm renting," she said, more for herself than her daughter, who had no clue what she was talking about.

"Still, he's so cool. You should marry him," she said, so offhandedly and annoyingly carefree.

But Lucy, she gasped. "What?"

Angie giggled. "You're so silly, Mommy. You sound like you saw a ghost."

She sounded like that because this was crazy talk. "Because you're crazy! Marry?" she laughed, her stomach going nuts. "Please, Benji wouldn't want to marry me."

"Why? You're so pretty," Angie said simply. "And he always stares at you."

"No, he doesn't."

"Yes, he does!" She laughed, smacking her thigh. "I'm gonna ask him."

"You better not," she warned, and Angie was full out laughing like they were in comedy hour.

"Ha! Mommy has a crush."

"Angela Lynn! What in the world? How do you know what a crush is?"

"I'm seven, Mom, not a baby."

"You are a baby, thank you," she said, breathless, pulling into the parking lot. "And I do not have a crush."

"Yes, you do."

"Angela! No, I do not," she said, by this point giggling as she parked. Why was she giggling? Stopping, she glared back at her daughter. "And if you say one word to Benji about that nonsense, I'll ground you."

Angie only snickered as she threw the door open and got out. Lucy, on the other hand, was shaking her head. Kid was going to give her gray hair before she was thirty. She swore it. She grabbed Angie's bag out of the back, and Angie met her by the trunk and bounced on her heels.

Wait. Did she say that because she wanted Lucy to get married? Crap. Looking over at Angie as she shut the trunk, Lucy found herself asking, "Do you think Mommy needs to be married?"

Angie shrugged. "Daddy is married to Heidi. And I don't know, I think it would make you happy."

Lucy bit into her lip. "But you're happy, right, baby?"

"Duh, I have the best mom in the world!" she gushed, giving her a half hug. "I just want you to be happy."

"I am."

"I know, but I think you need someone to talk to who isn't a kid, who loves you like I do."

"You are way past your years, Angela," she said, squeezing her baby to her side. "Plus, I have my mom, Jude, Jayden, and Jace."

Angie gave her a deadpan look as they walked up to the rink. "But they are busy with the people they love. You need someone to love."

"I love you!"

"Mom, come on. You know what I mean," she said, rolling her eyes. Lucy did, she just hated that her daughter thought this. What did she do wrong? Was she really that pathetic all the time? "There's Grandma and River!"

Running off like they hadn't just had a very eye-opening conversation, Angie jumped into River's arms, him throwing her up in the air before hugging her tightly. Smiling, Lucy made her way to them, catching the very end of River giving Angie a pep talk.

"Play deep, and when you get a chance, shoot. These girls don't even know what's in store for them! You know you're the best, so play it. Okay?"

"It's the peewees, River, not the NHL," Lucy sang and he grinned.

Angie giggled happily as Lucy's mom beamed. "Are you ready, sweetheart? I'm nervous for you."

"Mom," Lucy complained and she shrugged.

"What? You know how I am. My baby, come here. Let me hug you."

Angie went willingly as Lucy and River chuckled at how silly she could be. She was a mother hen, and her babies were just that, her babies. Hugging her grandma, Angie looked back at Lucy. "Mom, is Dad coming?"

Lucy swallowed hard, pulling her phone out of her pocket. "I told him the time. But it's still early, honey. I'll text and ask, okay?"

She looked dejected as she turned to Autumn. "You have your iPad, right? Uncle Jace and Jude want to watch the game."

Autumn patted her purse. "Done, River is gonna set it up."

"I wish they were here. I wonder where Jayden and Baylor are. And Benji."

Yeah, where was Benji?

Looking around, Lucy saw Jayden and Baylor coming from the concession stand. "There are Jayden and Baylor."

"Oh, yay! Oh, there's Coach Adler. I better go," she said, wiggling out of Autumn's arms and grabbing her bag. "Benji said he would be here, right?"

"Yeah, and I'm sure he will be," Lucy said reassuringly, but maybe she should text him, just to make sure.

Shit, maybe he wasn't coming.

No. He wouldn't have told her he was if he wasn't.

Nodding her head, Lucy bent down and patted Angie on the helmet since she had her cage on already. "Good luck. Love you."

"Love you," Angie said before running off. She fist-bumped Jayden and Baylor as Lucy watched, a grin on her face. When she ran past them, Benji all of a sudden came out of a side door, catching Angie midstride, lifting her over his head, her stick and bag hitting the ground as her laughter filled the room.

And Lucy's heart promptly exploded in her chest.

"You're here!"

"Duh," he said, hugging her tightly. Then they were talking, but Lucy couldn't hear them. As she headed toward them, her mother stopped her.

"Who is that tall drink of water?" she whispered and Lucy gasped.

"Mom!"

Autumn laughed. "What? Just wondering. Is that the famous Benji?"

Lucy's lips curved as he patted Angie on the head and they fist-bumped. "Yeah, that's him."

"He's adorable," she said as they closed the distance between themselves and Benji and Angie, but Lucy didn't verbally agree as Angie beamed back at her.

"Benji's here!"

Lucy grinned. "I see that. Hey, Benji."

He was wearing his thick, dark-rimmed glasses, his hair falling against them as his lips curved. "Ms. Sinclair."

"Silly, her name is Lucy!" Angie giggled, leaning into him. "Isn't she pretty today?"

"Angela," Lucy warned, but Autumn was beaming.

"You are looking extra beautiful today," she agreed and Lucy glared.

"Mom!"

Benji just grinned, though, his eyes bright as Lucy met his heated gaze. "I think you are completely right, Hart. Prettiest girl I've ever seen. Besides you, of course," he said, tickling her, and she dissolved into laughter on the ground. Glancing at her mother, Lucy found that she and River were laughing too. Why did this feel normal to her?

Shit, what was happening?

Picking her up by her jersey, Benji put Angie on her feet and then fixed her jersey. "All right, Hart, ready to win?"

"Yes!"

"Remember, play deep, right by the goal. Rebounds, you got them, right?"

"Yup!"

Benji tapped her helmet. "That's my girl. Go kick some butt."

Angie nodded quickly before dragging her bag with her toward where Shea was waiting for her. Looking back at Lucy, Benji smiled and her lips quirked as her mother held her hand out.

"Well, my goodness, you are wonderful with her. I'm Angie's grandma, Autumn, and this is my fiancé, River."

Benji reached for her hand, shaking it. "She's a great kid, lucky to meet her. But wait, did you say grandma? You mean aunt, right?"

Oh, her mom ate that right on up. Lucy rolled her eyes as he shook River's hand. "Man, it's wonderful to meet you. I really admire your game, mirror some of my play on yours."

Oh, yeah. Lucy had forgotten River was kind of a big deal—being a Stanley Cup winner from the Bruins and all. Grinning ear to ear, River nodded. "Yeah, Paxton, right? You play opposite to Sinclair."

Benji nodded. "Yes, sir."

When they started to talk hockey, her mother leaned to her. "He's amazing."

"Mom, stop."

"You should get on that."

"Mom, please."

"Lucy, he likes you. He keeps staring at you."

"Please, Mom, stop," Lucy begged but Autumn just grinned.

"Want me to ask him out for you?"

"Sweet Lord in heaven," she muttered before clapping her hands together. "I'm gonna go sit down."

Benji looked over at her and grinned. His eyes bored into hers, letting her know he'd be where they said they'd meet. But she had just left him not three hours ago. Surely, they weren't still meeting. "I'll meet you guys up there. I gotta make a stop."

"Okay," she said as she started to walk away with her family. But when she looked back at him, he waggled his brows.

Damn it. How was she supposed to get away?

Stopping at the bathroom, she waved her family off. "I gotta pee real quick."

They kept going, by the grace of God. She was convinced Baylor or her mom would decide they had to use the restroom. Her heart was pounding, and she was about to giggle because of how absurd this was. But they started around the rink for the home bleachers. Lucy waited, ready to take off. God, this was stupid. Closing her eyes, she felt so silly but at the same time, so damn giddy. Fighting back her grin, she made a beeline for behind the bleachers, praying no one saw her.

But when she found Benji leaning against the wall, looking all sexy and carefree, she all of a sudden didn't care who saw her. Reaching for her, he brought her in close, holding her tightly in his arms. As he moved his nose along her jaw, she melted in his arms while his heart crashed into hers. "I almost thought you wouldn't want to see me."

She rolled her eyes. "Oh, hush. I told you last night, or, er, this morning, that all that doesn't change anything."

Pulling back, he looked down at her, his thumbs moving lazily along her cheekbones. "Still, I was worried."

"Well, don't be."

"Okay," he said roughly and she smiled. "Are you okay? You seem nervous."

Was she? She was. Crap. "I hate lying to my family. To Angie. She asked me where I was last night."

"Oh. I'm sorry."

"Please. I came speeding over, literally."

He chuckled against her lips, but then he stopped, his eyes searching hers. God, she loved his eyes. They were so beautiful, so compellingly gray. Kissing her nose, he asked, "What else?" She made a face and he smiled. "Tell me."

"I'm worried Rick won't show up. She really wants him here."

He nodded, his grin dropping. "Have you texted him?"

"Not yet," she said, lacing her hands behind his neck. "I'm a little occupied at the moment."

His lips curved, his eyes darkening as he leaned closer. "Oh yeah, we have some kissing to do."

"We do."

"You look really hot," he murmured against her lips, his hands falling to her ass as she sucked in a breath.

"Yeah?"

"Yeah."

"Angie says you stare at me."

"Oh, I do."

"Do you?"

"Every chance I get," he murmured before taking her mouth with his. Her eyes fell shut as her heart pounded into her ribs. When she leaned into him, he deepened the kiss, his tongue moving against hers with heated need. She couldn't just kiss this guy. No, she had to consume him. Or he was consuming her, whatever, lots of consuming was going on, and it was freaking fantastic. When his hand squeezed her ass, his hard cock pressing into her stomach, she pulled back.

"Whoa, killer. We've got a game to go to."

"Hey, not fair. Come back," he muttered, but she shook her head.

"A kiss—one kiss—and you're two seconds from doing me right here."

He thought that over and then shrugged. "Am I supposed to be sorry for that?"

She laughed, rolling her eyes as she pulled away, fixing her shirt. "Give me a good three minutes before you follow."

He rolled his eyes in an exaggerated fashion and then grinned. "Or I can stick my hand in the pocket of those naughty jeans and walk out there with you."

She side-eyed him. "Want to piss on my leg instead?"

He scoffed at that as she shook her head, going to walk away. But of course, he pulled her in for one more kiss. A long, delicious one that she felt in her toes. She could kiss this man for the rest of her life and be completely fine with it.

Shit, did she just think that?

Crapola.

This time, he was the one to pull back, kissing her nose and then the side of her mouth before waggling his brows at her. "I think your mom likes me."

"Good Lord," she complained before pulling out of his arms and walking away. But she was smiling.

Hard.

Rushing to where her family sat just before Angie took the ice, she climbed the bleachers as Jayden yelled out, "Jeez, did you have to take a shit?"

She stuck her tongue out at him as all the parents around them laughed, and their mother smacked him hard on the arm. He, of course, was laughing like a hyena as their mom complained. "Jayden! Goodness!"

Rolling her eyes, she sat down beside her mother, crossing her legs, and pulling her phone out to text Rick.

"Honey," her mother said as she typed quickly.

Hitting send, she looked up. "Yeah?"

"Honey, your lipstick is smeared."

Her eyes widened as she wiped the side of her mouth quickly while her mother eyed her suspiciously. But of course, that wasn't the end of her embarrassment.

"Hey, Paxton, that red looks good on you, buddy," Jayden called out. And when she glanced up to see Benji coming up to them, her eyes closed.

Fucking hell.

His brow rose. "What?"

"You have lipstick all over your mouth," Jayden said dryly as Benji fell into the seat beside him.

"Do I?" he asked, wiping his mouth as Jayden chuckled.

"Yeah, jeez, who were you kissing?" Baylor laughed as Lucy died a slow and humiliating death.

"Funny, the same red that's on his lips is the same red that was on your lips, well, now the side of your mouth," her mother mumbled. But Lucy just kept facing forward, praying to God the subject would get dropped. "Wonder why that is?"

Still, she said nothing as Benji asked, "Did I get it all off?"

"Yup," Baylor said, then leaned forward to Lucy. "Did you want a napkin?

Since yours was smeared?"

Pressing her lips together, she wanted to die. "Nope, good."

When her phone dinged with a text, she thanked God before looking down at her phone.

> Rick: *I'll be there when I get there. Don't rush me. I do have a life.*

"Motherfucker," she murmured as Benji leaned forward.

"Ignore him," he said, shaking his head. "His life should be his daughter."

"I know," she said under her breath.

"You left—"

"Benji, shut up and watch the game," she demanded and he laughed, leaning back as she shook her head.

Her mother, though, was looking from her to Benji over and over again. Finally, she leaned to Lucy and whispered, "You guys would make beautiful children."

"Mother, please, just stop," she begged as Angie lined up for the drop of the puck. Lucy saw her look up, and she waved her hands in the air, yelling Angie's name. When everyone joined in, Angie beamed before looking back down at the puck. Lucy prayed Angie didn't notice Rick wasn't there, but once the puck was dropped, Lucy was sure she didn't care about anything else but kicking some ass.

"Why are we all the way up here?" Benji asked, but she ignored him, watching Angie.

"I don't know. I hate sitting so far away," Jayden complained.

"Come on, let's go down," Benji decided, and together they made their way down. Lucy did not watch Benji's ass that was clad in those damn sweat pants. Nope. She watched her daughter as Benji and Jayden went to stand behind the goal. She wanted to go down there with them, well, Benji. But she knew that her mother would know right away.

If she didn't already.

Which she probably did.

Damn it.

But soon, she wasn't worried about that, only about Angie playing. She was one of the fastest, on the line with the Adler sisters, and Shea loved playing them together. They stayed out there a lot. And when Shelli scored, the place lost it like it had been Shea Adler himself scoring. Standing up, Lucy cheered along with everyone else as Shelli and the rest of the girls hugged tightly before heading back to the bench. Two more shifts happened before Angie was back out, skating deep like she had been told by all the NHL'ers she was surrounded by.

"Angie! Sunshine! Look, left, cut left, there you go! *Shoot!*" Benji yelled, and Angie did, but the goalie blocked her and he clapped loudly. "That's all right, keep going! Attagirl! Yeah!"

Jayden was right next to him, hollering just as loud, and she thought it was really cute. That is until Jude asked from the iPad, "Who are the gorillas that are yelling for Angie?"

"Your brother and Lucy's boyfriend," Autumn said simply, jerking back and forth with the play.

"What? Boyfriend?" Jude asked. "Like someone she likes when she doesn't have to?"

"Like a real boy? Man? Manboy? Wait, what happened?" Jace asked, also from the iPad, and Baylor snickered.

"Mom, Benji is not my boyfriend!" Lucy complained, but it was like no one was listening because just then, Angie scored.

"*That's my niece!*"

Benji high-fived Jayden as they both hollered for Angie, who had just scored one sick-ass wrister.

"I taught her that!" Jayden yelled up at his family but they all rolled their eyes, and he was pretty sure he heard one of the Sinclairs on the iPad call him an idiot.

But in all reality, he was pretty sure he taught Angie that last week.

Not that he was going to say that.

"That's right, babe! Good job!" he said, pumping his fist when Angie looked back at them.

"Amazing! Good work," Benji urged as Angie grinned, skating back to the bench. As the play started back up, they stood in silence as they watched. Shea was loud, animated, and the girls loved him.

But that Elli Adler, she was the loudest one out there.

"That's my baby! Hit 'em! Get it, girl!" she yelled in her thick, country accent that had them laughing.

"Our boss is nuts."

"She sure is," Benji agreed as they looked back on the ice just as Angie got on. When she went behind the goal, getting the puck to send it back out, she grinned at them before heading to where she needed to be.

"She likes you," Jayden said, folding his arms over his chest as the whistle blew for offsides. "A lot."

"She's a cool kid."

"No, I meant Lucy," he said, chuckling. "I guess I never really paid attention but, dude, she's smiling up there."

He looked up to where Lucy was sitting, doing her damnedest not to look at him, and she was smiling. Did he do that? Chuckling, he shook his head at her bare lips. He hadn't even noticed her lipstick was smeared when she was walking away. He was too busy trying to get his desire under control. That girl drove him mad, and he sure as hell didn't feel the lipstick on himself. It was embarrassing, and he was really starting to believe Lucy when she said she had only bad luck.

It was kind of funny.

But he was pretty sure he was the only one laughing.

Bringing his gaze from hers, he looked at Jayden. "Yeah, that's my goal, at least."

Jayden nodded. "Good. She needs that, and so does Angie."

Benji looked out on the ice where Angie was lined up for the puck. She was breathing hard, her eyes on the puck. She was ready to go. He felt like a proud father, but he wasn't her father, he couldn't forget that. No, her dad was douche dude from doucheville.

"Where is the bag of dicks?" he found himself asking, his blood suddenly boiling. How dare he miss his kid's game? Angie deserved way better.

"Fuck if I know. I hate that dude," Jayden said, looking around, and then he paused. "Ah, he's sitting on the visitors' side."

Benji glanced to where he was looking, and there was Rick with a pretty blonde and a girl the same size as Angie, playing on her iPad. "Is that his wife and kid?"

"Yeah," Jayden said, his voice laced with acid.

That bothered him. The little girl looked Angie's age. Maybe older. He almost asked, but then Angie got the puck, a breakaway. She rushed down the ice, leaving everyone in her dust.

"Deke, deke, shoot," Jayden yelled and Benji scoffed.

"She's seven, dude!"

But Angie did what her uncle said. She deked left, then right, pulling the goalie completely out before lifting the puck into the goal with ease. As she threw her arms up, Benji was screaming so loud, he was sure he was going to lose his voice. Lucy was too, waving her arms and jumping up and down as Angie grinned big, turning to give him and Jayden a thumbs-up. They both gave her a thumbs-up, and she skated away with a grin nothing could touch.

"Hell yeah!" Jayden yelled and Benji was pumped. But when he glanced at Rick to see if he was cheering too, he found he wasn't cheering. No, he wasn't even watching.

His fury-filled gaze was on Benji.

Narrowing his eyes, Benji looked away as the buzzer rang and the game was over. The home side was cheering loudly as the girls all wrapped around each other, hugging tightly, and Shea fist-pumped from the bench. "Let's go over there," Jayden said, and together they headed over, reaching Shea as he was cheering the girls on.

"Great passing, great puck control, and, Hart! That breakaway, amazing! I'm so proud of you girls. You did awesome. Now, all together. Ready? On three. One, two," he hollered, and then together everyone said, "Glittery Butterflies!"

Jayden chuckled and said under his breath, "Ha, who would have thought that big Shea Adler would be coaching a team called the Glittery Butterflies?"

"I sure as hell did," Benji said between laughs, but when Adler glanced back at them, they both stopped laughing. "Great game, Coach!"

"Yeah, I hear y'all," he said dryly, but a grin pulled at his lips as Angie came toward them, waddling in her skates.

"Okay, that was awesome!" she decided, and Benji shook her by her shoulders.

"Awesome? That was freaking amazing! You're so fantastic!" he cheered and she beamed as he undid her helmet.

"How you feel, superstar?" Jayden asked as girls passed by, congratulating Angie on a good game.

"My feet hurt and I'm tired. A nap is in order for this glittery butterfly princess," she decided, and they both laughed as Benji picked her up, putting her on his shoulders, watching her skates so they didn't cut him.

"Well, then, glittery butterfly princess Angie, I'll shall carry you to your bag," he said and she giggled.

"Thank you, good sir. Man servant, my stick, my helmet," she said, handing Jayden her things and he took them, a grin on his face.

"Yes, yes, princess."

Dissolving in laughter, Benji's heart almost couldn't handle it. It was all too damn much. Too damn sweet and perfect. Man, this was the life.

As they walked together toward the door to leave, Angie replayed the game. While Benji listened, he saw that Rick was talking to Lucy, his wife and daughter behind him, everyone looking very awkward and uncomfortable. When Rick's face got red and Lucy glared, the hair on the back of Benji's neck stood to attention. He looked up to Angie, but she was too busy talking and didn't notice Rick, which was good.

Clearing his throat, he said, "Why don't you go change? You're all wet. Jayden will take you."

Jayden nodded, noticing where Benji was looking, and said, "Yeah, come on, glittery butterfly princess."

Carefully, Benji took her off his shoulders and she went with Jayden as Benji made his way to Lucy. Her mom and River were with her, and he was sure she was fine, but he needed to be there.

Wanted to be there.

Coming up just as Rick sneered, "You made a big deal about me being here, and she doesn't even care I was here. She didn't even look at me! Why did I come if she didn't care?"

"She did care! She looked at you twice. I don't know what you want, Rick. I can't make her get up your ass," Lucy snapped back as her mother's hand came down on her shoulder.

"Lucy, just come on."

"He isn't worth it," Baylor sneered, her eyes in slits.

"Whatever, you don't even know shit," Rick said to her, but then River was in his face.

"Watch it, buddy."

"Get out of my face, old man. This has nothing to do with any of you and everything to do with her," he said, pointing his finger to Lucy. "This is bullshit and you know it. Your family steals all my time. She doesn't even care about me half the time."

"Do you know you sound like a toddler right now?" Lucy bit out, her eyes flashing, and Rick stepped toward her, pulling up short when Benji came up beside her.

"All she cared about was—" he stopped and pointed to Benji "—this douche. Who are you? Why are you even here? You like little girls or something?"

"Rick! That's enough," Lucy yelled and the blonde behind him put her hand on his arm.

"Let's go say bye to Angie. People are watching," she said and Rick glared back at her, which made her snap her mouth shut.

"Buddy, you don't know me, but I'd watch it," Benji said sternly and Rick laughed.

"You aren't even on my radar, dude. You don't even matter. You're nothing, you don't know my kid, so go on somewhere else. This slut may be fucking you, but believe me, she'll be done soon. She doesn't last long. That door on her bedroom is revolving."

"Whoa, now," River yelled, pointing to Rick's daughter. "You are disgusting to talk like that in front of your child."

"He's worthless," Baylor mumbled, but Benji's gaze never left Rick's.

"What, big boy? Got something to say? That's what I thought," Rick said, and then his gaze went to Lucy. "Keep this dude away from my kid."

Before Lucy could speak, Benji said, "Not gonna happen, dude."

"What?" he roared, taking a step toward Benji. He went toe-to-toe with him, his hands shaking at his thighs. Rick was a good foot shorter than Benji, but he'd give it to him, the guy didn't back down. "What did you say to me?"

"I said, not going to happen. I not only coach Angie, but I'm friends with her mother."

"You mean, the fuck of the week? Listen, she's a whore—"

He was cut short when Benji's nose came toward his. "One more time. One more time, you disrespect the mother of your child, and I swear you'll never speak another word a day in your life."

"Benji," Lucy urged as she pulled on his arm.

"Rick, that's enough," his wife complained, pulling at him, but he shook her off.

"You think you're winning, dude? I had her before you. I know what that is. You're wasting your time fighting for her."

"You son of a bitch, you are a piece—" River pulled Autumn away as she kept screaming, Baylor going with them.

Lucy pleaded, "Please, Benji, he isn't worth it. You're only making it worse."

He nodded slowly. "You heard me. Don't ever disrespect her again."

Rick scoffed, backing away and shaking his head. "Got you a big ol' boyfriend. Think he can protect you? I'm already talking to lawyers, Lucy. This is going down."

She was shaking, her hands digging into Benji's skin as she glared back at her ex. "I don't know why you are messing with what we have. It's sound. Angie is happy."

"No, you have my daughter subjected to filth between that River bastard and this guy. She needs stability, and Lord knows that ain't you. We're done talking."

He stomped off, but his wife stayed behind, embarrassment all over her face. She looked to her husband and then back to Lucy. Leaning in, she said, "I'm so sorry, Lucy. I'll talk to him."

Lucy's lip trembled as she shook her head. "It's whatever. Did he tell you about dance?"

"Yeah, I pulled her."

"Thank you," she said, looking to Nina. "Hey, Nina."

"Hi, Miss Lucy," the little girl said in a small voice.

"Okay, well, sorry. See you guys later," Heidi said, walking away with Nina.

He could feel the anger and the embarrassment pouring off Lucy. When he looked over at her, she was fighting back tears as she slowly shook her head. Clearing his throat, he reached for her, but she put her hands up. His stomach dropped.

"Lucy?"

"No, I need a minute," she said, sucking in a deep breath and letting it back out. When a tear slowly slid down her face, he wiped it away and ignored her flinching, wrapping his arms around her and kissing her temple.

"It's okay. He's scum, baby, calm down," he said because she was shaking so badly.

"No, you shouldn't have done that," she breathed against his chest, her body shaking. "Damn it, Benji."

"He won't talk to you like that," he choked out as she pressed her nose into his chest. "I won't stand for it."

Slamming her fist into his chest, she shook her head before pulling out of his arms. "Yeah, well, thanks."

She turned on her heel, but he was right behind her. "What, you want me to stand by and not stand up for you?"

"I don't need anyone to stand up for me," she snapped back at him. "I've got this. I can deal with him. Just, shit!"

She opened the door but he pushed it closed, pulling her to the side. "No, don't walk away from me."

"I have to get to my daughter," she bit out, her eyes flooding with tears. "Before my family makes this even worse."

"Lucy, look at me," he demanded, but she shook her head.

"I can't. I just can't, okay?" she said, pulling out of his grip. He didn't want to let her go, but when he looked in the direction of her gaze, Angie was watching, her brows together. "I need some time."

"Time?" he bit out, his heart pounding in his chest.

"Yes, just…please," she said, moving out of his hold and walking to the door. She opened it and headed to where her family stood with Angie. Rick was nowhere to be seen, but Benji was frozen in place, unable to understand what he had done wrong.

He just wanted to be there for her.

How was that wrong?

No one should be able to talk to her like that. Maybe he had overreacted, but, no, that dick wasn't going to treat her like that. He did nothing wrong. Did he? Shit.

Turning, he reached for the door, pulling it open and walking through before running his hands through his hair, frustrated. He wasn't sure if he should leave or go to where everyone was acting like Rick didn't matter and was gushing over Angie.

He knew he couldn't leave without saying good-bye.

Walking to the group, he came between Autumn and Jayden, watching as Lucy helped Angie put on the clothes she had brought. When her mother's hand came to rest on his arm, he looked down to see her smiling at him.

"Thank you," she mouthed, her eyes full of appreciation. He nodded slowly, unable to speak as Angie rambled happily.

"I want Texas Roadhouse, River," she said and River grinned.

"Anything for the superstar."

She grinned and then looked to Benji. "You'll come to lunch, right, Benji? Or are you busy?"

Lucy's gaze cut to his, but then she went back to fixing Angie's jacket.

Shit.

"Of course he'll go," Autumn said, rubbing his back with a big smile on her face. "He's a big guy, he needs food. Right, hon?"

But Benji was looking to Lucy, waiting for any sign as to what he should say, but apparently that jacket was really important. Or the buttons were giving her a hard time. He wasn't sure, and he didn't know what to do. He didn't even know where he stood with her, but before he could even decide, Angie was practically begging.

"Come on, Benji, please!"

Swallowing hard, he smiled down at her and nodded. "How can I say no to the glittery butterfly princess?"

"You can't!" she cheered, wrapping her arms around Lucy's neck. "I'm so happy!"

Lucy smiled as she kissed Angie's cheek. "That's all that matters, baby."

But what about Lucy?

What about her fucking happiness?

Chapter
FOURTEEN

"**B**enji, can I ride with you?"

Looking over at Lucy, he found she wasn't looking at him or even at Angie, for that matter. She was carrying Angie's bag, her lips pressed together, her eyes on the door. God, he hated this. He didn't want her to be upset, and he really didn't like that he wasn't sure if she was mad at him or not. He just wanted her to talk. Tell him something.

When he looked down at Angie, her eyes were wide and hopeful, and Benji couldn't say no.

He was wrapped around her finger.

Hell, both of their fingers.

Insane.

"It's up to your mom. You both are welcome to ride with me," he said as he pushed the door open, holding it for both of them.

"Mom! Can we?"

"Angie, honey, I can drive."

"Yeah, but I want to ride with Benji. He has, like, this huge truck—"

"Honey, not right now," Lucy complained, rubbing her eyes, and when she looked down to see Angie's dejected expression, she let out a breath. "I'm sorry, honey. I have such a headache."

"More reason for Benji to drive."

Clearing his throat, he said, "I don't mind. I can bring you back to your car after lunch."

Sighing, she shrugged, and he could tell she just didn't want to fight. "Whatever. Stay with Benji. I'm gonna put your stuff in the car."

Sliding her hand into Benji's, Angie shrugged as they watched Lucy walk to her car. "Guess she's not feeling good."

"Yeah," Benji said, his heart heavy. He was pretty sure she was mad at him, and he still really didn't understand what he had done wrong. But he sure as hell wasn't going to apologize. Rick could suck it; he wasn't going to talk to Lucy like that. It was that simple. Clearing his throat, he gave her a weak smile. "She'll be okay."

Angie nodded. "Yeah, she always is. My grandma says she's the strongest woman she knows."

Benji agreed. But at what expense?

She always worried about everyone else and not herself. She felt she could handle everything, so fiercely independent. It was killing him. He wanted her to lean on him. Let him help. Let him be there for her. But then, who was he to ask that of her? He had just come into her life; she wasn't used to it. But he would do everything for her to know that he was there. That he wanted to help.

When she started back toward them, Angie's booster seat in hand, he tried to smile at her, but she ignored him, taking Angie's other hand. Giggling, Angie squeezed both their hands, looking at Benji then to Lucy.

"Aw, we're like a family!" Angie cheered, swinging their hands, and Benji smiled, while Lucy did not. "Isn't this nice, Benji?"

Benji nodded, but he didn't answer because Lucy warned, "Angela."

"I'm just saying," she said simply, but Lucy wasn't playing, and Angie's shoulders soon fell in defeat.

God, this sucked.

Reaching his truck, he opened the back for Angie and she hopped in with her seat, shutting the door. Lucy tried to get in, but he was blocking her on purpose. Turning to him, she gave him a look. "You're in the way."

"I know. Listen—"

"Not now," she said, her eyes pleading. "I can't right now. I'm doing everything to hold it together. Please, Benji. Not right now."

He could see it in her eyes and it gutted him. He wanted to wrap his arms around her, kiss her, tell her it was okay, but he wasn't sure if that was a good idea. "Do you need a hug?"

Her shoulders fell as her lip wobbled and she looked away. "I do, but not now. Not with Angie right here," she almost whispered and his heart sank.

"Rain check?"

"Yeah," she whispered as she pulled in another breath. He nodded, opening the door for her. She climbed in, and before he shut the door, he heard Angie ask if she was okay. Walking around the car, he saw Lucy reassure her daughter that she was. But he didn't think she was, and he also wasn't sure *they* were okay.

He wasn't sure which thing bothered him more.

But he knew he could deal with them not being okay; he could fix that. But he worried about her. Could he fix her? Would she even let him?

Swallowing hard, he started the truck as Angie asked, "Did you hear from Dad, Mom?" Lucy stiffened as she folded her hands in her lap. But before she could answer, Angie said, "I didn't see him. Sucks he didn't come."

Shaking her head, Lucy let out a long breath. "He was there. You didn't see him?"

"No, where was he?"

"By the visitors' side."

Angie thought that over for a moment. "Why didn't he say anything to me?"

Rage filled Benji's soul as he sucked in a frustrated breath. What a dick.

"I don't know, honey," Lucy said sadly, and Benji couldn't stop himself, he reached over and laid his hands on Lucy's. "I'm sorry he didn't."

"Isn't your fault," she said simply, and Lucy closed her eyes as Benji squeezed her hand.

"She's right, it's not," he said then, but Lucy didn't say anything, she just looked out the window.

And he wanted to shake her.

At lunch, she also had nothing to say. No one really did, though. Benji talked hockey with Jayden and River, while the girls gushed over Angie. Lucy, though, she just sat there, smiling when she should. But it never reached her eyes. He tried to enjoy lunch. Autumn was a hoot, and River was so doting on her and Baylor and really proud of Angie. He remembered the man to be so hard, but seeing him with his ladies was sweet. It was obvious he loved them all. Even Lucy. He wrapped his arm around her, hugging her, and she curled into his side. But she didn't say anything, just a weak smile that didn't fool anyone.

"Honey, eat," Autumn urged but Lucy shrugged.

"I'm fine, Mom, just tired. Not really hungry."

She was a horrible liar and everyone knew it, especially Autumn. To his surprise, though, she didn't say anything as she turned to look at Benji. "Benji, where are you from?"

Laying his fork down, he wiped his mouth and sat up straight. "Chicago, right outside the city in the suburbs."

"Oh, how nice. Is your family still there?"

Benji paused. He wasn't sure, but he assumed so. "Yeah."

"Is it just you? Or do you have siblings?"

He cleared his throat, Silas heavy on his heart as he tried to smile. "I had a brother, but I lost him in a car wreck when he was seventeen."

Angie's brows pulled together. "He died?"

Benji nodded sadly. "He did."

"That's so sad, I'm sorry. Isn't that sad, Mommy?"

Lucy looked up then, meeting Benji's gaze. "Yeah, it is."

He gave her a small smile and he picked up his fork as Autumn asked, "So are you single, Benji?"

"He is!" Angie giggled and Lucy cut her a look.

Autumn beamed as Benji laughed. "Actually, sunshine, I'm seeing someone."

Angie's eyes widened as she looked to her mom, and Lucy shrugged. "What?"

"Yup," he said as Lucy looked up, her eyes narrowing as he smiled. "She's this really awesome gal, makes my heart hurt at the sight of her. She has the best smile."

Angie looked bored. "Well, yay."

"Angela," Lucy scolded and Angie threw her hands up.

"I wanted him to take you on a date!"

Benji smiled as Lucy looked away, his smile slowly dropping as she said, "Enough, Angie."

She made a pouting face, leaning on her hand, as Autumn said, "Well, then, Angie, tell me about your breakaway."

Like the grandma she was, she knew what would liven Angie up. Angie sat up, excitedly giving a play-by-play. Jayden leaned in close. "You're talking about my sister, right?"

Benji looked over at him and nodded. "Yeah, trying to make her smile."

"Yeah, that asshole," Jayden basically growled, but he looked relieved. "Mom said you almost fought him."

Benji looked at Lucy, who was seated at the end of the table, her eyes on Angie before she glanced back at Benji. Her eyes were so sad, so tired. She needed to go home and go to sleep. "He had one more chance to say something shitty about her and I would have."

Jayden nodded as Lucy looked away. "She's pissed."

Benji let out a long breath. "Apparently, that was wrong."

"No, from what my mom said, Rick is trying to get their parenting plan changed. She's stressed. It isn't you."

When Benji gazed back across the table, Lucy looked over at him and then back at the food she hadn't even touched. "What do I do?"

Jayden shook his head as he met his eyes. "I don't know. Short of killing the dude, is there anything we can do but be there for her?"

"Will she let us?"

Jayden scoffed. "Nope. But we will try anyway."

It was clear that Benji was a part of that *we,* and it made him feel good. But did Lucy still see him that way? She wouldn't even really look at him, and it was killing him.

He didn't know what to do.

When they were done with lunch, they walked out as a group, Baylor limping behind, and Benji slowed to walk with her.

"When's the surgery?" he asked and Baylor shook her head.

"End of the month."

"When you hitting the ice again?"

Biting her lip, she shrugged. "I don't know if I will. Professionally, at least."

His brows came together. "Really?"

"Yeah, they don't know if I'll play ever again to my full potential."

Benji nodded slowly, thinking that over. "Do you believe that?"

Baylor met his gaze and held it for a second before shaking her head. "I don't."

Smiling, Benji cupped her shoulder. "Don't give up."

She smiled, the curve of her lips brightening her whole face before she nodded. "Thanks."

"Anytime," he said, squeezing her shoulder as Angie squealed.

She was up on River's shoulders when she declared, "Mommy! River is gonna take me stick shopping."

Lucy shook her head, though, her brows coming together. "No, she has a stick. She's fine."

"She has Jayden's old stick. She needs her own."

"She's fine," Lucy tried, but Autumn was already waving her off.

"We want to take her out, spend some time with her. We miss her."

"Mom, you guys see her all the time. Stop spoiling her."

"No, you go on. We'll bring her by Jayden's later," Autumn insisted, and River nodded while Angie pleaded with Lucy with her eyes.

"Yeah, Mom, go for a ride with Benji. Maybe he'll break up with his girlfriend and take you on a date if you're nice," she sang, and Benji chuckled as Lucy glared.

"Angela," she warned, but Angie was giggling with Autumn. "That's enough."

"She's right," Autumn whispered while Jayden and Baylor snickered behind Lucy.

"Mother, enough," she demanded and then let out a long breath. "Fine, y'all go. Text me later. I'm gonna head to the apartment and start packing."

"I thought we were doing all that tomorrow and Monday?" Autumn asked and Benji's ears perked up. She hadn't told him about this.

"Monday is my office, tomorrow is the apartment. I'm gonna get a head start since you guys are taking my daughter."

"So instead of going out with Benji, you're gonna pack?" her mother deadpanned and even Angie made a face.

"Bye, guys," she said, turning on her heel. "Be good, Angie. Love you. Come on, Benji," she called over her shoulder and Autumn set him with a look.

"Take her out."

"Yeah, to Chuck E. Cheese!" Angie said then and Benji chuckled.

"See you guys later. Good game, Angie."

"Thanks! But really, she loves Chuck E. Cheese," she stressed and Benji had to fight his grin as he ran off to catch up with Lucy. She was almost to the truck when he finally fell into step with her.

"Apparently, you like Chuck E. Cheese. You didn't tell me that."

She cut him a sideways glance. "I hate that place."

"Angie thinks otherwise."

She just shook her head as he reached for the handle to open the door. "They're all insane."

Stepping in front of her before she could get in, he held his arms out. "Time to cash in that rain check. Bring it in."

Sucking in a deep breath, she shook her head. "Not now."

But he wasn't taking no for an answer. Wrapping his arms around her, pulling her to him, he kissed the top of her head. Thankfully, she didn't fight him. "Yes, now," he whispered against her hair, and when her arms came around his waist, his eyes fell shut.

Nuzzling her nose in his chest, she drew in a deep breath and then let it out, holding him tightly. "Dealing with Rick just sucks ass," she whispered, squeezing her eyes shut, and he nodded.

"He's a dick, for sure."

Pulling back, she looked up at him and nodded. "I'm just so tired."

He smiled. He was tired too, but he would gladly be tired for the rest of his days if he got to spend every night like he had last night with her. "Me too."

He cupped her face, and she leaned into his hand as she closed her eyes. When she opened her eyes, he found them swimming in tears as her little lip wobbled a bit. "I'm sorry you had to deal with all that."

"You don't apologize for that fucker, Lucy."

She paused, looking up at him. "You're right. I'm sorry I snapped at you for just doing what a man who cares for someone would do." His heart fluttered as his lips curved. He held her gaze as she cleared her throat. "It just really hard with him, and I'm not used to someone wanting to stand up for me against him."

"Well, get used to it, baby. I'm not going anywhere."

She let out a long breath, shaking her head. "That's the thing, Benji. You can't. He will use it against me."

Benji gave her an incredulous look. "How in the world can he use me standing up for you against you? I don't understand. You don't matter to him. The only thing that should matter is Angie and her best interests."

When her lip started to tremble harder, he took her by her hips and a tear rolled down her cheek. Reaching up, he wiped her face free. "Don't cry, baby. Please."

But the tears kept coming. "He wants to go week on/week off with me. Where I would get her one week, he would get her the next, and so on. Angie can't do that. She needs stability. With her ADHD, she needs the consistency, the reassurance of permanency. She loves her school, they honor her 504 Plan, and we are comfortable there. He isn't in her school district. And I know he won't drive her, he'll try to get me to drive her to his school district."

"That's stupid, though. It's not ideal for Angie."

"It doesn't matter. He's doing this to hurt me. I know he is because he doesn't care at all about what Angie needs. He says that I used the ADHD as a shield, something to keep her in my clutches, when that's not it. I want her to have a daddy, someone who loves her and whom she can trust. But I told him I don't want her in dance, that she feels like she's being ignored., And he said he feels they can be better parents, and Benji—" Her voice broke and he took her in his arms, his heart shattering in his chest as she sobbed. Holding him tightly, she pressed her face to his chest, clenching his shirt in her fist. "I can't do that. I can't go week to week. If it would benefit her, then, yes, I could understand and I would deal. But it won't. She comes home from his house and it takes a day or two to get her back to who she is. Happy and carefree. She is better with me, I know it, and he makes me question that."

"Lucy, don't you dare," he said roughly against her temple. "That won't happen. He won't get her, there is no way. He's a dick—anyone can see that."

"Yes, I know. But he has the family—the wife, the daughter, a steady job. It makes me so nervous. He's looking for anything, and it scares me. It scares me so damn bad," she said, her body shaking as her words were muffled. He leaned in to hear her as she whispered, "He wanted me to keep River away from her. I refused and now he's added you." Pausing to sniff hard, she looked up at him and shook her head. "She would be devastated if I told her she couldn't see you."

"Me too," he admitted, his throat tight with emotion.

"And I would be devastated."

Holding her close, he leaned his head to hers, kissing her temple. "That won't happen. Remember that fighting you for you thing I have no problem doing? This falls into that category. I'm sorry, but I won't let you."

She tried to smile, but the tears came faster and she slowly shook her head. "I just don't know what to do. He scares the living shit out of me."

"He can't touch you, and he won't get Angie. It won't happen," he repeated,

holding her and kissing her temple. "I promise."

"Benji, you can't promise that."

"Well, I'm promising it," he said roughly, kissing her once more.

"He wants me to break up with you," she whispered against his neck and he froze. "He texted that at lunch."

He held his breath. "What did you say?"

"I told him to fuck off," she said softly. "And he said I better hope Angie never says that you touch her. He's such a fucking asshole!" she yelled against his chest, her fist balling up as her body broke with a sob.

His eyes fell shut as she clung to him, his fingers biting into her ribs as his heart ached. "Lucy, I'm sorry. I'm so fucking sorry. Tell me what I can do."

"Hold me. Just hold me."

"Done," he whispered, kissing her once more, and he did. He held her as she cried, and he really didn't know what to do. He had been sure she was going to throw the mom card in his face, but she didn't. She clung to him, needed him, and it pleased him to no end. But the issue of Rick was still so strong. He really didn't understand the dude. He had moved on, had a wife and daughter, so why was he so worried about Lucy? Why wasn't she allowed to be happy? To move on, too?

It was sad.

On one hand, he wanted to hunt the dude down and kill him, but he knew that wouldn't help anything. No, he'd have to be her rock, and he could do that. For her and Angie. Pulling back, he moved her hair out of her face and kissed her nose. Holding his gaze, she whispered, "Thank you."

His brows pulled together as he shrugged. "For what? Being here for you? That's a given, baby. Don't thank me for that."

"It's not only that," she whispered, her lip trembling. "I've never broken down about Rick to anyone but my mom. My brothers don't even know, more because I just don't think they'd understand. But you, it's easy, and that is such a comforting feeling. I don't think you realize how important that is to me."

Moving his thumbs across her cheeks, he kissed her lips softly. "Well then, you're welcome, Lucy."

"You scare the living bejesus out of me, Benjamin Paxton."

He scoffed. "Funny, you don't scare me at all," he said with a wink and she grinned, her dimples flashing as she leaned up to press her lips to his. Melting against her lips, he let his fingers bite into her hips as he squeezed his eyes shut. When he opened them, pulling away, she looked up at him with so much relief and need in her eyes that he found himself breathless. "You know, this shit with Rick… Let it go right now. Angie is with your mom and River, having a blast. There is nothing we can do now anyway, so how about we go back to my house and take a nap?"

She looked hopeful for one second, and then she shook her head. "I really need to pack. They need my stuff out by Tuesday."

He cupped her face. "And it will be. But today we nap. Tomorrow, we work."

But, of course, she protested. "No, you don't have to do that. You have stuff to do, I'm sure. I've got this. Jayden and River are gonna help. Go do what you need to do."

Benji nodded his head, already ready for her to try to deny his help. "Yeah, you're right. I do have something to do."

She nodded. "See, it's fine. I've got—"

Pressing his nose to hers, he said, "I have to help my girlfriend move her stuff out of her old apartment and office."

Her eyes darkened as her lips started to curve, only one dimple appearing. "Girlfriend?"

He nodded. "Yeah, I talked about her at lunch. She has this ass to die for," he said, his hands sliding to her ass. "These eyes that leave me speechless, lips that should be on lipstick ads, and a smile that honestly makes it hard to even comprehend how God could give that smile to only one person." Her lips fully smiled and both dimples appeared as her eyes lit up. Smiling, he whispered, "But thank God He did, because being on the receiving end of that smile… Heaven. Pure fucking heaven."

She held his gaze and his heart stopped in his chest as she said, "Wow, this girlfriend must be pretty lucky."

Leaning his head to hers, he kissed her nose, his eyes falling shut. It wasn't going to be easy loving this girl. No, between her shitty-ass ex and her way of dealing with things, it was going to be tough. She had a stream of bad luck that wasn't for the faint of heart. She sure as hell could start a fight in an empty room. But the thing was, he didn't care, because he was a pro at tough situations.

And she was worth the fight.

Pressing his nose to hers, he smiled as he whispered, "Actually, I think I'm the lucky one."

When her phone vibrated in her hand, Lucy made a face when she saw it was her dad.

Again.

What the hell?

She did not want to speak with him. No, she was way too busy. Plus, she just didn't want to hear his voice. Tucking her phone in her pocket, she looked around the room, confused as to what to do next. Her dad calling was messing

with her brain.

"Hey, babe. Am I taking the boxes in the back of my truck to your office or to the warehouse?"

She looked up from where she was staring at the floor to see Benji standing in the doorway, looking back at her.

"Sorry, what?"

He smiled and, God, he was so sexy. He was wearing a ripped up, dirty, white shirt with some loose jeans that hugged his massive thighs. Wearing a purple Assassins beanie, he was sweating from all the heavy lifting he was doing. She wanted to ask him to stop, that River and Shea could help, but he insisted.

And she was so damn thankful.

"Boxes in the back of my truck. Where are they going?"

"The office. Thank you. Wait, shit. What time is it?"

She looked around frantically, feeling like she was losing it. The day before, with the help of her family and Benji, they had packed up her whole apartment, taking most of it to the warehouse and the rest to Jayden's. They hadn't finished, though, and had been finishing up while getting the office done today. She tried to tell Jayden and Benji not to worry about helping since they had a game that night, but they wouldn't listen and had even brought Shea to help. By the grace of God, they were almost done, but she was going to lose it. She was sure.

"Baby, your phone is in your hand."

"Sweet Lord in heaven," she complained, looking down and then throwing her hands in the air. "I gotta go get Angie. Shit, I gotta help Shea and River. And then what time do you have to be at the arena?"

Closing the distance between them, he took her in his arms, cupping her face in his hands before kissing her nose. He had been just perfect the last two days. She was convinced he would run the other way after the shit with Rick or her vomiting her issues all over him, but he hadn't. He stood beside her, reassuring her everything would be fine, and she clung to him like a koala. It was crazy, and she sure as hell didn't like leaning on people, but she was leaning.

On Benji.

Especially with the move. It was hard getting everything together, and her emotions were all over the place. It was her first apartment after Rick, and she'd lost it. Yeah, it wasn't her fault and Benji stressed that, but she felt like a failure. Particularly since she was living with her brother at the moment. She should just dip into her savings and get Angie and herself a place. But everything that was by Angie's school was crazy-ass expensive and she just didn't feel right about it. She needed that money for a lawyer in case shit did get nasty with Rick. No, she had to figure something else out.

And having Benji there to bounce ideas off and to just talk to, she was finding was really freaking nice.

"Okay, you go to the house with Shea. Take my truck. I'll take your car, go get Angie, and then meet you at the house, take my truck back, and head to the arena. I have time."

She bit into her lip. It was a good idea, but was it okay for her to send him to get her child? Angie would probably eat it up, but should he do that? "Are you sure? That's kinda over and beyond the duties of a boyfriend, isn't it?"

Shit, she admitted the boyfriend thing, but he must have missed that because he rolled his eyes. "Angie is an extension of you, remember? I don't mind. If it's going to help you out, I want to do it."

She held his gaze and then nodded. "Thank you so much, and I promise sexual favors later," she said quickly and he waggled his brows.

"Shit, I'll be Angie's chauffeur full time for those," he said, kissing her lips quickly before taking her keys out of her pocket. He handed her his, and then kissed her once more. "Meet ya there."

"Okay," she said breathlessly as he rushed out, leaving her as her phone started to ring once more. Ignoring it, she rolled her eyes but then jumped when someone started squealing.

Her mother.

Shit.

"I knew it! He's just perfect. How long have you two been together? I just knew when he said that at lunch he was talking about you. Ah! Why haven't you told me?" she said, throwing question after question as Lucy moaned loudly.

"Mom, not now," she complained as her phone sounded with a text. "Why the hell is Dad trying to get ahold of me?"

That made her mom pause, her smile dropping. "Your father?"

"Yeah," she said, shaking her head and hitting the text.

Dad: Call me. It's about a contract that just came in for your new office. And then Rick's punk ass.

Her stomach dropped.

"Fuck," she muttered and her mother's eyes widened.

"What is it? And goodness, Lucy, your mouth. I'm sure Benji doesn't like that foulness."

But Lucy ignored her, hitting her dad's name. "He doesn't care. Hold on," she said, walking out of the building into the brisk, cold air. Winter was coming and she couldn't say she was ready. She hated the cold. As she cuddled into her coat, her father's deep voice came across the line.

"Lucy, how are you? How's Angie?" he asked happily, making her skin crawl.

"What contract? What about Rick?"

"Right to business, I see." When she didn't say anything, he cleared his throat. "Well, then. I got a contract from Paul Nixon, representation for Benjamin Paxton?"

"Yeah, that's who I'm renting my new office from," she said simply, her face twisting in confusion. "Why would you get that contract, though?"

"You have me listed as your lawyer on your website still."

Oh. Well, that needed to be changed. "Okay, anything wrong with the contract?"

"No, it's pretty cut-and-dried. But do you know this guy or something? This rent is way too low for a real office building."

Lucy's glare deepened. "Does that matter?"

"No, just making sure you aren't getting screwed over."

Her blood boiled. "Is the contract good or not?"

"It's good. It's fair, just really low for rent. Is it legit? Did you have it checked out?"

"Yes," she lied and then made a note to do that, even though she was already moving in to it.

"Okay, well, on to the next order of business," he said simply, unfazed the hatred in Lucy's voice. "That son of a bitch had his lawyer contact me about splitting Angie's time fifty-fifty. I asked what the reasoning was, and he informed me that his son of a bitch client doesn't like the way you are raising his daughter. I told him that he can take us to court, but he better have some solid proof to back up his claims. He asked to settle out of court. I told him to take a flying leap. Just wanted to let you know."

Biting into her lip, she closed her eyes, her body shaking with nerves. "Do you think he'll do it?"

He paused, letting out a long sigh. She could just see him. Sitting at his desk, his pen at his lips, really thinking. So many summers she had watched him do just that. "I don't think so. I told him he'll be paying all the court costs and everything else. That we are completely good with the parenting plan the judge decided. That dickface agreed, too, when the divorce was finalized. He'd be dumb to take us to court, honestly. You keep records of everything still? All the texts, emails, recordings of your phone conversations? Have you gotten anything from the school lately?"

Her stomach was still hurting as she cleared her throat. "Yeah, I'm still doing that. But, no, she's been doing great in school. The new medication is working wonders."

"Yeah, but you need to make sure you keep an ear out. Is she still shutting down when she gets home from his house?"

"Sorta, but hockey has been really great for her."

He clicked his tongue. "Okay, that's good. You are doing it right, Lucy."

"Should I be worried?"

He let out a long breath. "You know, Laney, I don't think so. But I'll keep you in the loop if anything changes."

Her heart skipped at the nickname he had for her. He hadn't called her that in years, and it hurt to hear it. Her dad used to be her hero, the person she loved most and looked up to. She had wanted to be a lawyer for so long because he was one. She would play hockey with the boys and him, just so she could be the center of attention. She was daddy's little girl. But when it came out that he was cheating on her mother, that he had a whole other life with another woman, he not only broke her mom's heart, he broke Lucy's too. That was the day her heart turned to stone and she never trusted a man again.

Well, until now.

Until Benji.

Clearing her throat free of emotion, she nodded. "Okay. Thank you."

"Of course. Call if you need anything."

She didn't answer, she just hung up and slowly shook her head, the nerves eating her alive. She wasn't sure if she should trust what her dad was saying. How would he know if Rick was going to take them to court? She knew he would fight. He loved Angie and knew what Rick had done to them, but still, neither of them knew Rick's financial status. Money talked, but she had so much on him. No, she was fine, but would he really do this?

Looking at her phone, she considered calling Rick, but it wouldn't end well. No, it would get nasty, so she called Benji.

"Hey, I don't have her yet."

"No, I know. You have like three minutes."

"Oh, okay, I was about to go in there and get her. I thought maybe I missed her or something. By the way, this school is swanky."

She chuckled. "Yeah, it's really good for her."

"Yeah, I can tell. But you need a BMW. Your Honda isn't cutting it."

She scoffed as he laughed. "I'll get right on that."

"Yeah, so what's up? You miss me?" he asked and she grinned.

"Always," she decided and his rough chuckle ran down her spine. "But, it's not that."

"Well, that's bogus."

She paused and then laughed. "You and your wack vocabulary."

"Hey, don't make fun of me!" She giggled, looking up at the sky as his laughter made her heart expand. "Anyway, what's up if you don't miss me?"

"I said I did, dork. It was just more than that," she said, rolling her eyes. "Anyway, my dad called me."

"Really?" he asked, surprised. "That's not normal."

"No, not at all. But apparently, Rick's lawyers have contacted him and they want to change the parenting plan. Which we already knew he wanted to do, but I didn't think he'd actually get a lawyer."

"Yeah, that's surprising. He seems like a lot of talk, no do."

"Exactly, but my dad told them to take a flying leap, that they can take us to court. But he doesn't think they will. Should I call Rick? Try to talk to him about this? Maybe we can work something out? I don't know, I just don't want to go to court. I don't want to do that to Angie."

He didn't say anything at first, and she'd almost thought she lost him when he said, "Yeah, Angie doesn't need to go through that. But do you think calling him would work?"

"I don't know. I'm sure it would end in a screaming match."

"Yeah, then what's the point, you know?"

"Yeah, I just wanted to make sure I was making the right choice. Ignore it."

"You know him better than I do. As a man, I would want to sit down and discuss it with you, figure out how to make it better for both sides. But he isn't a man, he's a disgusting waste of space, or at least, from what I've seen, he is. You don't really tell me much about him."

Biting the inside of her cheek, her stomach dropped. She didn't talk about it because she hated Rick. Still, she could understand his interest in it. "Do you want to know?"

"Well, considering it deals with you and Angie, I would like to know. Maybe I can better understand his idiocy."

Lucy sighed. "No, there's no understanding Rick Hart."

"Well, we can talk about that later. Angie is coming. I'll be at the house in a bit."

"Okay. Thanks, babe."

"Anytime," he said before hanging up. She dropped her phone to her lips, tapping them in deep thought. Surely, Rick wouldn't do more. Letting out a long breath because she just wasn't sure, she went to return inside. But when she turned, she ran right into her mother.

"Good Lord, Mom! How long have you been standing there?"

"Long enough."

She looked hurt and Lucy's lip curled. "I was coming inside."

"I know. But this bastard has contacted a lawyer and he thinks he's gonna get the parenting plan changed?"

Anxiety eating her from within, she nodded. "Apparently. From what Dad said."

"But your father has this? He feels good about it?"

"From what he said," she said simply and her mother nodded.

"He's a shitty person, but he's a good lawyer and he loves Angie. I think it will be okay. I don't think anything will come of it."

Lucy shrugged, hoping her mom was right, that Benji was right. "I hope so." Her mother's eyes met hers, searching them before taking Lucy's hands in hers. Lucy held her mother's gaze and then shook her head. "What, Mom?"

"You trust him?"

"Dad? I mean he's a law—"

"No, Benji."

Lucy looked down, her heart beating fast in her chest. For so long, she had been closed off from everything. She shared things with her mom, but it was mostly details about Angie—never deep, dark feelings because she wasn't really a sharing kind of girl. It sure as hell was never about a guy because no guy ever came along. But now one had, and while she was giddy about Benji, she didn't want anyone judging her. Because, yeah, it was moving fast. He was picking her kid up and giving her advice about an ex he didn't really even know anything about, but it worked for her.

They just clicked.

But would her mom get that? Lucy had rushed into marriage with Rick, and that had ended in a fiery heap of shit. Was she making the same mistake? As soon as she thought that, she knew she wasn't. First, she wasn't marrying Benji; they were dating and he was nothing like the sort of man Rick was. Things were just so much different with Benji. Still, it made her so damn nervous.

Meeting her mom's gaze, she shrugged. "Yeah. I do."

Aged from years of raising four hellions and going through a nasty divorce, her mother's face lit up as her lips curved, her fingers lacing with Lucy's. "How long have you been seeing him? I mean, how did I not know?"

Lucy bit her lip and looked away. "Because it's only been like two weeks. I know it's crazy and stupid and so new, but—"

"Lucy Lane, does he make you happy?"

She looked up, her eyes wide as her mother gazed at her, love shining in her eyes. Clearing her throat, she nodded. "Yeah, he does."

"Is he good to Angie?"

Lucy grinned and her heart skipped a beat thinking about how great he really was with her. Angie hadn't wanted to stay home the day before, and even though the apartment wasn't safe, Benji promised to keep an eye out so she could come. So she would feel included. "He is."

"Good, then it doesn't matter how much time it's been. It matters how you feel," she said.

"But I made mistakes before. Rick—"

"And you learned from them, didn't you?"

"Yeah."

She nodded, her eyes pleading with Lucy's. "You know, I've always been able to read people. I know a good person when I see them. I knew that Jude was going to marry Claire. That Jayden would marry Baylor, that Jace would marry Avery," she said, her eyes darkening with each word. "I knew when I looked at River, after I decided I wanted to move on, that he was the man for me. Lucy, honey, I loved him after our third date."

Lucy smiled, holding her hands. "Whoa, no love here, Mom. I really like him and I trust him, but whoa."

She laughed nervously and her mother smiled. "That's fine, but let me tell you, when you came home married to Rick, pregnant, I knew he wouldn't last. I didn't trust him as far as I could throw him," she said with all the vengeance in her voice. Lucy knew this. She had always hated Rick. Everyone did. "But when I saw Benji lift Angie over his head and how he looked back at you, his eyes just so full of love, I knew he was the one for you."

"Mom, be real. You just met him."

"And I know," she said with a nod of her head. "Watch, mark my words. You'll marry that man."

"Mom," she said, rolling her eyes.

"As long as you don't mess it up, that is," she said then, bringing Lucy's attention back to her.

Pulling her brows together, she glared. "What the hell does that mean?"

Her mother gave her a knowing look, but Lucy was confused. "You know what it means. You're your own worst enemy. You don't know how to be happy since that asshole, and it's scared me, Lucy. I thought you were gonna be one of those women who grow old alone. But when I see you with him, a little grin on that face of yours, I think you're learning how to be happy again. I can't describe how much joy that brings me. I love the guy just for making you smile."

Lucy looked away, sucking in a deep breath. Her mother was crazy, that was it. But yet, she found herself saying, "It's new. It's all shiny and shit, I don't know. He makes me happy."

"And I'm excited to watch you grow with him."

As she met her eyes, her mom smiled and Lucy couldn't help it, she smiled back. Because, like her mother, she, too, was excited for the future. Crazy since she had never cared before, but now, because of Benji, she was excited to see what would happen.

And if, by chance, she would fall in love with him.

Chapter
FIFTEEN

"**O**kay, woman, I have not seen you in three days and your office is behind my house. I call bullshit."

Lucy giggled as she drove onto the interstate. Glancing at Benji on her phone, she found him with a little grin playing on his lips as he lay back in his bed. "Hey, it isn't my fault you're a hotshot hockey player with things to do."

"Hey, this is not my fault. It's yours. You're all over the place, designing. And yet, my house has not been started, nor has a contract for it come through."

She rolled her eyes. "Didn't I say I was busy when you insisted on dating me?"

He gave her a look. "Fine. Where is my contract?"

"It won't be coming. I'm not charging you for my services, only for the supplies and crap I buy. Don't need a contract for that."

"Excuse me?"

"I didn't stutter," she teased and he glared. "Seriously. You've helped so much the last couple days with letting me rent your guesthouse and helping me with moving. It's the least I can do."

It was, and she should do more. He had been a godsend. He painted the whole office for her on Tuesday. Then, on Wednesday, he put together her office, with directions from Rayne, while she was out shopping and doing errands for one of the local restaurant's designs. She honestly didn't know how she could ever thank him, and she didn't like that. She hated owing people or putting them out to help her. She asked him not to help, but of course, he didn't listen.

But then, if he had, she probably still wouldn't be set up.

"You're so frustrating, you know that?"

She grinned. "I think you said that when I yelled at you for twenty minutes not to paint my office. I really thought you were going to throw the paint on me."

He scoffed. "I won't lie, I thought about it."

She giggled. "Figured."

"Yeah, so how much do you charge?"

"Why? I told you not to worry about it!"

"Fine, I'll call Rayne."

"Don't worry about it, please," she begged as she turned off at her exit. "It isn't like I can give you the blow job of your life since I'm so busy. Let me do this. I plan to start on Friday after I drop Angie off."

He paused, his eyes half-lidded. "So, wait, you're coming over Friday to do the design or to give me the blow job of my life?"

She grinned. "Well, play your cards right, Paxton, and it could be a mixture of both."

He thought that over for a moment and then nodded slowly. "I guess I can handle that."

She giggled again and a fluttery feeling went nuts in her belly as she looked at him on the phone. He was looking damn near irresistible. He had his black-rimmed glasses hanging low on his nose and his stubble was dark and thick. He was almost bursting out of his ratty tee and his jeans didn't even fit. No. He was sexy as hell. Or maybe it was because, like he said, they hadn't seen or touched each other in three days.

She was jonesing for some Benji Paxton.

"Why are you so hot today?"

"Whoa, don't steal my lines."

She laughed hard. "Please. I'm serious. Like, why? You got someone to impress?"

"Um, no," he said simply, looking down as he pushed his glasses up. Shit, even that was sexy. "I'm wearing some jeans and a work tee."

"Yeah, sexy," she said all rough, and man, he was.

"I see some cleavage. So who you trying to sell to?"

She laughed. "I was hoping to maybe see you today."

"Well, I have like an hour before I have to go to the rink. Come over," he demanded, waggling his eyebrows, and she chuckled, shaking her head.

"I can't. I have to get to this restaurant before the delivery gets there. Then I've got to get Angie and then go home and work."

"Home? Jayden's?"

"That is where I live." He made a little grumbling noise and she rolled her eyes. "Oh, goodness, are you pouting?"

He gave her a dry look. "Wouldn't it be easier to walk from here to your office?"

"Benji, we are on week three. I am not moving in with you."

They had been having this conversation a lot the last three days. Ever since she said she was going to get a hotel for her and Angie after walking in on Jayden and Baylor banging, he had been very persistent about her moving in with him.

"See, it wouldn't even have to be with me, like, in my room. I mean—"

"Please, if I lived in the same house as you, I'd be in your bed and you know it."

He paused, nodding his head. "This is true, but I don't want you getting a hotel."

She let out a breath. "I know, I'm not. Jayden already said he'd glue me to the house. He's psycho, but I swear, I see him banging his wife one more time—"

"You'll move in with me?"

She gave him a deadpan look. "Do I really need to throw the kid card up? Remember, I have one of those? She needs stability. I already feel like I'm fucking up by living with Jayden, but I can't dip into my savings. I almost have enough. And I'm definitely not taking money from anyone for an apartment," she added, since Jude had just called asking if he could pay for an apartment. But she wouldn't let him. She'd be damned. "With Rick and everything, I just feel better saving the money. Angie's with family, so we are okay for now. But if we move in with you, because it's *we*, you know that?"

He glared. "No, I completely forgot you had a child. Not that you don't bring it up all the time or anything."

She glared back. "If we don't work out, then I'll be moving out. And that's not good for Angie. At least now, I know we are good. If that happened, no telling what would happen."

Letting his head fall back, he moaned like a bored teenager. "That won't happen, though."

"You don't know that."

He gave her a look. "Maybe I do."

"How?" she laughed and he smiled before shrugging.

"'Cause I do."

Rolling her eyes, she shook her head. "Whatever, Autumn Sinclair."

His brows came in. "What does that mean?"

But she shook her head, no reason to bring up that little doozy her mother had predicted. "Nothing."

He eyed her and sat up, leaning into the phone. "Just think of how fucking great it would be? We could wake up together, eat breakfast together, you could go right out the back door to your office while I take Angie to school. We could be together. All the time."

She laughed. It would, and it would be so much easier, but she just wasn't ready for that. "I promise, I'm not that cool. You don't want to spend all your time with me."

"Negative woman. I think you're the coolest and I want you. Now. All the time."

"I swear you're like the chick in this relationship," she teased and he laughed.

"Maybe, but admit it. You'd love it here."

"In my dream home where the orgasms are endless? Um, yeah."

He threw his hands up. "See!"

"But…" she said and he held his hand up.

"But don't you think it just makes sense? We find each other, we click, you're homeless—"

"I'm not homeless!" she complained and he laughed.

"You are without a home, and I have one. I feel it's fate."

Rolling her eyes, she smiled. "I want this to work, Benji. I do. And I want us to be sure. We have to think of Angie. Don't rush it. If this is it for us, if it's *fate*, then we have forever."

He paused, sucking in a breath and then letting it out. "I don't like admitting when you're right."

"Another reason I can't move in. Let's be real. I'm always right, and you haven't accepted that yet," she teased and he rolled his eyes, running his hand down his face.

"Babe, I'm dying. I miss you."

Her lips quirked as she looked over at him for a second before looking back at the road. It sucked only seeing him on the phone, but she had to work. Now that she was getting the office back up and running, she would be hiring another designer. To afford to do that, she had to work. "I miss you too, I do. But I'm coming over tomorrow, and let's be honest, I probably won't leave till Sunday when I get Angie. Gotta figure out how I'm going to explain that to my brother."

"You act like everyone doesn't know about us."

She pursed her lips together. "I don't want to admit it and have them be right."

"You're impossible, you know that?" She stuck her tongue out at him and he laughed. "Anyway, are you coming to the game tomorrow?"

She paused. "Shit. I forgot you had a game. Do you want me to?"

"I'd love you to."

"Okay, I'll go, then."

"Cool, but since you won't move in with me, you and Angie can come over for dinner and a movie tonight."

She let out a long breath. "Benji, I haven't even told her about us yet."

"Perfect time. We can do it together."

He was so ready, so confident. If he had his way, they would come and never leave. It was really sweet and she loved how much he wanted them there, but shouldn't they, like, love each other before all that? It just seemed kind of crazy. No matter how great and amazing it sounded, she had to keep her head about this.

She had to be smart.

"Benji," she whined and he shook his head.

"Plus, I want to hang out with her before I leave. Starting Monday, I'm gone for almost two weeks."

She made a disgruntled face. He was leaving? Wait, she knew this. Jayden was leaving, too. "Boo."

"Yeah. So, tell me, what's your favorite food?"

She gave him a look. "I love all food."

"No, you have a favorite. What is it?"

She let out a breath. He wasn't going to take a no, plus, Angie would really like to see him before he left. But that meant Lucy really needed to tell Angie. She was leaving for Rick's the following day, and Lucy was sure he was going to bitch about Benji in front of her. He was just a dick that way, but she wanted Angie to hear it from her. It just worried her. What if she didn't take it well? Who was she kidding? Angie would probably pee her pants with excitement.

She loved Benji.

The problem was, if she told Angie, it was real. Her family knowing was one thing, but Angie knowing—that was real. She was doing this, she was trying, and there was no turning back. A part of her was still hesitant for good reason. Her track record in love was nonexistent, and she didn't like heartache. Plus, it all seemed too damned good to be true. Great guy who loves kids, who enjoys a lot of the same things she does, and just clicks with her? Yeah, that didn't happen to Lucy Sinclair. No, her life was hard, but with him…

It wasn't.

Clearing her throat, she shrugged. "I actually love chicken potpies the way my mom makes them."

"My specialty," he said simply, and her face twisted in disbelief.

"What? You cook?"

"Duh, I'm an alcoholic who did nothing before you. Of course, I learned to cook." She made a noise of appreciation and he grinned. "Still so against moving in?"

She laughed. "Hush. I gotta go," she said, pulling into the parking lot. "I'll call you later."

"Okay, babe, have fun," he said and she smiled before pushing end and getting her phone. She begged the butterflies to stop going crazy in her gut before she got out and went to work.

With Benji loud and clear in her mind.

Before she could reach the building, though, her phone chimed with a text. It was the dreaded group text with her brothers.

> *Jace: Rumor is Lucy is getting laid, by a real boy. Like a boyfriend.*
> *Jude: That's what I heard.*
> *Jayden: That's what I know. I saw them after they made out like little high schoolers at our niece's game.*
> *Jude: Wow. I'm speechless.*
> *Jace: Like, real life? She really kissed a guy? It wasn't a girl?*
> *Jayden: Nope, real dude. Superawesome dude too.*
> *Lucy: Really, guys? Go find something else to do other than talk about my love life.*
> *Jace: She doesn't deny it!*
> *Jude: Holy crap, our Lucy is growing up!*
> *Lucy: I hate you all.*
> *Jace: Man, he must be brave.*
> *Jude: Right? I'm surprised you haven't eaten him alive yet.*
> *Jayden: I think she tries but he puts her in her place. He's awesome, guys, really.*
> *Jude: He better be.*
> *Jace: Yeah, only the best for our sister.*
> *Jayden: Agreed*
> *Jude: Yup.*
> *Lucy: Okay, maybe I love you guys.*

They weren't really that bad, she decided as her heart warmed. She did deserve the best, and while admitting that Benji may be the best scared her, she was leaning toward that. He was great and he was so patient, but Rick still weighed heavy on her heart. He hadn't spoken to her since Saturday, even with her texting him to confirm a time for pickup. It wasn't like him to ignore her. Even if it was just a sly remark, he always answered. But all she got was silence.

It made her crazy nervous.

But then, thinking about what her brothers said and the fact that Benji would have dinner for her when she got to his house, she couldn't help but grin. Tucking her phone in her purse, she walked into the building. But once she was inside, the grin was gone and the stress was eating her alive. All the orders she had made for the job, with a company she had been using since she started her business, had resulted in their sending the wrong thing. And they couldn't get anything out for a week because most of it was on back order now.

"I understand mistakes, but this is a colossal one. I placed this order two weeks ago. You said I was good, but you sent the wrong items." Lucy said sternly, her body shaking with anger.

"We understand, but the person who took your order was new and ordered the wrong thing."

"I get that, but you need to make this right. I have to have this job done by this weekend. I want my product by tomorrow. You have to fix this, or I will be finding a new distributor."

"It won't happen by tomorrow."

"Oh, it won't? Let me speak to your supervisor," she snapped, and Tina's face was full of worry. She was the owner of the restaurant and it was her baby, one she had inherited from her grandma. She wanted to redo the whole place, give it a facelift. The grand reopening was set for the following Monday. It had to be done this weekend. "It's fine. Everything is okay," Lucy reassured her, but then she caught sight of the time, realizing that Angie had to be picked up.

Shit.

Putting her phone on speaker, she texted Jayden, but he didn't answer and her stomach dropped. Crap. Automatically, she hit Benji's name and texted him.

> Lucy: You busy?
> Benji: Never for you. What's up?
> Lucy: Can you go get Angie for me? I'm stuck at my job right now.
> Benji: Yeah, I'll leave now.
> Lucy: Thank you so much. I'm calling the school to tell them you're coming.
> Benji: Sounds good.

Putting the phone back to her ear, she picked up the landline in front of her, dialing the school and making the request. Thankfully, it was no headache. But when she hung up and the supervisor came on the line of her cell phone, Lucy was sure her head was about to be pounding.

As she yelled at the manager on the phone, she refused to even think about the fact she had just depended on someone, other than family, to pick her child up. Again.

Nope, she had way more to worry about. Plus, she knew Angie was in good hands.

"Benji! Hey!"

"Hey, sunshine," he said as the door was opened by one of the teachers who had checked his ID before Angie was able to get in. He still thought the school was extra swanky, and they weren't playing when it came to him getting Angie. He was pretty sure they were five seconds from asking for a hair sample. He appreciated it, though. It meant Angie was safe and that was good. He hadn't realized it would be this much security, especially as this was the second time he had picked her up. Maybe it was because he was in his truck and not Lucy's car with the school decal? He wasn't sure, but again, he appreciated it.

When Angie hopped into the back of his truck, exclaiming over the new booster seat he'd bought a few days ago in hopes of more outings with her and Lucy, he grinned back at her. "Your mom is working, asked me to get you."

"Oh, cool! So I get to hang with you?"

He nodded as the door shut. "Looks that way. Is that okay? Do you want me to take you to Baylor?"

"No way! Let's go!"

He chuckled as he waited for a signal to go, sending a quick text to Lucy that he had Angie.

> *Lucy: You're a godsend.*
> *Benji: Sexual favors?*
> *Lucy: Lots.*

Grinning, he put his phone down as the crossing guard started to wave him on. "How was your day? Do you have homework?"

"Yeah, I have a test tomorrow in spelling, but it was good. I played some knee ball in gym and learned some like factors. You know, elementary school. It's awesome."

"Good," he said as he chuckled, turning out onto Demonbreun. When his phone rang, he looked down to see it was Lucy. "Oh, it's your mom. Hey."

"Hey, so I don't know when I'm gonna be out of here. It could be another hour or two. Lots of stupid shit went down. Thankfully, I fixed it, but I have to wait for the next delivery. Can you take Angie to Jayden's? I don't know if we'll make it to your house tonight."

Disappointment flooded him. He'd really wanted to see her and hang with Angie. "Well, if it's cool with you, Angie wanted to hang out with me. I asked if she wanted to go to Jayden's, and she said no. So, I mean, I can keep her, and then you can come over and we'll have dinner."

"Oh, yeah. Let's do that," Angie called from the back and Lucy let out a sigh.

"I don't know. I'm not sure how late I'll be."

"It's fine, I promise," he said and then he turned so Angie didn't hear him. "I want to see you."

"Okay. I'll keep you updated."

"Cool, we will be waiting."

"Thank you. So much. Really, you really came through for me. Jayden was napping."

He smiled. "Anytime."

Hanging up the phone, he met Angie's hopeful gaze and he nodded. "We're good."

"Woo-hoo!" she cheered, bouncing in her seat. "Can we play some hockey?"

"Duh! Gotta study first and I gotta put dinner in the oven, okay?"

"Cool."

"Oh, I have to stop by the bank real fast."

"Boring," she sang and he laughed.

"It will be quick."

She nodded as he drove, heading toward the bank. "So are you still dating someone, Benji?"

He chuckled. "Why do you ask?"

"'Cause I think you should ask my mom out. I think she likes you. Don't tell her I said that."

"I won't," he laughed, shaking his head. "Why do you think that?"

"Because she smiles around you. Like, all the time. Grandma says it's nice and Mommy needs to smile more. I think so too."

"Well, I am noting your comment, and I'll report back, okay?"

"Cool," she said, nodding her head to the music. "She's really nice. And really pretty."

"I couldn't agree more."

"She's funny too."

"Is she?"

"Yeah, Grandma thinks you guys would be cute together."

"Does she?" he laughed and Angie nodded.

"River told her to stop worrying about it, but she called my uncles Jude and Jace and told them to say something to Mommy. Every time I try, she says she's gonna ground me. So I figured, since you can't ground me, I'd say something to you."

This girl was a mess. So much like her mother it was scary. The more time he spent with her, the more he fell for the mini Lucy.

As his lips curved, he scoffed. "I can't ground you?"

She paused. "Wait, can you?"

He laughed as he shrugged. "Probably, but I don't mind."

"Cool," she decided, looking out the window. "So is your girlfriend as pretty as my mommy?"

Pulling into the bank, he parked and shut the truck off. "Okay, let's go."

"You didn't answer me," she complained as he opened the door.

"Oh, my bad. Come on," he said, shutting her door and placing his hand on her back to lead her in. Pulling his wallet out as they went to the teller, he looked down at Angie and then to the teller.

"How can I help you?"

Handing her his bank card, he said, "Hey, my name is Benjamin Paxton, and I would like to open a savings account in the name of Angela Hart."

"Me?" she asked, her eyes wide, and Benji nodded.

"Yeah, for college."

"Ooh! I want to go to college like my mom and uncles did!"

"Good, 'cause you're going," he said with a nod before looking back at the teller. "A deposit of six hundred dollars will be made on the first of every month. Have that go straight into Angela's savings. Transfer five thousand into there now, please."

"Whoa! I got cash!"

Benji smiled as the teller typed away. "Yes, sir."

After getting all that taken care of, while Angie commented on everything and anything, Benji walked out, feeling on top of the world. When he told Lucy he'd do what he wanted with the money she paid him in rent, he knew it was going to go straight to Angie. Even if they didn't work out, he wanted to make sure Angie got a good start when she turned eighteen. He didn't get to give that to his beautiful Leary, who, if she were still alive, would be almost fifteen.

That hurt his heart.

Out of breath, he reached for Angie's car door and she hopped in, unaware of his internal struggle. When he got in, she asked, "Why did you do that?"

Putting the key in the ignition, he turned to look at her. "'Cause I want you to have that money when you get older."

"Yeah, but why?" she asked, smiling. "I mean, don't get me wrong, it's cool, I love money. But Mommy always tells me things don't come for free—there is always a catch."

He had to stop himself from rolling his eyes. That woman. Nodding his head, he held Angie's little green gaze. Her hair was down today, curls around her face. She wore a Taylor Swift shirt with pink leggings and sparkly silver cowboy boots. Looking at her, he wondered if Leary would have had that kind of style. Ava was very conservative. She never wore pink, or any colors, really, except black and white. Leary never wore glitter when she was a baby. Or maybe she did. He'd been too drunk to remember.

Clearing his throat, he smiled. "Your mom is very right."

"I know. She's always right. At least, she says so. Jayden says she's crazy, so do Jude and Jace. They all do. They fight a lot. Have you met the other two?"

He laughed, shaking his head. He was starting to realize the Sinclair family was a whole lot of crazy. "Not officially."

"Officially, what's that mean?"

"Like face-to-face. On the ice, yes, but not officially."

"Oh! My uncle Jace is the best player in the league."

It was like playing goalie for her; she was shooting stuff at him left and right. "I've heard."

"Yeah, so anyway, if people don't get stuff for free, then why are you giving me all this money for college? I'm seven. I've got like—" she paused to do the math "—eleven years till I go to college. Unless I graduate early like my sister, Nina. She's crazy smart and my dad says she'll graduate at sixteen. But he doesn't think I will. He said I'm lucky if I graduate, and man, that made my mom so mad. I thought she was gonna hit him. My grandpa almost did."

What a fucking slimeball. Really? Jeez. "I bet."

"I don't get to see my grandpa much. He works a lot, and he and Grandma got divorced. He's cool, though. I wonder if he'll come to one of my games."

"I don't know. I haven't met him."

"Yeah," she said simply. "So, anyway, ready to go? No, wait! Why are you giving me all this money?"

He couldn't help but laugh before setting her with a look. "Anyone ever tell you you're really awesome, Angie?"

She nodded. "Mom does and so do my uncles."

"Well, has anyone told you today?"

She thought for a moment. "Nope."

"Well, you're awesome, kiddo."

"Thanks! You too," she said, fist-bumping him, and his heart soared.

Clearing his throat, he reached out and moved a stray hair out of her face as she grinned up at him. She was missing the two teeth on either side of her front teeth, yet her smile could brighten his world. If he wasn't confident before about opening the account for Angie, he was now. It was to honor Leary's memory. "You remember how I told you about my daughter?"

Angie's brow furrowed. "Oh, yeah! Where is she? Do you not get to see her all the time?"

"No, sunshine. She died when she was two."

Angie's smile dropped and she leaned forward, her little body still as she gazed up at him. "I am so sorry, Benji."

Tapping the hand she had placed on him, he nodded. "Thanks, sunshine. But the reason why I'm giving you this money is because I never got to send her, Leary, to college. So I want to make sure that a little girl who is as awesome as she was gets to go to school."

Angie sat for a long moment, staring at him, and then she smiled. "I'm going to make you proud, Benji. I promise. For you and for your daughter."

Reaching out, he ruffled her hair. "Anyone ever say you're wise beyond your years?"

She nodded, exhaling a breath. "A few. I get that a lot. My grandma says it's 'cause I'm so smart."

Laughing, he turned in his seat. His heart was still pounding in his chest, but he felt good.

And, above all, he was starting to love life again.

"All right, Hart, let's go."

"Sounds good, Paxton."

When the doorbell rang, Benji rolled his eyes.

Surely, Lucy didn't just ring the doorbell.

"Someone's here!" Angie yelled from where she was playing NHL 15 in the living room. Shaking his head because he was pretty sure it was Lucy, he pulled the potpie from the oven and placed it on the counter, taking off his oven mitts before heading to the front door. Looking at Angie as he passed, he made a face. She was standing in his gamer chair, balancing as she played.

"Girl, sit down before you fall and bust your face," he said and she dropped down, grinning up at him as he reached for the door. Opening it, he found Lucy standing on the front porch, her hands tucked in her pockets.

"Really?" he asked and she shrugged.

"I didn't want to just walk in."

"You should have," he said as she walked past him, but she didn't get far before he took a handful of her ass. Looking back at him, she gave him a little kitten grin before Angie jumped out of the chair and went for her.

"Hey, honey, did you have a good day at school?"

"Yeah! Me and Benji played hockey all afternoon, but he made me study for, like, seven hours. I'm pretty sure I'm gonna get a hundred tomorrow."

Lucy smiled, moving Angie's hair out of her face before looking over at Benji. "That's awesome."

"Yeah, he said I can hang my test on the fridge if I do. But only if it's a hundred. Have you seen his fridge? It's huge, and did you know he cooks? Like, really cooks, Mom, like chops veggies instead of getting bags of frozen ones."

He smiled. "That was a big deal, apparently."

Lucy grinned. "I'm not much of a cook. Grandma always did all the cooking, huh?"

Angie nodded. "My grandma is the best cook ever. You should so come to dinner one night at her house."

"If I get an invite, I'm there. I love food."

"Me too!" Angie gushed, wrapping her arms around Lucy. "Mommy does too, huh, Mom?"

"I do," she said, kissing the top of her head. "I smell something yummy."

"Yes! Benji made potpie. Can you believe it? It's your favorite," Angie sang, hopping around before heading toward the kitchen.

Looking back at Benji, she smiled. "She's happy."

"Yeah, we've had a great afternoon."

She grimaced a little when Angie screamed her name. "Sorry if she's been a little wacky. Her meds usually wear off by six."

"She's been great," he reassured her, reaching out to squeeze her hand. "I can't kiss you, can I?"

She glanced to the kitchen as Angie yelled, "Mom! Come look!"

She looked back and he smiled. "Come on. I slayed that pie for you," he said, taking her jacket for her as she smiled a thanks. "Did you get everything finished?" he asked as he hung her jacket in the coat closet.

"Yeah, what a mess," she complained, shaking her head before they made their way into the kitchen. She explained how her distributor had sent the wrong items and told her they weren't going to fix it, but when she threatened to take her business somewhere else, they sang a different tune and found someone in town to deliver for her. "Thankfully, we got it done and everything is beautiful. I also get free Mexican anytime I want it."

"I love cheese dip!" Angie cheered from the counter as Lucy came to a stop at it.

"Wow, this looks amazing," she gushed and Benji smiled proudly. "Looks almost too good to eat!"

"That's what I said," Angie giggled and Benji nodded.

"She did."

Lucy laughed, her face bright as she cuddled Angie to her side. "Like mother, like daughter, huh?"

"Yup!" Angie agreed as she took the plates Benji had laid out. "Come on, let's eat. I'm starving."

Looking over at Benji, Lucy didn't move as Angie started to set the table. "It does look really good. Thank you for having us over."

"Anytime. I hope this can become a regular thing for us," he said and she grinned as Angie shrieked.

"Oh my God, please, Mom. I had so much fun today."

Lucy smiled as she took the forks and knives, heading to the table. "We'll see, okay? Benji is busy."

As he lifted the potpie, Angie looked at him and he shook his head. "Never too busy for you two."

Angie beamed before looking at Lucy hopefully. She rolled her eyes as she chuckled a bit. "Don't look at me like that."

"But, Mom! He likes us," she said in a mock-whisper and Lucy laughed, her eyes shutting as her heavenly, happy voice filled the room. Moving from the counter to the table, he stopped short, his heart jumping into his throat as Lucy laid the utensils down. She was laughing at Angie, who was grinning right back at her as she bounced in her seat. This was what he wanted. He wanted a family. He wanted laughter in his big house. He wanted late-night dinners with the people he loved.

He wanted this.

"Sit down, crazytown," she said, kissing Angie's head before falling into a chair. Angie sat her bottom in the chair. They both looked up at him and Lucy smiled. "Are you going to let us eat?"

He shook his head, remembering that he wasn't watching a dream—this was his reality. He walked to the table, setting the pie down before sitting beside Lucy. As he looked around, he saw Angie had started bouncing in her seat again before she held her hands out for Lucy's and Benji's. His heart was still in his throat as he took first Angie's hand and then Lucy's before closing his eyes and bowing his head.

Clearing her throat, Angie lowered her voice and said, "Thank you, Lord, for this nourishment and this wonderful food Benji has made us. Thank you for giving us the blessings you do, for allowing me to wake up and go to school. For my mommy's job and giving her everything she needs to make me happy. Please help my mom in finding us a house so that we aren't homeless—I mean, without a home—because Mom really wants us to have a house. Thank you for Benji, for him cooking for us and picking me up and giving me the best day ever. And maybe, Lord, if you could break him and his girlfriend up so he can marry my—"

"Lord Almighty, Angela Lynn!" Lucy screeched, and all Benji could do was laugh as he peeked up at Angie, who was wide-eyed and confused.

"What?"

"That is not something you pray for! Goodness me."

Angie's shoulders fell before she closed her eyes again. Benji grinned over at Lucy. She was shaking her head, her face bright red as Angie continued, "I'm sorry for asking for that, Lord, but I really like Benji and—"

"Amen!" Lucy declared and Angie's lips pursed in a pout as Lucy started serving them.

"I wasn't done, Mommy."

"Yes, you were," she said, still shaking her head.

Benji's groin tightened as he watched the curve of her ass when she leaned over to give Angie her plate. She was wearing one of those snug dresses with tights that he was really starting to like. Her hair was done in curls along her shoulders. She wasn't wearing that much makeup, but what she had on enhanced that already gorgeous face of hers. After she put a piece on his plate, she handed it to him and he grinned.

"Can I have two pieces?"

Lucy's lips curved before giving him another serving and then sitting down with her own piece. He waited for her to take a bite, and when her eyes fell shut, the look of pure bliss on her face as she nodded her head, he grinned.

"So, so good," she decided and Benji beamed, his chest puffing up as he took a bite.

"Thanks."

"Mom, this food is so much better than that takeout stuff Baylor is always getting."

"Angie, please," she said and Angie made a face.

"I'm just saying."

"Well, that's rude. Baylor and Jayden are giving us somewhere to stay."

Angie nodded, moving her fork through her food. "Well, if you married Benji—"

Closing her eyes, she pinched the bridge of her nose. "Angela."

"Sorry," she grumbled and Benji chuckled, until Lucy shot him a look. Snapping his mouth shut, he fought a grin as they ate. Soon they fell into easy conversation about their days, and Benji was on cloud nine. Honestly. He had never been so happy in his life as he was, sitting with two spunky girls. They were so animated, playing off each other, and it was beautiful. He wasn't sure how he was supposed to eat dinner in his big ol' house alone ever again. Not after all the laughing and joking he was being spoiled with.

When they finished, Angie ran off to play NHL 15 as Lucy started to clean. "You don't have to," he told her, but she ignored him, taking everything into the kitchen and then rolling up the sleeves of her dress before getting to work.

As he watched her, he wished he could convince her to just move in. Was it crazy? Yeah, but he really didn't care. He knew the moment he saw Lucy that she was different, and he wanted her more than he wanted anything in this world. It scared him and the guilt was there because he was really starting to think that Lucy was his soul mate. But if that was the case, then what was Ava? Because, back then, he was convinced she was the only woman for him. All that changed when Lucy came along. He wasn't sure, but he couldn't stop what he was feeling, and he wouldn't ignore it. He couldn't. He had to live; he had to be happy.

Lucy and Angie made him happy.

"Are you even listening to me?" she complained and he smiled.

"Starting my design Monday now."

She pursed her lips. "Yes, but goodness, you were spacing out. What are you thinking about?"

He looked down at his bare feet, tucking his hands in his pockets. "I don't want you guys to leave."

Chancing a look at her, he saw she was smiling and nodding. "Well, you've got Angie sold." He grinned as she shut the dishwasher. "But I need some time."

"I know."

"But this was great, really nice," she said, reaching out and taking his hand with hers. Lacing their fingers together, he moved his thumb along hers as she held his gaze.

"It was."

"Sorry we can't stay for a movie."

"No, it's fine. She's got school."

"Yeah," she said slowly. "But tomorrow, I'll have a sleepover bag, if that's still okay."

Moving toward her, he gripped her hips, pressing her into the counter. "More than okay."

Pressing her hand to his chest, she gave him a look. "Down, killer."

He chuckled, dropping a quick kiss to her nose before moving back. "When are you going to tell her?"

Lucy let out a breath. "I guess now. Shit. Why am I nervous?"

He laughed, suddenly nervous himself. "I don't know. Why? She's gonna be fine with it."

"Obviously, since she was praying for it," she said, rolling her eyes as Benji laughed, shaking his head. That girl kept him on his toes as much as Lucy did. "Angie, honey, come here."

Angie ran into the kitchen, coming to a halt, her brows rising. "Wait, am I in trouble?"

"No, crazy. Come sit down."

Angie looked from Benji to Lucy and then slowly moved to the barstool, climbing up onto it, and leaning on the counter. "Are you sure I'm not in trouble?"

"Did you do something?" Lucy asked and Angie's eyes widened.

"I-touched-Benji's-Pop-upstairs-but-it-was-a-pony!" she squealed and then slapped her hands to her mouth. "I couldn't resist. I'm so sorry."

Benji shook his head as he held in his laughter. Setting her with a look, he said, "It's fine. Don't do it again, though," he said sternly, and her eyes got even bigger.

Then she cut her gaze to Lucy's. "Can he ground me?"

"Yeah," she said and Angie's eyes widened more. "But really, don't touch his toys—er, collectibles." Angie snickered as Benji side-eyed Lucy. "Really, ponies?"

He shrugged. "I have all kinds. They're cool."

Shaking her head, she looked back at her daughter. "Anyway, we need to talk to you about something."

Angie just blinked. "What?"

"Um," Lucy said, smacking her hands together and then glancing over at Benji before looking back at Angie and clearing her throat. He looked to Lucy, waiting. Her face turned red as she struggled with her words. She was so cute when she was nervous. Finally, she spat out, "Benji and I, well, we're dating."

Angie looked from Lucy to Benji and then back to Lucy, her brow furrowed. "So you guys are getting married?"

Benji grinned as Lucy gasped. "No. Well, I don't know. Maybe. We are dating. That's it. He is my boyfriend."

Looking to Benji, she shrugged and he smiled. "We are getting to know each other, but we want you to know so if you see us kiss or hug, you won't be weirded out."

Angie made a face. "So you kiss?"

"Oh, Jesus take the wheel," Lucy muttered before covering her face.

"Sometimes, if she lets me," he said with a grin and Angie laughed.

"My dad and Heidi kiss all the time. It's gross, but I don't think it would be gross if you guys do," she decided and Benji shrugged.

"That's a plus," he said to Lucy, but she still had her face covered.

Bringing her hands down from her face, Lucy looked at Angie. "Like I said, we are dating. Is that okay? You don't have a problem with that, do you?"

Angie shook her head. "I thought you had a girlfriend?"

Benji smiled. "Yeah, your mom."

Her brow rose as Lucy glared at the side of his face. What? He wasn't going to lie to the kid.

"So you two have been dating, but no one told me?"

Still glaring, Lucy tore her gaze from Benji's to look to Angie. "We wanted to wait until we were sure we liked each other."

Angie nodded and then thought that over for a moment. Pressing her finger to her lip, she looked up at them. Benji smiled, but Lucy looked like she was about to have an anxiety attack. "So are we moving in?"

"Angela, no! We are just dating."

She squinted her eyes as she crossed her arms over her chest. "So what do I gain here? From him being your boyfriend?"

Covering her face again, Lucy moaned as Benji laughed. "You get a friend," he answered, ruffling her hair as she giggled. "Plus, I'll always make your mom smile."

She shrugged as Lucy looked over at him, a grin pulling at her lips. Angie smiled and then said, "Cool."

"Cool?"

"Yeah, cool," she said with a nod before sliding out of her chair. Lucy looked to Benji with wide eyes.

She's crazy, she mouthed and he grinned, nodding his head.

The girl was a handful for sure.

"And, Mom?" Lucy looked from Benji to Angie as she held on to the counter, rocking back and forth. "Told you prayer works."

As she walked away like she had just made the point of the century, Lucy glanced at Benji and shook her head, but he couldn't take it anymore. Reaching for her hips, he brought her in close and kissed her hard on the lips. Relaxing against him, she laid her fingers against his jaw as he moved his lips with hers. When he pulled back, he kissed her nose then her bottom lip before leaning his head toward hers.

"Was that so bad?" he asked, and she rolled her eyes.

"It was torture. That girl drives me to no end," she said, moving her nose along his, her fingers biting into his neck. "But I feel better. I don't like keeping secrets from her."

He nodded, kissing her top lip. "You know she's right."

"Good Lord, about what?"

"That prayer does work," he said, his lips curving. "'Cause I've been praying for you for the last ten years."

And thank God the big guy was listening.

Chapter SIXTEEN

Pushing through the back door, Lucy found Benji at the counter, looking up at her with wide eyes. Probably because she came through the back door like a bull in a china shop. Quirking a brow, he said, "Hey, you."

"Hey," she said, looking around frantically.

"Need something?"

"Scissors! I can't find mine anywhere."

"Did you look in the bottom drawer on the left on your workstation?" he asked as she came around the counter, searching his kitchen drawer.

She paused. "No."

"Well, they are in there," he said as she slowly rose to look at him.

"They are supposed to be in the right, top."

"Well, I didn't know that and put them in the left," he said, leaning over to kiss her cheek.

"Why didn't you ask me?" she asked, striking her hips, and he grinned.

"Because you weren't there, and I wanted it done so you could work." She rolled her eyes as he kissed her once more. "I like when you're frazzled. Really cute."

Giving him a deadpan look, she pursed her lips, eyeing the leftover potpie he was about to eat. All of a sudden, she was famished. Waggling her eyebrows, she nodded her head to it. "Hey, you gonna eat that?"

He grinned. "I am. There is some in the fridge if you want some."

She grinned, leaning into him, batting her lashes. "Can I have yours?"

He laughed. "Are you serious? Get your own."

"But yours tastes better," she whined, leaning into him more, nuzzling her nose into his jaw. "Please."

Letting out a sigh as his fork dropped, he pushed the plate to her. "You suck."

She giggled, taking the plate and the fork. "You rock. Thank you."

Leaning up for a kiss, she pressed one to the side of his face before going around the counter. "One day, I'll learn to say no to you."

Her eyes widened. "Oh, I hope not," she said with a wink, reaching for the door.

Taking a bite, she was almost out the door when he said, "Hey, want me to get Angie? So you can leave from here for practice? Or do you have it?"

She paused, thinking for a second as she chewed. She had a lot to do, but she didn't want to put him out. "If you can get her, that would make life so much easier."

He grinned, looking up as he placed a slice of potpie on his plate. "Well, I do like making your life easier, so I'll get her."

"Are you sure? No big deal?"

"No big deal," he promised, his eyes locking with hers. "I like picking her up. She's a hoot."

"She's something," she said around a bite. "Okay, I'll run by the house and get her stuff when I head to the warehouse. You are a lifesaver. Thank you."

"Anytime. Did Rick get back to you? Are you meeting him tonight, or is he coming up to the rink?"

She let out a frustrated breath, shaking her head as her heart pounded with anger. Rick never did this, never ignored her, and it was driving her insane. Communication, even if it was rude, was better than this silent crap he was pulling. "Not yet. I'm gonna call him in about an hour during his lunch break."

Benji rolled his eyes as he placed his plate in the microwave. "I don't know if I want you going alone if you have to drop her off. Maybe I can try to go. What time?"

She smiled sweetly. "Six thirty, you'll be at the rink."

"Shit. Yeah."

"Benji, I've been meeting this man for four years. I'm good. I promise."

He shot her a look as he leaned on his forearms on the counter. "That was before you had a boyfriend who refused to let you be disrespected."

Oh, heart. Yeah, I know you can't be still.

Shutting the door, she came to the counter as he watched, his lips curved before she leaned over and pressed her nose to his. "And while I love that my boyfriend wants me to be treated right and not disrespected, I can handle Rick Hart, believe me. But, thank you. For being you and for caring about me."

Moving his nose against hers playfully, he smiled. "Wow, are you feeling okay? Did you hear what you said? 'Cause I heard you actually like that I want to help and be there for you."

Meeting his gaze with a dry look, she rolled her eyes as the buzzer sounded from the microwave. "Way to go, ruin the moment."

When she tried to pull away, his hand came to the back of her head, holding her in place as he grinned widely at her. "Where are you going?"

"I've got to work, and since my boyfriend likes to tease me, I'm going back to my office. With my food."

"You mean *my* food," he corrected and she grinned as he kissed her nose. "And also, have I told you I really like when you say boyfriend? It gives me this little girlie feeling in my gut."

Grinning as she pulled back, she nodded. "Well, you are the girl, so it makes sense." As he glared, she shot him a wink before turning to go to the door. "See ya, hot stuff."

"I'll text you when I have Angie."

"Sounds good. Thanks again," she said, heading out the back door, but then she paused before shutting it. "And don't worry about Rick. I can handle him."

Looking back at her from the microwave, he shook his head. "It isn't that I don't think you can handle him, babe. It's that you shouldn't have to. That is what makes me mad and makes me want to tear him to pieces. You don't deserve that shit."

She smiled. "I know."

He nodded slowly, taking a bite of his pie. "Go to work before I take you upstairs."

She feigned shock before shaking her head. "Oh, no way, I'll never leave!"

"That's the point," he called as she shut the glass-paneled door. Holding his gaze, she turned her lips up as she waved and he grinned back. She headed for her office, not even wanting to go. She'd much rather go upstairs with Benji, lie with him, but she had things to do and she was sure he did too. With a little pep in her step as she inhaled her potpie, she closed the distance between his house and her office and realized she was smiling. For no damn reason but that Benji just made her happy.

It was odd, having someone who cared about her enough not to want her to be disrespected by anyone. Of course, her family didn't want that, but they were supposed to feel that way. She was their blood, but Benji had no ties to her. No reason other than he wanted to, and that just filled her with all kinds of feelings. To have someone want to be there. To offer to help and know they weren't put out by it. That they genuinely wanted to provide assistance, to make things easier, was really nice. And man, he loved Angie. He was just...he was just perfect and, God, that scared her to the core.

225

Because nobody that good existed.

Or at least, they didn't for Lucy.

It was sad, but she was just waiting. She knew it would happen, that moment when it would be too much—dealing with Rick, dealing with the fact that she had a kid and that Angie came first—and Benji would say to hell with it. A part of her wasn't even sure she was worth it. She was snarky, she was bitchy, but then, with him, she wasn't. Or at least, she wasn't that bad, mostly. But she knew he would run the other way sooner rather than later. For that reason, she was sure, she was hiding her heart. That was the main reason she held back from moving in with him even when it made so much sense and felt right. No, she had to be careful. Because as much as she wanted this to be forever, she was pretty sure it was only temporary.

And that made her smile disappear.

Pushing aside her worries because she needed to work, she headed through her office that was completely set up and beautiful. Benji had done an excellent job, and as Rayne sat behind her desk, a grin on her face as she worked, Lucy felt complete. She always wanted somewhere for her office that would feel like home. The little guesthouse that was now her office was home. It felt right. Just as Benji did. But she couldn't think of that right now.

No, she had work to do.

And she had to call Rick in an hour.

Deciding she really didn't want to do that, she tried to text him one more time.

> *Lucy: Are you meeting me at the rink to get Angie? She'll be done by six thirty.*

To her surprise, he actually answered.

> *Rick: That's fine.*

That's fine?

Nothing was ever fine with Rick.

As uneasiness filled her stomach, she considered texting him back. But what would that do? Nothing. It would be a waste of time, or worse, it would turn into a fight. Instead, she put her phone to the side, grabbed her scissors out of the wrong drawer, though it did make her smile, and got to work.

But the uneasiness never went away.

Especially when he got to the rink twenty minutes before he was supposed to. Her day was going so well; she had gotten a lot of work done, and Benji had hung with Angie before practice while she finished up. She hadn't even worried. She knew Angie was good, and watching Benji say good-bye, promising he would see her before he left on Monday, did things to Lucy's heart. It was a good day with the promise of a great night with his game and then having a late dinner with Jayden and Baylor.

She was excited, but one glance at Rick's face and she knew he was about to ruin her day.

He came toward her, and she held her breath as she tucked her hands into her pockets, her breath quickening as she tried to act unaffected. When he sat down, he leaned on his legs, looking out at the ice. Exhaling a breath while he shook his head, he didn't look at her as he said, "This really is a dumb sport. She's a girl—she needs to do girl shit."

Biting her top lip, she clenched her fists as she watched Angie shoot, making the goal. Shea tapped her on the head and she beamed before going to the back of the line. "She loves it. Whatever makes her happy, makes me happy."

"Whatever," he said, leaning back, his eyes still on the ice. "My lawyer contacted your dad."

"I know."

"Your dad, ever so nicely, told him to fuck off."

Nerves ate her alive as she nodded. "I know."

His neck started to get red but she didn't care. She wasn't going to just agree to something she knew would jeopardize Angie. "I feel we should do the smart thing and settle things out of court," he said.

"There is nothing to settle. Things are good the way they are."

He finally looked at her, his brown eyes blazing as he glared. "I want more time with my daughter. Maybe then you won't subject her to these men who do nothing but put thoughts in her head."

She looked away, her face scrunching up. "You have two weekends a month to spend time with her. And who are these men?"

"Any man you bring around her. She's starting to get mouthy, telling me to leave her alone, ignoring me and shit. That's not right. I want more time with her so she knows who to respect. Why won't you just give her to me?"

"Because I don't believe you really want her. To make sure she knows who to respect? Rick, she is the most respectful, sweetest kid I know. Yeah, she's wacky, but she's very respectful."

"She's insane. Always bouncing around and being so damn loud."

"Because she has ADHD. She can't help it!"

He rolled his eyes. "There you go. With your shield of made-up diagnosis… ses," he bit back and she glared.

"I'm not making up the *diagnosis*," she corrected. "It's the fucking truth. Maybe if you spent time with her, you'd realize what kind of kid she is. She tells me all she does is play with Nina when she's at your house. That you don't even really talk to her or deal with her, so I don't believe you. And if she disrespects you, it's because you don't have the time for her that is needed to establish boundaries."

"What?" he shouted. "You're gonna believe a seven-year-old over an adult?"

Lucy shot him a guarded look. "Believe my child who doesn't lie to me, who is a beautiful, God-loving child, over the man who cheated, lied, and smacked me around? Yeah, I think so."

He glared. "You are pathetic, you know that? You're just trying to keep her from me because you know she loves me more."

Lucy couldn't help it, she laughed, shaking her head. This dude was delusional. Looking at him, she held his heated gaze and her eyes pleaded. "Do you know how much I wish that were true? How I wished she loved going to your house? Spending time with you? How much I wish she didn't come home a different person because all you do is yell at her when she's there? I want you to have a relationship with her. I've wanted that, no matter what, because I know what it did for me as a child to have my parents both love me. But you care about Heidi and Nina more than you do Angie."

Her fairy-tale family ended when her dad cheated on her mom, but for a long time, Lucy loved the idea of love. Knew that she had two people behind her. Yeah, she was stubborn and did what she wanted. But she knew if she needed them, they were there. Both of them. All Angie had was Lucy...

And... Crap, was she really thinking this?

Benji.

Benji had been there more for Angie in the last three weeks than Rick had been in the last seven years.

She was going to hell for that thought.

Blistering with anger, he shook his head. "That's not true at all! I don't favor them."

"Really? Why didn't you say bye to Angie last weekend? She thought you weren't here, and that hurt her."

"That's a lie. She saw me."

"Apparently not. She asked me if you were here. I had to tell her you were because you didn't go see her."

He glared, his face flushing red as he spat out, "Because I was pissed at you."

"And because you are pissed at me, you hurt her? How does that make sense? Our issues are our issues. Don't let it bleed over to our child."

"Well, if you weren't such a bitch all the time, we wouldn't have that problem."

"Do you hear yourself? I shouldn't matter—"

"Well, when you're a shit mom and have your shit boyfriend try to cover for your crap, then, yeah, I'm gonna be mad."

"That's enough," she roared, her body breaking into a heat rash from the anger bubbling in her soul. "You will not talk to me like that. I am a good mother. I love our daughter, and she'll tell you that backward, sideways, and upside down. She loves me."

"Oh, yeah, mother of the year," he muttered, and she swore it was taking everything out of her not to beat his face.

But as she stared at the side of his head, she said, "Also, Benji has nothing to do with this. His concern is for our safety, the same way you wouldn't let anyone talk to Heidi the way you talk to me."

He scoffed. "Whatever, he's a wannabe daddy. Trying to steal my daughter."

"Are you serious? Benji would never. But, man, are you jealous, Rick? That I'm moving on? That Angie has a man to look up to?"

He scoffed. "Don't flatter yourself. I don't give two shits about you or him. And my daughter has someone. Me."

That was a lie and they both knew it. He wanted to control Lucy, he wanted her to be submissive to him, and he hated that she never was. Never would be. He was so far from a father figure for Angie, it was sad. In some fucked-up part of her, Lucy had thought maybe he could change. But the more nonsense that fell out of his mouth, the more she knew her baby daddy was a big, steamy pile of shit.

"See, I disagree. Because if you didn't care, you wouldn't worry so much about my personal life and would only worry about how our daughter feels."

"I don't, and I do only care about that."

"Then fix the problem. Make her feel welcome, and maybe I'll consider your request. Maybe we can make it a four-day weekend. But not until Angie is comfortable." She was trying to smooth things over. Trying to hold off because a custody battle was not what she wanted to get into with him. She wanted Angie to be happy. But the more and more she thought about it, the more she knew a custody battle was in her future. Because Rick was a lot of things, but he wasn't one to back down from a fight.

Glancing over at him, she found he was fuming, his fists clenched. For a second, she worried he was about to hit her. She could see it in his eyes, that hatred she had seen before. But he looked away, almost growling as he seethed. "She is comfortable. If she isn't, it's your fault."

"How?" she asked. "How in the world is that my fault?"

"'Cause you and your dumb family have turned her against me."

"You are delusional."

"It's cool. I'm documenting it, and I will get my daughter back."

"You never had her," she said simply. Really, she knew she should just let it go, but like him, she wouldn't back down either. Which was probably a big part of the problem. "This parenting plan has been in place since we split. Even in the beginning, when you told me you couldn't keep Angie the whole weekend 'cause it was too much on you and Heidi with having Nina, I let it go. I didn't demand my child support, I didn't push her on you guys, I raised our child. When you decided you wanted to keep her the whole weekend, I allowed it, because it was the parenting plan. I didn't ever complain; I let it be, especially when it took you two years to catch up on all the child support. I have been very understanding when I didn't have to be, when I should have had your ass thrown in jail."

He scoffed, shaking his head. "Why are you bringing up the past? It's over, and you weren't as easy as you said. You constantly reminded me that you always had her, that you needed your money and shit. Don't lie."

"Are you serious? I never reminded you. I was good. I worked, I went to school, and I took care of Angie and me. I didn't need you then, and I don't need you now. I just want Angie to be happy, and for some reason, I think having you in her life will do that."

She was starting to rethink that, though.

"You're wrong. Angie needs me. Mom and me both say Angie would be better off with me and Heidi."

Ah, his mom. The lovely Mrs. Hart. "Well, when your mom pushes Angie out of her twat, then she can have some say. But until then, we will follow the parenting plan."

Shaking his head, he looked out at the ice once more and scoffed. "What, you get a boyfriend and you're all high and mighty? All of a sudden you're good?"

Don't answer him. Ignore him, she begged herself but, yeah, it didn't help. "I don't need anyone. I've always been good on my own."

"Whatever, you're pathetic. You depend on your family for everything. Now you'll do the same to him, and he'll leave. No one can handle you."

Motherfucker. Glaring, she sucked in a breath and stood up, her body shaking with rage. "I'll get Angie."

"Aw. Did I hurt your feelings? Oh, wait, you don't have any."

Ignoring him, she walked around the rink, waving at Angie to come on. Shea looked over at her and concern filled his face. Skating toward her, he opened the side door. "You okay?"

"Yeah, Angie's dad is here. She's gotta go. Every other Friday, it will be like this."

He nodded slowly as Angie slipped past him. "See ya, Coach."

"Bye, Hart, see ya tomorrow."

She smiled as she nodded, heading toward the lobby to change. Looking back at Shea, Lucy smiled. "Bye, Shea."

He looked from Lucy to Rick and shook his head. "Bye, see you tomorrow. Her game is at ten fifteen."

He said it loud enough for Rick to hear it, but he was walking away, heading to the lobby. Nodding to Shea, she sent another wave and then followed Rick and Angie. When she entered the lobby, Angie was already almost done, putting all her stuff in her bag as Rick stood by, playing on his phone.

"Her game is at ten fifteen," Lucy reminded him.

Without looking up, he said, "According to the parenting plan, I don't have to bring her."

Lucy's brows rose as Angie's eyes widened in protest, looking between her parents. Holding her hand up to ward off Angie's potential freak-out, she glared at Rick.

"Yes, but I would think you'd want to bring her since it's something she enjoys."

"We'll see, but I have stuff planned tomorrow," he snapped, looking up and glaring. "Let's go, Angie."

"But, Dad, I want—"

"I said, let's go." His voice was chilly, his body rigid as he looked away. Angie looked to Lucy, tears in her eyes, and Lucy's heart started to jackhammer in her chest.

"Rick," Lucy called when he started to walk away. "You guys will be here at nine thirty, right? If not, I'll pick her up and bring her. She wants to come. This is important to her."

"Whatever, Lucy. I said we'll see. You're the one who wants to follow the parenting plan."

Fucking dick. "And I'm telling you she wants to come. This is important to her," she stressed, but Rick just rolled his eyes.

"Let's go, Angie."

"But, Dad—"

"I won't say it again, kid," he reprimanded and Lucy snapped.

"Don't take out your anger for me on her," she yelled and Rick glared, shaking his head.

"Goodbye, Lucy. Let's go, Angie."

"Wait—"

"Wait?" he seethed. "For what? You trying to not let me take her? 'Cause we can call the cops."

She scrunched up her face. "What the heck? I'm trying to talk to you!"

"Well, I don't want to talk to you. Now say bye to her so we can leave, Angie. Heidi and Nina are waiting."

Angie looked to her mother, fear in her eyes, and Lucy's heart dropped. This was such bullshit. "Hey, no worries, come here," she said, bringing Angie into her arms. "I'll see you in the morning. Call me if he can't bring you. I'll come get you. Okay?" Angie nodded, but she was on the verge of tears. "Hey, don't worry. You're good. Have fun, okay? Call me if you need anything."

Rick let out a frustrated breath, and Lucy kissed Angie's cheek hard. Lucy didn't want to give Angie to him. She felt in her soul it was a bad idea, but she had no choice. She wanted him to honor the parenting plan, which meant she had to too. Kissing Angie once more, she hugged her and then let her go, even though Angie kept holding on to her.

Rick had already started walking away when Angie looked up to her and asked, "Do I have to go?"

Lucy's heart just broke.

"Yeah, baby, I'm sorry," she said, her voice cracking as she hugged her tightly.

"But what if he won't bring me?"

"Then call me. I'll come get you."

"But what if he won't let me? Just take me home now."

"Honey, I can't. It's his weekend. It's fine. I'll see you in the morning."

Angie only nodded as Rick called, "Come on. Now."

Looking up at her, Angie pleaded with her eyes, but what was Lucy supposed to do?

She had to let her go.

Tapping gloves with his teammates as the Assassins gathered in the locker room, Benji went to his locker and sat down, a grin on his face. What a way to start the night. With a win. After kicking some Penguins' ass where Tate got a shutout, Benji was feeling good. He hadn't scored but he had four assists for the night, highest of his career. Which was freaking awesome. He was killing it, and he and Jayden were clicking better on the ice. Things were good.

Next stop, late dinner with his girlfriend and then a long night of sex.

Yes, Benji was a happy man.

"Great game, Paxton," Sinclair said, tapping his glove as he sat.

Benji nodded, feeling on top of the world as he threw his gloves to the glove collector to dry them. "Thanks, man. Great game."

Sinclair grinned as he leaned back, sucking in a long breath as Coach came in to do his end of game speech. When he singled out Benji, he beamed, feeling real good. He listened intently as Coach stressed how they needed to play like they had tonight for the next two weeks on the road trip. They were facing some tough competition during the road trip, but Benji had no worries. They were going to kick some ass.

But first, he was going to spend the weekend with Lucy. Man, he couldn't wait to see her. He was pretty sure he played so well because he knew she was there. Watching him. He still owed her a goal, but he had done well tonight. Hopefully, she enjoyed herself. When Coach clapped his hands, they all joined in as he walked out, fist-pumping in unison with them. Leaning back, Benji was all smiles as he exhaled a breath, reaching for his phone to text Lucy that he'd be out soon.

Peering over at him from his locker, Jayden asked, "Hey, bro, where we going to eat?"

But Benji wasn't listening. No, his shoulders had slumped as he read a text from Lucy.

> Lucy: I'm so sorry. I won't be at the game and I'm really not in the mood for dinner. Text me when you are on your way home and, if you want, I'll come over. I really would like to come over. I got into it with Rick.

"I guess nowhere," he said and Jayden's face twisted.

"I thought we were going out?"

"Yeah, I guess Lucy and Rick got into it. She doesn't want to go out. Wasn't even here tonight."

Jayden's face changed to concern. "Is she okay?"

Benji shrugged as he hit Lucy's name to call her. "Not sure."

Jayden let out a long breath, falling back into his locker. "I hate that dude."

"Hey," she answered and he leaned on his legs. "Sorry I'm not there."

"No worries, are you okay?"

She hesitated for a second, and he could hear the pain in her voice as she said, "Not really. I've eaten four boxes of Girl Scout cookies I had hidden away, but they aren't helping."

"Okay, I'm leaving in about thirty. Want to meet me at the house?"

"Yeah, I would really like that."

"Okay, I'll see you soon."

"I'm really sorry, Benji."

"Don't be. It's fine," he said and he wasn't lying. So she didn't come and they wouldn't go to dinner. That was all trivial to the fact that she was upset. "Is Angie okay?"

Her voice broke and it gutted him as she whispered, "I think so."

His stomach ached with uneasiness. "See you soon."

"Okay," she said as he hung up and then started getting undressed so he could shower.

"Well?"

"I don't know details, but she sounds crushed. I'm meeting her at my house."

Jayden nodded. "Well, let me know if we're going to go on a manhunt."

Benji nodded because, if he had his way, that's exactly what he'd want to do. He just wanted the dude gone, but he was sure that wouldn't happen. Throwing down his girdle, he reached for his towel and said, "Will do."

After getting dressed and saying good-bye to the guys, Benji headed to his house, anxiety eating him alive. He had no clue what was going on, but this was the first time he had heard Lucy that upset. She sounded helpless, distraught, and that wouldn't fly with him. He was really getting tired of Rick, and something needed to change. Like he needed to disappear or something. He was going to have to sit down with the guy. Or beat his face in. One of the two. He prayed it wouldn't come to the latter. He wanted to handle this like adults. The only thing that mattered was Angie.

Getting to his house, he found that Lucy was already there. Parking beside her car, he got out, locking his doors, and headed through the back door into the kitchen. The downstairs was dark, and that worried him.

"Lucy?"

"Upstairs," she called as he walked past her shoes and noticed her coat lying over the counter. Reaching for it, he took it to the coat closet and hung it up before heading upstairs. Taking the stairs two at a time, he got to the top quickly. When he looked down the hall to find Lucy lying on his bed on her belly with her face toward him, his stomach dropped.

She had been crying.

"Aw, you're not naked," he called teasingly, hoping like hell he could make her smile as he walked toward her.

She shrugged, not returning his smile, not that he expected her to. Still, his heart remained in his stomach. "Sorry."

Pursing his lips, he toed out of his shoes and climbed over her, taking her in his arms and cuddling her close. She wrapped her arms around his torso, nuzzling her nose into his chest, clinging to him. "What happened?"

Shaking her head, she sucked in a deep breath, filling her lungs before letting it out slowly. Closing his eyes, he listened as she told him what happened at the rink, what Rick had said, and how Angie had looked at her. He listened, he did, but it was hard when her voice broke and her tears soaked his tee. All he saw was red. All he wanted to do was rip Rick limb from limb. How dare he? How could he be so heartless to Angie? Hockey was important to her, and he didn't care? What kind of man doesn't care what makes his daughter happy? Benji would kill for the chance to make Leary happy again. And this man—no, this scum—was wasting this precious chance of loving a piece of himself?

It was sickening.

But what was more stomach-turning was listening to Lucy cry for her daughter.

"I didn't want to let her go, Benji. I didn't, but it's legal, you know? I can't say she can't go. No matter if I think she doesn't want to go. I'm not even sure if she has to go. I just don't know," she cried, clinging to him, and he held her close, dusting kisses along her temple. "I don't know what to do, and I don't know how to fix it. I don't understand why he is being like this. Is it you? Is it because I'm finally moving on? Or is it because he's just a jackass and he doesn't like that Angie is more vocal now? Telling me when she is not happy with him. I just don't know. He wants her to know to respect him."

"What a douche." It could be any of those reasons, and that was just sad. Angie was a great kid. Very respectful. Honest. Sweet. Wacky. The dude was worthless, and Benji hated that for both of them. "Lucy, I'm sorry. I'm completely speechless. He's such a dick."

"He is," she agreed, nuzzling her nose to his. When she opened her eyes, they were full of pain, watery, and just so damn sad it hit him straight in the gut. "What do I do?"

He could only shake his head. He had no clue. "Have you called your dad? Isn't he your lawyer?"

She looked away, her shoulders falling. "Not yet. I will tomorrow. I was too upset to speak to him tonight, and I just hate talking to him. I don't want to need him. Maybe I should find another lawyer?"

"Yeah, and I understand, but your dad knows the case. He's been there since the beginning, right?" She nodded, her eyes welling up with tears. "Then maybe you should stick with him. He'll fight for Angie because, surely, he loves her."

She leaned her head to his chin, and he just wanted to make her feel better. His heart was jackhammering in his chest, and he was unsure of what to do. He wanted to make the pain go away. He wanted her to smile. But how? What could he do?

"You're right, but it's just… I don't want to put Angie through all this. I don't think it's fair to her. She's at the age now where she knows what's going on. She knows when I'm sad, when I fight with him. And dragging him into court is going to put the spotlight on her. I just don't want to hurt her, but I also can't fail her."

He nodded as she sat up, crossing her legs and running her hand down her face. Moving his hand into hers, he laced their fingers. "But what is best for Angie?"

Her lip trembled as she shook her head. "I don't know. I want it to be easy. I want him to be a good man and love his daughter. I pray all the time that he'll change, but he won't. And I don't know if I'm hurting her more by leaving her there with him or taking her away. But the look in her eyes, Benji, it was like having the air knocked out of me."

"Does she want to go there?"

"I don't know. Some days I think so, but then some, I don't. Tonight, she most definitely did not want to go, but that's 'cause he was so iffy about hockey tomorrow, I'm sure." Running his hands through his hair, he met her worried gaze. "Am I jumping the gun? Am I freaking out for nothing? Maybe he was just being a dick, but tomorrow will be fine?" She was hopeful, but he was pretty sure the dude was a dick twenty-four seven.

"I don't know, babe."

She made a sound of frustration as she covered her face with her hands. "I just wish I'd never met him. No, I don't regret Angie, but damn him, I regret him. More than anything."

Now is not the time to ask. It isn't. Don't ask. Do not ask.

"Can you tell me what happened between you two, baby?" he asked and he cringed. Apparently, he didn't know how to talk himself out of stuff. She looked up and his eyes held hers. "'Cause I really don't understand how someone can treat their child and their child's mother like this. I cannot imagine."

"Because you're a decent guy, Benji. Not everyone is cut from the same cloth as you."

"I understand that, but if Ava and Leary were alive, and our situation was like yours, I would do right by them. I would be a man about it."

She looked down, moving her fingers along the back of his hand. "I know that, which is why I think you're really amazing."

"Well, thanks." As he watched her, she continued to trace the back of his hand, her lips moving but no words leaving her mouth. Her neck was turning red, her face flushed from her tears as she struggled with what she wanted to say. It was painful to watch, and finally, he said, "Do you not want to talk about it?"

"Not really."

"Okay."

His voice was rough, unsure what to say next. He wanted to know. He wanted to know that part of her not only so he would understand Rick, if there was a way to understand him, but because that was the last part of her he didn't know. He wanted to know everything about her. He wanted her to be open with him, to fully trust him.

He wanted to find a way to help.

"But I should," she whispered, leaning into his hand. "Because you deserve to know."

He looked up then as a tear rolled down her cheek. "I don't want you to tell me if you don't want to."

"No, I do," she said softly, another tear sliding down her cheek. "I just hate talking about him. About what he did to me and Angie. I hate strolling down memory lane when it comes to Rick."

He could tell, so bringing the back of her hand to his lips, he kissed it softly before saying, "Don't worry about it, then."

He wanted to know, but he refused to put her under any more stress than needed. Being Lucy, though, headstrong and stubborn, she shook her head and swallowed hard. He watched her as she sat for a moment, breathing in and out. When she looked up, a haunted expression swirled in those deep green eyes.

And Benji knew he was in for a doozy.

Chapter
SEVENTEEN

She cleared her throat, and Benji watched as she struggled with the words, his heart pounding in his chest.

"I met Rick in high school," she said then, exhaling his name, but not in a good way. Almost in a disgusted way. Like his name was just the nastiest thing she could have had in her mouth. "He was the bad boy from the trailer park who wanted to do bad things. With me. I was eighteen, straight A's, captain of the softball team, and I was going to go to law school like my daddy did. Problem was, I was also going through that rebel phase since my dad told me to keep my head in the game, not to veer off course 'cause I had law school to worry about. I didn't want to keep my head in the game, though. I wanted to have fun because, for the last four years, I had done what I was told and everything that was expected of me. Enter Rick. He had a motorcycle that, looking back, I'm sure wasn't safe, but I loved riding on the back of that thing. Pissed my parents off, but I was having fun."

A small smile pulled at her lips. "I was a relationship girl, didn't have sex until I was with the guy for a while. But Rick, he had me in the back of my car by day two. He just had a way about him. We had sex every chance we got. Young, stupid, kid sex that led to Angie. I freaked because I was supposed to go to law school and I had plans, but Rick promised we'd be good. That I had changed him, that he'd marry me as soon as he turned eighteen. He'd get a job and we'd be fine. Seemed like a sound plan, so I went home and I told my parents, and they lost their shit. They both hated Rick with everything inside of

238

them. Told me he was using me because he was the poor kid and I was the rich kid. Told me to dump him and they would help me raise the baby so I could still try to live my dreams. I was such a brat and said no, that I loved him. But, really, I didn't. I just didn't want to seem like a failure."

She exhaled, shaking her head. "We graduated and I was six months pregnant with Angie. We got married in a quick courthouse wedding that neither of my parents attended. Broke my heart. I stopped talking to them because of it. I moved in to his trailer with him and his mom. I think that's when things when south, when I lost my confidence, lost all hope. Because, Lord, she was awful to me. I know you may find this hard to believe, but I was pretty snarky and sassy all the time, and she hated it," she said with a grin and he smiled.

"You? Never."

Her smile fell off as she looked down at their hands. "She told him that no woman should talk to her husband that way, that he needed to put me in my place. Blah, blah, blah. She even smacked me once. Right across my face because I told her I wasn't cleaning up after all of them when they had a party the night before. I left when she did that. But of course, Rick talked me into coming back. Said our baby needed both of us 'cause he knew what it was like not to have a dad. But, in retrospect, I know that's when shit got really bad."

Looking up, she shook her head as she looked into his eyes. He was hanging on every word she was saying, unsure how someone as beautiful and strong could end up like that. "I was so stupid. I still can't believe I stayed as long as I did. I tried to go to school, I did. But it didn't work out 'cause Rick always had my car, going to 'work,' and I wouldn't have a way to school. It was sad, and I let him ruin my dreams.

"My dad offered to take me back in, that he'd pay for my schooling, the whole nine if I divorced Rick and came home. I was so stubborn that I wouldn't accept it, saying I loved him. At that point, I really think I might have. I'm not sure. And then when I was in labor and I had Angie, I was in the room with my family. They were all loving on us because not only was it a new baby, but because they hadn't seen me in months. A woman walked into the room—"

Her nose crinkled a bit as she shut her eyes, slowly shaking her head. "Heidi, it was Heidi who walked into the room. Rick was downstairs getting me something to eat—or really, hiding from my dad and brothers—and she walked in. She asked if I was Lucy Hart, Rick's wife. I had noticed her a few times; she lived about nine trailers down from us. She was a few years younger than us, went to school with us, but I never paid her any mind. I was living in hell, why would I?" she added with a humorless laugh. "But I said, yeah, that's me, and she goes, 'My name is Heidi Slattery, and I've been sleeping with Rick for the last eight months. We're pregnant.' She opened her coat, and sure as shit,

she was pregnant. Big and pregnant."

"What the hell, Lucy? Really?" Benji said then and she rolled her eyes. "So Nina and Angie are—"

"Two months apart," she said, shaking her head. "I wasn't even shocked. I didn't cry or anything, but my dad and mom freaked the fuck out. I mean, they were cussing, screaming, and my brothers, bless them, Jace had no clue what was going on, but Jayden and Jude did. They tried to fight Rick, but he left. Left me at the hospital."

"He left you?"

"Yup, and his brand-new baby. My dad convinced me to go home with them. I was about to leave, but Rick showed up the day I got released and told me that he hadn't come back before because of my family. That he loved me, to come home, that he was sorry, Heidi meant nothing to him, blah, blah, blah. It was a dumb mistake, he loved me. And my dumb ass believed him. I think I was scared. I didn't want to be the statistic. Now, I'm proud of my life and Angie, but then, I was scared. So I went home with him." Wiping away her tears, she looked up at him and all he could do was stare at her. She was so strong. So amazing, it blew his mind that she was that girl at one time. "For the first two years of Angie's life, Rick did nothing. He claimed he worked, but I never saw a lick of money. I was constantly borrowing money from my parents to get Angie the things she needed and working side jobs, tutoring the kids in the trailer park, and cleaning houses because I could take Angie with me. He hardly ever helped me. Bless her, she had such bad colic, and he would just leave. Let me deal with it as his mother yelled at me to 'shut that baby up.'"

When she paused, Benji was fuming, his body shaking with anger as he watched her come undone. Holding her breath, she let it out quickly and closed her eyes, shaking her head as the words played in her mind. He wanted to ask her to stop, but he knew she wouldn't. But yet, he said roughly, "Lucy—"

"He never hit me before, though," she said then, looking over at him, the tears spilling onto her cheeks. "Not really. He'd push me or act like he was going to, but he never did. I knew it wasn't right, and I knew I deserved better, but I didn't want my parents to look at me as a failure. I had already failed out of college because I didn't go, and I didn't want to disappoint them further with a failed marriage. So I figured I'd stay until I could save some money. But then I found out he was still with Heidi. Like full out. When he wasn't with me, he was with her, raising her baby. All his money went to her, and he was also promising her that he would leave me. That he felt sorry for me and he stayed 'cause my family had disowned me. Not true. I stayed because I was embarrassed. I heard it from her cousin whose kid I tutored. I know, it's like some backwoods reality show," she said, shaking her head as she scoffed. "I was trailer trash, and I knew it. Talk of the trailer park, Lucy Hart. Well, that was it. He wasn't going to do that to me. It was Angie's third birthday, and this wasn't going to go on any longer. I was going to confront him and he was going to choose us, or I was gone. I should have just left but, eh, you live and you learn. But he came home, I told him what was going to happen and, Benji…he whooped my ass."

Benji's fists clenched as he watched her close her eyes, the tears spilling down her cheek. Reaching out, he wiped them away and whispered, "Jesus, Lucy."

"Oh, yeah, he made sure I felt every punch, every kick, and every slam of my head into that wall. I actually put a hole in the wall with my head. My child sitting two feet away from me in her birthday dress, watching the whole thing go down. She didn't know what was going on—and doesn't even remember, praise God—but his momma saw it and she did nothing. It took the neighbor, seeing him punching me through the kitchen window, to come over. He pulled Rick off me and dragged him outside where he kicked his ass, from what I came to find out later.

"Apparently, his momma went out to help him, and I passed out from the pain. When I woke, the trailer was empty, Angie was still sitting next to me, crying, shit coming out the side of her training pants, and even though I couldn't see out of one eye, I packed all our stuff, called my mom, and I went home. Never looked back."

Reaching for her, he pulled her into his arms and on top of him, running his hand up and down her back. "I told Rick I never wanted to see him again, and that was that. Dad drew up the divorce papers, and he married Heidi after he signed them. I was convinced I'd never see him again, but then my dad put in the request for child support, saying Rick was going to pay for his child. But Rick said he wasn't paying for some kid he didn't see, so then he got visitation. I tried to cry that he had beaten me and I worried about the safety of my child, but because I didn't make the report when it happened and I had no proof other than my word, the court awarded him visitation. I thought I was done, but I wasn't. And now I'm paying for it. Every time I have to deal with that man."

"Lucy, you were young. How could you have known?"

"My dad told me, numerous times, the day I came home to go to the cops, but I ignored him. I was so embarrassed, my brothers were freaked out, my mom cried a lot, and my dad wanted to skin him. At first, Rick would only keep her for an hour at a time since he had a toddler at home too, and I never said anything. I got my kid and I was on my way. You know? I never pushed him for child support because I knew he didn't have it. I was deathly scared of him. That if I asked, he'd beat me up again. He wouldn't meet me at my mom's, and he had a restraining order on my family 'cause he claimed they threatened him. They had, and because of that, I had to go to him alone. I was terrified of him until Angie was about four. My dad was tired of me being scared, so he took me to get a gun, and that was that. If he touched me, I was going to shoot him, simple as that. I never had problems, though. He was always rude, calling me worthless and shit, but he'd be there to pick her up, and he dropped her off. Always on time, but he never asked for more time. Angie loved playing with Nina, so I figured we were good.

"But in the last two years, it's gotten worse. With the whole ADHD thing, her having anxiety, she was telling her teacher that she didn't want to leave me because her daddy was mean to her. Rick would tell her she was stupid and all this other crap. The school called DCS, and when they went to their home, Heidi lied, called my kid a liar, and Rick said I was brainwashing her. I wasn't, and when they came into my home with my family, they knew he was lying. But they didn't have proof, and all I had was hearsay. That year was hard. Lots of counseling and lots of documenting what was said between us because they wanted proof, something I still do. When they finally got her meds right, it was awesome. From then on, she was great and she was happy, but he tells her all the time that she's insane and that's why she needs meds. Says it's all my fault, which sucks, but Angie knows it's not. Or at least, she tells me she knows," she said with a smile, running her fingers through her hair.

"I've considered taking him back to court, to just cease everything, but Angie did like going over there. Though now, I'm seeing that things are different, and I'm going to have to have a talk with her, I guess, because I can't do this anymore. I won't do this anymore. But it freaks me out that he honestly thinks he can get full custody. Or fifty-fifty. His momma hit the lottery a couple years back, and now she thinks she has money to sling around. So I'm sure this is her doing because she hates me so, but it still makes me nervous. I'm not really sure what to do. I don't want to drag my kid through a custody battle. Not only for her sanity and well-being, but I don't want things to get nasty because—" She paused, looking away, the tears running down her face faster.

"Because?" he asked, lifting her face so he could see her eyes.

"Because, for once, I'm finally happy. And I'm sure he'll drag you into it, and then you'll be gone."

His brow furrowed. "Where am I going?"

She gave him a look. "The other direction, surely. No one wants to deal with that."

Still confused, he asked, "Are you in the other direction?"

"Benji, come on. You'll hightail it away from me and Angie. Haven't you seen custody battles? They are scary."

"No, I won't," he said, louder than he meant to. Her eyes widened as he held her gaze. "I'm behind you, a hundred percent. That dude won't chase me off. I told you, I'm digging you, and I'm not going anywhere. I'll be there for you and for Angie."

"You don't know that, Benji," she said then, shaking her head. "It's easy to say now, but it could all change when it goes down."

"Um, I do know, but I'm not arguing that with you. Here's what I think," he said as she looked back at him. "Let's see how tomorrow goes. If it goes the way you think it'll go, call your dad. If it doesn't, when Angie comes home Sunday—I'm going with you to pick her up—then you can talk to her and go from there. You know what's best, Lucy. You know what needs to be done, and no matter what, I'm here for you. One hundred percent." She bit into her lip as a tear rolled down her nose, dropping onto his. Smiling, he wiped it off and said, with the hopes of making that face shine, "You're snotting on me."

She nodded, her lips curving just the slightest amount as she nuzzled her nose into his chest. "Because you're so great. Really, thank you for listening to me."

"I'm great because I have someone I want to be great for. Thank you for opening up to me."

"It wasn't easy," she said and he grinned.

"I could tell."

"I bet you're disappointed in me, huh?"

His brows touched as he shook his head in disbelief. "Why in the hell would I be disappointed in you? You trusted him, loved him, and he fucked you over. How is that your fault? If anyone should be disappointed in anyone, it should be you in me. I'm the drunk whose family got killed because I'm an idiot."

She eyed him and then nodded. "I'm not disappointed in you. I'm proud, because you aren't that man anymore."

His heart stopped in his chest. "And I'm proud of you for getting out and becoming who you are. Which is one hell of a mom and a woman. You know what's best for Angie—you don't settle for shit. Don't forget that."

She leaned her head to his and closed her eyes. "I just don't want to hurt her."

"You won't. If anything, you'll make her life better."

"You think so?"

"I know so," he said sternly. "Like I said, you know what's best and what needs to be done. Ask your mom, your brothers, they'll tell you the same, Lucy. You're a strong woman. You've got this."

Her eyes were hopeful as she nodded slowly. "Yeah, I do. I've got this," she repeated, her words full of conviction as she held his gaze.

"Good. Now, come here. Give me a kiss and let's go to sleep."

She eyed him, her nose against him. "Go to sleep?"

"Well, I mean, I'm down for some loving if you are."

Threading her fingers into his hair, she smiled against his lips, but it didn't reach her eyes. "Well, you're in luck, 'cause I want the sex."

His lips curved, and his hands came onto her ass. He knew she just wanted the distraction, and that was fine. He could give her that. "Ooh, I like the sex."

Sputtering with laughter then, she leaned on him, kissing his nose. "Dork."

Rolling her over, he pressed into her. He figured he didn't have the right answers for her when it came to Rick, but he had the power to take her to another world. To make her forget, if only for a short amount of time. Looking into her beautiful face, he saw a gorgeous woman, but also very troubled one. He saw strength too, and he knew, like everyone always said, she was going to be okay.

But this time, he was aiming for something higher.

He hoped she'd be great, because he was going to be behind her, supporting her and loving her.

God, he loved her. He loved her so much it hurt, but as he gazed into those clouded green eyes, his heart hurting from the stress she was going through, he knew that his chance to tell her would come.

Kissing her nose, he smiled and whispered, "You wouldn't have me any other way."

"I sure wouldn't," she whispered back, her lips moving against his. "Thank you, Benji."

But before he could say anything, her lips came crashing into his, and as their bodies moved together, he knew he was going to prove her wrong.

That he wasn't going anywhere.

Well.

That was hard.

She'd laid it out there.

Every single thing.

The good…er…well, there was no good, just a whole lot of bad and ugly.

But she told him, and it felt good. Really good, and of course, that surprised her. Not even her family knew what really happened to cause Rick to beat her to a bloody pulp, only that he had beat her. But now Benji knew. She was worried he would judge her, think she was stupid to stay with Rick for as long as she had. Hell, she thought she was stupid. But he didn't. His eyes held nothing but concern and tenderness in their gray depths. He didn't talk; he just listened. He was her rock and it was so refreshing, so perfect. As she lay in his arms, looking into his eyes as her body still vibrated from her orgasm, his fingers moved along her jaw. She was pretty sure she was falling in love with him.

Crap. She was.

Her heart stopped as she wondered if she should let herself fall.

Don't. It could be a trap. He'll just leave. Watch.

Maybe he won't. Maybe he really is saying the truth when he says he won't go anywhere. That he wants you. Lean on him

No, no man has ever done you right. They all fail you. He will too. Don't lean. You are the only one who can take care of you and Angie.

But Benji is different. He's a good man. You deserve a good man. Let him in.

Closing her eyes, she squeezed them shut tightly, wanting the voices to leave. She didn't want this. She didn't want to go back and forth; she just wanted it to work. To be right. Thankfully, the voices left, or maybe she was done being crazy. When she opened her eyes, Benji was watching her. His eyes were half-lidded and oh so sexy as he eyed her.

"Internal struggle?"

She grinned. "Something like that."

"Tell me," he urged, his hands holding her close.

She smiled, nuzzling her nose against his chin, her eyes drifting shut. "Just thinking how great you were about the whole thing with Rick."

"How else would I be?"

"You could have judged me."

"That's stupid. Why would I do that?"

"'Cause I was an idiot."

"You were young, you didn't want to fail, that's understandable. You're still like that."

She smiled. "I think of it as driven."

"Yeah, to the extreme. You're so worried about failing everyone else that you don't think about yourself."

"Well, aren't you Mr. Know-it-All?" she accused, lifting her head to meet his smiling face.

"You also cover your real feelings with sass. It's pretty funny to watch."

She glared. "Are you teasing me?"

"No, just pointing out the obvious."

"You mean my flaws?"

He scoffed. "Those are not flaws, those are what make you unique, amazing, and beautiful."

Her lips curved as she slowly nodded. "Well, then."

He bit the tip of her nose, and her giggles filled the room. Moving her leg up his, she hooked the other one over his hip as his hand slid up her leg, his eyes boring into hers. "Here's a secret, but don't read into it. I think you're starting to let me in a bit."

She grinned, knowing he was right. "You think?"

"Yeah, I do," he said with a smug grin, leaning back into the pillows as his hand moved up and down her back. "I like it too."

"I bet."

Eyeing her, he shrugged. "Maybe you'll be ready to move in with me soon?"

She rolled her eyes, shaking her head. "Benji…"

"Come on, you know you want to."

"I'm not entertaining that right now," she decided and he laughed, rolling on top of her, falling between her legs before taking her by the ribs. Looking at him with wide eyes, she said, "You tickle me, I'm not in control of what I'll do. I have broken Jayden's nose twice. Keep that in mind, Paxton."

His face twisted in horror. "Twice?"

She nodded. "I don't like to be tickled."

"Jeez," he said, moving his hands up to her bare breasts, his weight welcome against her. "Fine, no tickling. But give me a time frame. What are you thinking?"

"Time frame for what?" she asked, laughing at his expression. He didn't have his contacts in or his glasses on, so he was squinting. Looking adorably dorkish with his hair falling in his eyes. Reaching for his glasses off the nightstand, she put them on his face, and he smiled.

"Thanks, but give me a date, a time when I can bring it up again. Or I swear, I'll ask you every day to move in with me."

"Benjamin, no!"

He paused. "That's hot, the way you say my full name. You should do that more."

"Jesus, you're infuriating!"

"Shh, give me a time frame. A month?"

She shook her head. "No."

"Two months?"

"Benji."

"Three months?"

"I swear, you are impossible. Why are you rushing this? Just let it ride."

"'Cause it's what I do. I rush the goal to score. You are the ultimate goal, and I want to score."

"You just did," she said dryly and he laughed.

"Plus, I'm tired of the expiration date you try to throw on us. I want something to look forward to, something we decide is the next stepping stone."

"Or," she challenged, "we can just let it happen."

He gave her a look. "If we did that, nothing would ever happen."

She considered that and then shrugged. "You could have a point."

"Exactly. No, come on. Three months?"

Rolling her eyes, she shook her head. "Yes. Three months. We will revisit this notion in three months, you crazy."

He nodded, visibly calculating in his head. "So end of February."

"Oh." She paused. "I thought you meant the length of time of us being together."

He liked that better, his eyes lighting up. "So, end of January. I like that."

She tried to act like it didn't give her butterflies or a gushy feeling as she nodded. If they kept on the way they were, she'd be living with Benji when she came back from Florida. Maybe he'd want to come? "I'm actually going to Florida to do the design for Shea and Elli. Maybe you'd want to go with us if you aren't in the All-Star Game."

"I probably won't be, so count me in."

"If we're still together."

"See! Stop trying to expire us," he demanded and she smiled.

"Yeah, yeah," she laughed, snuggling into his side. But then she paused. Her heart was pounding at the possibilities, but one thing was for sure. Lifting up, she looked down at him. "I want to be in love before we move in, by the way. I don't want us just moving in 'cause it's easy. I want it because we love each other and want to build a home together. If we aren't there at three months, then it's okay. Okay?"

As she gazed at him, his eyes were dark and she swore he was holding something back when he looked up into her face. His lips curved and he nodded before whispering, "Okay, but I want you to promise me something right now."

"Okay?"

"You stay with Jayden till then, or with your mom. But don't go get an apartment or a hotel room. Okay?"

"But what if we decide we don't want to live together at the end of January?"

His face was stone as he held her gaze. "We will."

"How do you know? You frustrate the hell out of me, you know that?"

He scoffed. "Good, I love the way you look when you're mad," he said, nibbling at her jaw. Rolling her eyes, she wrapped her arms around his neck as he looked up at her, his nose pressing into hers. "This is going to work. Me and you. Just accept it."

"Anything can become a factor, anything can break us."

"Not if we don't let it."

She eyed him, unable to understand how he could be so confident about them. "How? How are you so self-assured?"

"Because I met someone who, without even realizing it, reassures me to believe in us."

Her lips curved. "I do?"

He nodded. "Yup, every time you try to fight what's happening between us, it only makes me want to fight you harder for you. Just FYI, I'm a scrapper. I will win."

She grinned. "Yeah?"

"Oh, yeah," he said, rolling them over. "I beat alcoholism, I worked my ass off to earn my spot back in the NHL, and every day I strive to be a good man. It used to be for Ava and Leary, but now, I want to be a good man for you."

She paused, her heart stopping in her chest. "Do you still miss them?"

He met her gaze and he nodded, his pain visible. "I miss the stuff I can remember. I miss their smiles. The way Leary said 'Daddy.' How Ava used to look at me with love in her eyes when I was me, not the drunk. She hated the drunk. Can't blame her. I hated him too because I missed a lot."

"That's awful," she said, her eyes widening as he nodded.

"It is. I don't remember the cool things at all. Like Leary's first steps, her first words, or anything like that. It's sad and it's something I have had to learn to deal with. I asked for a lot of forgiveness. For the longest time, I blamed myself. But I was sick. So sick."

"Alcoholism is scary."

"It is," he agreed as her heart ached for him. "I know now, if I had a chance to go back to all that, to do it differently, I—" He paused, and she knew what he was going to say next. That he'd go back and do it all over again, that he'd be the husband Ava needed and the father Leary deserved. She expected it. It was who he was, a good man, no matter that she never would have had the chance to be with him. That she never would have had the chance to be fully happy.

Looking down, he cleared his throat. "I would have gotten divorced when Ava asked the first time, and then I would have been the father Leary needed once I got clean."

She exhaled deeply, surprised. He looked up, their eyes meeting. "I hurt them enough. I broke their trust. I lost my chance to be good for them. I know that now, and I'm not trying to disrespect their memory—"

"Never," she answered. "I would never think that."

"But they would have been better off without me."

Her heart was in her throat as she held him. "It takes a real man to know that."

"I've grown from it, accepted it, learned from it. And now, I just want to be better than what I was to them. I want to honor them by making you and Angie happy. I want to do right by you two."

Swallowing hard, she smiled. "I want the same."

"Good. You got it," he said, kissing her lips softly. But she didn't kiss him back like she normally did. No, she was too consumed with her feelings, her worries. When he pulled back, he looked confused as he asked, "What's wrong?"

She shook her head and she hated how the tears threatened to fall. "I'm worried about Angie."

His eyes filled with compassion as he held her gaze. "Me too."

"Do you think she's okay?"

"I hope so."

Emotion choked her as she closed her eyes. "Do you think tomorrow is going to be bad?"

Rolling them over, her body pressing into his hard one, he hugged her. "You know what? I don't know. I know that's not the answer you want. I know you want me to tell you it's going to go great. But I don't know, and I'm sorry I don't," he said, his mouth near hers as he spoke. "But I can promise you, no matter what happens, I will stand beside you, and I will be there for you through it all. Okay?"

Yeah, her heart was going nuts, and it took everything not to cry out in joy. If it had been her mother, she would have promised it would be fine. That everything would work out. But Benji didn't do that. He just promised he'd be there, and that almost made it all better.

Almost.

But even with the nasty feeling in her stomach, she knew she'd be okay. Not because she was always okay, but because she had Benji.

Chapter EIGHTEEN

Lucy was going to need Benji too.

Because when she got to the rink…

Rick was nowhere in sight.

"I don't understand why he isn't answering the phone," she said frantically, calling him for the ninth time.

"Maybe they overslept?" her mom said, hopeful and always so damn positive. "It's early."

But Lucy shook her head, dread filling her chest as it went to voice mail once more. It was taking everything out of her not to lose it. Not to scream. Not to drive over there and kick Rick's ass. She knew she couldn't do that, though, that it would only make matters worse. Plus, she was a fucking lady. Most of the time.

"God, Mom, weren't you listening to me? He's being a dick like always and not bringing her 'cause it's not in the parenting plan," she spat out as she called once more, again going to voice mail. Benji's arm came around her waist, pulling her into his side before kissing her temple.

"Breathe," he whispered against her ear. "Calm down. It isn't her fault."

"I know that," she bit out, only seeing red. "But I don't know if you know, but my daughter is not here when she is supposed to be."

Meeting her gaze, he held it as he nodded. The man had the patience of a saint because even she knew she was being a little hostile. "I know, but we knew there could be a chance he wouldn't show. Breathe."

Sucking in a breath, she let it out and then nodded. He was right. They had hoped Rick wouldn't do this, but she was pretty sure she'd always known he wouldn't show. He was more concerned with hurting Lucy than he was about caring for Angie's needs, and she was fucking done.

Her eyes still locked with Benji's, she said, "Sorry, Mom."

"Oh, it's fine, honey. I know you're stressed. I just wish that son of a bitch would answer the damn phone," she said, sounding as frazzled, if not more, than Lucy. Her mom was more than just a grandma to Angie; she was basically her second mom. She had cared for Angie since she was a tiny thing, when Lucy was going to school and work. She was a huge pillar of Angie's life, hell, of Lucy's life. Lucy needed to remember that and not snap at everyone. Before she could apologize once more, though, her phone vibrated in her hand. Lucy looked down to see it was a text.

> Rick: Jesus. I'm busy. What do you want?
> Lucy: Answer the phone.
> Rick: Busy.
> Lucy: Where are you?
> Rick: Out.
> Lucy: Are you on your way to the rink?
> Rick: No

She made a sound of distress as Benji hugged her. "Just breathe."

> Lucy: And why not?
> Rick: We are taking Nina and Angie to Chuck E. Cheese instead.
> Lucy: Angie wanted that?
> Rick: Yes.
> Lucy: Call me, let me talk to her.
> Rick: No.

"Motherfuckingasshole," she grumbled, dialing his number once more, but it went straight to voice mail. Looking to Benji, her eyes wide and full of tears, she asked, "What do I do?"

He shook his head, his eyes full of apprehension. "You call your dad."

She nodded, looking to her mom first. "He isn't bringing her. Says she wanted to go to Chuck E. Cheese, which I'm sure is a fucking lie!"

River struck his hips in frustration as Autumn muttered a curse. "He can't do stuff like that. I let the boys go early this morning so I could be here. People make plans for her. He can't just decide when she has somewhere to be," River barked and then he held his hand up. "I don't mean that at you, honey. I'm just fucking pissed."

Lucy's lip wobbled as she nodded.

"We all are," Benji said then, his arm snaking around Lucy tighter. "But it will get figured out."

Reaching out, Autumn pulled Lucy into her arms, hugging her tightly as she squeezed her eyes shut. "It's okay. He wouldn't hurt her. And if he does, I swear to God, I will kill him so you never have to see him again, Lucy Lane. I'll do the damn time to be rid of that filth. He's doing this to hurt you, I just know it."

"I know," Lucy mumbled, hugging her mother close.

"Don't you worry. It's gonna be okay. Okay?"

"I just know that he's lying," she said, holding back her tears.

"He probably is," River said. "Son of a bitch."

Pulling away from her mom, she looked at both of them. "I'm sorry to have had y'all come out. I should have called."

"No. No worries," her mom said, kissing her cheek before letting her go. "We don't mind."

"No, we want to be here to see her play," River said then, shaking his head. "I look forward to it, and it makes me sick that he doesn't realize how important this is to her. You need to get this fixed, Lucy. You need to just cut ties with him."

"Yeah," she agreed, but she knew she could never fully get rid of him.

"Well, let's just drop it. It'll get fixed. Angie is fine. Plus, we have a cake tasting for the wedding. Y'all should come. Free cake!"

Oh, God, no.

"We would love to," Benji said, his arm coming around her shoulders as she looked up at him, wide-eyed. "I love cake. Don't you love cake?"

She tried to tell him with her face that she'd rather eat a bullet than go taste testing with the almost newlyweds, but apparently Benji didn't know how to read her face. "Yes. I love cake."

"Great! It's at noon, over at Audrey Jane's. Jayden raves about her, and she is just cute as a button," Autumn gushed, taking Lucy's hands. "This will be good. Get your mind off of that trash and try to salvage your weekend."

"Nothing will salvage this weekend until I know Angie is okay," she said morosely, and Autumn begged her with her eyes.

"My heart can't take it, Lucy Lane. I need you to believe with me that our baby is okay."

"She's fine," Benji said then, lacing his fingers with Lucy's. "But maybe we can get your dad to call Rick's lawyer and demand a phone call."

"Oh, good idea," Lucy said quickly, pulling her dad's number up. "Mom, River, love you. See you at the bakery."

Hitting send, she heard Benji saying good-bye as the phone rang. When her dad answered, her stomach dropped. "Hey, honey, how ya doing?"

"I need you to tell me you can call my fucktard ex-husband's lawyer and demand I talk to my daughter," she barked into the phone.

"What's going on?"

She explained the whole thing, what had been said yesterday, and what was said just minutes before she called him. Her father listened. She could hear him taking notes, and he only asked a few things. But other than that, he let her do the talking. She was standing beside Benji's car when he walked up, leaning beside it and watching her. He was just as nervous as she was; she could see it all over his face. While that pleased her to no end, it also worried her. Was this the beginning?

The beginning of the fucking end.

Shutting her eyes, she pinched the bridge of her nose. "I don't know what to do, but I'm pretty sure shit's about to get nasty."

"Yeah," her dad muttered into the phone. "I'm looking over the parenting plan now, Lucy, and I really don't think he has to let her call you."

"What?" she roared. "Dad, I've got to talk to my daughter. I have to make sure she is okay."

"I must have missed this part when we were going over all the details four years ago, or maybe I just assumed he wouldn't be an asshole and not let her talk to you."

A tear leaked out of her closed eyes as Benji's fingers locked with hers. "Dad, please tell me what to do here."

"I'll call his lawyer, scare him a bit, see what I can get done. But I don't think he'll go along with it, especially since I told him to take a flying leap at the beginning of the week." He paused, the sounds of paper being moved around coming through the phone. "Lucy, what are you thinking? What are you wanting to do?"

"I don't know yet. I want to talk to Angie."

"Okay. Well, let me call the lawyer, see what I can do. I'll call you back."

"Okay, um, er, thanks," she muttered and then she hung up quickly, feeling dirty for even speaking to him. "I hate that I fucking need him right now," she cried, shaking her head. "I hate that I have to depend on him, but I know he'll get it done because he loves Angie."

Looking up, she found Benji watching her, nodding his head. "I know, baby. Come here," he said, bringing her into his arms and kissing the top of her head. "I'm sorry this sucks right now."

"I just want to talk to her."

"Can you try calling Heidi? Surely, being a mother, she'd understand."

That was another great idea. Her lips quivered as she nodded, pulling out of his arms to call Heidi. She answered right away. "Hey, what's up?"

"Hey! Are you by Angie? Can I talk to her?"

"Oh, no. She's at home with Rick. She got in trouble this morning for mouthing off or something, I don't know. So she didn't get to come with us."

Lucy began to shake. That liar. "What did she mouth off about?" she asked as calmly as she could.

"I really don't know. I was in the shower."

Covering her mouth, she closed her eyes, shaking her head. "She had a hockey game this morning."

"Oh? Rick said it was canceled."

I hate him. I hate him so fucking much. Clearing her throat so she didn't sob into the phone, she said, "Can you have her call me when you get home?"

"Sure, but just call Rick. He's home with her."

"I've been calling all morning. He won't answer my calls," she bit out, seeing red as everything inside her burned. She wouldn't bring Heidi into this. As much as she wanted to cuss the woman out and tell her to fix her stupid husband, she knew she wouldn't. Heidi was a doormat. She was worthless and did whatever Rick said. She wouldn't side with Lucy. Lucy was pretty sure Heidi wished Lucy and Angie would just disappear. But she saved face, tried to be nice, even though Lucy knew she didn't give two shits about her. Hell, she heard the shit that woman had talked about her and Angie, saying they were a problem since the very beginning.

When, really, Heidi had been the one who was the problem.

"That's odd. Did you guys get into it again?"

"You can say that."

"You guys need to stop all this fighting."

"Yeah, well, he needs to work on that."

"Or you do," she said and Lucy paused.

Taking a cleansing breath, she snarled out, "Can you please have her call me?"

"I'll try."

Exactly. Clenching the phone in her hand, she opened her eyes to meet Benji's gaze. "Thanks," she snapped and then hung up, shaking her head. Opening Rick's text conversation, she typed out a message quickly.

Lucy: *You are a liar and you best hope my daughter is okay.*
Rick: *Be real, she's fine. Wait, are you threatening me?*

Before she could type back what she really wanted to say, Benji's hand came over the screen and she gawked up at him. "Let it be. He is baiting you."

"Fucking shit!" she yelled, moving her phone out and typing him back.

Lucy: Can I please talk to her?
Rick: She's busy.

"Let it go. Hopefully, your dad can pull through," Benji said, his voice stern as Lucy felt like she was completely losing it. "Come on, let's go get some brunch and then we'll go have dessert with Autumn and River."

"I want to go home," she said, looking up at him. He was blurry because of her tears.

"Which is why we'll go out."

"Benji, you don't understand!" she yelled, shaking her phone at him. "I don't know what is going on with my daughter because her dad is a jackass." Sucking in a breath, she shook her head as she met his gaze. "I'm worried."

"So am I," he admitted. "But you've done everything you can. You dad will pull through, but I won't let you sit at home and stew in your worry. You'll drive yourself crazy."

"So I'm supposed to act like it's no big deal?"

"No. Not at all. I didn't imply that either. I'm just saying that sitting at home stewing and thinking of everything that could go wrong is going to make it worse." He paused as he looked at her with a serious expression. "Do you think he'd hurt her? If so, Lucy, I'll drive you over there, bust in that house, get her, and go to jail. I don't care."

Her stomach hurt, but she was pretty sure Rick would never physically hurt her. He had never laid a hand on her before, only Lucy, but it scared her to the core that he *could* do it. He had never done that before, though. He always let her talk to Angie or let Angie call her. What if she was calling for Lucy? What if she needed her? Her heart hurt. Should she drive over there?

When her phone rang, she fumbled with it, not checking who it was before answering, "Hello?"

"Honey, it's me," her dad said, and her body went rigid.

"Yeah, what did you find out?"

"He doesn't have to let you talk to her, and his lawyer pointed that out. I already knew this, though, and I said I'd send the cops over for a well-being check. The lawyer didn't want that, so he put me on with Rick over conference. I told him to call you. He said he wouldn't, that he was spending time with his daughter. I asked to speak with Angie. The lawyer said Rick didn't have to do that, but he did. She got on the line, and I asked if she was okay. She said yes. I told her you were thinking about her and missing her a lot. She said she missed you and loved you, that she missed me, and that she hoped I could come to one of her games. I asked if she wanted to leave Rick's house. But before she could answer, the lawyer hung up. So I don't know. It's a fucking mess, and I'm gonna go ahead and get a court date, I think. Some things need to change."

Lucy's heart was in her stomach, and she was pretty sure she was about to throw up. She didn't hear a lot of what he had said, except that Angie was okay. "So, she's okay?"

"She sounded upset, but she wasn't crying. I don't know."

"What do you think I should do? Should I go over there?"

"There is no point. He'll call the cops, and then someone will get arrested, more likely you since you'd be on his property."

Lucy looked down at the ground, sucking in a breath. "So just wait till tomorrow?"

"Yeah, talk to her tomorrow, and if you want to proceed, I'll arrange for a date."

"Okay," she said, nodding slowly and feeling a little better. Not much, but at least she wasn't about to lose her shit anymore. Clearing her throat, she said, "Thanks, Dad."

"Anytime. Keep documenting, Lucy. Everything. We'll get this fixed."

"Okay."

"And maybe you can get me that hockey schedule so I can come," he said and Lucy froze. She could tell him to fuck off, tell him to go to hell, but it wasn't in her. He didn't have to help her, especially with how hateful she had been since the divorce, but he was helping. He was there for her.

"Let me think about that."

"Of course," he said, and that surprised Lucy. She expected a fight. "Call me tomorrow."

"I will."

"Oh, are you dating someone?"

Lucy paused. "Why?"

"Lawyer says that Rick wants there to be a no-contact clause between the guy and Angie. That he is a pedophile. Since I know you haven't brought anyone around Angie since you left Rick, I'm sure this guy is decent. So I told him again to take a flying leap. I wanted you to know that, though."

Digging her nails into her palms, she shook her head. "He's not a pedophile, and that won't work, not only for me, but because Angie loves Benji."

"I figured. Call me tomorrow after you speak with her. We'll go from there."

"Okay. Thanks, Dad."

"Anytime," he said and then she hung up, looking over at Benji.

"What did he say?" he asked, tucking his hands into his pockets.

As she explained what was said, what her dad wanted to do, Benji listened and nodded. Throwing her hands up, she shook her head. "This is a fucking mess."

He nodded, pulling her into his arms. "It is."

"I don't want to go into a custody battle, Benji. He says you're a pedophile, and I swear he is doing this to hurt me. He knows I'm finally happy and that Angie is happy. It's such bullshit."

Looking up, she found anger in his eyes. "He can say what he wants, but we know the truth. Angie knows the truth."

Nodding her head, she bit her lip as she gazed into his eyes. She couldn't do this to him. It wasn't fair. He was such a good guy. Any girl would be so lucky to have him, and here she was, with her nails in him while the clusterfuck of her life unfolded. "This is your chance, Benji. Before it gets to be too much."

His brows touched as his lips curled. "Wait, what? No," he said, holding his hands up and glaring at her. "Don't tell me you're saying this is my chance to get out." She just looked at him and he shook his head, framing her face before pressing his nose to hers. "We've got this, *we*."

As she leaned into him, nuzzling into him, she was surprised.

Surprised—because she was starting to believe him.

"I want cake by the ocean."

Glancing over at Lucy as he drove to Audrey Jane's, he smiled as the popular song by DNCE played. Her fingers were laced with his, and while she was off in a distant world, Benji knew they were going to be okay. Nodding his head, he said, "Hey, we'll be in Florida in January, right? We'll have cake."

She exhaled a long breath. "Something to look forward to."

"Yeah, it will be great," he said, squeezing her hand. "I get to see you in a bikini."

She looked over at him and he waggled his brows. Thankfully, she smiled. "Will you wear a Speedo?"

He scoffed. "Dick's too big for that."

Snorting with laughter, she brought his hand between both of hers in her lap. "Of course, how silly of me."

"That's what I was thinking," he said and she laughed louder, her whole face bright as she leaned back in the seat, looking over at him.

"You're great."

He nodded. "I know."

But the tension of the situation with Angie still weighed heavily on both of them. He knew she wasn't his kid—he got that loud and clear—but that didn't stop him from loving her as much as he loved Lucy. He may have fallen for Lucy first, but Angie was right behind her. Since the beginning, though, he had cared about her. He understood her, enjoyed her silliness. He thought she was an awesome kid, and his stress, his ache in his heart, was more caused not because of how much he hated seeing Lucy so upset, but because he was afraid Angie was scared. He wondered if she knew she couldn't call Lucy. That Rick was keeping them apart.

It freaked him the hell out.

But he was going to stay strong for Lucy.

He would be her rock.

Turning into Audrey Jane's, Benji smiled up at the cute little posh bakery that Audrey Odder had built from scratch. Rumor had it that she used to make cupcakes just for her family and then for Tate. He pushed her to open her own place, and she was prospering. Making all the cakes for the stars and professional athletes. She made fabulous sweets, and Benji's favorite were her lemon cakes Crokmou that were inspired by *Game of Thrones*.

"I love Audrey's cakes. She's made Angie's birthday cake for the last four years," Lucy said as they parked beside River's truck.

"Yeah, I gained like ten pounds over break eating her lemon cakes."

She looked over at him, eyeing him. "The *Game of Thrones* one?"

He about melted at the mere thought of them as he nodded. "Yes."

"So good," she said, shaking her head as she got out.

"Best ever," he agreed, getting out and locking up. "I should see if she could make me a birthday cake out of them."

Lucy grinned. "That's a good idea. Or I can. When's your birthday?"

"Christmas."

"Really?" she gushed, leaning into him, and he nodded.

"Yeah, when I was a kid, my mom was awesome about making Christmas one thing and my birthday another. Now, I just buy myself whatever big thing I want and call it good," he said, wrapping his arm around her shoulders as they headed toward the entrance. "Last year, since I turned thirty-two and I had no clue what I wanted, I took thirty-two disadvantaged kids from Erik Titov's foundation shopping and bought them anything they wanted. It was really great."

She beamed up at him as he pulled the door open. "That's so awesome."

"Yeah, it was."

"Well, my friend, I can't separate your day this year because my mother is getting married, but next year, I got you," she said, flashing him a grin, and his lips curved.

"Wait? Did you just look to the future?"

She shot him a deadpan expression. "Shut up."

"Lucy! Benji! Over here, sweeties."

Lucy's shoulders fell at the sound of her mother's cheerful voice, and Benji had to hold in his laughter. He knew she didn't want to do this, but he didn't care. He loved cake, and he really liked Autumn and River.

"You owe me," she muttered as she turned to face them. Grabbing a hold of her butt, he nuzzled his nose in her ear.

"Oh, I got you later," he whispered and she giggled as they headed toward a grinning Autumn and River. Before they could reach them, Audrey Odder appeared, her face bright as she wrapped Benji up in a tight hug.

"Benji! I didn't know you were coming in. You should have called. I would have had some lemon cake ready."

Squeezing her, he pulled back, grinning down into her beautiful, wide face. She had lost a lot of weight since the birth of her son, but she still had that round face that made you crave cupcakes. Or maybe it was the way she smelled. Like sugar and happiness. He wasn't sure; he just knew he really enjoyed her cupcakes.

"I didn't know I was coming. Here to cake test."

"With the Moores? Jayden and Baylor's mom and dad? How do you know them?"

Benji grinned as he pulled Lucy into his arms. "I'm dating Jayden's sister."

Audrey lit up, bouncing on her heels as she clapped her hands. "No! Yes? Ah, that's so awesome. Oh my God, isn't he the sweetest? I just love Benji," she gushed, squeezing his arm, and Lucy grinned.

"He's all right," she teased and Audrey laughed, nodding her head.

"Honestly, one of the best guys I know other than my husband, and that says a lot 'cause I know a lot of Assassins men. But Benji, he's a good one. You're very lucky."

A little red dusted her cheeks as she beamed up at him. "I know."

"Eek! I'm so happy for you. Maybe we'll do a cake testing for you two next," she said with a wink, and Lucy's eyes widened.

"Whoa, lady. Calm down."

Audrey didn't care, though. She giggled happily as she waved Lucy off. "You'll see. Okay, let's taste test!"

By the time they finished tasting all the cakes, Benji was ready to puke. He didn't turn down cake, and Lucy and Autumn would only take a bite or two, so that left lots of cake for him and River. It was fun, though. River and Autumn were really something. Funny, and so into each other, it was refreshing. It gave him something to look forward to. They also treated him like family. Like they'd already decided he wasn't going anywhere. They spoke to him the way they talked to Lucy, which was with nothing but love and support. It was great. After being so alone and only having the guys from the team when he allowed himself to be around them, to now having Lucy, Angie, and her family, it was just nice. Really nice.

"So do your parents visit much, Benji? You said you're from Chicago, eh?" River asked and Benji nodded, feeling Lucy tense up next to him.

"Yes, sir. Um, but I don't speak to my parents. Haven't in a really long time."

Autumn's face twisted. "My goodness, can I ask why?"

"No, Mom," Lucy said, shaking her head. "That's his business."

"No, it's fine," he said, but Lucy gave him a look.

"Please don't think you have to say anything to them because of me, really. Just tell them to butt out," Lucy said, and he laughed as Autumn tsked at her.

"That's not nice," she said and Lucy shot her a look.

"Mom, you're asking him something personal."

"Because I like him. We are friends. And he's dating you!"

Benji laughed as River rolled his eyes. "It's fine, really."

"Whatever," Lucy decided, leaning against him and nibbling on the last piece of cake. "She's nosy and she won't stop."

"Lucy Lane!"

"Just saying."

Chuckling, Benji looked over at Autumn and he sucked in a deep breath. He understood their interest and appreciated it, but it was never easy speaking of the family he'd lost. "My family wasn't there for me when I needed them. I had a drinking problem, and instead of supporting me and being there for me, they kicked me when I was down, blamed me for stuff, and basically told me they wished I had died instead of my brother. At the time, I agreed with them. But now, I know they were just shitty people. Because of that, I live by the motto, 'If you don't add to my life, you're out of my life.'"

"Wow, that's deep," Lucy said with a nod. "Great motto."

"Yeah, one life to live, you know. I want it to be the best I can make it."

"Exactly. That's why I'm marrying this gal right here," River said, pulling Autumn into the crook of his arm. "She's the best."

"Gag, get a room," Lucy teased, but Benji didn't think they heard her as they kissed sweetly. "Mom, you guys decide on a cake?"

But Autumn ignored her, looking at Benji. "So if you don't mind my asking, why are you still single?" Lucy started to choke on the milk she had just taken a drink of.

"Mom!" she gasped, before choking a little more, and Autumn waved her off.

"We're friends, remember?" Autumn said and then she pointed to him. "Plus, he's amazing. Such a sweet guy, so doting on you, and great with Angie. So why hasn't anyone scooped you up yet?"

Benji smiled as Lucy muttered a curse. "Mom, leave him be!"

"No, it's fine," he said, his hand sliding across her back to rest against her shoulder.

"She won't stop."

He heard her loud and clear, but he honestly didn't mind. "I was married before."

"So you're divorced? Hm, I didn't think that about you. You seem like the kind of guy who won't back down from a fight," River said and Benji nodded.

"No, I'm not," he said simply, and there was a flicker of confusion in Autumn's eyes. "My wife and my two-year-old daughter were killed in a car crash about twelve years ago."

Lucy blew out a breath as both Autumn's and River's faces changed, sorrow deep in their eyes. "My God," Autumn gasped as River shook his head.

"I'm very sorry," he said seriously and Benji nodded. "I hadn't realized that."

"Thank you," he said with a soft smile. "I never remarried. Never found the right girl."

His gaze drifted to Lucy, and her face filled with heat as she shook her head. "Don't look at me like that."

Chuckling, he leaned into her, kissing her temple as Autumn asked, "So you lost your brother too, all to car crashes?"

Benji nodded, meeting her sad gaze. "Same car crash. All three of them."

"My goodness, bless your heart," she was almost crying and Benji nodded.

"Enter drinking problem," River stated with a nod. "Been there. Done it."

Lucy's eyes widened. "You did?"

"Oh, yeah," River said, holding Autumn closer. "Baylor's mom left me, and I left the NHL. I was depressed to no end, turned into a functioning alcoholic, and I thought I was good. But then I met your mom and things just changed. I didn't need to be numb—I wanted to feel everything because I loved her."

"Gagging, but wow, that's sweet," Lucy said, sending her mother a grin, but Autumn was too busy beaming up at River.

"Yeah, mine started when I was younger, but it got worse. Took me a long time to come back from that, but I'm coping. And while I didn't stop for a woman, I stopped because I wanted to be a good guy, someone people could depend on, and maybe one day, love." Looking over at Lucy, Benji found her lips quirked at the side, watching him with dark eyes.

"Well, I think you're a great guy," Autumn decided and Benji smiled.

"He's okay," Lucy said, and Autumn tsked her as River chuckled.

"Yeah, I think I'm finally enjoying life. And when you enjoy life, you become the person you want to be."

River and Autumn both grinned at Lucy as she groaned. "Ugh, stop, guys." That made them all laugh as Benji held her close.

"Well, I've been around Ms. Lucy Lane for a little over a year now, and I can say I've never seen her smile or laugh as much as she does when she's around you," River said, toasting his cup of milk to Benji.

Lucy rolled her eyes, her face filling with color as she looked across the table at her soon-to-be stepdad. "Never had anything to smile or laugh about,

unless Angela Lynn had something to say." That made all of them smile, but the tension was back. All of them worried about spunky little Angie. Lucy eyed Benji, a grin pulling at her lips. "But maybe I do now."

"Well, I'd say so," Autumn gushed, beaming ear to ear as River nodded happily. "So, Benji, tell me, what are you doing on Christmas?" Autumn asked and Benji shrugged.

"Well, I was hoping I could score an invitation to hang with you guys at apparently the coolest wedding ever."

"Done. The whole family will be in. Jude and Jace will be excited to meet you. So please come."

The thought of meeting the other Sinclair brothers as Lucy's boyfriend kind of made him nervous, but he wouldn't miss it for the world. "I'm there."

Lucy grinned as she leaned on the table, his arm falling to her hip. "It's his birthday," she said as Audrey came to the table.

"Is it?" Autumn exclaimed, looking up to Audrey. "We need to have that lemon cake he keeps talking about as a side cake for one." Benji wanted to protest, but he knew Autumn would ignore him. She was Lucy's mother, very headstrong but not as angry, and he was finding he was starting to care for the sweet lady. "It'll be Benji's birthday."

When Autumn flashed him a grin, squeezing his hand, Benji smiled.

And he felt like, maybe, he could really belong to this family one day.

Chapter
NINETEEN

As he pressed Lucy into the wall, Benji's fingers bit into her ribs and he got lost in her kisses. She tasted like cake, Audrey's fabulous cake, and he honestly wasn't sure if he liked the cake more on a plate or on her mouth.

One thing was for sure, he wasn't about to stop.

Lifting her up, he pressed himself into her as her fingers threaded through his hair, arching her chest into his. He held her ass and she gasped against his mouth, pulling away as his lips trailed down her jaw.

"I'm gonna put a sectional over there."

He couldn't fathom why she wanted to talk about the design right now, but he was too busy to stop her. Dragging his teeth down her throat, he gasped against her as she squeezed her legs around his waist.

"It's gonna look great... Oh God, yes," she moaned as he dipped his tongue in the V of her shirt. "But, but, can we pause?"

"No," he said against her skin, nipping her collarbone before grazing his teeth against her jaw. "No shits are given about design right now. All I care about is getting inside you."

She gave him a serious look. "But I want to tell you."

"And I want to fuck you," he said desperately. "I leave in two days. I won't get this ass for almost two weeks. Talk later, okay?"

When he went to kiss her, she put her hand up, stopping him. "It will take me five minutes, and then you can have your way with me."

He paused, thinking it over as he held her gaze. "Actually, I can have my way with you without listening because I'm pretty sure you can't say no to me."

She scoffed. "Don't get me confused with yourself," she said, patting his chest and wiggling out of his grasp, her feet hitting the ground. "Now, as I was saying…"

Groaning loudly, he leaned into the wall, his cock throbbing in his pants. He didn't want to wait. But like she said, he couldn't say no to her. As she moved away from him, pointing to the long wall that held all the big windows, she said with a raspy voice, "This is where the sectional will go." He nodded but it was hard, especially with his heartbeat roaring in his ears and all the blood in his body going right to his cock. When she started to remove her shirt, throwing it down on the spot, he paused. He drank in the sight of her pale skin against the dark red of the bra she wore, and his groin tightened as she moved to the corner. "Here will be the big, man recliner. Sorry, the gamer chair is going upstairs in the toy room." She undid her pants, pushing them down her thighs. His mouth went dry as she turned, bending over to give him one hell of a view of her plump ass with only a peek of a red string thong.

Choking on his words, he said, "You mean collectibles?"

She nodded, looking over her shoulder at him. "Oh, of course," she muttered, turning and going to the TV. "This will be wall-mounted." With her eyes holding his, she undid her bra and hung it over the TV. "Good spot, huh?"

But Benji couldn't speak. He was aching to touch her breasts, and he had almost closed the distance between them, but then she was walking toward him. Strutting in the wickedest way, she paused beside him, running her hand down his chest, his stomach, and pausing at his cock, squeezing it through his jeans.

"Damn," he wheezed and she grinned, her eyes wicked as she held his.

"Wanna see what I'm gonna do to the stairs?"

He swallowed hard as her hand moved along his hip before she headed to the stairs, bending over to pick her coat up off the floor. Hanging it up, she started up the stairs.

"I'm gonna put up pictures of you playing," she said roughly, her eyes never leaving his. Then she paused, pushing her panties down and laying them on the banister, her eyes half-lidded as she said, "Maybe some jerseys. Not sure yet."

Before he knew it, he was moving.

Her lips curved as he stopped in front of her, his face at her breasts since he was down a stair. "Sounds great."

"I thought so," she said, moving her hands down her body. "Wasn't it worth it to listen?"

His eyes narrowed as he wrapped his arms around her butt, holding her to him. Looking up at her, a breast on either side of his face, he grinned. "Yeah, now can I make love to you?"

Her brow quirked. "Oh, make love now?"

He nibbled at her breast. "Yeah, decided I wanted more than just a fuck."

"Just now deciding that?"

"Well, you are designing my house. Might need to throw in some deep, soulful kisses."

She nodded in agreement. "Maybe a little gazing into my eyes to make me feel like I mean something to you."

He tried not to laugh. "Yes, of course, a lot of caresses too as I move into you ever so slowly."

"Yes! And promises of tomorrow."

"And beyond," he cheered, and she dissolved in giggles as he threw her over his shoulder. "I don't want some cheesy romance novel. I want you."

"Well, good thing 'cause I'm more smutty than cheesy."

Grabbing a handful of her ass, he squeezed as he said, "Just the way I like you."

"Take me upstairs, Benji. Make love to me," she said in her best heroine voice and he grinned.

"All right, milady," he said roughly, smacking her ass hard. She squealed as he laughed before running up the stairs and down the hall to his room. As he threw her on the bed, she grinned up at him while he removed his shirt and tossed it on the floor. Reaching for his belt, he pulled it out in one fluid movement, his gaze on hers as he ran his tongue along her lips.

Slapping the belt to his palm, he winked. "Maybe we can move into some BDSM."

Her eyes widened as she scoffed. "And maybe I can kick you in your dick if you come anywhere near me with that belt."

He paused. He wasn't sure why that surprised him, but it did. He was soon laughing so hard, he was crying as he fell onto the bed beside her. Giggling with him, she reached for his pants, undoing them as she shook her head.

"Jeez, disabled by laughter," she teased as his chuckles subsided and he looked up at her.

Cupping her face, he grinned. "You're insane."

"Eh, been told that a time or two," she said with a grin before getting off the bed and yanking his jeans and boxers off. "Lazy! Make me do all the work."

"Hey, damn right. Now climb up here," he demanded, stroking his cock, his gaze locked with hers. "I want to be inside you."

She moved toward him, coming between his legs, her fingernails running along his thighs before she stopped, her lips curving. Taking his cock in her hand, she dropped her mouth to him, sucking the head of him between her sweet lips. Breathing out her name, he threaded his hand into her hair as the other clenched above his head. He swore she had the hottest mouth, and he

almost couldn't handle it. Especially when she got a good rhythm, moving her hand and mouth in perfect unison, taking him deep to the back of her throat and then back out, driving him absolutely crazy.

"Babe, come on. I'm going to come," he warned, his hand fisting her hair. "I can't take it."

She paused, looking up at him, his cock deep in her mouth, her green eyes bright.

Fuck, she was gorgeous.

Ever so slowly, he bit into his lip as her lips moved up his cock until he was out of her mouth, her hand still moving along his bulging shaft. "Do you want me to stop?"

"Fuck no," he scoffed. "But I really want to be inside of you."

She shrugged. "Fine. Whatever you want," she said before dropping her lips to his head, making him jerk from the sensation as she kissed him lightly. Climbing up his body, she moved her pussy along him as her mouth met his. Her legs fell to either side of him as his hands came up to hold her thick, sweet ass. She was wet. So fucking wet, causing him to moan against her mouth as she moved herself up and down on top of him.

Driving them both mad.

Kissing his jaw, she used his chest to sit up, going up on her knees before directing him inside of her. As she slowly lowered her body, his eyes drifted shut and he disappeared inside of her, filling her to the hilt.

"God, you feel so fucking good," he grunted, one handful of ass and the other holding her breast. "I can't get enough."

She could only nod as she started to raise and lower herself on him, her rhythm painfully slow, but he loved it.

He loved her.

Squeezing her ass, he thrust up into her, stealing her breath as she started to bounce faster on his dick. Holding his shoulders, she rode him like a champ. And when she cried out, stretching her body up and grabbing her own breasts, he could only drink in her beauty as he fought for breath. As she moaned, her pussy clenched around him and that did it. His toes curled, his breathing stopped, and her name fell from his lips as he came from what he was sure were the depths of his soul.

She fell onto him, and he wrapped his arms around her torso as their mouths met, her pussy continuing to squeeze him as he filled her. Closing his eyes, he pressed his face into the crook of her neck and shoulder and breathed her in. He never wanted to forget anything about this gorgeous woman. He doubted he ever could. Her breath, her smell, her sweat, her kisses were absorbed inside of him. Seeping into his soul. God, he loved her.

He kissed her ear and then her cheek, and she moved her head, meeting her mouth to his. As his fingers threaded back into her hair, he moved his tongue against hers, his body vibrating with the aftershocks of his orgasm but also with the love he had for her. When she pulled back, that little kitten grin on her face, her eyes locked with his and he felt it. He knew she was going to say it. Say the words he so desperately needed to hear from her.

"Thank you for today," she whispered against his lips, her eyes searching his. "I really couldn't have done it without you."

Even though those weren't the words he wanted, they meant almost the same thing. "I'm not going anywhere."

She smiled, her eyes drifting to his lips as she ran her fingers along his jaw. "I'm starting to believe that."

Curving his lips, he closed his eyes. "We're making progress."

She nodded her nose along his. "We are."

Rolling them to their sides, he moved his hand along her cheek, looking deep into her eyes. The sun was shining brightly into the room, making the lighter parts of her hair look almost red. Her face was flushed, her body red with splotches from where he had held her, kissed her.

"You're so beautiful."

Grinning, she pressed her forehead into his jaw and exhaled loudly. "I don't think I'll ever get used to hearing that."

"You'd better 'cause I think it's a shame that someone hasn't been saying it your whole life."

Pulling back to look at him, she pursed her lips. "Shut up."

He scoffed at that, holding her close as he kissed her temple. "Tell me something."

"Okay?"

"What do you want to do? You pick, we'll do. Movie, dinner, more sex—I'm down for whatever you want."

She beamed up at him. "Anything?"

"Anything."

"Even dancing?"

He cringed since he wasn't much of a dancer, but he nodded. "Even dancing."

She bubbled with laughter. "But you'd much rather get a root canal."

He shrugged, chuckling. "Eh, maybe not that far, but I would go to Walmart instead."

She giggled, leaning into him. "Okay, well, how about we order some Chinese food for dinner and binge-watch *Game of Thrones*? Since I haven't seen it and it's apparently your favorite thing in the whole wide world."

Yeah, he would marry her tomorrow. "Well, maybe not my favorite thing, but, yes, that sounds like the best night ever."

She grinned. "Thought so. But if it's not, then what is your favorite?"

He gave her an expectant look and cupped her face. "You."

She shook her head, her face deepening with color as she pushed him away. "Come on, you've got my heart going crazy."

"Good, get used to it," he said, rolling off the bed and heading toward the bathroom. "Shower?"

"Yes," she said, climbing off the bed and following behind him. When he stopped, she wrapped her arms around him from behind and kissed his back. "I like the way you make me feel," she whispered against his hot skin.

With a grin pulling at his lips, he covered her hands with his. "And how is that?"

"Happy."

Closing his eyes, he let his head drift back, resting against hers. He may have made her heart go crazy, but she made his race. That's all he wanted. He wanted to make her happy, to make her smile, to make her feel good. He knew she was still worried about Angie, about the potential custody battle. What she didn't realize was that his love for her and Angie roared louder than any demons in her life.

More than Rick.

And nothing could ever stop it.

When Lucy woke the following morning, the first thing she saw was Benji, sleeping soundly beside her. He was naked, the blanket only covering a little as he lay sprawled out in the bed. His lashes were kissing his cheeks, his hair in disarray, his breaths deep and strong. Marks from their lovemaking were on his chest where she had bitten and scratched him the night before. They made her blush as she drank him in, but then, she was also proud of them.

He was hers.

The night before had been almost like magic. She'd worn his shirt and boxers while they ate and binge-watched *Game of Thrones*. She wanted to say she loved it, but truth be told, she couldn't even pay attention. Between her hot boyfriend and the fact she had no clue what was going on, she missed a lot. But she would rewatch it later since her mind just hadn't been into it. She didn't want to go anywhere; she just wanted to chill with him.

She couldn't stop thinking about Angie. Her stomach hurt with worry, but at the same time, her heart was full of happiness from her night with Benji. She almost felt guilty. Did that make her a bad mother? It couldn't, because if she'd honestly believed Angie was in harm's way, she would have gone over there.

Benji was just so great. Every laugh, every touch, every locked gaze, it was like a fairy tale. And if she felt that good while also distracted, then no telling how it would be when everything was right in the world. When it was just her, Angie, and Benji.

A family.

What?

A family?

Fuck, she was falling for him.

Hard.

And it scared her because she had no clue what was going to happen with Rick. But a part of her didn't care because she prayed and hoped that Benji was true to his words and he would be there for her. Stand with her. Somehow she had come to lean on him. Depend on him.

And that had never happened before.

She wouldn't let that scare her. She thought about how he fought to be clean, to be healthy, and to be ready for love one day. How River cleaned up just for her mother. How Jude, Jayden, and Jace did everything they could to be good men for the women they loved. Love was such a beautiful thing, and she had the chance to have it. She actually didn't hate it any longer. Didn't reject it. No, she wanted it, and for once, she felt like this was her chance. She couldn't sabotage that, she just couldn't. She had to let it happen.

She had to think of herself, like Benji had told her so many times.

And to do that, she had to have Angie and Benji.

Reaching out, she traced his jaw, his lips, and then his nose, causing him to twitch and make faces. Smiling, she pressed her body to his, kissing him underneath his jaw as his arms came around her, squeezing her close to him. "I don't like being woken up," he muttered against her lips and she smiled.

"Oh, really?"

"Yeah, I hate it."

"Well, excuse me," she muttered back and he squeezed her, her breasts pressing into his chest. Moving her fingers through his hair, she closed her eyes as she traced her lips along his. As she hooked a leg over his hip, he captured her lips with his and exhaled loudly.

"Okay, maybe it isn't so bad," he muttered before rolling onto her. "At least, I'm waking up to you."

Grinning up at him, she ran her fingers over his cheeks as his lips pressed to hers. Leaning his head to hers, his body pressed into hers as he whispered against her lips, "Did you sleep well?"

"I did."

"Good," he said, moving his nose against hers. "This could happen all the time."

She rolled her eyes. "Yeah?"

"Yeah, I can have a key made for you."

"January," she said and he wrinkled his face.

"Fine," he exhaled, nuzzling his nose against her jaw. "When do we meet Rick?"

"In an hour."

"Are you okay?"

She shook her head. "Nervous."

"Don't be. We'll be together. Nothing will happen."

She hoped he was right. "Oh, I know. I just worry about Angie."

"She's okay and this will go well."

He sounded so sure, but she wasn't. Yet, she nodded and said, "Okay."

Closing his eyes, he nodded his head, his lips resting lightly against hers. "Well, let's go get ready, make some breakfast, and go face the dick."

Neither of them moved, though. Meeting her gaze, he smiled as he pressed himself against her. He was deliciously hard, and of course, she wanted him. It killed her that he was leaving the following day, and she wasn't sure if they'd get a moment free later since she was getting Angie. She also needed to take the edge off. So arching her hips against his, she whispered, "Or, we could pick up breakfast and coffee?

With a half-lidded look, he nodded. "Good idea."

Smiling against his lips, Lucy closed her eyes and couldn't agree more.

But neither of them was smiling when they pulled into the parking lot of Walmart. The tension in Benji's truck was thick, and Lucy was convinced her heart was beating so hard it was going to shatter her eardrums. With his hand in hers, Benji followed her directions, parking in the back where she always did. Rick wasn't there yet, and that made Lucy's heart race. They were only two minutes early, but it wasn't like Rick to be late on drop-off days.

"What if he doesn't show?" she asked, her heart pounding against her ribs.

"Then we drive over to his house," Benji said simply, looking out the window, for what, she wasn't sure. He didn't know what Rick drove. "He'll be here."

Before she could say anything, she saw his car coming down the lane and she sat up straight. "There he is."

Opening the door, she got out, meeting Benji at the front of the truck as Rick parked. Before he could even get out, though, Angie was out of the car and rushing to Lucy, wrapping her arms around her waist. "Mommy," she breathed, her face in Lucy's stomach, holding her so tightly she almost knocked the air out of her.

"Oh, honey, I missed you," Lucy said, holding back her tears as she kissed her daughter's head.

"I want to go home," Angie whispered, and Lucy nodded.

"Of course," Lucy said, but Angie didn't let her go. "Are you okay?"

"I just want to go home," she said once more, and then Benji was crouched down beside her, his hand coming to rest on her shoulder.

"Hey, sunshine," he said and Angie peeked out.

"Hey."

"Wanna get in the truck? I think your mom and dad need to talk."

She nodded. "Can I play with your phone?"

He held his arms out. She went to him and he lifted her up. "Of course."

Tearing her gaze from them, Lucy pinned Rick with a look that was straight from hell. He was glaring, his fists clenched as he watched Benji put Angie in the car. He didn't even say good-bye; he was just glaring like a son of a bitch. When she heard the door shut, she cleared her throat.

"Why is she upset?"

"Who knows?" he said, meeting her gaze. "She's always bitching about something."

"Shouldn't that make you realize something is wrong?"

He just shrugged. "What do you want, Lucy?"

She took a step toward him, her fists balled at her thighs. "You ever do that shit again, I will come to your house, and I will—"

"Stop," Benji said as he came up beside her.

"Yeah, better listen to your boyfriend there, Lucy, even though we all know no one can control that mouth of yours," he said, his gaze meeting Benji's. "I wouldn't even try."

"Listen, buddy—"

"I'm not your buddy," Rick snapped and Benji nodded. "And we have nothing to say to each other."

"No, we do," Benji said sternly, and to her surprise, Rick's lips pressed together as he sized Benji up. She wasn't sure what he was thinking. Benji could kill him; he had at least a foot on him and also sixty pounds. He was a tank, while Rick was a smart car. Well, he was stupid, but size-wise, the comparison applied. With a calm but firm voice, Benji said, "I don't know how we got off on the wrong foot, but we need to fix this. For no one else but Angie. I don't care that you don't like me, because I sure as hell don't like you, but I refuse to have what happened this weekend happen again. You can't keep a mother from her daughter, and I know Lucy would never do that to you, no matter how much she hates you."

"Not that you call, anyway," Lucy added, and Benji shot her a look that she shrugged off. She understood his cool, calm approach, but she wasn't going to let the bastard off without knowing she could and would cut him.

"I mean, this is all pointless. Nothing is going to change. I'm not taking her to hockey, and I'm not letting you speak to her. That's final," Rick stated, and while Lucy was ready to fly off the handle, Benji spoke first.

"Why is that?"

"'Cause I don't want to. She's with me. Don't cut into my time."

"It's two hours on a Saturday! Hell, you can keep her two hours later on a Sunday if that will make it better."

"No," he said simply and Lucy's blood boiled.

Benji, on the other hand, was cool as a cucumber as he said, "Okay, I understand that you want your time with her. But what about what she wants? She loves hockey, she wants to play, and Lucy paid a lot to get her started, I'm sure. So can we at least pick her up for hockey? Bring her right back?"

"We?" Rick asked and then he laughed. "Dude, I'm trying to make it so you never even see my daughter."

Sucking his teeth, Benji glared and Lucy saw him cracking. "And why is that?"

"Because you're a fucking alcoholic who preys on women with kids to replace the family you fucking lost," Rick seethed, taking a step forward and leaving Lucy gasping for breath. How in the fucking world...? "And that little girl is mine. You can have Lucy. I don't want her, but Angie, you can't have her."

"What in the hell? How dare you?" Lucy yelled and she was going to kill him, rip him limb from limb. But before she could even get close enough, Benji had his arms around her, stopping her.

"Lucy, stop!"

"He can't talk to you like that. You don't even fucking know him. He is twenty times the man, hell, the father figure to Angie, that you'll ever be," she yelled, her body shaking with anger.

"Lucy, Angie can see you. Stop," Benji demanded as Rick laughed, and Lucy went still. She looked back, and thankfully, Angie was looking down. But he was right. She couldn't be acting like this. Letting her go, Benji turned, looking at Rick. "While you are right, I am a recovering alcoholic and I did lose my family, I don't want to steal your daughter from you. I just want her to be happy. And I'm asking you, please, work something out here."

But Rick shook his head. "Want to work something out? Take me to court."

"We would like to avoid that, for Angie's sake," he tried, but Rick shook his head.

"I don't care. I want full custody."

Lucy laughed out loud. "Over my dead fucking body."

"Fine, we'll see in court."

"Yeah, we will," Lucy snapped, her eyes blazing, and Rick's brows pulled together, surprised. "Let's go."

Benji paused, though, and turned to Rick. "Are you sure? Because she'll be on the phone with her lawyer as soon as we get in that truck."

Rick just glared, shaking his head. "Fuck you. You know nothing about me. I'm loaded now, and I'll hire the best lawyers to get my daughter—"

"We're done," Benji said, turning his back and leading Lucy to the truck, but Rick was apparently not done.

"You won't get what you want. Who is going to let you stay around a kid when you're an alcoholic? A sleazeball, washed-up hockey player? They would be stupid to—"

But before Rick could finish, Benji slammed her door shut, and Lucy couldn't hear Rick since Benji had the music up. She watched as Benji went around the car, Rick still yelling. But Benji seemed unfazed as he got in, slamming the door behind him. Putting the car in drive, he pulled away, his grip on the wheel so tight, his veins started to pop up.

"I'm so—"

"Don't," he said sternly as he stopped at the intersection. Turning in his seat, he looked back at Angie. "You all right, sunshine?"

"Yeah," she answered, her voice full of despondence. "My dad wouldn't take me to hockey yesterday. Coach Adler is gonna be so mad."

"No, not at all. I'll call him, don't worry," Lucy said quickly. She turned in the seat as Benji took off. "Or Benji will call since they're friends."

Angie didn't look up as she shrugged. "He grounded me because I screamed at him for wanting to go. Then he wouldn't let me call you and I cried, and he screamed at me that I was a baby. Then Nina and Heidi got to go shopping and to Chuck E. Cheese, but I had to stand in the corner."

Lucy's heart stopped. "The corner?"

"Yeah, 'cause I'm bad."

"You're not bad," Lucy said, rubbing her daughter's knee. "You're perfect."

"I don't know, Mommy. He was so mean to me and wouldn't let me do anything. I told him I wanted to go home, and that only made him madder."

"I'm sorry."

Still not looking up, Angie shrugged. "I don't know why he has to be mean."

"I don't either."

"But Grandpa did call me," she said, looking up then, and her sweet face was flushed, visibly upset. "It was nice to hear from him."

"Yeah," Lucy said, reaching out and rubbing Angie's face. "Maybe he'll come to the game Saturday."

"Cool." Then she looked to Benji. "But you're leaving tomorrow, so you

won't be there, huh, Benji?"

"No, I won't. I'm sorry, but maybe I can get your mom to FaceTime me?"

Angie smiled. "I'd like that."

"Me too," he said, flashing her a smile in the rearview mirror.

Looking back at Lucy, her eyes welled up as she let out a long breath. "I don't want to miss hockey, Mom, but Dad said he won't take me."

Rubbing her thumb along her daughter's cheek, Lucy fought back tears. "I'll see what I can do. Maybe I can talk him into letting me get you."

"I just don't want to go back," she said, the tears spilling over her cheeks. "I hate it there. All he does is yell at me, only Nina and Heidi matter. And now Nina doesn't even really talk to me. Heidi took her out all weekend. I just don't want to go back. Don't make me go!"

When she balled herself up, Lucy panicked, undoing her seatbelt and climbing in the back. Wrapping her arms around Angie, she kissed her the top of her head as her own tears started to fall. She couldn't promise she wouldn't have to send her back to Rick's. She wasn't sure what was going to happen, but one thing was for sure, she was going to fight Rick Hart tooth and nail. No one made her baby cry.

"How about we go get some ice cream? Wanna go to Chuck E. Cheese, Angie? Maybe shopping?" Benji asked and Angie peeked her head up, wiping her face. "I'm leaving tomorrow, and I need to spend the whole day with my girls. So how about we go have some fun?"

She nodded. "Really?"

"Yeah, us three? You gotta dry up those tears, okay? Know that Mommy and I will get everything fixed, okay?"

"Okay," she said, wiping her face as her little lip wobbled. "I don't want you to go, though."

"I know. Me either, sunshine. That's why we'll have so much fun today that it will last for the next two weeks. Okay?"

She nodded and looked up at Lucy. "Want to, Mommy?"

"I would love to," Lucy said, her tears begging to fall. As Lucy kissed her head, Angie leaned against her chest and Lucy slowly shook her head. What the hell was she going to do? How was she supposed to let Rick have her? This was going to get worse before it got better, and crap, Benji was going to be gone the whole time.

Damn it.

When she met Benji's gaze in the rearview mirror, her lip trembled as he tried to send her a smile. His gaze was so tender, so loving, but she could see the worry in the depths of his gray eyes. Her heart just couldn't take it. He was too good to them. Holding Angie closer, she closed her eyes and she knew Benji was there. He was going to be the rock she needed.

Together, they were going to be okay.

Chapter TWENTY

"I feel guilty."

Benji sensed Jordie looking over at him as Melissa, the AA leader, met his gaze. "Why is that, Benji? You look great. You seem so much happier, so much more open than the last time I saw you. It's almost like I'm seeing a whole different person."

She was beaming, excited, and he knew her words were true. Because he was. He hadn't seen her since they played the Kings at the beginning of the season. Both Benji and Jordie really liked the LA AA chapter and made sure to stop in when they were in town, but in this meeting, Benji's heart was heavy.

"She's right, dude. What in the world do you have to feel guilty about?"

"I know, but I met someone—Lucy," he said, more to Melissa and the three other professional hockey players who sat in the room. Another thing he liked about this chapter was it was only for athletes. Last time, there were some football and baseball players, but apparently they had stopped coming. It was sad, but it happened all the time.

Alcoholism wasn't easy to beat.

"She's spectacular and we click. She makes me laugh and she's just awesome," he said, his lips curving into a grin. "She has this little girl, Angie, who just lights up my world. I've been gone six days, and she FaceTimes me every day when she gets home, just to tell me how her day was. She looks forward to talking to me, and I love it. I love them. So damn much, but I feel so bad because I think Lucy is my soul mate, that they were meant to be in my life and to love me. And for me to love them. But if that is the case, then what about Ava and Leary? Am I disrespecting them by thinking that? By thinking that Lucy and Angie are the loves of my life? Because, looking back, I know Ava wasn't the one, she was the safe option, but I feel horrible for that."

Melissa nodded slowly as Jordie leaned on his legs. "But, didn't you say before that you know you and Ava should have divorced before the accident, but you couldn't let her go?"

"I didn't want to be alone," Benji said with a nod. "But I feel like I'm not honoring their memory by falling so hard for Lucy and Angie."

"But you are, Benji," Melissa said, bringing his attention to her. "You still think of them, you still miss them, and I'm sure Lucy and Angie know about them."

He nodded. "They do."

"Exactly. So you are doing right, Benji. You have to move on. You can't let the past hold you down."

"No, I'm not. I am moving on. I love Lucy, I love Angie, that's not the problem—"

"Have you told them?"

He paused. "No."

"Why not?"

He shrugged, shaking his head. "I don't want to say it and scare her. She'll think I'm moving too fast."

"Or is it because you've never told anyone but Ava and Leary you loved them?" she asked, holding his gaze, and he swallowed hard. He hadn't thought of that, but that didn't seem right. If he wasn't ready to move on, then he wouldn't feel the way he did for Lucy and Angie.

"No. Lucy was in a shit relationship. She's divorced now. And she was so hesitant about being with me that I think the reason why I haven't told them is because I don't want her to freak out on me. I still love Leary and Ava, I will always love them, but I know I am moving on. I just have this guilt I can't seem to shake, and I don't know what to do."

"I think it's because you haven't fully forgiven yourself for the accident," Jordie said before Melissa could say anything. "I think you still think you don't deserve this love, these girls."

Benji nodded, meeting his friend's gaze. "Absolutely."

"Well, until you forgive yourself, Benji, you'll never be able to shake the guilt," Melissa said. "Just look how far you've come. You are the poster boy for recovery. I love your story, and it pleases me to no end that you have found love again. I want you to remember how much you deserve this. Deserve them. And I want you to forgive yourself."

Biting the inside of his cheek, he looked away as he shrugged. "I'm trying."

"That's all you can do," she said. But was it enough? Was he not trying hard enough?

Moving the puck back and forth behind the goal, Benji waited as new forwards hit the ice. He noticed that the Kings took that chance for a fresh line too. Clearly this was the time to go. Banking the puck against the boards, hard, it went center ice where he thought Erik would grab it, but he didn't.

Jude Sinclair did.

"Fuck!" he yelled, coming out and rushing toward him to block him since Jayden had been at the blue line, waiting for Benji to come out. Jude was on a mission, though, and when he went to shoot, Benji dropped down, using his body as the puck came crashing into his chest guard.

Still knocked the breath out of him, though.

Luckily, Jayden had made it back, getting the rebound off of him and taking the puck up as Benji slowly got up, wheezing for breath. Skating toward the bench, he climbed over as the whistle blew. When he heard singing, he turned to see Jude, singing with his gaze on him.

"What the hell?" Sitting down as Jayden sat, Benji looked over at him. "Is your brother singing to me?"

Jayden rolled his eyes, gasping for breath as he took a long pull of water. "He's an idiot. Sings to people on the ice."

Jude scoffed at that since he was in earshot, still singing. Benji continued to look puzzled. "What's he singing? Who sings on the ice?"

"He does. It's insane, but I think he's singing the Beach Boys."

"The Beach Boys?"

"Yeah, he told me he was gonna sing 'Don't Hurt My Little Sister' to you to throw you off your game."

Benji's face twisted as he looked out at the ice, Jude skating off as he moved his head to the beat in his mind. "Lucy wasn't kidding when she said he wasn't the sharpest tool in the shed, was she?"

Jayden chuckled. "Nope, not even kinda."

Benji ignored Jude and the game continued, the Assassins down by two. It had been a tough game. They had their backup goalie in, Dylan Alexander, and he was doing fine, but it was easy to see he was rusty from not playing for a while. Leaning on the boards, Benji watched as the Assassins fought into the Kings' zone, shooting pucks left and right. When one of the Kings' players cross-checked Jordie into the boards, the bench lost it in protest. Thankfully, the ref saw it and threw his hand up.

Power play.

"Paxton, Sinclair, go," Coach yelled, and they jumped over, heading to the face-off circle.

When Jude skated by him, grinning like a fool while singing, Benji shook his head. Would Lucy be mad if he pummeled her brother? He wasn't sure if he cared, because the dude was getting on his nerves. When the puck dropped, though, Jude stopped singing and tried to win it. But Anderson was fast, kicking it back to Benji, who sent it to Jayden, who shot wide. Going around the boards, Benji rushed to get the puck before it went over the line, getting there just in time to send it to Anderson, who sent it to Titov, who shot, but the goalie batted it away. Right onto Jayden's stick. Instead of shooting, though, he whizzed it to Benji, who was ready for the one-timer, and when the red light flashed, he threw his arms up.

There was Lucy's goal.

"Fuck yeah!"

As his boys wrapped him up in a hug, he somehow met Jude's gaze. He was just grinning, nodding his head as he headed to his bench. Benji wasn't sure what that meant, but he didn't feel comfortable about it.

But he didn't have time to worry about Jude because as soon as the next line went out, the Kings scored again—in the end, winning the game. Benji hated losing, hell, everyone did, but it really sucked since it was the Kings, Jude's team, that had kicked their asses.

Defeated, the Assassins headed back into the locker room. And when he sat, Coach came in with the usual get-your-shit-together speech. When he called Benji out, saying he wasn't in the game, he was right. Between fucking Jude and the fact he was still thinking about what had happened in AA, he didn't know what to do. He needed to figure it out. Because things were happening.

Lucy had called her dad once they had gotten in the car and told him to get her a court date. It was only to get the parenting plan revised, but apparently, Rick's lawyer said they would be asking for full custody. His heart hurt remembering how hard Lucy had cried in his arms. She didn't want to do this—she didn't want to put Angie through it, and Benji got that—but Rick was a douche and needed to be put in his place. He knew it would turn out in Lucy's favor, but he worried about what that would do to Angie if Rick stuck around. He seemed like he already had one foot out the door, only hanging in to hurt Lucy, and that was mind-blowing to Benji.

How do you claim to love someone but be a complete asshole and not want to support what they love? Especially someone as amazing and sweet as Angie. Benji did not believe for a second that she had been bad or mouthy. She was always so good, yeah, a little nutty, but she was a kid and did normal kid stuff. Didn't Rick want a relationship with his daughter? Or was he too concerned with hurting Lucy because he couldn't control her? Benji didn't know, but he sure as hell worried about Lucy's sanity and Angie's heart.

It wasn't fair.

Life wasn't fair. If it were, Ava and Leary would be alive. But then, would he be where he was now? It was just all such a mindfuck because, while he didn't wish away his time with Ava and Leary, he couldn't fathom his life without Lucy and Angie. Maybe this was his normal, though. Maybe this was how his life would always be. Feeling bad for one thing, but happy about another. Could he live with that regret? If it was really regret. He wasn't sure. But one thing *was* for sure, he would talk to Lucy about it.

"Paxton, Johansson, you two are up for an interview," one of the media folks said, and Benji rolled his eyes.

He didn't like doing interviews.

Vaughn, though, he loved them, but today he looked pissed.

"You good?" Benji asked as they walked together to the hall.

"Don't want to do this today."

Benji could only nod as the media guy stopped him and Vaughn went ahead. Brie Soledad, the Assassins' new locker-room broadcaster stood with her mic up at her mouth, talking about something. She was adorable; Benji had always thought so. At one time, he had wanted to holler at her, but that was while he was actually searching for what turned out to be Lucy. Watching as Vaughn towered over her, Benji wanted to laugh. She was so little, maybe five feet, with big, blue eyes and long, brown hair that had blond at the ends. She was on the thicker side, almost like Elli Adler, but she pulled it off and all the guys liked her. She was nice, but apparently Vaughn forgot that as he stood before her, his hands on his hips, annoyance rolling off him.

"Tough game, Vaughn. Tell me, what could your team have done to win tonight?"

"Well, Brie, don't know if you were actually watching the game, but we weren't playing," he said simply, and her eyes widened as Benji held back his laughter. "We fucking sucked out there. The defense was off, the offense wasn't even doing anything. We can't win games playing like that. We have to be better."

And then he walked away.

Like he had dropped the mic.

Poor Brie looked stunned, and all Benji could do was laugh. Vaughn was in so much trouble. As he expected, Benji's interview was very short and then he headed down the hall. The media team was tearing a new one into Vaughn, just as Jude Sinclair was heading toward him.

"Hey!" he called out and Benji paused.

He looked around. He wasn't sure, but he'd thought maybe the guy wouldn't talk to him. Pressing his finger to his chest, he said, "Me?"

"You're the one dating my sister, right?"

Benji nodded, a smile pulling at his lips. "I am."

"Awesome. Well, then, yes, you," he said holding his hand out and Benji took it. "How's the chest?"

"Stings."

"I bet," Jude laughed, and he looked so much like Lucy. The whole Sinclair resemblance was a bit scary. He'd thought that Jayden and Lucy could be twins, but Jude looked so much like his brother, Benji was now convinced their genes were some scientific marvel. "Hate that we can't get together. Get to know each other."

Benji nodded. The Assassins' bus would be leaving soon for San Jose. "Yeah, but we have the wedding."

Jude gagged visibly and then nodded. "So you're going?"

"I am," he said, nodding his head.

"Awesome, my mom loves you. Like, I think she wants to marry you instead of River," he joked and Benji laughed.

"She's awesome."

"She is," he added, his face clearly full of love for Autumn. The same look Lucy always got for her mom. "But, yeah, it was great winning against you," he said with a wink.

Benji rolled his eyes. "We'll get you next time."

"Yeah, yeah. But, hey," he said, looking Benji right in the eyes. "Don't hurt my sister, okay?"

Benji wanted to laugh as he held Jude's green gaze. "Not that I would, but I'm pretty sure she'd kill me if I did."

"Oh, no doubt," he laughed, nodding. "She sure would. But, really, please don't. Not only do you seem like a good guy and I don't want you to be killed since my mother talks about you all the damn time, but Lucy's had it rough. From what I hear, you make life great for her and for Angie. Those two…it's been hard, and I want you to keep doing that. Hell, I'll pay you to keep doing that."

That made Benji laugh as he shook his head. "I don't want your money, bro. Don't worry, I love your sister, and I'm going to do everything I can for her so she can always be happy."

Jude's eyes were wide as he held Benji's gaze. "You love her? Lucy?"

Not realizing he had said that, he smiled. "I do. She doesn't know that, though."

"Oh, okay, because I don't think she loves anyone, not even me."

"Who could? You're a dipshit," Jayden said, coming up to them and putting his arm around Jude's neck. "I don't even love you."

As they tussled with each other, Benji watched and he shook his head.

These Sinclairs were crazy. When they broke apart, Jude scoffed. "Whatever, dude. I'm your favorite."

"No, Lucy is," he said with a wink for Benji and he smiled.

"Ha, well, did you hear? Paxton here loves our sister."

Jayden looked to Benji and he shrugged. "It's true."

"Well, duh, I knew that from the rip. Question is, does Lucy love you?" Jayden asked, shaking his head. "I told you, I don't know if she knows how to love."

Benji wasn't sure and was unable to answer as Jude shook his head. "Well, for her sake, let's hope so. She told me she loved me yesterday, and I think she meant it," Jude said and they laughed. "Maybe our sister's cold, dead heart is coming back to life."

"You guys are too hard on her. She's really great," Benji said. He knew they were tough on her. It was some weird Sinclair thing they all did, but he felt he needed to defend her. They both looked at him like he was crazy, though.

"Shit, he is in love," Jude laughed, smacking Benji on the back.

"Right? Scary. You should see them together. It's like Mom and River, just less gagging 'cause I want Lucy to be happy," Jayden added with a grin on his face.

Jude liked that and nodded. "Cool. Let's hope it works."

"It will," Benji said confidently.

He just hoped he was right.

"Now, Mom, Dad is coming and I know—"

But her mother held her hand up, her other one laced with River's. "As long as he makes sure that piece of junk does not get our baby, then he can come to any game he wants. I'll even invite him to my wedding."

"Well, I mean, let's talk that over for a second," River said. Lucy nodded since that was the last thing she'd expected her mother to say, but she was thankful.

Because she was legit losing her shit.

She hadn't wanted to invite her dad to the game—she'd much rather keep it strictly professional—but he was going above and beyond for Angie. After fighting Rick's lawyer about court dates, he finally got one that was good for both parties. Apparently, Rick was leaving for Christmas, which was good for Lucy since Angie wouldn't have to go to his house after this next time before the new year.

But she did have to go.

Lucy couldn't bring herself to tell her.

Her father had tried everything, talking to Rick's lawyer and even Rick himself, but he wouldn't just let her be. He was forcing her to come to his house, and it scared Lucy to her core. Especially with Benji being gone. Stress was eating her alive, and she was so worried. She wasn't sure how, but during all this, she was still working to her full potential.

She had hired a new designer, Meg Patterson, and Meg had taken on a lot of the work. That was great because Lucy could focus on Benji's design. She had maybe three more days on it, and while it was coming out perfectly to her specs, she was nervous he would hate it. She was sure he'd lie and say he loved it, but still, it worried her.

And she was so troubled about Angie.

Angie just wasn't herself. She was withdrawn and scared, and it was killing Lucy. The only time she was the child Lucy recognized was when she was on the ice or talking to Benji. Did Angie blame Lucy for the Rick thing? Did she hate her mother because she knew she had to go back? Lucy wasn't sure because when they went to therapy on Wednesday, Angie only spoke about how she loved Lucy and didn't want to leave her. Lucy was a mess for sure, but her only saving grace was calls from Benji.

He was just so damn good to her. He did everything to make her laugh. To joke with her, to turn her on, and to tease her. He was everything she could ever need and she missed him dearly. She was ready for the next seven days to zip by so she could hold him.

Hug him.

God, she needed a hug from him.

"Oh, baby, come here," her mother said before pulling her into her arms and kissing her hard on the cheek. "It's okay. Don't worry. You are amazing, Lucy, and such a good mom. Please remember that."

Lucy's mouth curved as she closed her eyes. It wasn't Benji's hug, but it was pretty damn close. Benji had told her almost the same thing that morning, but there wasn't a time these days when she didn't need to hear it. Especially when Rick was singing a different tune.

"I love you, Lucy Lane."

"I love you, Mom," she said softly, hugging her tightly. When River's hand came to rest on her back, she looked up at him, smiling as his lips turned up. "You too, Riv."

He smiled gently, patting her back. "Back at you, sweetheart."

Sucking in a breath, she let it out slowly, still holding her mom. "I wish Benji was here."

She didn't miss the little happy giggle her mother did before she wrapped her up tighter in her arms. "You should marry him."

"Calm down, woman," she said, breaking out of her arms and shaking her head. Pinning River with a look, she said, "Ask the woman to marry you, and now she's marrying all of us off."

River scoffed. "Don't act like she hasn't been trying to marry you off the whole time I've known you."

"Touché," she said as she saw her father walking through the doors with his child bride on his arm, Ellen. "Shit, he's here," she muttered as he came toward them. Her father was a handsome man; there was no denying that. He was tall, with dark hair and green eyes. His face was weathered from the stress of his job, but he was still a good-looking man. When he met Lucy's gaze, his eyes shone with love. Still. It was insane, and it made her heart hurt. She had loved that man with everything inside of her. He had been her rock through the divorce from Rick, and he'd loved her so much. She was his little girl. But he'd betrayed all of them and she couldn't let it go.

Coming to a stop before them, he smiled, his whole face lighting up with the movement. "Hey, everyone."

"Hey, Dad," Lucy said, tucking her hands into her coat pockets as her mother was stone-faced.

"Mark."

"Autumn, you look great, a lot slimmer. Are you not feeding her, River?"

He meant it as a joke, but River didn't even crack a smile. "She eats just fine."

"Oh, good, that's good," he said, looking to Lucy. "You remember Ellen, my wife?"

Ellen, with her big, blue eyes and even bigger breasts that were on display in the middle of a freezing cold rink—not that it was any of Lucy's business—grinned over at her. Lucy tried to smile, she did, but it didn't work. "Hey."

"Hey! I'm so excited to see your daughter play. Mark talks fondly of her."

Lucy nodded, taking in a breath. "Yeah, she's amazing. Oh, they're hitting the ice. Let's go sit down," she said, turning without letting anyone object. Her mother walked beside her with River on the other side as they climbed the bleachers. When they got to their normal spot, the one Benji hated, she sat down and turned her phone on to call him.

Before she could, though, her father cleared his throat. "Laney, before I forget, next week when you go to drop Angie off, make sure you call me, keep me on in your pocket so I can hear everything that goes down. If Angie doesn't want to go, don't make her—make him make her. You just stand there. I know it will be hard, but you don't stop him."

Lucy's heart dropped, but before she could say anything, River asked, "How can she do that? That will be heartbreaking. Not to mention, unfair to Angie."

Her father nodded, his face stricken. "I know, but it's in the parenting plan.

Lucy doesn't have to force her to go, but she does have to drive her there and Angie has to be the one to say no. What Rick does is on him, which is why I want to be on the phone."

Autumn took in a quick breath, tears in her eyes as Lucy's own started to flood. When River's hand came onto Lucy's, she looked at him. "No worries, we'll go with you. We'll be with you. Don't you worry."

"I can't stop him?"

Her father shook his head. "No, honey, no one can. It's on him."

"Even if he's hurting her?"

"That's why I'll be on the phone."

"She'll hate me."

"No, just talk to her," he stressed as a tear rolled down her cheek and her heart ached.

"I can't do it," she whispered, and before her mom or dad could say anything more, she got up, heading down the bleachers as more tears threaten to fall. Her heart was pounding. It wasn't even exchange day, but she was about to have a panic attack. She couldn't watch Rick force her child to leave. She knew he would do it just to hurt her. And she couldn't do anything about it? No. She couldn't fucking do that.

Reaching the fresh air, she lifted her phone up and dialed Benji's number.

When his face came over the phone, he was smiling, but then his grin disappeared as he stared back at her. "What's wrong? Are you okay? Angie?"

"No," she cried, shaking her head just as her mother put her arm around her.

"Lucy, baby, what's wrong?"

How she was able to tell him what her father said through her tears would always be a mystery, but she did, her heart breaking in her chest as what she had to do tortured her. How was she supposed to tell this to Angie? Wouldn't that be betraying her daughter? "How am I supposed to do this, Benji? How? Tell me how?"

Shaking his head, he ran his hand down his face as he sucked in a deep breath. "Fuck, baby, I don't know," he pulled in a deep breath as she cried, leaning into her mother. "I can't come in early—we have a game Friday night and Saturday afternoon, or I would be there," he said and she nodded.

"I know."

"I want to be there. Can River go? And your mom? Can you guys go, Autumn?"

"Yeah, we'll be there, honey," her mother said, but Lucy wanted Benji. He knew what to do, how to calm her and handle Rick. Her mother and River might fly off the handle, and then everything would be a fucking mess. Even though it already was.

"I can't do this, Benji. Explain how I am supposed to do this."

"Like the strong woman you are," he said simply, holding her gaze. "You can do this. You will do this. You will be strong for Angie. You will tell her it's only two days and then she's back home with us for the rest of the month. She is as strong as you, baby. She's got this. She was raised by you," he said, his voice breaking, and Lucy swallowed a sob as he had to look away. Looking back at her, he tried to smile, but it didn't reach his eyes. "She is the best thing in this world, and she's got this. I know she does, as I know you have it. You hear me?"

Her lip wobbled as she nodded. "Yeah, I hear you. I wish you were here."

He paused, letting out a deep sigh. "I wish I never had to leave. I'm sorry I'm not there."

"It isn't your job—"

"Shut up," he said simply and she laughed, her face brightening as her tears rolled down her cheeks. Looking into his eyes, she felt her heart yearning for him. He was so amazing. "Now, go watch her kick some ass and position the phone so I can see."

"Okay. I miss you, Benji. I'll call you back in a moment. I'm sure my mom wants to cry all over me."

Autumn laughed against her shoulder. "I do."

"See?" she said dryly and Benji laughed.

"Fine. Hurry, though. I don't want to miss much, but I do I miss you more, baby."

She smiled as she nodded. "Be back soon."

He waved and she hung up, turning in her mother's arms and hugging her tightly. Autumn's tears wet Lucy's face as she kissed her cheek. "He's right, Lucy Lane. You are so strong and you've got this. You do. I know you do. But man, it's gonna be hard."

"It is," she agreed, nuzzling her nose against her mom's shoulder. "It's going to gut me."

"Me too," her mom whispered as she hugged her tightly, kissing her one more. "But damn that man for being just freaking perfect! I've never crushed on a man, but Benji Paxton has my heart."

Closing her eyes as her mom held her, Lucy smiled. "Me too, Mom. Me too."

The rest of the week went by quickly. While Lucy was thankful for that since Benji would be home the following day, her heart was aching because she knew she had to take Angie to Rick. She hated it. It was December; she was supposed to be excited for Christmas, for her brothers coming in town, and for all of them being together for her mom's wedding. But she was so stressed out she hadn't done a lick of shopping and all she could think about was watching Angie being forced to go with her father.

It was heartbreaking, but she had to follow what her dad had said.

And jeez, he was a whole other issue.

He was great at the game, and Angie just ate it up that he was there. He was extremely sweet to her and actually very nice to River and her mom. She didn't know what he was up to and hated that she assumed he was up to something since he had been so helpful, but it wasn't like him. The last three years had been hell. He had manipulated all of them and burned his relationships with his sons, so she was sure she was next.

Leaning on her hand, she dreaded every hour that passed. The closer to meetup time, the more her belly hurt. Her mom and River were meeting her at the rink where Angie would only have an hour practice since Rick said he wouldn't meet her there. It was frustrating because Angie wanted to practice, but what could she do? It was his time, and he was following the parenting plan like he had told her many times.

When her office door opened, she looked up as Rayne came in, her brows pressed together. "Hey, Lucy."

"Yeah?"

"So, I know it's none of my business," she said, falling into the seat in front of her desk. "And usually, I would ignore it, but—"

"What's going on?" Lucy asked, her heart kicking into high speed at Rayne's worried expression. She was usually so happy-go-lucky, but she looked troubled.

"Well…" She paused, handing Lucy a piece of paper. But when she looked down, she wasn't sure what she was looking at. "I follow Nikky Jiggler's Blog of Puck Bunnies. I know, it's trashy and just something I find hilarious. This chick goes around and sleeps with all these hockey players and then writes up these insane blog posts about them. It's very funny, but also pretty scandalous."

Her stomach dropped. *Please don't say what I think you're about to say.*

Swallowing hard, Lucy looked down, and there it was, Benji's name.

"She doesn't have a blog post yet, but it's just his name and the words 'To Come,' so I don't know. I don't believe it, but I thought you should know."

Letting out a long breath, Lucy shook her head. "Fucking figures. I have the worst luck in my life. I don't need this." Rayne nodded as Lucy got up, her heart pounding. "Thanks for showing me this. I gotta go get Angie."

"Are you okay? I'm sorry."

"No, don't be. And I've been better, but it's nothing I can't handle," she said as Rayne stopped her.

"I don't believe it, though. Benji isn't that guy."

Lucy only nodded, patting Rayne's hand before heading out of her office and out the door. She couldn't believe this. Getting in her car, she put her phone in its holder and FaceTimed Benji.

"Hey, baby," he answered as she backed out of the driveway. "Off to get Angie?"

"Yeah," she said sharply as she put the car in drive to pull away. "Do me a favor. Go to NikkyJiggler.com."

He made a face. "Why in the hell would I go on that filth's website?"

"So you've heard of her?"

"Everyone has heard of her. She's trash," he said simply. "Why?"

"Go look."

He didn't say anything for a moment, and when she looked over at him, he was staring at his computer. Making a face, he looked back at her. "Okay, do I need to defend myself here, or are we good and you know this is complete bullshit?"

Her brow furrowed. "I mean, what do you think?"

"I think it's a pile of bullshit. But that doesn't matter. What matters is what you think."

"I don't believe it, if that is what you're asking. But it would make sense."

"Excuse me? Make sense how?"

"I'm the queen of bad fucking luck. Finally find this guy I'm really digging and he cheats on me with some whore. Figures."

"Well, you're actually in luck, my love, 'cause my heart only wants you and that's it. This is bullshit, and I'll be calling my lawyer as soon as we get off the phone."

She nodded, shaking her head. She already knew that. Benji wouldn't cheat on her. He wasn't that kind of guy. Still, it was nice for him to reiterate that, though. "Okay."

"I'm sorry this came up now."

She shrugged. "My luck. But like you said, it's bullshit. I'm not worried about it."

"Are you sure? Are you okay?" he asked, and she shook her head again.

"No, I'm not."

"Do you want to talk about it?"

"No, 'cause it won't do anything," she said sharply, feeling bad for it, but she was just pissed. Stupid Nikky Jiggler. Stupid Rick.

"Okay," he said slowly as she pulled into the school parking lot. "You look beautiful today. At least when that douche is being an asshole, he'll have regret for ever treating you wrong."

Her lip quirked as she put the car in park. "Just what I want."

"I know, baby, I'm sorry," he said as her eyes met his. "I wish I was there."

"Me too. I haven't even really talked to her about it. I told her that we had to meet him, and she had to tell him she didn't want to go. She didn't like that, told me she's scared of him, Benji. How can you be okay with your daughter being scared of you?"

He shook his head. "Baby, I don't know. It's killing me. It really is."

"I just— Shit, she's getting in the car. Hey, honey bun!"

"Hey, Mom!" Angie jumped in, leaning over the seat and giving her a kiss. "Hey, Benji! You come home tomorrow, right?"

"Yup. We're still having that dance party Sunday?"

"Duh! You better be ready."

"Oh, I am," he promised and Lucy grinned as Angie snatched the phone and sat down.

As Lucy pulled out, Angie said, "Hopefully, I'll see you Saturday. Mom says I have to tell my dad I don't want to go to his house."

"Yeah, I know, sunshine. Are you okay with that?"

Lucy's heart broke as Angie said, "Not really, but Mom says I have to."

"You do. It's legal adult crap that you shouldn't have to deal with. But do me a favor, honey," he asked, and Lucy caught Angie grinning in the mirror.

"Anything!"

He chuckled and it made Lucy's heart swell. "No matter what happens, you're coming home Sunday, and you don't have to go back till after the first of the year. So just remember that and try to have fun."

"But, Benji! He won't take me to hockey and he yells all the time."

"I know, sunshine, so just be strong, okay?"

When a tear slid down Lucy's face, she wiped it away as her baby said, "Okay, I can do that."

"All right, I miss you and can't wait to see you Sunday!"

"Me too! I love you, Benji."

That stole her breath and Lucy gripped the steering wheel as Angie grinned at the phone. Did her baby just say that? Holy crap, she did, and when Benji spoke, his voice was hoarse and full of emotion. "I love you too, sunshine. Be good, and I'll see you soon."

"Okay! Win some games, okay?"

"Of course. Hey, let me say bye to your mom."

"Okay. Here, Mom," she said, handing the phone back.

Holding it in her lap, Lucy felt him looking up at her but she couldn't put him in his spot yet.

"I'm driving, sorry you're getting my double chin."

He laughed. "No, all I see is my gorgeous girlfriend."

She grinned as she turned onto his road. "Yeah, yeah, sweet-talker. I'm almost home."

"It could be your home," he suggested and she shook her head.

"Shh, you. Can I call you later? I gotta get inside to do some work before taking Angie to practice."

"Yeah. Listen, I'll be at the game, but I'm gonna call you before we have to hit the ice. To check on you."

"Okay," she said, pulling into the driveway.

"It's gonna be okay. Call me before if you need me."

"I will," she promised as she parked and held the phone up. When she saw he had tears in his eyes, she was breathless. He loved Angie so much, and he was just as pained as Lucy was. She prayed what he said was true. That they would both be strong through the ordeal, that it was going to be okay.

But she was pretty sure it wasn't going to be.

Chapter
TWENTY-ONE

Lucy's heart was in her throat.

Her body was vibrating with nerves.

Her stomach was a mess.

And she was two seconds from falling apart.

She couldn't do this.

No. She *could* do this.

She *would* do this.

Mindlessly, she stroked the back of Angie's head as she looked out the window, hoping that Angie couldn't sense her anxiety. She was sweaty, a little stinky, but Lucy didn't care. She needed her to know she loved her because she was terrified that Angie would hate her after this—if this went the way her father said it would. How was she going to stand there and allow Rick to take her away? God, this was going to suck.

But maybe he would just let her be.

"Grandma, why are you coming?" Angie asked then, bringing Lucy's attention back to her.

"We are going wedding shopping after we drop you off. So we figured we'd take you so I can make Mommy go," she said with a laugh and Angie smiled.

"I want to go wedding shopping! Maybe Dad won't make me go with him," she said, her eyes full of hope as she met Lucy's gaze.

"Yeah, let's hope so," River said before Lucy could. "But remember, baby, there is a chance he will and you'll have to go."

"But I don't want to," she said simply and Lucy's lip started to quiver. She hated feeling so fucking weak. Why couldn't she control this? Why couldn't anything go the way she wanted? The only good thing was Angie and Benji. Well, when they were both with her.

"I know, baby, but we might not have a choice," Autumn explained, turning in her seat.

But that didn't work for Angie. Turning to Lucy, her gaze bored into her mother's as she asked, "Mommy, you won't make me, will you?"

She shook her head. "No honey, I won't. I promise I won't. But he can make you."

Angie's face twisted in confusion and maybe a bit of horror as she looked at her. "So I might have to go?"

Lucy's eyes started to flood with tears and she cupped Angie's sweet little cherub face. "Yeah, but remember what Benji said? It's only two days and then you'll be back home."

Angie bit into her lip as she looked out the window. "Okay."

"I'm sorry, Angie. I wish we could just go shopping."

"Me too," she answered, and then Lucy's stomach dropped when she realized they were in the parking lot of Walmart.

No. Not yet. Fuck. Shit.

When her phone vibrated, she looked down to see it was a text from Benji.

> *Benji: You've got this. Keep your cool. Don't give him any fuel for his fucked-up fire. Okay?*

She was shaking too badly to text him back, and when she looked up, she saw Rick's car. Her heart dropped into her stomach as River stopped in the spot beside him. Lucy hit her dad's name in her phone and he answered but she didn't speak, holding it in her hand. She went to turn, tell Angie that she was sorry again, that she loved her, but Angie took a deep breath and opened the door, her chin held high. Lucy almost lost it. She felt like she was falling apart, and she knew she would never remember getting out or walking around the car.

Before Rick could say anything, Angie took Lucy's hand and said, "I don't want to go to your house, Dad."

He snorted, folding his arms over his chest. "That right? Your mom tell you to tell me that?"

"No," Lucy said, her hands shaking at her sides as her mom and River got out of the car.

He laughed. "Brought the cavalry, I see. Where is that boyfriend? He off cheating on you again?"

Lucy's head tilted to the side, her eyes narrowing. She'd had no reason to assume so, but now she was pretty sure Rick had something to do with that website. With Nikky Jiggler. "Why would you say that?"

"Word on the street—or blog, I guess," he snarked and Lucy's glare deepened.

"So you're following hockey blogs now?"

He shrugged. "When they have the name of the dude who's trying to play daddy to my daughter, yeah, I do."

"Well, that's fine. But one thing is for sure, Benji is not you, Rick," her mother spat, but she pressed her lips together when River squeezed her hand.

"Aw, I don't miss you, Autumn. Why are you here?" he sneered at her and then he rolled his eyes. "Angie, let's go."

"No. I don't want to go."

"Get in the car, Angela," he said more sternly, his eyes boring into Lucy's.

"No, Dad. I don't want to go. I want to stay with my mom," she said louder. "Go home, go to Disney World with Heidi and Nina."

Lucy looked up. "What? That's where you're going for Christmas?"

"Yeah. So?"

While she didn't want Rick to take Angie anyway, he couldn't even want to take her? "You didn't tell me this."

"Why would I?"

"Um, I'd assume you'd take Angie."

"No, I can't afford it."

"Wow, Rick, that's low. Even for you."

He scoffed. "What?"

"You don't think she'd want to go? You can't make that work?"

"I can't make money appear," he said simply and Lucy shook her head.

"But you have all kinds of money for all these lawyers?"

He rolled his eyes, taking a step forward. "Angela, let's go now."

"No!" she yelled and his face started to turn red.

"I won't tell you again, Angela Lynn. Now."

"I said no," she said, wrapping her arms around Lucy's waist.

Meeting Lucy's gaze, he pointed to Angie. "Let her go and make her get in the car."

Lucy only shook her head no, her tears spilling over her cheeks. "No. According to my lawyer and our parenting plan, I don't have to force her to go with you."

"You stupid bitch," he muttered, pulling his phone out.

"Watch your mouth, Hart," River warned and Rick laughed.

"Shut it, old man. You don't even belong here," he spat back, and Lucy looked back at River, shaking her head.

River sucked in a deep breath as Rick yelled into the phone. "She won't fucking come. What? No, this is my time. No, I'm sure her mom talked her into this. Whatever. Okay."

He hung up and then looked over at Lucy and Angie, his eyes full of anger. "Get in the car, Angela, or I'll make you."

Angie's eyes widened as Lucy's heart broke into a million pieces. This was really about to happen. Holding her breath, Lucy looked down at her daughter as Angie said, "I don't want to."

"I don't care what you want. Get in the car." Rick practically stomped his foot.

"No!"

"Lucy, make her get in the car!" he yelled, his fists clenching at his sides, his voice rattling her soul.

Lucy's lips trembled as she said, "No."

"Lucy, be a fucking adult here and give me my kid."

"I don't have to," she said simply, trying to keep her cool, when she really wanted to rip his head off.

"Mommy, don't cry," Angie said then, her arms tightening around Lucy. "It's okay. I'm not going."

"Yes, you fucking are," Rick said, grabbing Angie's arm and yanking her to him. Lucy cried out, wanting to hold on to her, but she couldn't.

She fucking couldn't.

Pulling away as hard as she could, Angie dug her fingers into Lucy as she screamed, "Mommy, make him stop!"

"I can't, Angie. I'm so sorry," Lucy sobbed as River came to her side, hugging her shoulders and kissing her cheek.

"It's okay, honey, breathe," he soothed. But she couldn't. She couldn't do this.

"Leave her alone!" Lucy yelled and Rick yanked once more, but Angie wasn't letting her go.

"Mommy! No!"

But then Autumn bent down, her hand on Angie's back as Rick screamed at her. "Let go!" he yelled but Angie wouldn't let go.

"Two days, my love. Just two. Just go," Lucy heard her mom say. "Just two."

"Grandma, I don't want to!"

"I know, my love, but you have to," she said softly.

Rick was breathing hard, glaring at Lucy. "This is all your fucking fault," he seethed, but she shook her head.

"No, it's yours. You've made it to where she doesn't want you," she spat back, her heart breaking.

"Mommy, I don't want to go," Angie cried, her fingers still biting into Lucy's

waist.

Lucy looked down at her sweet baby and slowly nodded as she cupped her face. "I know, baby. I'm so sorry." Angie's little lip quivered as her tears rushed down her cheeks. With all the strength she had, Lucy whispered, "Only two days."

"And then Benji will be home?"

"Who the fuck cares? Get in the car!" Rick yelled, but Lucy nodded.

"He will be and he'll be so proud that you were strong and went. We both will."

Angie's bottom lip puckered out and then she nodded slowly, letting go of Lucy. Rick went to grab her, but she moved out of his way, glaring up at him. "Stop! You're so mean."

"Get in the car, now."

"I'm going!" she yelled back, her tears streaming down her face. Angie shook her head and looked back at Lucy. "I love you, Mommy."

"I love you more," she said, her voice breaking as the sobs suffocated her. "I'm so sorry."

But Angie just shrugged resignedly, grabbing her bag from Autumn and then walking toward his car. Getting in, Rick looked back at Lucy and glared.

"Thanks for ruining our fucking weekend."

"If anyone ruined anything—a weekend, a relationship—it was you, Rick Hart, and you'll have to live with that," Autumn spat at him. "You will be completely alone one day, and then what?"

"Whatever, lady. You watch—when I win, I'll make sure you never see her again."

Autumn took a step toward him. "Bring it, asshole."

Rick laughed, stepping back as Lucy clung to River, crying so hard, it hurt everywhere. As Lucy watched Rick drive off, Angie looked back at them, her little tears falling as she waved slowly.

It was enough to make Lucy wish she were dead.

It was almost midnight when Benji FaceTimed her.

When she hit answer and the little box of herself appeared in the corner, she could see she looked like death. Her face was red and swollen; she had cried until she couldn't cry anymore, and her heart just ached.

"Hey, baby," he whispered and she tried to smile, but nothing moved. No, she was frozen in a state of turmoil. "It didn't go well?"

"No," she answered, shaking her head as she rubbed her face against his pillow. "He tried to yank her away from me, Benji. And she clung to me, crying for me not to make her go. I couldn't do anything. I just cried and, River, bless him, he was holding me, telling me it was okay, but it wasn't. It was horrible."

Benji's brow furrowed as he shook his head. "I'm sure you handled it like a boss, but still, I'm so sorry, baby."

A certain kind of calm washed over her, her heart slowing a bit as she nodded. "She was so strong, though. She let me go and she went of her own accord."

"Of course, she did. She's your child."

"She is," she agreed, wiping away a tear. "I hate him so much, Benji. You know where he is going for Christmas?"

"Where?"

"To Disney World, but he can't afford to take Angie."

Benji scoffed. "Thought he had all kinds of money."

"Apparently not."

"That piece of shit. Whatever, that's fine. We'll take her to Disney World, and you better believe I'll make sure she sleeps in Cinderella's castle."

Lucy smirked. "Only, like, celebrities can sleep in there."

He made a face. "I'm a professional athlete. Don't you worry, I'll get us up there."

She smiled, shaking her head. "You're crazy."

"About you, I know," he said with a wink and her heart fluttered. Shaking his head, he curved his lips as he whispered, "I don't know how I am going to make it until tomorrow. To see you."

"I don't either."

"It will be hard."

"But we'll make it."

"Yup," he agreed, lying back in his bed, his hair falling in his face. "Are you at my house?"

She shrugged, a grin pulling at her lips. "Yeah, I didn't want to go home and have Baylor be all over me as I cried."

"Yeah, I mean, you can move in tomorrow if you want."

She rolled her eyes. "Anyway...great game."

He chuckled as his lips turned up in a big grin. "I got four penalties 'cause every dude I saw was Rick."

"That's awesome in my opinion."

He laughed as he nodded. "I guess. Your brother was just as bad. Apparently your mom called all the boys, crying 'cause you wouldn't answer the phone. She told Jayden you were so strong and she was so proud of you and Angie, but he didn't give me details."

"She was great, but she did try to make me come home with her and River.

Had to get out of that quick."

He chuckled. "Yeah, you've seen enough family members having sex."

"Right? Gosh," she said as she ran her fingers through her hair. "I have such a headache and I'm so tired."

"Go to bed. Or better yet, go take a bath."

She shook her head. "I don't want to move, and I also don't want to drop my phone in the bathtub."

He grinned. "Shoot, I was hoping to see you naked," he said with a wink, and she smiled back.

"Perv."

"Only on days that end in 'Y.'"

Rolling her eyes, she laughed. Leaning back into the pillows, she smiled as she held his gaze. She missed him so much and couldn't wait for him to be home. Clearing her throat, she said what she had been thinking about like mad when she wasn't thinking about killing Rick. "I was pretty surprised to hear Angie tell you she loved you."

He smiled, his face brightening before her eyes. God, he was so beautiful when he looked at her like that. "That girl. Man, she has my heart."

Grinning, Lucy nodded. "And I think you have hers."

She wanted to tell him he had her heart. That she loved him. But she wanted to do it in person. She wanted to feel his skin under her fingers as she whispered the words. She wanted to see his eyes get brighter, feel his kisses after he whispered the words back to her. Because she was pretty sure he was in love with her too. No, she knew he was, and it was insane and crazy, but he was her insane and crazy. And she loved him.

With everything inside of her.

"I hope so. I promise, Lucy, I just want to do right by you guys."

"You are," she said, her throat thick with emotion.

"Good," he said with a nod.

"You'll be a great dad again one day, Benji. That's for sure," she said. She wasn't sure why she'd said that. She just knew it, though. She prayed that one day was with her, but there was a chance it wouldn't be. She hated that she still thought like that, but maybe she was just one fucked-up chick. Who knew? But, Benji, he grinned at the possibility.

"I hope so. Which, by the way, you're down for more kids, right?"

She laughed, making a face. "Whoa, what?"

"Whoa, what, what? You're the only one I'm making babies with."

Her eyes widened. "Me?"

"You. How many?"

She giggled. "I don't know, crazy!"

"Really?" he asked and she shook her head, her laughter subsiding. She had always thought she would have a big family like her mom did.

Swallowing hard but feeling completely silly, she said, "No, I do want more kids."

"Like five more."

"Jesus take the wheel. Benjamin, are you insane?"

That had him laughing from the gut. "Okay, four."

"One more."

"What? Two more," he persisted and she laughed.

"How are we planning kids when, one, we aren't married, two, we aren't even living together, and three, we haven't even proclaimed our love for each other," she asked.

When he went to say something, she stopped him. "And if you are in love with me, do not—and I repeat, do not—do that over the phone."

He nodded. "Fair enough."

Fair enough?

She glared. "Great. Now I'm going to analyze that."

He laughed. "As long as you're smiling, you can analyze anything you want."

Grinning ear to ear, she and her heart couldn't handle it. This was too deep, too serious, and she just couldn't right now. "Fine, lower that phone so I can analyze what's in your pants."

His cheeks reddened a bit. "Who's the perv now? Pervie McPerv."

Leaning on the pillows as she laughed, she knew she would never love anyone the way she loved Benjamin Paxton.

Now she just had to tell him that.

In person.

When Benji saw his house, he was nearly bouncing in his seat.

It had been thirteen long days without Lucy's kisses and Angie's hugs.

He was ready to be home.

To be with his girls.

The Assassins did great, winning seven of the nine games they played on the road. The defense was getting their shit together. The boys were finally playing as a team, and while he was proud of them, he just wanted to be home. He wanted to see Lucy; he wanted to take her in his arms and tell her he had loved her from the moment he saw her. He wanted her to know that he would stand beside her and support her through all the shit with Rick.

He wanted her to move in.

Marry him.

Have his babies.

Crazy, yes, as fuck, but he didn't care. Lucy Sinclair was his soul mate.

The love of his life and nothing could ever change that.

Was there guilt? Yes, but he was going to have to deal with that because God gave him Lucy and Angie. Maybe as a reward for cleaning up and being a decent man. He wasn't sure, but he wasn't letting them go. He hoped, prayed that Ava and Leary were up in heaven, happy for him, and he hoped one day he would get to see them again and apologize for everything. But until then, he was going to live the greatest life he could with Lucy and Angie, honoring their memory in the process.

Pulling into the driveway, he could see the lights were on downstairs. He saw Lucy moving through the living room, and a grin pulled at his lips. She had said the design was done, and while he was excited to see it, his only concern was her. Getting out of the car, he left his bags and all but ran to the front door. Before he could open it, she did, her face so bright and happy, he couldn't speak.

He reached for her, pulling her against him as his lips crashed into hers. Wrapping her arms around his neck, she kissed him hard, their hearts beating together as one. Nuzzling her nose in his neck, she whispered, "I needed this hug."

"Me too, baby," he said roughly against her shoulder. "So fucking bad."

He squeezed her once more and she smiled against his neck as she hugged him back. He just felt right.

He was home.

Pulling away, she grinned up at him. "Now, before you take me up against whatever surface you can find, please let me show you this design. I'm so proud of it."

He eyed her. "Will you be naked at the end?"

"No, but that's because I need you to focus," she added when he groaned.

"Can't we bang for a couple hours and then come and look at the design? Thirteen days, Lucy. Thirteen."

"Can we not talk about banging where the neighbors can hear you?"

"No," he said bluntly and she laughed.

"Dork! I get it and I want you, but I really want you to see what I've done. Angie helped too."

He shook his head. "Dirty, throwing Angie in like that."

She grinned. "I know, come on," she said, pulling him inside. When she closed the door behind her, his lips curved as he took in his now grown-up living room. She had done an amazing job, the light and dark grays playing off each other with the dark gray sectional. "So everything is superchic. Like, this is top-of-the-line awesomeness, and let me just say, that TV was a pain to hang. I had to hire four dudes to do it," she said, running her hand along the bottom of the TV as he laughed.

"Should have seen me and Shea carrying that sucker in."

"I bet! So I left space on the walls for maybe one day hanging candids of you and people you love and shit," she said offhandedly, but before he could say anything else, she was pulling him into the kitchen. She had done it with a very clean, slick look and it shone in there. "This is my favorite spot," she said, pointing to the little nook where she had put a big, fluffy chair and side table. "Figure when I come over, I'll be here."

He nodded. "Looks perfect for you."

"I thought so," she said with a wink, dragging him back into the living room and over to the stairs. "Another favorite part."

He looked up at the wall next to the stairs and every single hockey picture she could find was hanging up along the stairwell. "Wow."

"Yeah, isn't it amazing? And let me say, you pack like a man."

He scoffed. "I am a man."

"Whatever," she said, pointing to a frame that had a very elaborate drawing of him in it. "Angie did that for you."

His face broke into a grin as read the little message she had put on it. "'My favorite player, Benji Paxton. #20. Love, Angie. But don't tell Jude, Jayden, or Jace.' Well, at least she covers her bases."

Lucy nodded. "She's a smart girl."

"Yeah, she is," he agreed as they went into his collectible room. "Wow, Lucy," he said, taking in the glass cases she had installed with his collectibles on display in all their glory. On the south wall was another big TV and his gamer chair. "This is my man cave."

"Yeah, and apparently, these toys are a big deal. The guys I hired were annoying about them all."

"They are," he said dryly, smacking her butt playfully when she rolled her eyes. "Collectibles."

"Yeah, okay, come on," she said then, laughing as she pulled him into the first bathroom and then the first bedroom. "So, I know this is silly, and you said you wanted this to be a guest room, but I figured two guest rooms were unnecessary, so I left it empty in here."

He nodded. "For Angie, when you finally decide to move in."

"Okay, so that wasn't silly of me?"

"No, you should have just moved her stuff in."

She rolled her eyes. "Let's wait and make sure."

"What in the hell are we waiting for?" he shot back at her, but she shook her head, moving down the hall.

"Anyway..." she said, blowing out a long breath and flashing him a grin before leading him to the other bedroom that was a guest room and his office.

More sports memorabilia was hanging on the walls and it was awesome. He loved it. But his bedroom was probably his favorite. She had done lots of blues with accents of white and gray.

It was perfect.

He smiled up at her, but then something caught his eye. Going around the bed, he looked at the wall that held a picture of a very young version of him and how he remembered Ava, her blond hair up in a messy bun, sweat dripping down her face as she held a brand-new Leary. He gripped his chest, emotion choking him as took in the beautiful picture. It was the day Ava had given birth to Leary, after a long and horrible labor. Leary had gotten stuck and it was scary, but Ava had been a champ. He could still remember her cries as she pushed their daughter out, and how afterward, he had gone out and gotten shit-faced to celebrate Leary's arrival.

He was so pathetic.

It was almost too much to bear and his eyes flooded with tears. "That day was awesome. Leary was so beautiful," he whispered.

"She was."

"I went out and got drunk that night. Didn't even go back to the hospital, stayed at a buddy's house. Ava was so mad at me, for good reason."

Coming up beside him, Lucy reached out, straightening the frame. "Well, she would be proud of who you are today."

His lips curved slightly as he took in the picture, his heart aching.

"I hope you don't mind, though, that I hung it. I found the picture in the shed, had it enlarged, and then framed it. I thought it was nice and a good memorial for them. And then, I added us," she said with a laugh. He looked down at the picture of Angie, Lucy, and him getting ice cream two weeks before. He choked on a sob as he nodded. It was a great picture, all of them making silly faces, and God, he loved them.

"It's perfect," he somehow forced out. "I went to AA when we were in LA, and I talked about you, Angie, Ava, and Leary. How I felt guilty."

His voice broke, and Lucy's hand came to rest on his. "Why would you feel guilty?"

Glancing over at her, his eyes were hazy with tears as he whispered, "Because I never thought I could let go of my first love, that I could actually meet someone, and then that I could love that someone. Until I met you and Angie."

"Oh, Benji," she said, her eyes clouding as he turned, taking her face in his hands. "You can't feel guilty for that. You have to do what makes you happy."

He nodded. "And that's you. Lucy, I love you so much it's dangerous," he said roughly, his thumbs moving along her cheeks. "It's dangerous because it consumes me and it happened so damn fast. I swear I fell for you the moment you looked at me with that furrowed brow and snapped at me. You made me suffer for a week until, finally, I got you. And then you thought I was going to let you go? Please, you were mine. From that moment on. I swear on everything, my heart, my soul, my body… I'm yours until the day I take my last breath. I love you. I love you so fucking much."

When a tear rolled down her face, his heart swelled in his chest as she held his gaze. "I think I've always loved you, but I fought it. I'm sorry I'm a pain in the ass, but I love you too, Benji. More than you love me."

"That's debatable," he muttered against her lips, his lips curving. "But it's something we can debate for the rest of our lives."

"Agreed."

Pulling out of his arms, she lifted her shirt, pulling it over her head. While he loved her naked body, he was confused. "What are you doing?"

"You have to ask? I'm getting naked. I want you, Benji Paxton, and I want you right now."

"I thought we were talking about our feelings."

She made a face. "I thought we were done! How many feelings you got?"

He laughed. "A lot."

She grinned. "Well, I've got them too, but we don't have to talk. Let's do."

Grinning, he pulled at his shirt, and they undressed quickly. Taking her naked, sexy body in his arms, he lifted her off her feet as their mouths met in a heated tangle. His heart was soaring, his soul was happy, and God, he would never love anyone like he did her. Carrying her to the bed, he laid her down, covering her body with his as he drew the hot, sexy kisses out of her. Tearing his mouth from hers, he kissed down her neck as her hands moved up his back, gooseflesh appearing under her touch. As he fell between her legs, she arched against him, lusciously wet. His mind went wild. He wanted this to last, the feel of her, her kisses… He wanted to be inside the woman he loved.

He pushed her leg up and her fingers came to his chest as her brows rose. "What in the world happened here?"

Benji scoffed at the bruise on his chest. It was fading and hardly noticeable, but it still stung a bit. "Blocking your brother's shot."

"Which one?"

"Jude."

She winked exaggeratedly. "I'll beat him up for you."

"Good looking out," he muttered against her lips before directing himself into her body, their whimpers mingling as his eyes squeezed shut. "Fucking hell. Never, ever will this be something that I can get used to."

Arching against him, she moaned against his lips. "Benji."

"I love you, Lucy."

"I love you more."

Her toes curled against the bed and his heart jackhammered in his chest. He was pretty sure he would never get used to hearing those words from her sweet mouth. Moving out and then slowly back in, he caressed her lips with his, something more happening than just making love.

They were becoming one.

And it was too much for a lost soul like Benji to have ever asked for.

It was almost like a dream.

But as he reached his point of no return when Lucy squeezed him, his eyes met hers and he knew this wasn't a dream.

It was his forever.

Chapter
TWENTY-TWO

When Rick's car pulled up, Benji had to take a cleansing breath.

He wanted to get out of the car, pummel the dude's face, and throw his body in a ditch somewhere, but that wouldn't help their situation.

Their.

Lucy and Angie and *him*.

They were his everything, and he could still hear them telling him they loved him. Over and over again, and he swore it was like his own version of alcohol. Their love. It was addictive, and hearing Lucy whisper it against his lips, he knew he would never find another high like that in his life. Never.

"If there is even a mark on her, I swear, Benji, do not hold me back from scratching out his eyeballs."

Benji scoffed as he reached for the door. "I'll hold him down."

She flashed him a grin and he shot her one back. "I love you, guy."

He chuckled. "I love you more."

But she was right, if Angie got out of that car with any marks that shouldn't be there, Benji wouldn't be in control of his actions.

Because Rick Hart would be a dead man.

To say he was still fuming from hearing about their previous meetup was an understatement. He wanted Rick dead, but he would let the courts take care of it.

As long as Angie was okay.

Slamming the door behind him, he went around the car as Angie shot to

Lucy, wrapping her body around her mom, hugging her tightly. "I don't ever want to go back," she whispered, and Lucy held her daughter's face, searching her eyes.

"Are you okay?"

"Yeah, but he wouldn't let me out of my room, and—"

"She kept screaming at me," Rick said, crossing his arms over his chest. "I won't stand for that shit."

"You were screaming at him?"

"He locked me in my room and wouldn't give me any toys. He gave all my toys to Nina!" she said, her eyes welling up, tears falling down her cheeks.

"Please, she had a notebook and crayons."

"Yeah, that's enough for a whole weekend," Lucy spat back, kissing Angie's forehead.

"He wouldn't give me my medicine either," she said then, and Benji looked up at Rick.

"She don't need it," he said simply, but even Benji knew that wasn't true.

"So you locked her in a room, unmedicated? How could you do that to her?" Lucy asked, her voice dripping with acid. "Angie, get in the car."

Angie nodded and then she looked over at Benji. Her face lit up and she ran to him. He lifted her up into his arms, hugging her tightly. Planting a big kiss on his cheek, she said, "Oh my God, I missed you!"

His heart couldn't take it. "I missed you too, sunshine," he said, hugging her again and kissing her temple. Carrying her to the car, he said, "I think you got bigger."

"I did! And stronger! You gotta see my slap shot. I watched you do it for like an hour last week, and I think I perfected it."

"Awesome," he said, putting her in the car. "You'll have to show me later."

"We are still doing our dance party, right?"

"As soon as we get home," he said with a nod before handing her his phone. "Sit here for a minute, okay?"

She nodded, pushing at his phone as he shut the door and walked around to hear Lucy say, "You basically had her in a room with nothing to do, and you expected her to be okay? Her mind is going crazy, and she has nothing to distract her? No outlet? How dare you? That's child abuse," she accused and Rick rolled his eyes.

"Please. It's no big deal. She don't need the meds."

"She does, Rick," she stressed, her voice full of emotion. "Her ADHD is serious. I don't understand how you can just overlook that."

"'Cause it's some made-up shit you are trying to use to cover up that she's a bad kid," he spat back and Lucy's eyes widened.

"A bad kid! Are you fucking kidding me?" she roared, but when she went to step forward, Benji stopped her.

"Let it go. You know that's untrue," he said quickly, taking her hand in his. Looking over at Rick, he cleared his throat. "We will have the doctor write up something in simple words for you so you can see this is a real issue that Angie is dealing with. Since, apparently, Lucy's word is not enough."

"He's seen the paperwork. He should have come to the appointment, to therapy, but he's too fucking busy," she spat from his side and Rick rolled his eyes.

"I have a life, Lucy."

"Angie should be a part of it!" she shouted and Benji shook his head.

"Babe, come on. It won't help," he stressed and she looked away, swallowing hard. "Then what do we need to do to help you understand her need for the meds? Do we need to add that into the parenting plan?"

Rick scoffed. "Dude, there won't be a parenting plan when she's in my custody. Everything will be under my control."

"Do you know how stupid you sound? No one is going to give custody to you. You are wasting everyone's time," Lucy yelled at him, shaking her head. "We'll go to court, add your latest bullshit, and that will be it. The judge will laugh at you, especially with all the information I'm bringing. You'll be lucky if you get to see her every other month after this weekend. And add in the fact she doesn't even want to see you at all."

"I'm bringing stuff too. Don't forget that," he spat back and Lucy shook her head.

"You have nothing—"

But Benji stopped her, shaking his head before looking back at Rick. "Okay, then. So we'll factor that in, no big deal."

"It ain't no *we*. You aren't a part of this," Rick hollered at him and Benji held his hand up.

"I am. The sooner you realize I am a part of their life, the better. The easier this will be for everyone involved."

"Please, you'll be gone soon. I can promise you that," he warned and Benji glared.

"Good to know you're a psychic. Did you see that my lawyer will be contacting yours for invasion of privacy? To have you sign a nondisclosure agreement since you took it upon yourself to dig up my past? You had no right to do that. I—"

"I have every right," Rick said, and he looked nervous as he shook his head. "You are trying to be a dad to my kid."

"I mean, someone has to," he said simply and Rick's eyes widened.

"So you don't deny that you are trying to take my kid from me?"

Benji shook his head. "Would I rather be her dad than you? Yeah, I would adopt that funny, amazing, sweet, beautiful child in a second. I'd give her my name, and I'd love her more than you can even imagine. More than you're capable of. But I'm sure you'd rather run us through a nasty custody battle and hurt her in the process. So instead, where you lack in the father department, I'll excel. And Angie will grow to be a happy, well-adjusted girl who knows who her *real* dad is."

Rick didn't like that at all and came toe-to-toe with Benji, his eyes blazing with anger. "You don't matter."

Benji shrugged. "To you, no, but I think Angie and Lucy would sing a different tune."

"You'll be gone soon, so you're just wasting your time."

Benji sucked in a deep breath as Lucy watched him. This dude did not scare him, and all he was really doing with his idle threats was annoying him. "I'm not going anywhere."

"You'll see," he said, shaking his head and stepping away. "See you after the new year. Enjoy the time you do have with her."

He couldn't understand Rick. It drove him crazy because how could a man act like that about his child? Still, though, Benji wanted to give him a chance. So he asked once more, "Are you sure you don't want to just fix the parenting plan? Skip this charade of a custody battle?" When Rick went to snap at him, he held up his hand. "Not for us, please, we can handle it. But for Angie. You've already ruined so much with her. Don't you want to try to make your relationship a little better instead of putting her through this?"

Lucy looked up at Benji, her eyes full of love before she looked back at Rick. "You should want be to be a part of her life, but I can't do this, Rick. I can't put her through all this and urge her to want you in her life," she said as calmly as she could, and Benji was proud. "You don't deserve her, but you are her father and I have no problem with you being one—as long as you are going to be one. What you are right now is a douche."

Rick held their gazes and then slowly shook his head. "Fuck both of you. You both think you've already won. I'm better for her than both of you combined. A drunk and a bitter bitch? Please!"

Benji let out a long breath and nodded. "Have a great vacation with your family," he said simply, guiding Lucy to the truck before she clawed the asshole's eyes out.

"Yeah, whatever, dude."

But Benji ignored him as he opened the door for Lucy and helped her in. Once in the car with them, he started the ignition as he exhaled once more.

"You're a good man, Benji Paxton," Lucy said, lacing her fingers with his.

Bringing the back of her hand up to his lips, he kissed her and then nodded. "I try," he whispered. Lord knew it wasn't easy. He wanted to rip that bastard to pieces, but there was no point. Rick was just an idiot and not worth his time.

"You sure you don't want out?" she asked as he pulled onto the main road.

He rolled his eyes. "Do you really need reassurance, Lucy? 'Cause you frustrate the crap out of me when you do that. Here, let me give you some," he said, his voice full of frustration. "I love you. I'm not going anywhere. It's me, you, and Angie, and I guess, that dude, for the rest of my life. The latter until Angie turns eighteen. He doesn't scare me. I don't care one bit about him. Stop asking if I want out. I don't. I want you and Angie. I'm yours, baby."

"Mine too," Angie said from the back and Benji grinned. "You're mine too, right, Benji?"

"Absolutely, sunshine," he said, looking over at Lucy. "You two never have to ask again."

"Okay," Lucy said and she smiled. "I won't ask again."

"Thank God," he said, flashing her a grin before he looked at the road. Was this easy? No. Did he hate it? Yes. But what was he supposed to do? He wouldn't turn his back on them; he loved them. But, man, it would be so much easier without Rick in the picture. Though, like he said before, he didn't mind one bit fighting for Lucy and now Angie.

He'd fight for the people he loved.

He looked in the rearview mirror at Angie. "Hey, Angie, you wanna go out, do something?"

He was hopeful she would. But like he expected her to, she said, "Nope, I want to have a dance party!"

Lucy scoffed as Benji nodded, groaning inwardly and wishing like hell he hadn't agreed to this. "Dance party it is, then."

"But you hate dancing," Lucy said and he shrugged.

"When you love someone, you do things you aren't comfortable with to make them happy," he said simply and she beamed as Angie cheered.

"I bet you're a great dancer, Benji!"

"That's a big no, sunshine, but let's do this."

Lucy brought their hands into her lap and squeezed his hand. "I love you."

He smiled as his heart exploded in his chest. The way she said it was so beautiful. So sweet, and he was convinced he couldn't get enough of those three words. "I love you too."

"I love you both!" Angie giggled from the back and he couldn't grin wide enough.

He was complete.

Benji really hated dancing.

As he shimmied from side to side, Lucy leaned against the island, laughing so hard, she was crying.

"You're doing great. Try this," Angie said, spinning like a crazy person and Benji laughed.

"How about this?" he said, doing some break-dancing that was so bad, he almost smashed his head against the table.

But Angie ate it up. "Awesome! Mommy, watch!"

She did the same as Benji, and they looked ridiculous, but Benji had never had so much fun in his life. As he spun around on his ass, kicking his legs in no particular way, he looked up to see Lucy grinning, bubbling with laughter as she held her phone up, taking pictures. She looked so beautiful, so fucking happy, and while he really didn't want anyone seeing him like this, he didn't stop her. He wanted her to document this moment.

When he tried but failed very badly to spin on his head, he lay on his back, watching as Angie swung her arms around like an orangutan, laughing and having the time of her life. He wondered how many dance parties she had with Rick. How many times did Rick make her laugh like Benji made her laugh? He wondered why Rick even wanted to fight for her when he didn't even try to make her happy. When Angie looked over at him expectantly, he laughed.

"I'm old," he decided and she laughed, pulling him up.

"Never! Dance!"

Popping and locking, well, actually, he looked like he was having a conniption fit, he heard Angie laugh, the joyous sound filling his once empty house. When Lucy snorted, shaking her head, he grinned back at her as the music died down, changing to a slow song.

"Then There's You," by Charlie Puth.

He had heard it many times, liked it because it made him think of Lucy. When Angie went to turn it off, he stopped her. "No, honey, let's slow it down."

"Okay," she said, coming to him.

"Come here," he said, picking her up. She wrapped her arms and legs around him, laying her head on his shoulder. Closing his eyes, he cuddled her to him as he moved her through the kitchen, thankful for the break. He might have killed himself if he'd tried another headstand. When he turned, facing where Lucy stood, he saw her lips were curved and her eyes dark as she watched him.

"Come here," he demanded, holding out his arm. She shook her head.

"No, you two have fun."

But Angie didn't like that. "Come on, Mommy. Dance with us!"

"Ugh, fine," she said, laughing as she came over, tucking into his side, holding Angie as she laid her hand on his chest.

Exhaling a long breath, Benji closed his eyes and he leaned his head to Lucy's, kissing her forehead. Nothing could have ever prepared him for this. To feel so overwhelmed and in love from the bottom of his soul. Living life with no purpose had been scary, but now he had purpose, he had meaning, and he was holding it in his arms.

His girls.

Angie may never fully be his, but he was okay with that. Because when she was older and she graduated, she would thank Lucy and Benji, her parents. When some idiot assumed he was going to marry her, he would ask Benji, not Rick. And when it was time to give her away, Benji would be the one to do it. But if Rick got his shit together and he became the father Angie needed, then Benji would have no problem being number two. As long as Angie was happy and she knew he loved her too.

That was all he cared about.

Kissing Angie's head once more and then Lucy's, he smiled as the song played and they cuddled against him.

"This is awesome," Angie said softly and Lucy nodded.

"It is. I think he's a good dancer."

Angie popped up at that. "The best ever!"

Benji's body shook with laughter as she hugged him tighter. Another slow song came on, and still the three of them stayed wrapped together, swaying to the music. At that moment, Benji decided, as much as he hated dancing, he'd do this every day if he could.

As long as it was with these two.

When Lucy looked up, her face bright and happy, he smiled before kissing her nose. "Love you."

"Love you," she whispered, her eyes locking with his as she exhaled happily.

Holding her gaze, her gorgeous green eyes burning into his, he couldn't take it. He wanted this. Every day. He wanted to wake up to her beautiful face, to hold her sweet body when he slept. He wanted them over for breakfast, to share dinner with them. He wanted his family.

Angie and Lucy.

His voice thick with emotion, he whispered, "Move in, Lucy. Tomorrow. I don't want to wait till January. I love you, I love Angie, and this is right. We are right."

She searched his eyes, and he could feel her heart pick up in speed, beating against his chest. He figured she would fight him, tell him to hush, but to his surprise, she nodded her head and whispered, "Okay."

And right then, Benji decided that "Okay" was his second favorite phrase to ever leave Lucy's mouth.

"Baylor, thank God, she's leaving!"

Lucy shot Jayden a dark look as she handed Benji the last of the boxes. Standing in the front yard, all of them freezing their butts off as they packed Benji's truck with their things, Lucy shook her head. She was going to miss them.

"Har-har-har," she said and Jayden laughed, wrapping his arms around her waist before picking her up off the ground and shaking her.

Like he had been doing since they were kids.

"Put me down, you big oaf," she demanded as her feet hit the ground.

Kissing her on the cheek, Baylor smiled. "We'll miss you guys."

She went to her sister-in-law, who had just had surgery a week before, and hugged her tightly. She was on crutches so it was awkward, but she was thankful for such a good woman for her brother. "Thanks, Baylor."

"Any time," she said, squeezing her arm as Angie came over to hug her tightly.

"Now, Benji, there is a no-return policy on her. No take-backs on the little one either," Jayden teased as Angie climbed up his back and Lucy punched him in the chest. Wheezing for breath, he said, "Okay, we'll take Angie back, but not that one."

Benji just laughed as he jumped out of the back of his truck, wrapping his arm around Lucy's shoulders. "No worries. Didn't need the policies anyway," he said, kissing her cheek as she looked up to where all of her and Angie's belongings were in the back of Benji's truck. If she had been smart, she would have waited, done it all right, planned to move everything out of storage and all that, but Benji made her impulsive. So, like a crazy person, she packed up and moved in the following day. She knew it was outrageous, but she prayed it was going to work.

Because she really saw no future unless Benji was in their life.

They would be fine if he weren't. They were always fine, but they'd never truly be happy the way he made them happy. Because of that, she was ready to move in to her dream home with her dream man. It was simply ludicrous, when only a couple of months ago, she was just gliding through life, following Angie and only caring for her, to now, not only caring for Angie *and* Benji, but herself.

Love. Crazy thing, that love.

"When do we get my bed?" Angie asked as she sat up on Jayden's shoulders.

"Tomorrow," Lucy said, leaning her head to Benji's shoulder. "We have the Assassins' Christmas party tonight. You still wanna go, right?"

"Duh, Mom," she said dryly and Benji laughed.

"Yeah, duh," he teased, kissing her head before slapping his hands together. "So come on, ladies. Let's get home and unpacked. Home. I like that," he said, grinning over at Lucy and she smiled.

"Me too."

"Me three! We aren't homeless anymore!" Angie cheered as Jayden laughed, putting her on her feet.

"Angela," Lucy scolded, but she ran around her, jumping in the truck, saying good-bye to Jayden and Baylor before slamming the door shut.

Laughing, Benji leaned against the doorframe as Jayden teased, "You know you're gonna get shit for this from Jude and Jace."

Lucy rolled her eyes. "I don't care. I'm happy."

Jayden nodded before coming over and wrapping his big arms around her, hugging her tightly. "Good. That's all we want," he said and then he dropped his mouth to her ear. "I love you, Lucy, and I want this for you. Don't fuck it up."

Laughing, she pushed him away. "Thanks, asshole."

"God, I love you," he said as she met his gaze. He meant it, she knew that, but he drove her insane. Still, though, there was no way she was doing anything but grinning ear to ear.

"I love you. You too, Baylor," she called as she walked around the truck, and Baylor smiled.

"Love you. Don't be a stranger. I'm lonely now, all by myself until this leg heals."

"Which won't be long," Benji said with a nod. "We'll see you on the ice in no time."

Baylor beamed, but Lucy looked to Jayden to see how he felt about that. Her brother was grinning, his eyes full of love, and that was her answer. As much as he worried about Baylor, he loved her and he wanted her to be happy.

The ice and Jayden made her happy.

Waving, Lucy got into the car as Benji said good-bye and got in himself. Looking back at Angie, he said, "You ready to go home, sunshine?"

Lucy looked back at her daughter who looked just as happy as she felt. Angie threw her hands up and waved them wildly. "So ready!"

"Me too," he said, starting the car. He glanced over at Jayden's house before looking at Lucy. His eyes were dark, and her lips quirked at the side as he held her gaze. "The first time I pulled into the driveway to give you your bag, I sat right here and thought, do I really want to go in there and convince that girl to love me? Let me tell you, I didn't even have to think it through. I got out of this truck, went up to that door, and that's when it started. Our love story."

Breathless, she shook her head. "I thought it started when I said, 'And you think I'm gonna trust you with my kid?'" she said.

From then to now.

Wow.

Other than her family, there was no one else she trusted more with Angie than Benji.

He thought that over for a moment and then winked. "You're right. I like that better."

Grinning, she leaned over, kissing his cheek as he put the car in reverse to head home.

Home.

Their home.

When they got back to the house, it was crazy getting everything where it needed to be in a rush and convincing Angie that the guest room would be fine until they could go get her bed.

"It's fine. I'll go get her bed after the party," he suggested, but Lucy shook her head.

"That's silly. She's fine and she hasn't slept in it since we moved out of my mother's house. You can sleep in the guest bed."

"But I want my bed, in my room," she complained with typical seven-year-old urgency, and Lucy rolled her eyes.

"Angela, come on—"

But Benji was there, lifting her up and onto his shoulders. "It's really no big deal. We can grab everything that we two can get," he said then and smiled at Lucy. "Don't be mad. I want this to be fun, and if we would have planned better, she would have her bed."

Lucy glared. "Stop spoiling her."

He grinned. "But I spoil both of you."

She rolled her eyes. "It'll bite you in the ass when she's sixteen, I promise you," she warned, but all he did was laugh. Rolling her eyes, she turned and headed down the hall to get her bath box, the last box that was downstairs. She heard Angie say something about playing, but she ignored them, thinking they were going to drive her up the wall. She knew he didn't mean any harm, but he couldn't just roll over for that girl. While it was sweet and adorable, Angie had that man wrapped around her finger, and Lucy would need to untie him before Angie had him building her castles in the skies.

Knowing Benji, he'd do it.

Fool man.

And boy, did she love him.

As she walked through their home, she felt good. She felt complete and already thinking of little things she would hang to add pieces of Angie and herself to the home. She couldn't wait. A part of her was sure she'd designed it in a way she liked so that when she finally gave in and moved in, like she had wanted to do from the beginning, it would be hers.

And it was.

Grinning, she grabbed the last box and headed upstairs, but she heard

Benji's voice full of shock as he gasped, "Um, Angie, I don't think Mommy wants us playing with these."

Her heart dropped.

Please, God, no.

Rushing up the stairs and down the hall, she turned the corner just as Angie swung one of her dildos at Benji's face. "It's a sword! A weird looking sword, but come on. I like this one 'cause it's longer, but yours is sparkly."

Benji, bless him, was trying not to laugh, but Lucy was horrified. "Angela Lynn!"

Throwing the dildo in the box, she spun around, her eyes wide. "Mommy, I just want to play!"

"Go to your—er, the guest room. Right now! I've told you twice not to touch those."

Angie looked back at Benji as he held Lucy's sparkly vibrator in his hand. Inwardly, Lucy died as Angie looked to him, but he just shook his head. "She told you twice, dude. I can't help you."

"Ugh," Angie complained, stomping past Lucy and into the guest room, hopping on the bed and letting out a wail of protest. "I just wanted to play!"

Ignoring her, Lucy looked at Benji, her face beet red as she pointed to the sex toy in his hand. "Put it in the box, and please, for the love of God, forget this moment right now."

He didn't hold in his laughter as his head fell back, the rough sound filling the room as Lucy died a little more. "You're into sparkling cock?" he said in a low whisper. "Want me to throw some glitter on my dick? Would that turn you on?"

"I swear to God, I will stick that thing down your throat if you don't put it in the box right now," she warned, his laughter running up her spine. Shaking his head, he leaned over, throwing it in the box. But when he came back up, he had her longer one.

"And this one. Jesus, I know it doesn't fit," he said, swinging it around playfully. "I barely fit!"

Mortified, her eyes widened as she shrieked. "Benji!"

"What? It's like a python," he said, jabbing it at her.

Batting it away, she cried, "It was a gift. Please put it away."

"A gift?! Who gave you a giant cock?" he asked, making sure to keep his voice down. "I guess it is the gift that keeps on giving. If you can get it to fit…"

She couldn't help it, she dissolved in laughter, bending over as she wheezed with hilarity. Only Benji could make her laugh so hard she cried. When she looked up and he was holding it to his leg, shaking his head, she couldn't take it. This man was a mess. Fixing his glasses, he made a face as he tried to wrap his hand around the girth of it. "I mean, who could this fit in?"

Unable to speak, she just closed her eyes as her happy tears leaked out of her eyes and down her face.

She loved this adorable man.

Her dorky, inappropriate geek.

After getting everything set up the way they wanted, and even stopping by the warehouse to get Angie's bed, they made their way to Luther Arena for the Assassins' Christmas party for the families. When Benji asked her and Angie to go, she hadn't hesitated to say yes, but now as they started up the many stairs to the arena, a little nervousness settled in her stomach.

She was just the girlfriend with a kid. A kid who wasn't Benji's. What if everyone thought it was wrong of him to bring them? What if they didn't accept them as part of him? Of course, she knew some of them because of Jayden, but they were his sister and his niece. They weren't coming as that; they were coming as Benji's family.

Crap on a cracker.

She looked over at Angie, who was oblivious to Lucy's internal struggle, bouncing around, hockey stick in one hand and skates in the other. She was so excited to play with Shelli and Posey, along with all the other Assassins' kids. There were a lot of them, for sure. While Lucy was thrilled for Angie to play and have fun with the rest of the team, her own nerves about being accepted were almost a little too much to handle. Which she didn't understand. She'd never cared what anyone thought about her. But then, it wasn't about her, it was about Benji.

She didn't want to embarrass him.

Glancing up at him, she saw he was grinning, his hand in hers as they walked through the front doors and were greeted by the staff of the arena. He was so sweet, wishing them all merry Christmas, asking about their families and just being a genuinely nice guy. The best part was when he introduced her and Angie.

"This is my girlfriend, Lucy, and my little ray of sunshine, Angie."

Angie, of course, beamed at that, and so did Lucy. She felt…she felt fucking perfect. Fantastic, even, and her nerves settled a little. Well, that was until they entered the rink and all the Assassins and their families or plus ones were there.

"Oh, we need to get you skates. Angie, go down and get ready, I'll be right back. There's Jayden. Hey, Sinclair, can you get Angie while I get Lucy some skates?" he called down to her brother. Jayden nodded as Angie skipped happily down to him.

But Lucy stopped Benji. "It's fine. I don't like skating anyway."

He paused, his face twisting in complete confusion. "Excuse me?"

She smiled. "I'm not very good."

"You grew up with three boys playing hockey, and you aren't a good skater?"

She shrugged. "I'm good at hockey on my feet, but skates and ice…eh, not good."

He rolled his eyes. "Come on," he said, pulling her along despite her protest. "My woman will skate well."

She laughed at his silliness as they went back out to the lobby and then down to the locker room, where the skates were lined up for everyone. She noticed Lucas Brooks bent down, tying his wife's skates.

"Lucas, that's tight," she complained as Benji got Lucy some skates.

"I know, babe, it's supposed to be," he said, grinning up at her, waggling his brows. "You know, *tight.*"

"Freaking sicko," she muttered as her eyes widened. "Aiden James! Grab Emery before she tries to eat that whole thing of popcorn, please. Stella, love, come here. You can't spin in skates on carpet. Asher! Come on, those are stairs," she complained. The oldest one, who was very handsome, turned, looking at her wildly.

"Mom, this kid is nuts! Go give her back to the wolves," he said, snatching the littlest one up and holding her over his head. She was adorable, so pretty. Hell, all the kids were cute as all get-out.

"They won't take her back. Come on. Please!"

"Fallon, gorgeous as ever," Benji said, unlacing the skates.

She grinned up at him. "Why couldn't I marry you, Benji? I picked this lug who knocked me up four times with a bunch of hellions."

Benji gave her a toothy grin as Lucas laughed, "'Cause it's a joy for me. And she's the damn leader of the hellions."

Smacking him, she smiled as Benji said, "Well, Fallon, when you have such a gorgeous woman that you love, it's bound to happen. Just wait, Lucy will be just like you soon enough."

Lucy's eyes widened and she scoffed. "The hell you say!"

Fallon laughed at that as Lucas stood, grinning over at Lucy. "Ah, the girl who has changed Benji's world. Whoa, I know you. You're Sinclair's sister. Ha!"

Lucy's cheeks reddened as Fallon wobbled on her skates. "Well, I love her already if Benji is head over heels for her. Hi, I'm Fallon Brooks."

"Lucy Sinclair. It's nice to meet you."

"You, too," Fallon said, giving her the once-over. "Just wait, everyone will be gushing over you soon enough. Everyone loves Benji. Knowing he's finally found himself a girl will be big news."

That's what she was worried about.

As Lucy sat down like Benji told her, Fallon said, "See y'all out there."

He started tying her skates, and she watched as Fallon and Lucas rallied their kids together and headed back down the tunnel to the ice. Looking up at her, Benji grinned. "Didn't freak you out with that comment, did I?"

She shrugged. "A little, but I'm not having four kids."

"We'll see," he said with a wink as he tightened her skate.

"Ah, that's tight." He grinned and she smacked him. "Don't."

"Hey, I'm not the one with the monster dick in a box," he said and then he paused. "God, I'm hilarious."

"You're a dork," she said dryly, shaking her head.

He moved to her next skate, and she watched as he tightened it, making sure it was good before tying them securely. Wiggling her toes as he sat down to put his skates on, she decided this would be okay. She was a horrible skater, but at least Benji couldn't leave her alone for everyone to swoop in and give her the third degree where she could possibly embarrass Benji.

She should have just stayed home.

"What's wrong with you? Are you nervous or something?"

She looked over at him. "What?"

"You are nervous. Why? Everyone is great. I promise."

She shrugged. "I'm kinda standoffish, and what if I embarrass you?"

He laughed. "Just have fun. I know you won't. Now come on, let's get to the ice," he said, standing and helping her up. She was hesitant, but she made it out on her own. She even skated a bit before she went crashing down in a heap of legs and arms. Standing above her, Benji shook his head. "That was pathetic." She glared up at him as Jayden came to a stop beside them. "How does your sister not know how to skate, but your niece does?"

"'Cause she wouldn't go. It's all her fault!" he accused and skated off, going after Angie.

Bending down, Benji helped Lucy up as she grumbled, "I told you I suck at this."

"Come on," he said laughing, kissing her cheek before they skated together. He was patient and sweet, encouraging her. But she could see it in his eyes, he found this hilarious. As they skated, his big hands holding her, she decided she was okay with not being good. It meant he had to hold her, and she liked that a lot. Leaning into him as cheerful Christmas music played in the arena and children's laughter was at every turn, Lucy couldn't be happier.

But the nerves were back full force when he stopped where a group of women stood by the bench Baylor was sitting on. Lucy held on to the side as all the ladies looked over, their faces brightening as they called Benji's name.

For a guy who claimed he wasn't a ladies' man, these Assassins wives sure did love her boyfriend.

And she would not be jealous of that.

Nope.

Okay, she was.

A little.

Just a smidge.

Elli Adler beamed. "Well, aren't you two just absolutely adorable!"

Lucy smiled as she looked up at Benji, who was just grinning like a fool. "He is, isn't he?"

"Wait? Are you two together?" one of the ladies asked. Lucy was pretty sure it was Piper Titov, Reese's twin sister, who was Jude's wife's Claire's aunt.

Wow, mouthful there.

"Yeah, Piper, we are," he said, cuddling her closer as Piper squealed.

"About damn time!" she decided, smacking the boards. "Though, now I worry you won't come cook for us."

Benji laughed as Lucy smiled and offered, "You guys will have to come over for dinner, then."

Hey, she was doing well! *Go, Lucy, go!*

Piper loved that as she nodded. "We would love to! Is that your darling girl, the one with my daughter, Katarina?"

Lucy looked out where Angie was on her knees, playing with a sweet little girl who had a spurt of hair on top of her head. "I think so."

"Well, isn't she just adorable?"

"Thank you, I was thinking the same of yours."

Piper beamed as Benji cleared his throat. "Okay, let me introduce you to everyone," he said, pointing to Elli. "You know, Adler, my boss. You know your sister-in-law. Now, Piper, who is married to Erik Titov. Then we've got her sister, Reese, but you know her because of Claire, Jude's wife?"

Lucy smiled as Reese grinned over at her. "We do."

"Okay, cool, then we have Audrey. You just met her—"

"And I love her," Audrey decided, which made everyone laugh.

Lucy grinned as Benji nodded. "And then we have my boy Karson King's wife, Lacey. She's the one who owns the lingerie store, y'know, for breast cancer survivors?"

Lucy met Lacey's gaze and nodded. "Yes, I love your work."

"Well, I love your design for Reese's house. I need your number for some changes to our house," she said, moving her blond hair off her shoulders before rubbing her belly. She must have been pregnant, though, she didn't look it. "Sorry, I'm queasy today. Found out we're expecting."

"Oh, congratulations!"

"Thanks," she beamed as her lips quirked. "You have a lot of catching up to do once y'all marry and start. We average about three kids a family."

"You guys are also insane," Lucy said simply, and that had everyone chortling as Benji grinned. She wasn't joking, but they had to be—not only for the number of kids, but hadn't they just met her? How did they know she wanted kids and marriage with Benji?

"She's funny, right?" he teased, skating over to a very tall and very muscular woman who was holding a baby on her hip. "Anyway, this is Kacey, my boy and roommate on the road, Jordie's, wife and her little nugget, Ella. Let me see her," he said, taking her and kissing her loudly on the cheek, which made her giggle adorably as all the women grinned back at him. "These are the core Assassins wives who run shit and the woman in charge of it all."

"Basically," Reese laughed as everyone agreed.

When Benji skated off, Lucy wanted to chase him, but knew she wouldn't get far as Kacey said, "I guess I'm not getting my baby back."

"Probably not," Baylor replied as Benji skated.

"He just loves kids," Piper added while everyone watched him. He was great, skating with Ella before handing her off to the really big mountain man she knew to be Jordie Thomas and then chasing after Angie.

"He does," she found herself saying, and they all beamed back at her. "What?"

"You know he hasn't dated anyone since we've known him," Reese said, waggling her brows, and Lucy shrugged.

"I've heard."

"You know that means you're what he was waiting for," Elli announced then as Audrey giggled happily beside her.

"For real. Benji always said he was waiting for the one," Fallon said and Lucy hadn't even realized she was sitting beside Baylor. "You're the one."

Lucy's lips curved as she shrugged. "I've heard that too."

That made all of them sigh dreamily before they turned to watch the guys skate with the kids. They were all big kids themselves. Shea Adler was riding on Jordie's back as he raced down the ice against Karson and Lucas. Somehow, though, Benji had passed them with Jayden on his back while Tate watched with baby Ella in his arms, laughing.

Bunch of nuts.

"Good group we got. Great job, boss lady," Fallon said then and Elli nodded.

"Yeah, I think so," she said before turning to Baylor. "I need my girl, though. How're you feeling?"

Baylor looked up and smiled, even though it didn't reach her eyes. "I don't know, boss. Not sure I'll be back. It isn't official, though."

Elli looked sad but she nodded. "I know, honey. I hate that for you."

"We all do," Fallon said, wrapping her arm around Baylor as her youngest daughter took off out of the bench area. "Crazy ass," she muttered before chasing after her as some of the ladies laughed.

"Yeah, I'm accepting it," Baylor said, but Lucy knew she wasn't. Very slowly, she moved into the bench area and sat beside Baylor, hugging her.

"Well, you're a hero in my eyes," she said and Baylor grinned over at her.

"I mean, I lived my dreams. I wish it would have lasted longer, but I think I'm gonna teach some kids, push girls to live their dreams. That they can make it."

Kacey nodded her head. "Good idea. I mean, you did what I always wanted to do. You'll always be my hero."

Baylor's face reddened as everyone agreed. Lucy hated this for her sister-in-law, but in a way, she was okay with it. Baylor could take it easy, and Jayden wouldn't worry so much. That dude worried so much about everyone, and Lucy was convinced one day he'd have a heart attack. This was good—it sucked and she hated it—but it was good in the long run.

As they all fell into easy conversation, Lucy's nerves were gone and she felt at home. Within seconds, she loved all the ladies and all of them wanted her to come over so they could cook for her, Angie, and Benji. It was just so easy. They all accepted her and Angie without a bat of an eye. She hated that she had thought they wouldn't. That was the Assassins team. They were a family. Benji loved them, so they all loved him.

It was refreshing.

When people started going their separate ways to spend time with their families, Lucy soon found herself sitting alone with Baylor as she talked about the upcoming wedding. "I am sure I'm going to cry my eyes out."

Lucy chuckled. "God, me too. I never thought I would want my mom to remarry after my dad, but I love River a lot."

Baylor smiled as she nodded. "I love Autumn, always have, so it will be great."

"It will," she agreed as they watched Benji and Jayden play some intense two-on-two against Aiden and Lucas Brooks.

When Baylor cleared her throat, Lucy looked over to find her looking at her. "I know we aren't close—"

"What? I love you, Baylor," Lucy said quickly, but her sister-in-law was right. They weren't close like she and Avery were, but that was mostly because Baylor was so driven to succeed and Lucy was a bitch. She was too busy trying to not hate life that she had never had time for anyone else.

Baylor waved her off. "No, I know you do. But I mean, we aren't really close, close, and I want to change that," she said, looking up as Jayden threw his hands in the air after scoring a goal. "I want you to know that I've always loved you, but I really love who you are now. When I first met you, I was honestly scared of you. Jayden and the boys all talked so roughly about you, how you hated everyone. But all I saw was someone who needed to be loved, and Benji is that for you. We are all so happy for you. All Jayden ever wanted was someone to love his sister. You know how he worries like an old lady."

Lucy smirked, nodding her head. "Yeah."

"We're just so happy for you, and I feel like now that I'm retiring and stuff, I want to have a closer relationship with you. I've always considered you a sister, Lucy," she said awkwardly, her lips curving as she sighed. "I'm not good at girls."

Lucy laughed. Baylor was right; she had been playing and growing up with guys her whole life. She didn't have many female relationships, and while Lucy really didn't bother with them either, she would for Baylor. It was easy to see that she needed a friend. "No, it's fine. And, yeah, I would love to be closer to you. I just adore you."

"Thanks," she said, leaning into her. "Can I tell you something? No one knows."

Lucy's brow quirked. "Oh, so we are doing this now. Yeah," she teased and Baylor smiled as Lucy chuckled. "Tell away."

Looking down, Baylor bit into her lip. "The reason why I'm retiring and everything is not only because I have a bum leg—let's be honest, I could rehab that and figure out a way to be okay with being just okay—but I found out yesterday that I'm pregnant."

Lucy's jaw dropped. "What?"

"I know, crazy, right?"

"But you just had surgery!"

"I know, and I told them I wasn't pregnant. The chick said she did a pee test and it came up not pregnant. But when they got back my full blood work, they called me in and told me I was."

"Oh my God, is the baby okay?" Lucy asked, her heart pounding and Baylor shrugged.

"They said they think I'm good. I didn't actually take any of the meds, 'cause I'm that asshole who doesn't think they need pain medication. So that's good. We saw its heartbeat. I haven't told Jayden yet. I don't want to disappoint him if I lose it."

Lucy could only blink. "So this is real life?"

She smiled. "I'm eight weeks."

"What the fuck? You never knew?"

"My periods have always been wonky, and I thought I was sick from the pain. And even though I only had the surgery meds, it still scares me that they could have affected the baby. But the doctors are going to monitor everything, and they don't seem too worried. Crazy, right?"

"Um, yeah," Lucy said, her eyes wide.

"And the thing is, I wasn't upset when I found out. I always thought I would be mad because it wasn't something I wanted. But then I love seeing Jayden with Angie and Ashlyn, and I love Angie and Ashlyn. I don't know, I kinda want this baby no matter what it means for my career. And if for some reason I lose it, I think I want to try again."

Lucy was completely speechless, but then she was bursting with excitement. "This is happening?"

Baylor smiled. "It is."

"Then, hell yeah, let's do it!" Lucy gushed before wrapping her arms around her sister-in-law and hugging her tightly. It was crazy and Lucy prayed that the baby would be healthy, but she knew Baylor and Jayden would be wonderful parents.

"What are you two hugging about?" Jayden asked as he came up against the boards.

Pulling back, Lucy grinned and shook her head. "Nothing."

Baylor smiled as she looked up at Jayden. "Girl stuff."

His face contorted in horror. "I don't like the sound of that."

As he skated off, they laughed, and Lucy was convinced that life couldn't get better. Especially when Angie had Benji acting as if they were figure skaters, frolicking around the ice. When he lifted her and she kicked her toes, Lucy shook her head.

Her big and little dorks.

Her family.

Chapter
TWENTY-THREE

"What if he proposes? Wouldn't that be amazing?"

Lucy leaned into the closest person, Avery, and groaned at her overzealous mother. "Mom, Benji isn't proposing!"

"But y'all didn't exchange gifts," she pointed out as Claire did her makeup. Lucy rolled her eyes.

"Because we are doing it at home tonight with Angie, since you insisted that Santa came to your house," she said, holding Ashlyn close to her. They had done their Christmas morning celebration that morning and it was wonderful. She loved being with her family, but what made it ten times better was that everyone loved Benji. They treated him just like family, and she couldn't have been happier. While, yeah, she and Benji hadn't exchanged gifts, and they were waiting to go home for Angie to open hers from them, she knew he wasn't proposing.

It just wasn't time.

Looking down at Ashlyn, she kissed her forehead. She was convinced her little niece was the prettiest baby ever. Such wide eyes and just adorable. She was wearing her little rose-colored flower girl dress with a big, huge, over-the-top rose bow. Both Lucy and Jace had protested the bow, but Avery and her mom loved it. Smiling at her, she decided it was pretty damn cute and popped her nose. "Pretty baby."

"Because he's gonna propose!"

Rolling her eyes, Avery grinned over at her, and Lucy shook her head as she took in her sister-in-law. Her hair was styled in a beautiful updo that had pieces falling along her shoulders, and her makeup had been applied by the amazing Claire to be soft and feminine. She was wearing the same rose-colored dress as Angie, Ashlyn, Baylor, and Claire, since her mom wanted everyone to match— except Lucy. Her dress was, in her opinion, way prettier, mostly because she had picked it. Instead of the lace and flowing style the other girls wore, hers was form-fitting with no lace, and it also made her boobs look great. She was sure Benji was going to just eat it up, if her mother would ever let them leave her sight. The woman was driving her bananas today! Angie was lucky to have escaped with Benji and the boys as soon as she was dressed.

"Don't you think he's a doll, girls?"

"I do. He's really nice, Lucy," Claire said, and Lucy was surprised how much that meant to her.

"I think he's fantastic," Avery announced, and Lucy smiled. Avery knew everything that had happened between her and Benji, so to have her finally meet him was really great. She got to see firsthand what Lucy got to see daily. "So really, though, you think he's proposing?"

Lucy shook her head. "No. I'd know if he was. That dude can't keep anything from me."

Baylor smiled, glowing in her dress. It was funny how since Lucy had found out about her pregnancy, she saw her sister-in-law in a new light. Had she always been that glowy? She wasn't sure, but man, she wanted to tell someone. It was killing her, but she kept her promise. Hadn't even told Benji.

She felt she deserved cookies or something.

"It would be great if he did, wouldn't it, Mom? All your kids married and happy," Baylor said then and her mom beamed.

"Oh, I would be so full of love. Just need Lucy to bite the bullet and get it done."

Lucy exhaled loudly. "Maybe I don't want to get married again."

That had everyone turning to look at her and she rolled her eyes. "God, yes, I want to, but I'm not rushing it! We've only been together a little over two months."

"But it seems like forever. You guys are awesome together," Baylor said and Lucy shot her a look.

"I know, but we aren't ready."

"I think you are," Autumn said then and Lucy leaned back in the couch, Ashlyn cooing against her.

"I'm glad you know what I need, Mom."

"Anytime."

Frustrating woman, that Autumn Sinclair soon-to-be Moore was.

"Is he going to come down to Florida with you?"

Lucy nodded, running her finger along Ashlyn's fat cheeks. "Yeah, unless he gets invited to play in the All-Star Game."

"Oh, when do those invites go out?"

"The beginning of the month."

"Fun! Well, hopefully, he can come. It will be nice to hang out."

Lucy nodded. "I'm sure Jace will get invited."

"Eh, we'll see," Avery said with a fond little grin on her face. She always got that look on her face when it came to Jace. "Any word from Rick? Has he called Angie for Christmas?"

Lucy let out a long breath and shook her head. "Nope, and what upsets me the most is that Angie hasn't even asked. I mean, what father does that to his kid? Benji was so pissed and has been just so sweet to her all day. Not that he isn't all the time, the girl has him wrapped around her finger, but still, he's making sure her Christmas is extra nice."

While it was wonderful that Benji was doing what he was doing and she loved him even more, she couldn't believe Rick. Despite being a lowlife, he made a point to call her on her birthday and holidays if Lucy had her, and she did the same. She didn't understand how he could be like that. But then, she really didn't understand where he got off thinking he was going to get custody of their child. Who knew? The dude was borderline certifiable.

"So Benji is in this to win it, huh?" Claire asked, looking over at her. "Like legit, Angie is his kid, kind of thing?"

Lucy shrugged. "Yeah, I think so."

"That's so awesome. Because, let me tell you, no one ever wanted my mom because of me. Or maybe it was the kind of men she brought around. But no one ever looked at me the way Benji looks at Angie, until Phillip. That's basically his kid."

Lucy smiled as Autumn beamed. "Isn't he just perfect? He loves that baby, and it just pleases me to no end. 'Cause Lord knows she needs a good man to love her momma and her."

"Mom, I don't—"

"You tell me you don't need Benji Paxton and I will smack you. Don't lie to me, honey. Can you see your life without him?" she snapped and Lucy's eyes went wide.

Lucy looked to Avery, but she laughed as she looked away. "Don't look at me."

"I mean, shit, Mom. Yeah, I can't see my life without him now, but it's because I want him. Not 'cause I need him."

"Same thing," she decided and Lucy scoffed.

Crazy woman.

"I think it's great. He's wonderful for you, and I can't wait to see y'all grow," Claire said, sending her a grin. "I'm just happy you're happy."

"Me too," Baylor and Avery said at the same time, flashing grins at each other as her mom started to tear up.

"Well, we all know how I feel. Don't let that man go, Lucy Lane. Don't you dare let that man go."

Grinning like a Cheshire cat, Lucy nodded. "No plans for it."

She watched as Angie pulled Ashlyn down the aisle in a wagon, and a tear rolled down Lucy's face while she stood with her three brothers and their mother between them outside the venue. Autumn held on to Jude and Lucy, while Jace held on to Lucy and Jayden to Jude. It was really freaking sweet, but she knew they looked silly as hell.

"So Lucy's next, huh?" Jayden said, and she flashed him a dark look.

"No way, Benji won't marry her. He's only staying 'cause he's scared of her," Jude quipped and Lucy rolled her eyes.

"He'll probably figure out that she doesn't know how to cook and he'll run," Jace added, grinning, but when she looked at him, he looked away. "Or, I mean, he'll be lucky to marry our amazing, beautiful sister."

"Pussy," Jude whispered at him, and their mom smacked him.

"Jude! We are in a church."

"We are in a barn on church grounds, Mom."

"God can still hear you, boy," she snapped as her grip on them went tighter. "Now, shut up. I'm nervous."

"Nervous?" Lucy asked, confused. "I thought you wanted this?"

"If you don't, Mom, I can cause a distraction. Jayden will get you out of here—no wait, Jace will. And we'll have Jayden tell River while Lucy grabs the kids," Jude decided and everyone nodded, while Lucy was convinced she was related to idiots.

"Are you crazy? I am in love with that man," Autumn declared and all four of them gagged, on cue, simultaneously. Lucy was quite impressed. "We are doing this. I'm just worried he won't like my dress or something."

"What? You're gorgeous," Jude said.

"Prettiest woman I've ever seen in my life," Lucy agreed.

"He's a lucky dude, Mom. You're beautiful," Jayden said.

"What they all said. I'd say you're hot, Mom, but that's kinda gross," Jace said simply and they all shook their heads. But like they wanted, their mom smiled.

Holding on to them, she cleared her throat before saying, "I just want you four to know I love you. So damn much. And I'm so proud of the people you have become. I hate that it's not your father, but, well, he didn't want me. But

River does, and he's such a great guy. So thank you for walking me down the aisle, and thank you for loving and supporting me," she said. And of course, Lucy started to cry.

"Is Lucy crying?" Jude asked.

"She knows how to do that?" Jayden asked as the boys gawked at him.

"Man, Lucy, are you pregnant?" Jace asked and she threw her hands up.

"No, assholes. I'm happy for our fucking mom, okay?" she snapped just as the door to the barn opened.

Everyone, including Pastor Dwayne, looked at them with wide eyes. Like always, because it was just her luck, Lucy wanted to die.

Cracking up beside her, Jace said, "God sure heard that."

Kill me now.

With a bright red face, Lucy's eyes met Benji's as he sat with Angie in his lap, and a grin covered his handsome face. He was wearing a dark blue suit, a rose-colored bow tie, and he hadn't shaved since Tuesday. She knew this because she was living with the man and waking up every morning to that face. It was glorious, and she knew she couldn't be happier.

That was until he mouthed, "You're fucking hot."

That made her grin.

Big.

When her mom started down the aisle, Lucy's gaze went to River.

He was a bubbling mess of tears, and that only made Lucy cry harder.

"Coach is crying," Jace whispered. "I'm scared."

"Shut up," Lucy snapped, wiping her face.

"You guys are a bunch of babies. It's a wedding, not a funeral," Jude called over and Jayden scoffed.

"Dude, you cried at your wedding," Jayden accused.

"Did not!"

"Good Lord, you guys bicker about everything. Shut up, I'm trying to get married," their mom barked and all four of them snapped their mouths shut, fighting back their laughter. It felt like when they were kids, but they weren't kids anymore. They were four different personalities, all grown-up, paving their own ways. For once, Lucy didn't feel like she was missing out on anything.

Looking back at Benji, who had his arms wrapped around Angie as they watched, she curved her lips into a satisfied grin.

She knew she had everything she never knew she needed.

Benji had never seen a set of siblings bicker and pick at each other the way

Lucy did with her brothers.

"Benji, I shit you not, she still picks her nose," Jude decided.

"I saw her do it before we walked out, and she cussed in front of God and everybody," Jace added. "She's gross."

"She stinks too. Believe me, she farts like a dude," Jayden teased, holding back his laughter as Lucy glared.

"I've never seen or smelled either of those things, but thanks, guys," he said and Lucy shook her head, her eyes dark with annoyance. Though she was still gorgeous. Her hair was down in curls along her shoulders. The dress she wore was simply lethal, and he was convinced she was the most gorgeous woman in the world. She was hotter than the bride, and he knew that was taboo to say, but she was. The wedding, though, had been amazing. Benji even shed a tear or two for the beautiful couple. It was clear how much River loved Autumn and her in return. It was gorgeous. Their vows were sweet, and looking over at them, he couldn't help but smile.

Relationship goals.

That's what they gave him.

"I got you three, I really do," she said, and they all laughed her off. "Fine, Jude would crap his pants, and instead of going to my mom to get cleaned up, he and Jayden would paint with it."

"Ew! Lucy, I'm eating," Claire complained while Angie giggled loudly.

"You played with his poop? Not even your own, but his?" Baylor asked as Lucy grinned.

"I was, like, one."

"Three."

"You were crapping your pants at almost five?" Claire asked, horror all over her face.

"I had digestive issues, thank you," he said simply while Jace laughed like a hyena.

"And that one used to eat dog food," Lucy said, pointing to Jace, who stopped laughing immediately. "And I mean, dog food, the treats, the soft food, hard. Jace was basically a dog."

Avery made a face. "I'm never kissing you again."

"Ha! Please. Come here," he said, pulling her to him. She tried to resist him, but then she pressed her lips to his as everyone laughed.

"But that's not all—"

"Shut up, Lucy!" Jayden yelled and she smiled.

"Don't want me to tell everyone how you and Jude used to play with dog poop, too?"

Benji shook his head, laughing as Angie balked. "Ew, guys!"

"What was your thing with poop?" Baylor asked and Jayden shook his

head.

"I hate you," he said and Lucy grinned.

"Don't try to embarrass me in front of my boyfriend, then," she said plainly, and all three boys looked away, shaking their heads.

"Are you sure you want to be with her? She's mean," Jace called over to him. Benji smiled as he wrapped his arm around her shoulders.

"Yeah, I love her, the mean side too."

"She bites, did you know that? Like, I still have the scar," Jude said, pulling his shirt up, and sure enough, right by his ribs was a bite mark scar.

Benji looked over at Lucy and she shrugged. "He tried to tickle me."

"She broke my nose. Twice!" Jayden yelled and Benji laughed.

"I won't even try to tickle her, she's like a ninja." Jace shook his head, looking to Avery. "Like, really, she's evil."

"I feel like I should try. Get you down one good time and tickle the heck out of you," Benji said and she grinned up at him.

"Please. Try."

The challenge was in her eyes, and he almost wanted to do it until Autumn said, "Benji, honey, I like you a lot. Please don't."

He looked back at Lucy wide-eyed and she smiled. "I knocked her tooth out."

He gasped as Autumn nodded, pointing to the front one. "Fake tooth."

Looking back at Lucy, he said, "You are mean!"

That had everyone laughing as the server came by to refill their drinks. They were at Catbird Seat, some ritzy place Autumn and River really enjoyed. But Benji was still hungry and he had already eaten all his plate and most of Lucy's. It had been a great Christmas, though. For the first time in forever, he felt at home. He felt wanted being with Lucy's whole family and watching her with them. As much as they picked on each other, the love they showed for one another was almost suffocating. Benji had never been intimidated by anything, but he was by her love for her brothers. It was like they almost did no real wrong. They were idiots, she'd say, but they were her idiots. It was sweet, and he loved watching her interact with them and their wives.

Especially baby Ashlyn.

She loved that baby like she loved Angie, and it was easy too. The little nugget had dark black hair, big green eyes, and the brightest red lips he had ever seen. She was adorable, and when he finally got to hold her, he wasn't about to give her back. Even if he was hungry.

"Isn't she pretty?" Angie asked as she stroked her little head. "She's my favorite."

"She is pretty," he agreed and Angie smiled.

Leaning toward him, she whispered, "I'm still hungry."

He nodded. "Me too."

"Can we go stop to get some more food before we go home?"

"Yes, ma'am," he said and she grinned as she leaned into her grandma, Autumn taking her in her arms and kissing her hard on the head.

"You look great with a baby in your arms, Benji. Plans to have some?" Avery asked, her lips curving up when Lucy glared at her. For being so young, Avery was wise beyond her years and very intelligent, but apparently she had a little bit of a teasing streak.

Nodding his head, he looked back at Lucy and shrugged. "Got to get her to marry me first."

"Oh my God, are you asking?" Autumn practically screamed, fumbling for her phone as the boys and Lucy all groaned. "Let me get my phone. Pictures. River, get your phone, honey."

"Sweetheart, I don't think he's proposing," River said and Benji laughed.

"Not now. One day," he said, looking back at Ashlyn. "She says I rush into things."

He felt Lucy glaring at the side of his head, but he just kept grinning at Ashlyn as Avery said, "Sometimes, the best things are rushed."

"I loved rushing. Even though, I think it took you like a month to agree to date me," Jace said and she grinned.

"But, hey, didn't take that long to get pregnant," she said with a huge, exaggerated wink and Benji was sure he was missing something, but that didn't stop Lucy from snickering or Jude and Jayden from laughing hard.

"Nope, one and done," Jace said proudly and Benji grinned.

They were young, but they sure were in love. "How long have you two been together?"

"A little over a year," Jace said, kissing her head. "We moved fast, so I got you on the whole rushing thing."

Benji chanced a glance at Lucy and she shook her head. "Look the other way, Paxton."

Another round of laughter came and Benji really felt like he was fitting in. Like he was family.

"So I guess it's official," Jude said then, and everyone looked at him.

"What's official?" Jace asked, looking around. But everyone was confused. But Autumn's face lit up. "You're pregnant!"

He made a face and Benji chuckled as Jude shook his head. "No, woman. Shit," he complained as Claire laughed beside him. "I was saying that it was official that our brother, Jayden Mitchell, is now legally married to his stepsister."

Benji sputtered with laughter as Jayden and Baylor glared. He hadn't even thought of that.

Jace laughed, "How does it feel? Is it weird?"

"Eff off, dude. Shut up," Jayden spat and Baylor glared.

"I can still kill you," she warned and Jace laughed.

"When you guys have kids, though," Lucy said then to Jayden, and Benji didn't miss the way Baylor's eyes widened. What the hell was that about? "Will the baby call you Daddy or Uncle?"

That had the whole table losing their shit. Well, everyone except for Baylor and Jayden. "I hate you," Jayden declared before glaring at his mother. "Really, Mom? Had to marry my wife's dad?"

"You mean your stepdad," she teased, and again, everyone lost it laughing.

When Lucy stopped laughing, though, Benji looked over at her as Angie yelled, "Grandpa!"

He looked back to see Angie pop up and run around the table to a tall, dark-haired man who looked a whole lot like Lucy's brothers. When he picked Angie up, kissing her hard on the cheek, the whole table was full of tension.

Lucy's dad.

"Hey, love bug, how ya doing? Merry Christmas. Did you open your presents yet? You like what I got you?"

Angie shook her head. "Not yet. We had Christmas at Grandma's this morning, and Santa brought me a bike! We are opening the rest of our presents at home after dinner. And we're gonna have another cake for Benji's birthday. I love cake! Grandma got married to River today! Isn't she so pretty?"

Lucy's father looked up and smiled. "Way prettier than she was on our wedding day. Congratulations, Autumn, River."

"Thank you, Mark," Autumn said tightly.

"Well, just wanted to wish you guys a merry Christmas. Ellen and I were having dinner when I heard you guys. Always the loudest, ya know," he laughed but no one laughed with him. Benji looked around and almost no one was even looking at him. Only Lucy, Autumn, and River were.

As his laughter died down, Angie asked, "Have you met Benji, Grandpa? He's Mommy's boyfriend."

"I have not," he said and Benji handed Ashlyn over to Jace before standing up. Benji didn't miss Mark's eyes intently following the path of his newest granddaughter. Meeting Mark midway, he shook his hand.

"Benji Paxton, nice to meet you."

Mark held his gaze, the same green eyes as Lucy. "You too. Mark Sinclair. Heard a lot about you."

"Probably bad, I assume?" Benji asked and Mark laughed.

"Yeah, but Lucy redeems you. Hope what she says is true," he said, almost like a warning, and Benji nodded.

"I think so," he said as Angie came over to him, taking his hand.

"He's my favorite."

"Hey!" all three boys sang out, and she grinned back at them.

"Shh, you guys are my first favorites," she said in a mock whisper but Benji just grinned, his feelings not hurt.

"Well, it was great to meet you, but I've got to get back to my wife."

"You too," Benji said as he made his way back around the table.

"Again, merry Christmas and congratulations."

Autumn said thanks, but the boys said nothing while Lucy said, "Merry Christmas."

He sent one last grin and walked away. While Benji knew the dude was bad news and had done some wrong, he kind of felt bad for him. The boys, though, they cared not one bit before looking over at Lucy.

"You're talking to him?" Jude accused.

"He bought something for Angie?" Jayden asked.

"I have to, he's helping me with Angie," she snapped back and Jayden looked down, shaking his head.

"Be careful," Jace warned and she glared.

"I am," she shot back as Autumn snapped her fingers at them.

"He is not ruining my dinner. You four let go of that, and you enjoy our family time, you hear me?"

"Yes, ma'am," they all agreed, but even Benji knew the mood of dinner had changed. As they cut into Audrey's delicious cake, it livened up a little bit but not much, especially when the topic of Rick came up.

"Has you know who called yet?" Jayden asked, and Lucy shook her head while Benji's blood boiled.

"Nope."

"You should fight for full custody," Jude said. "He doesn't deserve her."

Benji looked over at Angie. She was sitting in River's lap, playing on his phone with him as Lucy said, "You think I don't know that? She needs a father in her life."

"Yeah, a good one," Jude said. He pointed to Benji. "Marry that guy. I've only been around him the last two days, and I've seen him do better for Angie than Rick ever has."

Lucy set him with a look. "I hear you, but don't employ Benji to step up. It's not his job."

Before Benji could argue that, say that he wouldn't mind, and it would be his life's greatest pleasure to be a father to Angie, Jace said, "Can't we just hire someone to get rid of him? Or can we not now that it's been brought up? Shit, I should have just hired someone."

"Or can we pay Benji to beat him up? He's a big dude," Jude added and Benji smiled.

"It won't do anything. He's an idiot. We just have to deal with him," he said as the waiter came up. "Can I get the check?"

"Benjamin! No! We're paying," Autumn said, but Benji waved her off.

"Our gift to you," he said, bringing Lucy into his side.

"But it's your birthday." Autumn frowned as Benji smiled at the stack of presents the Sinclairs had brought for him.

"But I want to do this for you," he said, sending her a pleading look, and thankfully, she agreed, shaking her head.

"Fine, fine," she said, waving him off. "But we are taking you to dinner one night this week."

"Done," he agreed, holding his card up, but the waitress shook her head.

"Actually, Mark Sinclair paid for dinner and told me to tell you guys merry Christmas and congratulations."

The table went quiet as Benji smiled. "Well, thank you, then."

"Absolutely. Can I get anyone anything else?"

Everyone declined as Autumn cleared her throat. "Well, that was nice of him."

No one really agreed as Lucy leaned on her forearms. "Yeah, it was, Mom."

"Lucy, really?" Jace said and she shrugged.

"He is honestly going above and beyond for Angie. Really. Maybe he's trying to mend fences."

But the boys didn't look convinced. Jayden announced, "Well, if he gets that guy gone, then maybe I'll consider thinking that. But until then, he's dead to me."

"Me too," Jace and Jude said. Benji looked to Lucy, her face full of apprehension. He knew the upcoming court date wasn't for another three weeks, but it was weighing heavily on her. He wished he could alleviate some of the burden, but she wasn't like that. She only leaned when she needed to, and so far, she was good.

But when she wasn't, he'd be there, and he'd bear the burden of all of it as long as Lucy would let him.

"My mom thought you were going to propose to me."

Wrapping his arms around Lucy's waist as Angie played with the new indoor hockey set Benji had gotten her, he kissed her shoulder. "Did you want that?"

She shook her head. "God, no, we aren't ready."

"No?"

"No, crazy. Jeez," she said, gawking at him. "Plus, I love my new bracelet and earrings. I've never had diamonds before, I didn't even have an engagement ring."

He made a face. "No?"

"Nope, we were poor," she said with a grin. "Plus, I never needed it. Angie was my main concern, or maybe I knew that Rick wouldn't last. I don't know," she laughed, leaning her head against his as she drank in the stunning set he had gotten her. When he saw it, he knew she'd love it, and while she thought it was too early for them to be engaged, it hadn't stopped him from picking out a ring for her.

Not that anyone knew that.

He hadn't bought it, but he found the one he wanted for her. It would fit her hand perfectly, a simple three carat diamond in a platinum band. He knew she'd love it, but he'd wait until he knew she wouldn't say no.

Kissing her jaw, he said, "Well, I'm getting you a ring."

"Later."

"Later? Like, how later?"

"Why do you need times for everything?"

He grinned. "So I can do it before then," he said with a wink and she laughed.

"I don't know, a year?"

He made a face. "No."

"No? You can't just say no."

"A year is too long."

"You are crazy. It's been little over two months, Benji. That's like ten weeks," she stressed and he shrugged.

"When you know, you know."

She made a face. "So you'd marry me tomorrow?"

"Hell, I'd marry you right now. I mean, it would be an excellent bonus birthday present…" he said and she made another face.

"You're insane."

He grinned as she cuddled into him. "But I'll admit, it's sorta cute."

"And hot, right? You want to bang me?"

She sputtered with laughter. "I always want to do that."

Smiling against her hair, he kissed her head as he held her. He wasn't playing. He'd marry her that second; all she had to do was say yes. Until then, though, he'd hold her, he'd love her, and life would be good. As they watched Angie bat the ball with her stick into the wall, he held her tightly. She whispered, "Benji?"

"Yeah, baby."

"I'm worried about court with Rick."

"Don't, it's three weeks away."

"What if, by some crazy chance, he gets her?"

"Then we will fight for her back, but I highly doubt that I will happen."

"It scares me," she whispered and he nodded, kissing her head.

"Don't be, I got you."

She let out a long breath, fisting his shirt as she looked up at him, her chin touching his. "Sometimes, it's hard to find words to tell you how much you mean to me. Most of the time, I don't say anything at all because I don't share the way you like to," she said and he smiled, getting lost in her eyes. "But I hope you know that having you and Angie is what I live for."

His lips curved even more as he dropped his mouth to hers. "I know exactly how you feel."

Her eyes shone with love as she cupped his face. "Merry Christmas, Benji."

"Merry Christmas, my love," he said before pressing his lips to hers.

"Benji! Come on, let's play! You said you'd be my goalie," Angie whined and then she stomped her foot. "Ugh! All you do is kiss."

Grinning against each other's lips, they pulled apart as his heart burst in his chest. "I'm being beckoned."

"I know."

"But I love you."

"I love you more, birthday boy."

And what a feeling that was.

Chapter
TWENTY-FOUR

ourt day.

Benji had been waiting for this day for weeks. He was ready to get it over with. Shut Rick up and get what Lucy had been wanting, what Angie needed. As he watched Angie kick her legs back and forth in the chair she was sitting in between Lucy and her grandpa, Benji's stomach was a mess. He was surprised how, even though he was ready for this, he was nervous. Probably because Lucy was so anxious. While she looked beautiful in a modest dress that came to her knees with black tights, her hair up in a nice bun, he didn't miss the way she had bitten her nails almost to the quick. Or how she kept moving her fingers together, lacing them, unlacing them, and then sitting on them. She was freaking out, and it was killing him not to be able to touch her.

Angie, though, she was just watching. Taking in everything about the room and the judge and drawing. No cares in the world. Like her mother, she looked adorable in a yellow dress that really made her his little ray of sunshine. Her hair was down, straight along her shoulders. She glanced back at him, and he smiled. She grinned before she mouthed, "This is boring."

Nodding his head, he pressed his finger to his lips, and she turned back around as the judge spoke. "Counsel, this court date was set to alter the parenting plan for Angela Hart, parents, Lucy Sinclair and Rick Hart?"

Lucy's dad stood, clearing his throat. "Yes, sir. Ms. Sinclair would like to change and add a few things to the plan."

"That being?"

335

"The biggest issue we are having now is that Angela does not want to go to her father's anymore. For the past two months, on Mr. Hart's weekends, he has physically forced her to go to his house. We would like to add to the plan that if she doesn't want to go, she doesn't have to. She is at an age where her wishes should be taken into consideration."

It was downright disgusting is what it was. It had taken everything out of Benji not to rip Rick apart the last time. He was mad the whole weekend and actually said sorry to some of the guys he knocked into on the ice. It was painful, and he hated seeing Angie being put through that.

The judge nodded as he looked up at Angie. He was a big man with a heavy beard and thick bifocals. "Angela, you don't want to go to your father's. Why is that?"

Mark looked down at Angie, and she looked from him to the judge. "He's mean," she said in a very small voice.

"Mean, how?"

"He is always yelling at me, telling me I'm a bad kid, that my sister is better. He's really mean about my mom and Benji—"

"Who's Benji?"

"Benjamin Paxton, Ms. Sinclair's significant other," Mark said then, glancing up at the judge.

The judge nodded. "Has he laid a hand on you, Angela?"

Angie looked down and Benji's heart stopped. She looked so pained as Lucy's gaze shot to her, her eyes full of concern before Angie nodded. "Sometimes."

Red-hot rage.

Lucy drew in a sharp intake of breath as she looked down, shaking her head. Angie hadn't told them that. Why hadn't she told them? Glancing over at Rick, who was watching them with narrowed eyes, Benji wanted to get up and beat him stupid. He completely understood Angie needing her butt spanked when she misbehaved. Lucy had had to do it before and it sucked and killed him a bit inside, but he doubted that Rick had reason to discipline her. Why? He had her for two days every other weekend. She shouldn't even have time to be bad if he was loving her the whole time.

"Why?"

She shrugged. "He said I was bad."

"Were you?"

She shook her head. "I don't think so."

"Okay," the judge said, writing some things down. "Other changes."

"If we cannot get Article One changed about the visitation, then we would like to add that Mr. Hart has to allow communication between Angela and her mother—"

The judge looked up at Mark. "What do you mean?"

"Since the end of November on Mr. Hart's weekends, he will not allow Angela to call her mother or for her mother to talk to her while she is in his custody."

The judge looked over at Rick, as did everyone else. "Is there a reason for this, Mr. Hart?"

Rick leaned back in his chair. He was wearing a dingy white button-down with black pants, his hair brushed to the side. Heidi was nowhere to be seen, which surprised Benji. Wouldn't she want to support him in this matter? Lucy had said she didn't expect Heidi to be there, that she didn't care about Angie anyway. Benji guessed she was right, and he wasn't sure how he felt about that. He got that Angie wasn't Heidi's, but she should love her. It was the right thing to do. Clearing his throat, Rick shrugged. "It's my time, I don't think Lucy should get to talk to her."

"She's her mother," the judge reiterated.

"And I'm her father," Rick spat back, and then his lawyer cut him a look that had Rick snapping his mouth shut.

The judge let out a long breath before waving his hand. "Continue, counselor."

"Thank you, sir," Mark said, moving a piece of paper around. "We ask that he should honor Angela's wishes for her extracurricular activities. Angela is very active in the hockey community and has practice on Fridays from five to seven, and games on Saturdays. We ask that the new pickup time be at seven thirty on his weeks to allow for that. Also, he needs to either take her or allow her to be taken to games on weekends she is in his custody."

The judge nodded, writing down the items. "Next."

"We have submitted that Angela suffers from ADHD and is medicated, per her doctor's orders. It has been brought to our attention that Mr. Hart will not give her the medicine she needs when she is with him. Angela has said that he locked her in a room with nothing to do, unmedicated, on one of his weekends. I have documentation from her therapist on that matter, sir," he said, walking up and handing the judge the paper. The judge's face reflected his annoyance as he looked over the paper and then back to Angie.

"Is this true, Angela?"

Angie nodded. "Yes."

Scratching his head, he looked to Rick and then back to Mark. "Anything else?"

Mark glanced to Lucy and she was biting her lip. She looked as if she were going to cry, but instead, she shook her head. Mark sucked in a deep breath and shook his head. "At this time, no, sir. But if Mr. Hart proceeds with the threats he has made against my client, her significant other, and myself, then we will have more changes."

The judge was a little taken aback as his head tilted to the side. "Threats?"

"Yes, sir. All documented," Mark said, walking to the judge and hanging him another sheaf of papers.

He let out a long breath as he read the documents, and Benji figured he was frustrated. Like everyone else. Looking over at Rick's lawyer, the judge asked, "Mr. Holloway, do you need a moment to speak with your client on the requested changes to Angela Hart's parenting plan?"

The lawyer didn't hesitate. "No, sir. My client does not want to change the parenting plan. He only wants to alter the physical custody of Angela Hart."

The judge leaned on his hand. "How do you mean?"

Rick's lawyer swallowed hard. "Mr. Hart would like to request full physical custody of Angela Hart."

Benji looked at the judge as Angie asked Lucy, "What does that mean?"

But Lucy shook her head, holding Angie's hand as Mark stood. "Judge, obviously we have a problem with that."

"I'd say," the judge said, letting out another breath. "Mr. Holloway, reasoning?"

Standing too, like Mark, he nodded, holding a sheet of paper in his hand. He was a small man, kind of scrawny, not sure of himself. Unlike Mark, who stood proudly and took up the whole room with his presence. It was hard not to appreciate the guy, not that Benji would make that public knowledge if he was around a Sinclair.

"My client feels that Ms. Sinclair isn't raising Angela the way he would. He feels she is spoiled and rude. That the diagnosis they have is fake—"

"I have paperwork saying otherwise," the judge interjected and the lawyer nodded.

"Yes, but he feels that Ms. Sinclair paid to have that written up."

The judge looked to Mark. "Where did you get this from?"

"I had the doctors and therapist fax the paperwork to me. The cover letter is attached and the medical professionals have affixed their seal to each page."

Man, Mark Sinclair didn't play.

Shifting the papers around, the judge nodded. "This paperwork seems accurate to me, Mr. Holloway. Anything else?"

Rick looked pissed, probably because the judge thought he was a joke. Or maybe that was just Benji's feeling. He wasn't sure, but when Lucy looked back at him hopefully, he smiled.

"We got this," he mouthed and she nodded before looking up at the judge who was waiting for the lawyer to speak.

"Yes, sir. He has an issue with Ms. Sinclair's boyfriend, Benjamin Paxton."

Well, shit.

He knew Rick would bring him up, but it still made his stomach drop.

"Okay? What's the issue with him? You know what? Wait. Angela, tell me about Mr. Paxton."

Angie sat up and Lucy smiled as she leaned on the table, her little feet kicking. "Benji's the best," she said and the judge smiled. "He plays hockey with me, and he teaches me how to do different things. He leaves a lot 'cause he's a pro hockey player, like, the best in the league. He had two Stanley Cup rings, and they are so huge! They don't even fit my fingers. It's crazy, but…" She paused, her little feet still kicking happily as she leaned on her hands. "He loves me so much, tells me all the time. And he plays with me, we have dance parties, and he picks me up from school—and he's just great. I want him to marry my mom so he can be my dad."

Sucking in a breath, she went to say more, but the judge stopped her as Benji's heart took flight. To be that girl's father would be an honor.

"So you like him?"

"Oh, yes, sir! I love him! He's amazing and so funny," she giggled, looking up at Lucy, who beamed. Benji couldn't stop grinning, his heart skipping a beat in his chest. When Angie glanced back at him, he winked, and she smiled so wide he could see the tooth she had lost the night before.

Man, he loved that little girl.

The judge nodded before looking back at Rick's lawyer. Rick was fuming, his whole face red, as his lawyer fumbled with papers. "As you were saying, Mr. Holloway?"

Benji watched as he cleared his throat, holding the paper in front of him while Rick glared over at him. Benji rolled his eyes as the lawyer said, "Mr. Paxton is an alcoholic—"

"Recovering. He's been clean twelve, going on thirteen, years, your honor," Mark corrected and the judge nodded. "Hasn't had any run-ins with the law. I have documentation of his stay at the Rehab Center of Chicago, documentation from his AA leader, who says he is a good man. Even letters from his boss and some of his fellow players. Everything is here if you need to see it."

The judge motioned for him to bring it forward as he said, "Thank you. Mr. Holloway, next complaint against Mr. Paxton?"

"My client feels he is trying to steal his daughter. That he is trying to buy her off, to make her love him."

Benji's face twisted, matching the judge's as he shook his head. "Proof of this?"

When the lawyer actually got up, Benji's heart stopped as his eyes widened. What the hell?

Lucy looked back at him, her eyes full of distress as Mark looked over at her. The lawyer said, "There was a savings account opened in her name where he makes regular deposits."

The judge looked at the paperwork and then up at Mark. "Counselor?"

Mark looked over at Lucy and she panicked, looking back at Benji.

Leaning toward Mark, he said, "It's for Angie, for college."

She made a face as Mark cleared his throat. "Apparently, it's an account that Mr. Paxton opened for Angela for when she goes to college."

"Yeah, it's to give me a great start when I'm older like he wished his daughter would have had," Angie said then, everyone looking over at her. "Leary died when she was two, and Benji wants me to live all my dreams like he had wished for her. So we went to the bank, and Benji put a lot of money in it for me."

"That's nice, Angela. Thank you," the judge said before looking to Mark. "But your client did not know about this?"

Mark looked to Lucy and she swallowed hard. "No, sir, I didn't."

Benji's heart was knocking against his ribs as the judge looked over to Benji. "Did you open this account, Mr. Paxton?"

Benji nodded. "Yes, sir."

"Is what Angela said true?"

"Yes, sir. We opened it about three months ago."

"How much is in there?"

"Almost seven thousand. Her mother is renting an office from me, for which we have a contract. The money she pays me in rent, I put in the account for Angie, I mean, Angela."

The judge nodded as Lucy gawked back at him, her eyes narrowing, and he knew he had just fucked up. He should have told her so she could have told Mark, but he had honestly forgotten about it.

"I do not see this as evidence that Mr. Paxton is trying to buy the child off—which is a downright silly thought anyway. I see no problem here, and it's obvious Angela cares for Mr. Paxton, so unless you have something else, I'd like to move on."

"We have nothing else."

"Okay, well, I deny your petition for full custody. I would like to approve these changes if you agree."

Holloway leaned to Rick, but he was already shaking his head. "I want full custody."

The lawyer said something Benji couldn't hear, but Rick shook his head. Looking back to the judge, Rick's lawyer said, "Judge, we do not agree, and we would like to further seek full custody of the child."

But the judge shook his head before looking to Angie. "Angela, how old are you? Seven?"

"Almost eight," she said with a smile and he smiled back at her.

"Oh, a big girl, then."

Angie beamed. "Yes, sir. I'm almost strong enough to hit the puck like

Benji."

Benji grinned as the judge nodded. "Good. So tell me, who do you want to live with?"

Her legs stopped kicking. "I live with my mommy and Benji."

"Do you want to live with your dad?"

"No, sir," she said simply. "I don't want to leave my mom or Benji. Mommy, I don't have to, do I? Am I going to live with Dad?" She looked to Lucy, her voice panicked.

Lucy shook her head quickly. "No, honey, he's just asking you what *you* want."

"I don't want to leave you or Benji."

"I know, baby. It's okay," Lucy said, wrapping her arm around Angie and kissing her head. Glancing back up at the judge, who was writing some things down as he nodded, Benji held his breath as the judge looked back to Rick and his lawyer.

"I usually don't ask children their wishes, but I wanted you to hear her response, Mr. Hart. I urge you to not proceed for full custody because that isn't what your child wants. She seems happy, and unless you can come to me with real evidence that Ms. Sinclair is mistreating her, especially when the evidence seems to indicate your misdeeds, or that Mr. Paxton is a negative influence, then, I'm sorry, I have no other choice but to deny your request and approve the changes to the current parenting plan."

Everyone looked to Rick as he shook his head. "I want to proceed with the full custody part."

The judge's face changed to displeasure as he looked down. "Fine, I want everyone back here in two weeks. Maybe that will give you all time to think. Mainly you, Mr. Hart. At that time, if nothing further has been brought to my attention, then I will decide what is best for Angela Hart, since I'm sure we won't come to an agreement otherwise."

"Judge, Angela is to go to her father's this weekend. Can we request that she does not go until after the next court date?" Mark asked quickly before the judge stood.

He took in a long breath and then looked to Rick. "Do you want to see your child, Mr. Hart?"

"Yes."

"Then we will honor the current parenting plan. Maybe he'll see that putting Angela through this isn't something a seven- almost eight-year-old should have to deal with," he stressed before standing up.

"Sir, I'm sorry, but I'd like to request that you reconsider," Mark tried and Benji was hopeful. He had to leave with the Assassins this week for a four-day stint before the All-Star break and had been hoping that Lucy wouldn't have to deal with the handover, but the judge shook his head.

"Mr. Sinclair, as much as I agree with you and believe what I'm certain you're thinking, I want to give Mr. Hart a chance to do right by his child. But I will say this, if Angela wants to speak to her mother, you must allow her."

Rick rolled his eyes and let out a long breath. "Fine."

"Don't make me regret this choice," the judge warned before slamming his gavel to the desk. "See everyone in two weeks."

Mark turned to Angie and picked her up, kissing her cheek before looking over at Lucy. "It's fine. We'll have this taken care of in two weeks. No big deal."

Lucy didn't look convinced as she slowly nodded and reached for her purse. "Thanks, Dad."

"Anytime, honey," he said, squeezing her arm. "Don't worry, okay? He has nothing on you guys."

"Okay," she said as Angie took her hand. "Let's go."

"Benji! Let's go to lunch," Angie decided as she broke free from Lucy, going for him. He picked her up, kissing her cheek as he nodded.

"Sounds good to me, and then we gotta go home so I can pack. Gotta leave this afternoon."

She made a face as they walked down the aisle, Lucy and Mark behind them. "I don't want you to go."

"I know, but it's only six days, and then we leave for Florida."

"Woo-hoo!" she cheered, laying her head against his shoulder as they walked out to the truck. "Grandpa, wanna come with us?"

"Sorry, love bug, I can't. I've got another case," he said almost automatically. Benji wasn't sure if he was being truthful, but he knew that Lucy didn't want him to go. He could see it all over her face. She was still holding him at arm's length, which Benji guessed she always would. He had done some major damage to his children.

"Aw, okay, I'll see you soon," she said, wiggling out of Benji's arms and going to Mark to hug him.

Moving around all of them, Lucy went to stand by the truck, opening the door before saying, "All right, Dad, thanks again. I'll be in touch."

Benji looked back at Mark as Angie got into the truck. He looked sad as he nodded. "Of course, honey. Talk to you soon. Benji, good to see you again."

"You too," he said before turning and getting into the truck himself. When he started to put his seat belt on, though, he could see that Lucy was mad and he was pretty sure it was directed at him. He looked over at her and she had her legs crossed, leaning into the door, the farthest she could be from him as she stared out the window. "That went really well," he tried, and she just nodded her head.

"Yeah."

Okay, then.

"Do you want to go to lunch?"

She shook her head. "No."

Angie went to protest, but Benji stopped her. "Honey, Mom is tired. That was exhausting. Let's go on home. I'll make you a peanut butter sandwich."

She nodded. "Okay."

His stomach was uneasy as he drove back to the house. When Lucy went in without a word to him, he bit into his cheek as he went into the kitchen to make Angie some lunch. He really didn't want to fight with her before he left, but it was looking like that was exactly what was about to happen. As Angie popped around being her usually silly self, Benji made her a sandwich and then set it on the island. Climbing up into the chair, she put her iPad on the counter and then looked to him.

"Am I going back to school?"

"Probably not."

"Cool, can we shoot around some before you leave?"

He nodded. "Yeah, sunshine. Let me go and make sure Mom is okay."

"Okay," she said before hitting play and starting a movie. Washing his hands, he wiped them off before heading upstairs where Lucy had gone. When he hit the hallway, he could see her sitting on the bed, her eyes on him.

"So I'm apparently in the dog house," he said as he headed down the hall, his eyes on hers.

"Yeah," she said, her sass in full force.

"Because of the savings account?" he asked, shutting the door, and she stood.

"Yes! What were you thinking? Why didn't you tell me? And I can send my kid to college, myself. You don't have to do it. I'm not helpless!"

He nodded, pressing his palms into his hips. "You're absolutely right. I should have told you, and I know you can put her through school. But I told you when we signed the contract for the office that I would do with the money what I wanted. So I opened Angie an account, and I have the money you deposit transferred every month. I also put the five thousand dollar design fee that you wouldn't let me pay in there too," he said. That made her brows go to her forehead, steam all but coming out of her ears. "I did it for no other reason than to help put her through school."

"It isn't your job, Benji! It's mine. I'm her mother. You're not—"

She paused, her eyes widening, and he watched her. He knew what she was going to say, and he tried not to let it hurt his feelings. But he knew he failed a bit as he held her gaze. "What? Not her dad, just the boyfriend? Yeah, I know that."

She looked away, her lips trembling as she shook. "I don't need anyone

helping me with my kid."

"I wasn't trying to help you. I was doing it for Angie."

She shook her head, a tear running down her cheek, and he waited. He knew how she worked. She needed a second, and as he expected, she soon looked up at him. "I'm sorry. I'm just mad because Rick tried to use that against you like the foul asshole he is, and I hate that I didn't know what was going on. I was completely surprised, and I hate that. I need to know what is coming at me so I can fight it. I couldn't fight that, and for a second there, I thought I was losing everything."

"I completely understand, and I'm sorry for not telling you. I honestly forgot about it."

She looked up at him, tears spilling out of her eyes as she threw her hands up. "Why are you staying around? I'm an asshole—"

"Because I love you," he said, taking her hand and pulling her to him. "Your stress level is borderline 2007 Britney Spears right now, and I get it. But, Lucy, I want to help you. I want to be there for you." He wrapped his arms around her, kissing her temple as she leaned into him.

"I didn't mean what I said to you. You don't deserve that. I'm sorry. You know I hate handouts. I'm just so fucking scared, so mad at Rick, not you. Fuck, I'm sorry."

"I know, baby," he whispered against her head as she wrapped her arms around him, holding him tight. "It's going to be okay. But I won't lie, Lucy, you almost broke my heart there. You really need to think before you speak."

She nodded against his chest, moving her nose against him as she hugged him tighter, almost like she didn't want him to let her go. He wouldn't. Not every man could deal with her tantrums, but then not every woman could deal with the shit she dealt with daily. If he couldn't love her through her hard times, why should he be allowed to love her during her good ones? So he would cut her a little slack. It wasn't easy for her right now, but it would be soon.

"I know. I'm so sorry."

"Forgiven."

"I don't deserve that forgiveness," she whispered and he kissed her nose. "I just hate how I feel so helpless. I never needed anyone. Not my dad, not a man, but now I need him and I fucking need you. I'm starting to need you to keep me grounded. I'm used to being so independent, only worrying about Angie. But you…I can't let anything hurt you or mess up what we have." She paused, sucking in a breath as a sob burst from her. "I want him to go away so it can just be us. So you can one day be Angie's dad. I just have so many fucking feelings and I hate them. I hate feeling like this."

"Do you want to go back to the way it was before?" he asked, and she looked up at him. "Lonely, only worried about Angie? 'Cause I sure as hell don't want that for you. I love you. I don't want anything but for you to be happy."

She shook her head. "For once in my life, I don't have to fake like I'm happy or force myself to feel that way. When I'm with you, I'm just blissful and I feel like nothing can touch me. So, no, I don't want to go back to my life before, because that life wasn't something I wanted. You are something I want in my life."

Looking deep into her eyes as they swam in her tears, he smiled. She didn't share much, but when she did, it hit him straight in the gut. "Then why are we still talking? Kiss me."

She cried out before his mouth came crashing against hers, and he got lost in her kisses as he held her close, his heart pounding in his chest. He knew this wasn't easy now, and while he hoped, in two weeks, Rick would be gone, he knew he wouldn't be.

No, Rick would always be a thorn in their sides.

But like he had been doing since the beginning, he'd be there for Lucy.

Because he loved her, and he knew there was no other love like hers out there.

Chapter
TWENTY-FIVE

Sitting at her desk, Lucy leaned against her hand as she read through emails. She was supposed to be at the house packing, so when Benji got home that night, they could meet him before heading to the airport. But Lucy was dragging ass. Not only had she not slept much that weekend with Angie and Benji both being gone, she was stressed with work. The other designer had fucked up on a job and Lucy had had to refund the client, which sucked ass. Now, she was considering letting Meg go and hiring someone else, but she had three open jobs right now. Lucy sure as hell didn't have time to take them on, so she'd have to let Meg finish them.

Then maybe she'd fire her.

It was a mess, and she couldn't wait to be on the beach. While, yes, she would be working, she would also get to just hang and bum it in the sun. A nice, relaxing vacation before court with Rick the following week. It was just what she needed. Surrounded by the people she loved with her toes in the sand. Glancing at the picture on her desk of Angie and Benji, of course, making silly faces—she swore they couldn't take a picture of themselves actually looking normal—she smiled. Even though Angie was only at school, she missed her dearly.

The past weekend had been hell once more. Rick had brought Heidi, for what reason, she wasn't sure, but she stood by as Angie threw a fit, not wanting to go at all. Angie begged him not to make her, but he was hell-bent and made her leave, ignoring her bag with her medication. Even when Lucy tried to give it to him, he just drove off. Lucy had always hated him, but she was really starting to loathe him, and she really didn't like that.

She wanted that co-parenting thing that everyone on Facebook raved about. She had never even had an ounce of that. Rick had been a dick since the beginning, but Lucy had wanted to believe that maybe she could have that. That they could be adults. She had hoped he wanted to be a father, a good one, but she was starting to realize that Rick Hart would never be a father to Angie.

But Benji could be.

She knew it was insane to think about it, but he was just so great with her. Yes, the bank account thing pissed her off, but it was sweet. It was Benji. Always wanting to help, be there for everyone. But his main concern was always Lucy and Angie. He loved her girl as much, if not more than she did—not that that was possible—and she couldn't ask for more than that. Because Benji didn't have to love Angie. Hell, Heidi sure as hell didn't love her, but Benji did. With all of himself.

God, she missed him. She couldn't understand how she'd gotten so lucky to meet a man like him. But she loved him more than she could ever express. The way he understood her, was so patient with her—she swore he deserved a medal. She sure as hell didn't deserve him, but somehow, she had him.

He was hers.

As she leaned back in the chair, a knock came and then the door opened. Rayne smiled as she came to the desk, laying a piece of paper down in front of her. Picking it up, Lucy looked it over as Rayne said, "Nikky Jiggler has not said anything about Benji since that post. It has since been deleted, so I emailed her and asked when that article would be published. She wrote that back."

Lucy looked down and shook her head as she read.

> *Rayne,*
> *I didn't sleep with Benji Paxton. I was paid to put his name on the blog by someone. Because of that, no article will be posted. It's dumb, but hey, a hundred bucks is a hundred bucks. Especially when I still got paid after having to take it down. Thanks for asking, tho!*
> *Love,*
> *Nikky*

"Well, that was short and to the point."

"Yeah, so at least you know," she said, and Lucy nodded. She was pretty sure she knew who had paid Nikky, and she would fax this to her dad just in case. She didn't understand what Rick thought he was doing. Why couldn't he just leave them alone? Let them be happy.

"Thanks," she said as her phone started to ring. "You rock." Rayne flashed her a grin as Lucy reached for the phone, seeing that it was Rick.

What the hell?

Answering it as Rayne left, she said, "Hello?"

"I need to see you. Where are you?"

She paused. His voice was hard, to the point. Quickly, uneasiness settled in her stomach. "At my office."

"Text me the address."

"Why?"

"'Cause I need to talk to you. Now."

He hung up and Lucy's heart was in her throat. She dialed her dad's number on the landline, and he answered right away, "Hello?"

"Dad, Rick just called me, wanting to come to my office."

"Did he say why?"

"No."

"Okay, stall him a bit, and I'll be right over. What's the address?"

She told him and then hung up, waiting a few minutes before texting Rick her address. As she waited, she paced. She wanted to call Benji, but he had press and wouldn't be able to talk. Thankfully, though, her dad arrived quickly. But before they could even really talk about anything, Rick walked in.

Shutting the door behind him, Rick rolled his eyes when he saw her dad sitting in the corner, his arms over his chest. "Why's he here?"

Her dad shrugged before setting him with a glare. "I'm here to support my daughter."

She really didn't like that answer since she wanted him there as her lawyer, but she wouldn't address that. Her dad's statement sure didn't make Rick want to talk either. "I want to talk to her alone."

"Oh. Well, then, I'm here for my client. No can do, buddy."

Glaring, Rick looked to Lucy. "I need to talk to you about that lowlife you have around my daughter."

She scowled at that. "Benji is not a lowlife. He is good to her."

"Oh, is he? I told you he was a pedophile," he spat back, doing something to his phone and then holding it out so Lucy could see. Mark came over as he pushed play. In the video, Angie sat fidgeting on the couch. It was clear she wasn't medicated, her body twitching and her hands moving as she bounced in the seat.

But most of all, she was terrified.

Tears welled up in Lucy's eyes as her heart started to thump in her chest.

Glancing at Rick, she glared. "What the hell is that?"

But he shook his head as his voice came over the video. *"Does Benji give you money?"*

Angie nodded. "Yeah."

"What for?"

"For whatever I want. I don't know. Can I go to my room?"

"No, tell me."

"Stuff."

"Has he touched you?"

Lucy's heart stopped. She looked to her dad, and he was glaring, his neck turning red as he held on to the desk.

"Dad, please. I want to go to my room."

"Answer me! Does he touch you?"

"Yes!"

"So he kisses you?"

She made an obvious face. "Yeah?"

"Does he make you touch him?"

"I don't know! Can I go?"

Before he could ask anything else, she got up and ran.

The video went black and Lucy was fuming.

"What the hell are you implying?" she spat out, her eyes burning into his. He had a smug look on his face as he shrugged.

"Pretty obvious."

But it wasn't and Mark started yelling. "That doesn't mean anything. Of course, he touches her. He hugs and kisses her. He lives with her. He is like a father to her."

"He's a pedophile, and this is what I need to get custody of my child," Rick snapped back at him and Lucy just shook her head as she stood, her body shaking with anger.

This was not happening.

"He is not. That video is bogus, and you know it. How dare you?" she roared as Mark laughed.

"That won't hold up in court, you idiot. Do you know what will happen if you bring that forward? Lots of investigations. Do you want that?"

"I don't care. They need to happen because my daughter is important," he said, his eyes narrowing as he sneered at them. "I mean, tell me, what man just automatically takes to someone else's child? Moves them in in a month? They've only been together for three months."

"Because he is a good guy! Is that what this is about? You're jealous?"

"Bitch, please. I don't give two shits about you," he sneered and Mark shook with anger.

"You are about to cause a big fucking mess, Rick. Don't show that in court. It's a lie and you know it."

"All I know is that bastard is raping my kid."

Rage. That's all Lucy saw.

"You stupid son of a bitch," she screamed before lunging at him. She slammed her knee into her desk but that didn't stop her. Jumping onto him, she whaled on him, slamming her fist into his face as he tried to push her away. "Benji would never," she screamed, her fist coming down against his mouth before her father pulled her away. "How dare you? You are scum. You are worthless. You piece of shit!"

Rick laughed as he slowly got up, wiping his mouth as he shook his head. Mark's arms held her tightly as she thrashed against him, nowhere near done. There was no way she would let him do that. Accuse Benji of something so horrible.

Not listening to her, though, he yelled, "And now I have an assault to add to the list of reasons my daughter needs to leave you, you stupid bitch."

"Rick, I swear to God, if you don't stop this, you will lose her. I promise you," she warned but Rick just grinned.

"Who has the proof? This guy. Fuck you, and fuck you, Mark. See you guys in court."

As he walked out, slamming the door behind him, Mark let Lucy go. It took everything out of her not to crumple to the ground. This wasn't happening. It couldn't be. This was a joke. The video was a joke, but the allegation wouldn't be good. Turning to her father, she pleaded with her eyes as she asked, "Does he have grounds?"

Mark shook his head. "That video is bogus, Lucy, we know that," he said and she exhaled loudly. Oh, thank God. When he cleared his throat, she looked back at him and knew there was more. Shit.

"But, they're going to investigate for sure, and that's going to be bad for Benji. It will hit the media, I'm sure, and then everyone will know. This won't stay quiet. Fuck, this is complicated."

That's what she thought. As her body went numb and the tears rushed down her cheeks, she closed her eyes. This couldn't be happening. They were happy. They were together. Damn it. Crouching down, she covered her face as she cried into her hands.

What in the hell was she going to do?

Sitting on her and Benji's bed, she felt the tears drip down her face as she stared down at her phone. He and Angie looked back at her, making pig noses. She'd cried the whole afternoon. When she picked Angie up, she couldn't even look at her, only sent her to her room to pack. She wasn't sure what she was doing, but she had to do something. After talking to her father, and his calling Rick's lawyer, she knew it was a done deal. Rick was going forward with the video to open a can of fucking shit. Her heart was aching, her eyes hurt from crying, and she couldn't do this to Benji. She couldn't. She thought about calling her mother, but she knew that would lead to everyone in the family knowing, and she didn't want anyone to know what Rick was trying.

She wouldn't let Benji's name be tainted.

No, she would handle this herself.

She would be okay.

She was always okay.

Dialing his number, she held her breath as she waited. When he answered, her eyes fell shut.

This was going to suck.

"You're calling me. That's weird," he said, and his voice made her heart skip a beat. "Did you hit the wrong button?"

She bit into her lip as she held back the tears. "No, I'm in a rush."

"Oh, okay," he said slowly, and she knew he was aware of the lie she was telling. But he went with it and asked cautiously, "What's up?"

"Um. Well…" she started, but then she couldn't do it. She clammed up, her heart in her throat, and she just couldn't do it. Why would she do this over the phone? And did she really want this? But she had to. She couldn't put him through this. "I…ugh…"

"Lucy, babe, what's going on?"

As the tears rushed down her face, she squeezed her eyes shut tightly. She had every intention of breaking up with him, but she just couldn't. She loved him so damn much, and she just couldn't bring herself to break his heart and annihilate hers. Losing Benji would destroy her. But what was she supposed to do? She couldn't let Rick do this to him. To his career. Maybe if she told Rick Benji wasn't in the picture, he would stop all this and be gone.

But wouldn't that let him win?

What other choice did she have?

God, she just needed to fucking think!

Clearing her throat, she held in her sob as she said, "I need some time."

"Time?"

"Yeah, to think."

"Um. Okay? I don't understand. What's wrong?" he asked, his voice filling with nervousness. She hated to worry him, but she knew him. He wouldn't let her go if he knew the truth. "You're worrying me here, Lucy. What's going on?"

"I'm going to go to Florida with Angie, alone," she said then. It suddenly seemed like a genius idea. She'd go, clear her head, figure it out, come back, and let Benji go. Then she'd fight Rick by herself. The thought sucked and it hurt, but she had no choice. She loved Benji way too much to put him through that shitshow. She didn't care how much he said he would stand by her. No one deserved that.

She wouldn't do that to him.

"What? Why?"

"'Cause I need time to think."

"About?"

"Us."

"Us?"

"Yeah."

"Why?"

"'Cause." She paused. "I just do."

"No, what the fuck is going on, Lucy? Tell me," he said roughly. "Can't you wait till I get there?"

"No, we are flying out early," she said then, even though it was a lie. "I need to clear my head, and I need to do it alone."

He didn't say anything for a long time, and each second that passed, her heart broke even more. "I feel like you're breaking up with me."

"No," she tried, but it sounded more like a sob. "I just need to think."

"I don't understand the needing to think thing. We were fine four fucking hours ago when I talked to you. What the hell is going on? I have a right to know," he said, his voice full of panic. "You know what? Stop, just stop. I'll be home in a couple hours and we'll talk."

But she knew she couldn't do this face-to-face. She couldn't walk away, and she knew she'd let him talk her into letting him go through what Rick was about to do. No, she couldn't do that to him. It wasn't fair.

Life wasn't fucking fair.

Nothing ever was.

She had everything she ever wanted, and just like that, it was about to be ruined.

But that was her life.

She'd always said, if she didn't have bad luck, she'd have none at all.

Such bullshit.

"I can't. I already paid, and Jace and Avery are expecting us."

"What? Did I do something wrong?" he asked, and she came undone, holding the phone from her face as she cried into her legs, her body shaking with the pain. "I mean, I know I'm a little dense sometimes, but I thought we were good. Are you still mad about the bank thing?"

"No, I just need to go."

"Without me?"

Her lips quivered as she shook her head. But she said, "Yes. Just me and

Angie. I need to focus on us for a few days."

She heard his voice break and everything inside of her went dead. What was she doing? How could she do this? But, how could she not? Breaking his heart was one thing—he could come back from that. But ruining his career, his name… That wasn't something he could come back from. She had to do this. "So you are breaking up with me." He said it so calmly, so painfully that Lucy was speechless. "Just tell me the truth. Is that your intention?"

"No, that's not what I want."

"Then what do you want?"

"I want time. I need to think."

"And you can't tell me about what?"

"No, I need time."

He growled, but it wasn't out of malice, it was in complete frustration. "I have no clue what to do here."

"Let me go for the rest of the week. To think."

"No," he roared, and her tears came faster down her face. "I won't let you just go and be fine with it. I'm fucking pissed. My chest hurts and I'm scared when you come back, it will be to pack up your shit. So, no, I won't just let you go. I'm going to ask questions. I'm going to try to figure this out. Shit, I might still fly down there to talk to you if you don't give me something to work with here."

She should have known he would. Closing her eyes, she whispered, "Do you love me?"

"Of course, I fucking love you, Lucy. What kind of question is that? Is that what the problem is? Baby, I love you," he stressed and she bit into her lip so hard it hurt. "I love you so damn much, and I swear, I'm here for the long haul. What the hell is going on?"

"I love you," she said. "So please, let me go. Let me think."

Sounds of frustration met her as he said, "Do I have a choice here?"

He didn't, but she wouldn't say that. Instead, she whispered, "I love you, Benji. I'm sorry."

"You're sorry? For what?"

"For all of this," she said, and as he went to say more, she hung up.

And felt nothing but complete and utter heartbreak.

What had she just done?

Chapter
TWENTY-SIX

When Benji got home, for some reason, he was convinced that Lucy would still be there.

She wasn't.

Neither was Angie.

Not that he assumed she would be, but it still hurt to find she wasn't. Thankfully, though, all their things were still there that they didn't take to Florida with them. Lucy's boots were in the corner where she had left them last week. Angie's hockey set was all over the place, and while the mess made his eye twitch, it was their mess.

His family's.

Or so he still hoped. He didn't have a clue what was going on, but he was going to find out. One way or another. Looking down at his phone, he swallowed hard and dialed her number. She had been ignoring his calls. It had been two hours since the last time he'd called since it took him that long to fly in from New York. Instead of calling as soon as he landed, he figured he'd check the house first. But as soon as he pulled up and found her car gone, he knew she wasn't there.

Hitting her number, he waited as it rang and then her voice came over the line. "Are you home?"

"I am. You're not, though. Did you make it there okay?"

"Yeah, about an hour ago. Angie is already in bed."

"Oh, I'm sure she's exhausted," he said and it irritated him. Why were they

354

making stupid idle chitchat?

"Yeah. We both are."

Swallowing hard, he said, "I can fly out tomorrow."

"Don't."

Letting out a long breath, he ran his hand down his face. "Why not, Lucy?"

"'Cause I need to think."

"About what, baby? Please, I'm dying here. Let me help you fucking *think*," he yelled, hating that word. "I don't know what I did, how to make it better. Please, give me something here."

"You did nothing, Benji, I promise. I just need to think through some things. I'm going to be working. It just doesn't make sense."

"It made sense a month ago when you wanted me to go. When Angie and I planned to make a mermaid castle. I mean, shit, Lucy, what changed?"

His heart was pounding so hard, he was sure it was going to come out of his chest and melt right in front of him. He had never sweated like he was at that moment because, as much as she said she wasn't breaking up with him, he truly believed she was, and he didn't understand. This wasn't her. She wasn't one to hold back on anything. What in the living hell happened?

"I just need—"

"I swear to God, if you say 'time' one more fucking time, I'm going to lose it. What you need is for me to come down there, wrap my arms around you, and then you tell me what is wrong so we can fucking fix it together. That's what you need."

"You don't know that."

"No, I fucking do," he stressed, feeling like he was already losing it. "Do you hear my voice, Lucy? I'm dying here. I miss you. I miss Angie. I want to be with my family." That was when a sob left her lips and her soft cries filled the line. Closing his eyes, his heart just shattering in his chest, he whispered, "Lucy, baby, please, tell me what to do here."

"Stay home," she cried. "Just stay there. I'll see you in a few days."

And then the line went dead.

"Fuck!" he screamed, his ears rattling as he covered his face with his hands. Should he just fly down there? But he didn't even know where Jace lived. "Fuck."

Letting his head fall back, he swallowed hard and picked his phone up once more. "Bro, tell me you know what's wrong with your sister?"

Jayden paused. "Um. No? I thought you guys were leaving for Florida?"

"She left without me."

"What? What happened?"

"I don't fucking know. She says she needs time."

"For what?"

"I don't know, Jayden! Have you not heard anything? Your family is one big

grapevine."

Jayden's voice was full of worry as he said to Baylor, "Mom tell you anything about Lucy?"

"No, what's wrong?"

"I have no clue," he said into the phone. "Let me call my mom."

"No, I will," Benji said and he hung up, dialing Autumn's number. It was late, but thankfully, she answered. "Have you talked to Lucy?"

"No? Why? Is she okay? Are you guys engaged?"

He fucking wished. "No, Autumn, she left for Florida—without me. Claiming she needs time. I don't know what is going on."

"What in the world? No. I don't know anything. Let me call her."

"No," he said quickly. That wasn't what he wanted. "She'll get pissed that I called you. I just was hoping maybe you knew something."

"No, sweetheart, I don't, but I'm still calling her," she said and then the line went dead.

"Fuck!"

Dropping his phone to the island, he let out a long breath as he rubbed his eyes, asking God what the hell he should do. This made no sense. It didn't seem right, and he couldn't even think of what he had done. He had been gone, so he knew that he didn't leave the toilet seat up or use her toothpaste. He had only talked to her, and he had been checking that whore Nikky Jiggler's site, and nothing. What in the world could be going on?

When he opened his eyes, he looked down, thinking maybe he could get Jace's number from Jayden and call him, but something caught his eye. The paperwork from court with Mark Sinclair's business card stapled to the top.

Could this have to do with Rick?

Turning the folder so he could see the number, he dialed Mark's number, but he didn't answer. Setting his phone down, he figured he'd try again tomorrow since it was almost midnight. He needed to go to bed. This had been his roughest Assassins road trip to date. He was aching everywhere from the hard-fought games against the Bruins, Islanders, Devils, and Rangers. They had won two of the four, but he was exhausted. Plus, he was worried, feeling like everything was just falling apart. He knew sleep wouldn't come easy.

When his phone sounded, he looked down to see a text from Lucy.

> Lucy: I'm going to kill you for calling my mom.
> Benji: I'm desperate. Talk to me.
> Lucy: I can't. Not yet.
> Benji: What the hell does that even mean?

He waited, but nothing came. Not even a little text bubble that signaled she was writing him back.

Nothing.

Complete silence.

The only sound he could hear was his heart breaking.

Benji didn't fall asleep until six a.m. He had watched his phone until it died and then as it charged, until he finally fell asleep. He felt pathetic, but he couldn't help it. He felt like he was losing everything with no clue as to why. He was pissed. So damn pissed at Lucy for doing this. He didn't understand what she was holding back. What she was hiding and why? Didn't she understand that he loved her unconditionally and he was going to support her no matter what?

What in the world had her running like this? Hiding?

The only thing he could come up with was fucking Rick.

Rick had done something, and it was taking everything out of Benji not to find that bastard and kill him. He considered driving to his house, but then he didn't know where the asshole lived. He also didn't have his number, so he was stuck. As he stared up at the spinning ceiling fan, he couldn't take the coldness that he felt. The way the house felt empty without them. How he had no clue what the hell to do. He was a fixer, he was a doer, but at that moment, he felt like a loser. With no clue how to rectify that.

As much as he wanted to believe she would come home and they would be okay, he knew they wouldn't. Not after all this. No, she wanted to break up with him. She just couldn't do it. While that should have pleased him, it just broke him more.

What in the world had he done? Or what had happened to make her want to leave him? To take away her love and Angie's? It was unfair, and in a way, he was convinced it was fucking payback for Ava and Leary. It had to be. Why else would he feel like this? Feel like he wanted to down a whole bottle of vodka and just die. Never in his twelve years of sobriety had he truly wanted a drink, but he could use one now.

But even he knew that nothing would dull the pain inside of him.

No, only Lucy could make it better.

Rolling over, he brought her pillow into his arms, nuzzling his nose into it, hoping to get a whiff of her. Taking in a long pull, her flowery scent intoxicated him and everything hurt.

Why couldn't she just talk to him?

When his phone rang, he scrambled to get to it, almost falling off the bed before getting his phone in his hand.

But he didn't recognize the number.

Hopeful, though, he answered. "Hello?"

"Hey, this is Mark Sinclair. This number called me last night."

"Yes!" Benji said, sitting up. "This is Benji. Benji Paxton, Lucy's boyfriend."

Or was he?

The thought made his whole body ache.

"Hey, Benji, what's up?"

"Um, well, funny you should ask," he said, exhaling hard. "Lucy left for Florida—without me—and I really don't know what's going on. And I was wondering, hoping, actually, maybe you knew something about this."

Mark paused, and Benji could hear him clicking his pen against something. "I'm sorry, what do you mean, left? I thought you all were going."

"Yeah, I did too, but she called saying she needed time to think. Whatever the hell that means."

Mark made a disgruntled noise and muttered, "Fool woman."

Benji panicked. "Listen, I know you don't owe me anything, that you don't have to tell me anything. But, if I'm losing my family, I need to know. I need to fix it. Save this before I can't."

Mark chuckled. "Boy, you love those girls."

"Like you wouldn't believe. Both of them."

"I can tell. I can hear it in your voice."

"Then you know I have to know what is going on so I can fix it. I can't lose my family, Mark. I can't, not again," he said, his voice breaking as the tears flooded his eyes.

When Mark cleared his throat, Benji held his breath. "All right, son, listen. I'm gonna give you my address and you come on over, okay?"

Benji was out of bed and getting dressed before Mark even finished his sentence. He wasn't sure what this would help, but it was clear Mark knew something. Getting the address, Benji rushed out of the house, into his truck, and then across town to Mark's office. Knowing that Mark could possibly help him gave him renewed hope he could fix this. But when he got there, nothing could have prepared him for what Mark had to say.

Blinking, completely speechless, Benji just looked across the desk at the older man, unsure what to do or say.

"It was fake, though. Completely. I saw that with one look at it."

"So he's trying to say I touched Angie inappropriately?" Benji asked, choking on a sob. He would never. Who would even think to accuse someone of that?

A fucking sicko, that's who.

Mark held his hands out, shaking his head. "I know, crazy. But since he has the intentions of making the allegation formal, it will be investigated. They will question Angie, they will question you, and Lucy, if it makes it to court."

"So you think it won't," Benji said, his mind racing, and Mark shook his head.

"Let me tell you something about my daughter," he said then, leaning back in his chair. "Lucy isn't dumb. She's a survivor and she protects the ones she loves. She thinks if she cuts all ties with you, goes to court and says you two aren't together any longer, that it will be a dead end. What she doesn't realize is they're still gonna investigate the allegation, which will run your name through the mud. It'll hit the media, for sure. I've already contacted your lawyer this morning. It's going to get nasty if it goes to court."

And then it all made sense. She was doing this to protect him. That damn, crazy, gorgeous, fool woman was willing to break them up, and it still wouldn't stop his name from being ruined, no matter what she tried. Didn't she realize he was nothing without her? He was going to shake some sense into her when he got his hands on her, which would be right as soon as he left Mark's office. But something was bothering him about what her father had said.

Benji's eyes narrowed as he held Mark's gaze. "You keep saying 'if it goes to court.' What does that mean?"

"It means that, just like Rick, I know how to hire a PI. And what my PI found will confirm that he is the lowest piece of shit imaginable."

"Okay," Benji said slowly, shaking his head, confused. What in the world was Mark implying?

"I can't go to him with this, being a man of the courts, but you can. You and Lucy together can urge him to keep his bullshit-ass video out of court, so that his dirty laundry doesn't fly free. 'Cause I'll fly it, loud and proud, to ruin that fucker," he said, acid dripping from his voice. "My hope for court next week is that we walk in, everything goes in our favor, and that's the end. I had planned on calling Lucy and telling her this today, but I have a feeling I won't need to do that."

Benji shook his head. "No, sir, I plan to take care of it."

Mark nodded. "She's lucky to have you."

Benji's lips curved. "Funny. Usually, I say that."

He nodded, looking down before pushing the file to Benji. "Well, Benji, I'm depending on you to take care of her."

"I don't have to; Lucy takes care of herself. But if you want me to love her, support her, be there for her, and never break her heart, I can do that."

Mark smiled. "That sounds even better," he said roughly, his voice breaking. "You know, I've done wrong to my family, and that's something I'll live with. But Lucy, she's always been my sweet baby girl, and when I failed her, broke her heart, I think it was worse than when I broke Autumn's heart." He paused,

clearing his throat as he met Benji's gaze. So much pain was in the depths of his green eyes. "I'm not much of a man and I know that, but you are, and I am so thankful that my daughter has found you. So, thank you. And please, fix this. Get her to get her head out of her ass and make that bastard go away. I'm depending on you."

Benji nodded and he knew that was his cue to leave, but he couldn't will himself to do so yet. Instead, he held Mark's gaze. "I know the story, hell, everyone does. No one really speaks fondly of you, except Angie. But I think Lucy still loves you. She's just so upset by your betrayal, and I can't blame her."

"Neither can I. I messed up."

It was that simple, and Benji was glad he owned up to it. "But, like I said, she loves you. And I think it would mean a lot to Lucy to know that I wanted to ask you this."

Mark's brows pulled together. "What?"

"May I marry your daughter?"

Mark leaned back in his chair, a chuckle leaving his mouth as he looked up at the ceiling, smiling. "When Lucy was a teenager, we watched this silly chick flick, *The Wedding Date*. There was this part when the guy—he was a gigolo the girl had hired to go to the wedding with her, but he actually started to feel for her. Well, he asked her dad if he could date his daughter. Totally cheesy movie, but I liked it because when that part happened, Lucy looked at me and asked, 'Do guys really do that, Daddy?' And I shrugged, told her I had, and I hoped the man that she would spend the rest of her life with would do it for her. She told me she hoped so too 'cause that's a real man." He paused, her eyes clouding with tears as he met Benji's gaze. "Rick never asked. She had asked me if he had before they ran off, and I told her no because I was so mad. I think she hated me for that. I think she wanted me to lie."

Benji watched him, his heart hurting for the man who just wanted to fix his mistakes. His love for his daughter was obvious, but the cuts he made were too deep, and Benji feared he'd never be able to mend them. Too much hurt, too much pain had been caused, and while Benji had no issue with the man he knew now, he knew that Lucy and her family did.

Mark shook his head and smiled before glancing back up at Benji. Clearing his throat, he said, "I couldn't lie to her, though. I hated that boy, man, whatever. But now, looking across at you, seeing how much you love her, love Angie, I have nothing else to say other than, yes, son, you can marry my baby. Because I don't think there is anyone else in this world who is meant for her but you."

There wasn't.

Now he just hoped Lucy knew that.

A vacation was where she was supposed to relax and have fun, and Lucy decided she sucked at vacations. Because, even though this was a work vacation that was more lie on the beach than work, she was a mess. A big ball of emotion who cried at the drop of a hat. She just hurt. Her soul hurt. Everything ached. She missed Benji. She felt bad for hurting him, for worrying him, and she hated most of all that she was allowing Rick to win. But she honestly saw no other choice in the matter.

It just wasn't fair.

She wanted to call Benji, tell him what was going on, ask him what he thought they should do. But he would want to push through. He wouldn't want to do the smart thing, which was to break up and let each other go—because that wasn't him. Hell, it wasn't her. She finally had the person she wanted for the rest of her life, and she couldn't even keep him? How fucked up was that? But that was her life. Rick was a constant villain who was hell-bent on ruining everything.

Why hadn't she kicked over his motorcycle instead of getting on it all those years ago?

Thankful for the sunglasses she wore, she watched as Angie threw sand in a bucket in a cute little two-piece that made a starfish across her belly. But when Lucy looked at her face, she was scowling.

She was not happy with Lucy.

"Mom. Where is Benji? Can I call him? We had plans here," Angie said, frustrated, and Lucy shook her head.

"Honey, he's busy," she said once more, her voice breaking a bit. She didn't miss the way Avery looked at her, shaking her head. Avery was the only one who knew what had happened, and Lucy had threatened her life if she uttered a word to anyone. Even to Ashlyn.

"This is so stupid! He promised me he'd be here to help me," she complained, throwing her bucket down and letting out a long breath. Lucy's heart broke a little. Shit, she was hurting everyone. This was so stupid. Maybe she should just call him. But how could she own up to this? Now it was her pride. She couldn't call him and ask for help after she ran, thinking she could handle it all on her own. No, she had made this bed, she was going to lie in it and fix it.

She just didn't know how.

Avery let out a knowing sigh, shaking her head once more, and Lucy cut her gaze to her. "What? Got something to say?" she asked and Avery shrugged her shoulders, checking on Ashlyn, who was sleeping in her little sand crib, a shade over her.

"Oh, nothing. It's none of my business," she said, holding her hands up. She still must have been upset from when Lucy snapped at her over breakfast. She just didn't want people telling her what to do. Especially when she already knew what to do.

Call Benji and tell him she was an idiot and she needed his help.

"One thing is for sure, you need to get the sand out your vag," Avery said before standing up and pulling her bottoms out of her butt.

"There isn't any," she snapped back and Avery scoffed.

"You need to check. I think a whole sand castle is up in there," she threw back as she stood before Lucy in all her beautiful glory. It made Lucy sick that she was still so skinny after having a baby. Not one stretch mark. Bullshit. "I'm going to go make a sand castle with my niece 'cause she's nice. You're a brat."

"Well, if there is already one in my vag, why build one?"

Avery glared back at her. "Because we don't want your stinky, angry one."

She almost laughed, but she didn't want to give Avery the satisfaction as she went over to Angie, sitting down to help her. When Angie looked to Avery, her little face sad, Lucy felt like shit as she asked, "Do you know where Benji is?"

"No, honey, sorry," Avery said. But then Angie stood, her face changing as she waved her hands above her head.

"There he is!" she screamed, running past Avery and toward the house. Lucy turned, and she wasn't sure why she was so surprised, but there he was.

Benji.

Angie jumped toward him and he caught her midair, kissing her hard on the cheek as she hugged him tightly. How did he find them? What was she going to do?

But, oh, thank God he was here.

Lucy looked back to Avery, shocked. But Avery must have thought her look was accusatory because she shook her head. "I promise I did not tell him."

"Benji! Where have you been? I missed you sooooooooooooo much," Angie stressed, her body wrapped around him like a koala. "I thought I was going to have to make this castle by myself, and I was so mad you weren't here. Where were you?"

"Sorry, sunshine, little miscommunication. But come on, let's make this castle," he said, carrying her toward them. He looked gorgeous. No shirt, his muscles rippling and bunching as he walked in a pair of swim shorts. He had a hat on and a pair of sunglasses, a careless grin on his face, like he was supposed to be there.

And he was.

If Lucy hadn't told him not to come.

Even with the sunglasses, though, she felt his gaze on her as he stopped beside her, bending down while still holding Angie to press his lips to hers.

Closing her eyes, she almost cried at the feel of his lips before he pulled back, looking deep into her eyes. "Hey, sweetheart."

Breathless, she swallowed hard. "Hey, I thought you weren't coming."

He smiled. "Yeah, your mom said to tell you she loves me more."

That stunned her for maybe three seconds before she glared. That Autumn Moore! As much as she wanted to be mad at her mom, she couldn't be. She wanted Benji there. She was just too damned proud to admit it.

She watched as he carried Angie to the sand mound she had made. He put her on her feet before looking back at Lucy. "Nice suit."

His lips curved and she fought a grin as she covered her chest with her arms. She was wearing a suit he had picked out for this trip, and while it pleased her that he liked it, she still wasn't sure what to do. He was acting as if everything was fine, but what did that mean? Did he know what was going on?

"Hey, Benji," Avery said as she stood, dusting sand off herself but he stopped her.

"You don't want to build?"

She laughed. "I was the stand-in till you showed up," she said with a grin before patting his back. "It's good to see you."

"You too."

Lucy watched as Benji bent down, getting to work with Angie as Avery came back to sit down. Leaning back in her chair, she said, "Maybe he can clean the sand out of your vag."

"And maybe I can bury you in it," she said, glancing over at her sister-in-law.

Avery grinned. "Love you, sister."

"Love you."

"Now why don't you go build a sand castle with your daughter and your boyfriend?"

"'Cause I'm probably not invited. They've been talking about this mermaid castle for, like, a month," she said as Benji started to stack buckets upon buckets. "Plus, I'm sure he's mad at me."

"Probably," Avery said simply. Lucy glared over at her and she shrugged. "I was agreeing!"

"Mom, come on!" Angie yelled, waving her arms wildly at her.

Benji looked over at her too, his naughty eyes drinking in her figure. Her body was hot in an instant, but she wasn't sure what to do. He was probably mad, but even when they were mad, they still wanted each other. "Yeah, come on, babe. Come build with us. You can sunbathe later."

"Go," Avery urged.

"Yeah, Mom, come on!"

She hesitated, but then something in Benji's eyes told her to get up and

come on. He was acting normal. He didn't want it to seem weird for Angie, like he had always promised, and that kind of hurt. Was he going to break up with her?

Jeez, what a mess she had caused.

Angie cheered as she came over, dropping into the sand to help. As they got started, she decided they would figure this all out later.

Right now, she was going to make a sand castle with the two people she loved most.

As Lucy took in the overextravagant castle they had built, Angie was bouncing with excitement. It honestly looked like a bad version of a superawesome sand sculpture, but it didn't matter that half of it was falling and that no mermaid would choose it as her castle, because Angie was beaming.

"It's perfect."

"It is," Benji agreed, rubbing her back. Looking over at Lucy, he smiled. "What do you think, Mom?"

Why did that make her tear up? Crap. "It's beautiful," she croaked out and he smiled as Angie giggled.

"Let's go swimming!"

"Angie, it's too cold right now," Lucy warned. "That water is ice. Maybe tomorrow when it's a little warmer."

She looked to Benji but he shook his head. "I don't like cold water."

She pouted and he laughed, picking her up to hug her tight. "How about this? You go change, and then we'll all go to dinner at that supercool Chuck E. Cheese I saw?"

"Sweet Lord in heaven," Lucy muttered, but Angie was all for it.

"Yeah! Avery and Ashlyn too, right?"

"Of course," he said and she grinned as Avery smiled.

"Yes!" Angie said before he put her on her feet and she ran off to the house.

Avery stood slowly, picking up Ashlyn. "I'm going to go and change and keep Angie occupied since I'm sure you two need to talk about things that aren't my business."

Benji chuckled as Lucy glared, looking away as her face warmed. When his hand came into hers, she looked at their hands before looking up at him. "Let's walk," he said, and she bit into her lip to keep a sob in as she nodded. The surf was running up on their toes as they walked, the sun shining. This was what she wanted. She wanted to be with Benji on the beach—but not with the stupid stress Rick had caused. It was eating her alive, and she couldn't bring herself to unload on him like she wanted.

It wasn't fair.

"I missed you," he whispered, leaning down to her to kiss her cheek.

She tried to smile but it didn't work well as she leaned into him. "I missed you too."

He led her down the private beach that Jace and Avery's house sat on. Lucy's toes sank into the sand as they walked in silence. She wasn't sure what to say. Sorry? Would that even cover it? What else could she say but the truth? But how could she tell him that Rick was planning on running his name through the mud with a lie? A video. A disgusting, sad video of her sweet daughter that Angie had told her on the plane Rick had forced her to do. She had texted her dad that this morning, but he hadn't gotten back to her. Which was odd. She didn't talk to him often, but when she did, he usually got back to her quickly.

When Benji suddenly stopped, Lucy looked back at him, turning to face him as he took his glasses off, tucking them in his pocket. "I talked to your dad."

Oh. Well, there was the reason she hadn't heard from him. Looking at her, Benji shook his head as his eyes bored into hers, disappointment flooding his eyes. She sucked in a deep breath and nodded. "So you know what's going on, then?"

"Yeah. Lucy, why didn't you just tell me?" She looked away, but he brought her face back up, his hands cupping her chin. "Don't hide from me. You've done that enough. Tell me what you're thinking. What made you run like that?"

Her lips trembled as she shook her head, the tears welling up in her eyes. "I knew you'd tell me we can beat him together. That it didn't matter what he did, that you wouldn't leave me. I can't do that to you, Benji. I love you too much."

"Damn straight," he said, his own eyes filling with tears. "And I love you for wanting to protect me. But leaving me, taking away your and Angie's love, that won't make it better. It will make it worse, because I don't care about my name if I don't have you two. I'm nothing without you two."

She shook her head. "Benji, he's accusing you of the worst thing. That isn't fair. A normal man would run for the hills."

"Not this man."

"But your career—"

"Is nothing without you," he stressed as a tear rolled down her cheek. "You give me purpose, Lucy. You make me excited to live. And why have a job that, yeah, I love, if I can't come home and share my accomplishments with you? And that house isn't a home without you and Angie. You two made that place so full of life. You think I can go back without you? Just because some dude is threatening us with what your dad says is a bogus video? I don't care about Rick and his lies, I care about you. About us."

Closing her eyes as his nose touched hers, she shook her head. She had known he was going to be like this. So fearless, impatient to take Rick out. "He could ruin you."

"I don't care," he said simply. "I'd rather lose all that other stuff and still have you and Angie. Because with you two, I have it all." Her lips trembled as she held his eyes. "I understand it. The love you have for me and wanting to protect me. Believe me, I'd do the same for you, but instead of doing it all alone, let me help. Let me be there with you. Let's be there for each other."

Biting into her lip, she slid her hands across his bare back, pressing her lips to the middle of his chest. His skin broke out in gooseflesh and she closed her eyes, knowing she couldn't leave him if she tried. Well, she had tried, and look at how that turned out.

"What have I told you from the beginning, Lucy?

She opened her eyes, looking up at him. His eyes had so much love, so much meaning, and she knew what he was talking about. "That you're not going anywhere."

"Exactly. So do me a favor and make the same promise. If you want to, that is," he added and she just stared at him. Of course, she wanted this. Him. She was just scared.

"I couldn't do it. I couldn't break up with you. When I got here, I thought I would figure it out. And, yeah, it's only been a day, but all I wanted was you—to call you and tell you so that we could figure it out. I shouldn't have run *from* you, but *to* you."

He smiled against her lips. "And I would have caught you. I would have hugged you," he said, wrapping his arms around her, nuzzling his nose into her neck. "And I would have told you I love you, that we've got this."

"I know. I was just so scared."

"You don't have to be scared, because I will help fight those demons. Fight Rick. He can't beat us if we stand together," he said, pulling back to look at her. "You are my slice of heaven, Lucy, and the thought of not having you is what terrifies me."

"Me too."

"So no more disappearing acts, okay?" he said, kissing her nose, and she smiled.

"I can make sure that never happens again." He smiled back as he dropped his mouth to hers, kissing her ever so slowly, her toes curling in the sand. She had missed him so damn much, and she was pretty sure that his kisses and hugs were what she lived for. As he pulled back, looking down at her, he shook his head. Moving her hand up to his face, she touched him softly, her thumb gliding along his cheek as she held his gaze.

"I'm just so scared, Benji," she whispered and he kissed her forehead. "I don't want anything to hurt you. You've had enough hurt."

"The only thing that can hurt me is losing you and Angie. Remember that."

She smiled, her eyes glossing over. "I hit him. Like, legit slammed my fist into his face because of what he was saying about you."

Benji's body started to shake with his laughter. "I'm jealous."

She smiled against his chest. "I just got so mad, and I couldn't believe the rage that filled me."

"Probably the same rage that filled me when you wouldn't tell me what was wrong."

She chanced a glance at him and he was looking at her, his eyes filled with the hurt she'd caused. "I'm sorry."

Cupping her face, he smiled before moving his nose with hers. "Forgiven."

She inhaled and then let it out, shaking her head. "No normal man would stick around for this crazy train."

"Lucy, I'm not normal, and I love crazy," he said and she grinned.

That was one of the first things he had ever said to Angie.

"What are we going to do?"

He smiled. "Don't you worry. I've got a plan."

Melting against his chest, she felt her tears start to fall. "Will we be okay?"

He smiled, his eyes burning into hers. "More than okay. We're going to be great."

It was a promise.

One she knew he would keep.

Chapter
TWENTY-SEVEN

With Angie in the back of the Jeep he had rented when he came to Florida a few days before, Benji was all smiles as he drove to his destination. The sun was shining, the clouds were fluffy, the sky was blue, and Benji felt fucking good. The happiest and the most relaxed he had felt in years. After telling Lucy everything that Mark had told him, she'd finally smiled. He knew the stress she was feeling was gone, and she was ready to fight. He just wished she had done all that before. He wished she'd come to him, but that woman never did anything easy. She always wanted to do things the hard way, but even she knew that had to change.

She needed him as much as he needed her.

From that moment on, though, their vacation had been great. He had spent his time on the beach with his girls, lazily lying around—well, when Angie let him. And when Lucy had to go work, he and Angie would explore the city of Ft. Lauderdale. He felt a little outnumbered with all the ladies since Jace had been off kicking ass at the All-Star Game and was awarded MVP, but Benji wouldn't change a thing.

He was too fucking happy. Too excited.

But even with the amazing week, he was ready to make it even better. He wanted to end this trip with a bang, so when they got home and faced Rick, Lucy would do it with nothing but a smile.

Yup, he was ready.

Singing along with Adele and Angie, Benji belted out the song at the top of his lungs as Angie matched him with full hand movements and lots of fist pumps. She was a nut, but she was his nut. His sunshine.

When they reached their destination, he parked and shut the car off, much to Angie's protestation. "Benji! I was getting down."

"Yeah, yeah," he laughed, getting out. "Come on. I want to talk to you."

"To me? Ooh, ice cream!" she gushed as she hopped out the side like he did.

He reached for her hand and they walked together to the little ice cream shack, getting a frozen treat before walking onto the beach to sit down and watch the waves. Angie's hair was down and she looked adorable as the strands flew all over the place.

"Ah! It's getting in my ice cream," she complained and he laughed, handing her his ice cream after getting the hair tie off her wrist. He wasn't sure what he was doing, but he threw it all on top of her head before wrapping a rubber band around the bunch like he had watched Lucy do a lot. Moving some stray strands behind her ear, she grinned up at him as he took his ice cream back.

"There."

"You're the best," she said, plopping down and taking a lick of her ice cream. "It's so pretty here. We should move to Florida."

Benji smiled. "But then what about Grandma and the Assassins? We can't leave them."

She thought that over and then nodded. "Then we should buy a house here for the summer."

"Whoa, living large, aren't you?" he teased and she grinned.

"Hey, I got money in the bank," she reminded him and he shook his head. "For college."

"Yeah, yeah," she said, sounding just like her mother as she grinned over at him. "I wonder when Mommy will be done."

"Probably around three."

"Cool. Do you think we can hit the beach before we have to pack to leave?"

He nodded. "I'm sure we can, but I think we're gonna take some pictures."

She made a face. "Why?"

"'Cause I think Mom would like them." She exhaled loudly and he smiled before brushing another stray piece of hair back. "Hey, let me ask you something."

She looked over at him, her green eyes sparkling in the sun. "What?"

"You know I love you, right?"

She grinned. "Yes!"

He grinned back as he nodded. "Well, you know I love your mom a lot."

"You guys kiss all the time." She scrunched up her face.

"We do, but that doesn't bother you, does it?"

She shrugged. "It's gross."

"Is that all?" he laughed.

She thought for a moment and then nodded. "Yeah, but I don't care, 'cause Mom is always smiling too."

Looking out at the ocean, he nodded. She did always smile, and he loved that smile with everything inside of him. Turning back to Angie, he grinned. "Yeah, but how would you feel about me asking your mom to marry me? Me becoming your stepdad?"

She held his gaze, and he wasn't sure what she was thinking. But then she was shooting questions at him left and right.

"Do we get to live with you forever?"

"Yes."

"Do I get to wear a dress to the wedding and throw flowers?"

"Yes."

"Can we get a puppy?"

"Ah, I don't know. We'd have to ask Mom."

She nodded and pressed her finger to her lips as she looked up at him. "Can I call you Dad, instead of Stepdad?"

His heart stopped. Right there. He was sure he was about to fall over dead on that beach. But what a way to go. As the emotion choked him and tears filled his eyes, he nodded. "I'm completely okay with that."

She got up then, sitting in his lap before she leaned against him, nodding her head. "Then, yeah, marry her."

"Thanks, sunshine," he said, his voice rough.

"Do you have the ring? You got her a ring, right? You can't ask her without a ring, Benji!"

"I got one!" he laughed, pulling it out of his pocket and opening it to show her. As she oohed over it, Benji grinned at how perfect it was. It was a simple princess-cut diamond in a platinum band, but he was convinced it was Lucy. It just screamed her, and he couldn't wait to see it on her hand.

Hear her say yes.

With lots of sass, he was sure.

"She's going to pee her pants, that's so pretty."

Grinning, he kissed Angie's temple before putting the ring away. But he pulled out another small box out that held a little hockey stick bracelet he had gotten Angie because he wanted her to have something too. When he opened it and put it on her wrist, she eyed it, her eyes twinkling. "This is something to remind you how much I love *you*."

"You got *me* something?" she gushed, holding it up and gasping at it. "Oh wow, it's sparkly and hockey!" She giggled as she looked it over, her eyes bright, and he nodded.

"And a number twenty for me and a number fourteen for you," he said, pointing to the little numbers that hung by the hockey stick. She grinned over at him and then kissed his cheek.

"It's awesome, thank you."

"Good, I'm glad you love it."

"I do," she decided with a nod. "I love you too."

"That's always a good thing. Because, not only do I love you, but I need your help," he said with more dramatics than needed, but he was trying to keep from breaking down and crying from the overwhelming love he was feeling. He never thought this could happen, to not only have a good, strong woman who loved him, but a beautiful, spunky little girl.

He really did have it all.

Her eyes widened as she sat up straight, ready. "Oh, I love helping!"

"Now, this is important," he said, holding her gaze. "How should I ask Mom to marry me?"

She popped up, her ice cream flying before she held her hands out. "Oh my goodness! I thought you'd never ask," she shrieked, hopping on her heels as she held his gaze. "First, we get a dolphin and then we have Mom come stand on the beach. And you ride in on the dolphin, the ring in your hand with rockets going off and glitter falling out of the air before me and the fairy mermaids come out of the ocean and we all say 'Will you marry Benji?' Insert more glitter, some more rockets, and lots of ice cream, 'cause Mom loves ice cream!"

Benji could only blink.

Well, that was one way of doing it.

When Lucy pulled into the driveway of Avery and Jace's house, Benji met her out front.

"Okay, don't get mad."

She rolled her eyes, and he swore that simple movement was hot to him. She had been gone all morning doing the final touches on Shea and Elli's beach house. It was looking awesome, and he was sure they would love it, but like always, Lucy was nervous about it. She wore the stress all over her gorgeous face. "I always get mad when you start it like that."

"I know, but…" he said, flashing her a grin, "I thought since it's our last night, we can have some pictures done on the beach. So we can have nice family pictures for the house. You always say our pictures are too crazytown."

She looked torn, letting out a long breath. "But, Benji, I'm tired."

He smiled. "Please."

She didn't even really think about it; she just nodded and he laughed. "Let me go change. Are you wearing that? What's Angie wearing?" she said, passing by him on her way into the house. As he followed her inside, she looked at Angie and shook her head. "Come on, let's go get ready."

"I am ready!"

"Angela, come on. I have two white dresses we can wear. Come on," she said and Angie followed as Benji smiled.

"That was easier than I thought," he called down the hall, and she grinned back at him.

"I wanted to do it anyway."

"Then why fight me?" he asked and she shrugged.

"I like to see you beg," she teased, her eyes full of heat, and his lips curved into a smirk.

Before he could say anything else, though, Ashlyn started to cry. She was in her playpen right beside him, so he picked her up as Avery and her friend, Mekena, who was taking their pictures, came through the back door. They had gone to college together, apparently, and when Avery moved down to Florida with Jace, Mekena decided to move too. She was nice but really quiet, very much stayed to herself, while he was trying everything he could to talk to her, to make sure she got the right shots.

He was worried, but Avery guaranteed him everything would be fine. Mekena had a part-time job taking pictures at the mall, and she had done all their pictures and Ashlyn's. The pictures around the house were gorgeous, so he felt a little better, even though Mekena wouldn't look him in the eye. But he had to make sure he documented what was about to happen. Jordie had made such a huge deal about how important it was to have photo evidence of these kinds of things. It seemed to work for him, and Benji sure did love the big print in the Thomas's house of Jordie and Kacey kissing after he had asked her to marry him.

"Oh, thanks, Benji. She's hungry. Let me make her a bottle."

"No problem, I like the little stinker," he said, kissing her head as she smacked his face playfully. She looked just like her daddy. The genes of the Sinclairs continued to scare him.

When Lucy came down the hall, her eyes wide, his brow quirked as he took in that her dress was half on. "Hey, now, Avery's in the kitchen, and I'm holding a baby."

She rolled her eyes as she ran toward him, coming right up to him before going up on her toes and whispering in his ear, "I have to tell you something, but you can't say anything, okay?" He only nodded, his heart picking up in speed. Did Angie tell her their plan? Shit. "Baylor is pregnant."

He looked back at her, his eyes wide. "No way."

She nodded her head wildly as she pulled him back. "Yeah, she's, like, thirteen weeks, and they did an ultrasound and the baby looks wonderful, healthy."

Pulling back to look at her, he was shocked. How could no one know? Her family basically called when one of them took a shit. But when he saw the tears in her eyes and he smiled, he knew why. "You knew."

She nodded quickly. "I'm so happy. I've been so worried."

"You never said anything."

"Sworn to secretly. Still sworn, but I had to tell someone!"

He leaned over, kissing her mouth. "That's awesome."

"I know! She's telling Jayden today. Eek!"

"Telling him what?" Avery called and Lucy shook her head.

"Nothing. Hey, is Markus coming up tonight?" she asked, obviously changing the subject.

"Who's Markus?" Benji asked and Lucy looked back to him.

"He's a friend of Jace's," she said as Avery shook her head.

He noticed Mekena looked relieved as Avery said, "No, he isn't going to make it."

"Oh, that's crappy. I haven't seen him in months. Whatever, I'll give him shit later. Okay, five more minutes."

"What was that about?" Avery asked as she came over, taking Ashlyn, and he shrugged.

"I don't know, she's crazy."

She side-eyed him. "Secrets don't make friends, Benji."

He grinned and she smiled back as she started to feed Ashlyn. "Who's this Markus guy? Should I be worried?"

She rolled her eyes. "You're about to propose," she whispered as she shook her head. "Worry about that, not some guy who means nothing to her. He's just a family friend."

"A douche," Mekena said and Benji's eyes widened.

"That too," Avery agreed and Benji knew there was more to that story, but he was too caught up in his own thoughts to worry about it. Sitting down across from them, Benji looked down at his phone, his heart pounding in his chest. Trying to keep his mind off what was about to happen, he thought about Baylor. He couldn't believe it, but at the same time, if she had to leave the league, he would rather it be on her own terms, for a good reason and not because she was forced. Having a baby, yeah, that was a damn good way to go out. Wow, he was so happy for her and Jayden.

And damn, he wanted the same thing.

He just hoped Lucy would say yes. She was a prickly little thing, and he was sure she would say it was too early, but man, was he ready. So damn ready to make that woman his. He wanted to build a life with her, have a baby one day, and he couldn't wait for the chance to hold a little baby that looked just like her. Or maybe, he'd get lucky and his genes would pull through. Not likely, but he just wanted the life he wanted.

With Lucy.

And Angie, of course.

The door opened and Angie came running out in a beautiful white lace sundress with her hair in pigtails. She stopped in front of him. "I look like a baby."

"I think you're adorable."

She made a face as he looked up to see Lucy walking out. His next breath was promptly gone as she moved toward him. She was in a matching white lace sundress; her hair was pulled to the side in a braid with a big, white flower over her ear. She had redone her makeup, a light pink shade on her lips. It wasn't the red he loved, but she was simply gorgeous.

"Wow," he murmured and she grinned, her eyes sparkling.

"Yeah, yeah, come on," she said, lacing her fingers with his and then heading out to the beach. "We're losing sun."

"For someone who was tired, you seem pretty eager to do this," he accused as Mekena followed with Avery and Ashlyn in tow.

"Because every picture we have at home is of us sticking our tongues out. I swear, if either of your tongues come out, I'm smacking you," she warned, and just like that, Benji and Angie stuck their tongues out at her at the same time. She glared. "Really?"

Glancing at each other, they laughed as he snaked one arm around Lucy's shoulders and held Angie's hand with the other as they headed to the beach. He wanted to say he was calm, that he was ready to pop the question. But as they posed in different positions, Mekena snapping away, Benji was ready to have a panic attack. He had this crazy feeling she would say no—which was probably insane—but it still freaked him out.

"Let me get some of just Angie doing some cute stuff. I want one of her and Ashlyn too, for Mrs. Moore," Mekena said, and that was his cue.

Shit.

His heart was in this throat.

"Oh, that would be wonderful," Lucy gushed as Avery grinned.

"Right, Benji," Avery said, widening her eyes to Benji because he was supposed to take Lucy away.

Crap.

Reaching for her, he took her hand. "Hey, come here."

"Why? I want to watch this."

"I know, but I want to talk to you. Over there."

"Why? Talk later. Let me do this," she said, turning around, but Avery shook her head.

"Lucy, go. I've got this."

Lucy made a face. "What in the world? I can talk to him later."

Everyone just stood there, no one knowing what to do.

"Lucy, damn it, come on," he said, and she raised a brow.

"I mean, what is so serious that you have to talk to me right now?" she complained, and he almost said it. Almost yelled that he wanted to propose, but he just held her gaze.

"Please, walk with me over there."

She let out an annoyed breath. It figured this wouldn't be easy. When was anything ever easy with Lucy Sinclair? As he reached for her hand, she took his reluctantly as they walked toward the shore. "I don't know why this couldn't wait."

"'Cause I want to talk now," he said, stopping and then sitting down. "Sit."

"Ugh," she complained and he wanted to strangle her, but he couldn't help but chuckle.

When she sat down beside him, he took her hand in his, lacing his fingers with hers before kissing the back of her hand. "I love you," he whispered, and her little scowl flattened some as she smiled.

"I love you too," she promised as he leaned his head to hers. "But you could have told me that later."

He rolled his eyes. "I wanted to tell you something more," he started, his heart jumping in and out of his throat. "Do you remember the first time we met?"

She smiled. "It was only a little over three months ago, so, yeah."

He glared. "Okay, brat. I meant do you remember what you thought when you saw me?"

She laughed. "Not something nice."

He closed his eyes. He was going to kill her before he could even ask. "Well, when I first saw you, you were looking down at Angie, panic in your eyes as you searched for how to dress a seven-year-old for hockey on YouTube. Your brow was furrowed and your lips were pursed, and I was stunned. I just stood there, staring at you and thinking how in the world could someone so beautiful walk this earth and I didn't know about her."

Her lips curved as she leaned into him. "Well, that's nicer than my thinking you were a creep."

"I'd say so," he laughed and she grinned, giggling against him. He cleared his throat. "I remember the first time you touched me. It was just a simple touch to my arm when you laughed about my collectibles, but it seriously rocked my soul. I think that's when I knew this was different, when I knew I was falling in love with you."

She eyed him. "You brought me out here to talk about this? I thought we were good. Did I do something?"

He made a face. "What are you talking about? I'm sharing my damn soul with you."

"Yeah, but why?"

He just looked at her, stunned. "Lucy, shut up for a minute," he said, and she snapped her mouth shut, her eyes bright as she tried not to smile. "Now, as I was saying... When I slept with you for the first time, I swore I would never feel like that again—"

"Wait, are you asking me to marry you?"

"Jesus Christ, Lucy!"

She eyed him skeptically when, thankfully, Mekena came over. "Can I get a picture of you two like this?"

"Yeah," he groaned, shaking his head as Lucy watched him, her brows pulled together. He leaned his head to hers as they had planned, but he was sure that was the only thing that would go as planned because nothing ever went right when it came to Lucy Sinclair.

"Wait, are you?" she asked once more.

"Smile, Lucy," he demanded and she did, but when Mekena gave them the thumbs-up, Lucy was back to eyeing him.

"Are you?"

Benji looked to Mekena for help and she spoke. "I'm going to go from behind and get one of the ocean, can you lean together again?"

But Lucy didn't move, she watched him. "Why aren't you answering me?"

"Because I'm trying to pose for a damn picture," he spat back.

He heard the camera clicking and all he could think was how these pictures would be a great thing to explain to their kids when they were older.

And this is Mom and Dad, fighting before he popped the question.

"Can you guys kiss?"

He leaned to her and she shook her head ruefully, letting out a breath before pressing her lips to his, the camera going off behind him. "You better not be asking me," she warned as they parted, and he let out a long breath.

When he pulled back, he held her gaze. "Do you know you drive me crazy?"

She laughed. "I thought you liked that about me."

"I do."

"Okay, guys, look back at me," Mekena called, but Benji didn't move. His eyes stayed on Lucy as she looked over her shoulder where he knew Angie was standing with a sign that said, *"Will you marry Benji?"*

As he wanted, she took in a deep breath as her eyes widened.

The tears filled his eyes at her shocked expression, her jaw dropping as she covered her mouth. He pulled the ring out of his pocket before holding it up. When she looked to him, tears were glistening in her eyes as she gazed deep into his, shaking her head.

"You."

"Me."

A tear rolled down her face, though her gaze didn't leave his, her lips moving as she whispered, "What happened to a year?"

"Couldn't wait that long."

Glancing down at the ring, she came undone as the tears rolled down her face faster. She sucked in a breath as she shook her head. "It's beautiful."

"Not as beautiful as you," he said, his voice breaking. "Before you decided to ruin my whole speech, I had planned to tell you that I'm glad we had that week of me being gone after we first got together to get to know each other. To fall in love. I fell in love with *you*, not just with the way you made me feel, and I will always be thankful for that."

Her lips trembled as she held his gaze. Reaching up, she wiped away one of his tears as her lips curved. He started to speak again. "I don't look forward to tomorrow as another day; I look forward to it because I get to wake up to you. I get to feel your lips against mine and I get to hear Angie's laugh. My life is nothing without you two, and I can't go on another second without knowing you are going to marry me. That Angie will be my stepdaughter, and that we will fight every single battle that comes our way, together. Because, together, nothing can come close to bringing us down."

"Really, Benji?" she cried, throwing her hands up. "How am I supposed to make you wait like I should? Who gets engaged so quick?"

"I married your brother and got pregnant all in a month or so," Avery volunteered, tears dripping off her chin, and Lucy glared.

"You're not helping. This is crazy! You're crazy," she accused, her grin taking up her whole face and he smiled.

"About you. Only you."

"Benji! How am I supposed to say no?"

"You can't," he said simply. "Because you want to be my wife as much as I want you to be."

"I do," she challenged, her lips curving, and he nodded.

"You do," he whispered as he leaned his head to hers. "Now, Lucy Lane Sinclair, the love of my life, will you marry me and make me complete?"

Looking deep into his eyes, she grinned from ear to ear as she pressed her nose to his. He almost thought she was going to say no just to be a brat, but when she slowly nodded, her nose sliding against his, he smiled as she whispered, "Guess you're not the only one who can't say no to the one you love."

And Benji saw no problem with that.

None at all.

Chapter
TWENTY-EIGHT

When Lucy opened her eyes two days later, Benji was fast asleep, his mouth parted, his lashes kissing his face as he drew in deep breaths before letting them out. Her hands were against his chest, the left one on top, her engagement ring sparkling in the sunlight that was streaming in across his beautiful body.

Holy crap, she was engaged.

To Benji.

And she couldn't be happier.

While it was early, and people would think she was crazy to be engaged to someone she hadn't even hit the four-month mark with, she really didn't care. She was happy, and that was all that mattered. Of course, her mom was bubbling with excitement. Already planning the wedding Lucy wasn't even ready to think about. She wanted to enjoy Benji and Angie. She wanted to take her time, have the wedding she dreamed about. The one she deserved. This time, she'd do it right.

With the man she loved more than anything she could ever describe.

Not even the fact that they were meeting Rick that afternoon for lunch could wipe the grin off her face. Could everything blow up in their faces when they showed him what her father's PI had found? Yeah, it could. But would they be okay?

They'd be great.

"I really hate when you stare at me while I sleep," he murmured and she grinned.

"But you're so cute," she giggled, cuddling into him, and he threw his arm around her, kissing her nose.

"Shh, I'm tired. Tell me we don't have to get up yet. I don't hear Angie. Surely, I have another hour."

She laughed. It was so funny how he hated waking up. He and Angie were the same in that respect. "I don't know."

"Shh, go to sleep."

"But I love staring at you and my ring," she said and his lips curved then. He opened his eyes to meet her gaze. Taking her hand in his, he kissed the palm of her left hand.

"Are you happy, baby?"

"I am," she answered automatically. And how could she not be? She was engaged to the most gorgeous and thoughtful man on the planet. Her daughter was happy and healthy, and hopefully, they could get the Rick thing taken care of that afternoon. Her business was thriving, her mom and River were blissfully happy, as were Jude and Claire, off in California doing big things. Jace and Avery were raising Ashlyn and totally in love, living the life they wanted. Baylor and Jayden were having a baby, and it brought tears to her eyes remembering hearing her brother's voice break as he told her the night before. He was over the moon.

No, Lucy Sinclair was one happy woman, and nothing could change that.

"Good, go make me some breakfast," he muttered against her lips and she scoffed.

"What?"

"I'm hungry."

"You're asleep!"

"Feed me."

"Mommy! I'm hungry," Angie said then, climbing into their bed and nuzzling her way between them. Wrapping his arm around Angie, he waved Lucy off.

"Go cook."

"Benji!"

"Mommy, please. Bacon and eggs."

"Really, guys?" she asked, but she was ignored as they fell back to sleep. "Brats."

Getting out of bed, she reached for her robe, turning to put it on as she looked back at her bed where they lay. Angie's head was against Benji's face, her hair caught in his beard as they both slept soundly. As a contented sigh left her lips, she grabbed her phone and took a picture. It was too cute not to. When she navigated off her camera, the picture of her and Benji grinning at the camera with Angie behind them, holding the sign asking her to marry Benji appeared as her wallpaper. She almost couldn't believe that had been only two days ago.

She still had that fluttery feeling. That unbelievable feeling of love.

Smiling, she headed down the hall, picking up hockey sticks from their nightly knee ball game and putting them back in Angie's room. Walking downstairs, she started breakfast with a grin on her face. While she hated cooking, she loved Benji and Angie, so bacon and eggs it was. As she fried the bacon, it didn't fail that Rick reared his ugly head into her mind, but she shook her head. She wouldn't be nervous about their lunch.

It would go great.

When her phone rang, she looked over to see it was her dad. Unlike how she usually did, she didn't groan as she answered. "Hello?"

"Hey, did I wake you? I just realized it was only eight."

"No, I'm cooking breakfast."

"Oh, good. I wanted to make sure you called me after the lunch. Let me know what is said."

"Yeah, no problem. We are dropping Angie off with Baylor and Jayden before heading to meet him."

"Okay," he said as she put the biscuits in the oven. "So everything is good with you and Benji?"

Lucy smiled. "Yeah, they're great. He asked me to marry him."

Her dad let out a whoop. "You said yes, then?"

"Yeah, I did."

"Good, he's a great guy."

"I think so too," she said, and she was surprised how unawkward it was to say that to her dad. Maybe she was still on her little, happy, glittery, pink cloud of engagement or something.

"Hey, you remember when you were like fifteen, I think, and we watched that movie, *The Wedding Date*, together."

Lucy paused, leaning against the counter as a smile crept over her face. She was surprised he remembered that movie. But why was he bringing it up? "Yeah, I do."

"You remember how it was such a big deal for your husband to ask me to marry you?"

Her breath caught as she stood up. "Yeah."

"He asked, Lucy, and I said yes, even though it wasn't really my place to anymore, but I did," he said, his voice rough as Lucy's eyes started to cloud with tears. "I'm really sorry, honey, for betraying you like I did. I know you looked up to me, and I really failed you. Hell, I failed you all, and I'm sorry. For as much as it's worth, I really am."

When a tear spilled over and rolled down her face, Lucy closed her eyes.

Ever since she'd found out about her father's whore on the side, all she'd wanted was an apology, for him to own up to what he did, and she finally had it. "Thanks, Dad."

"Of course."

"And thanks for telling Benji he could marry me."

He scoffed. "Now, I don't think anyone is good enough for you, honey, but that man…he could prove me wrong."

When Benji and Angie entered the kitchen acting like zombies, she couldn't help but think they looked like zombies too, with their hair all over the place and drool on their faces. And still, she grinned at them.

"Yeah, maybe."

Her dad laughed. She stood up when Benji came over, wrapping his arms around her waist and kissing her neck. "Well, I'll let you go. Call me later."

"Will do. Thanks, Dad."

"Anytime, honey."

And then he hung up.

They weren't fixed. Lucy wasn't sure if they ever would be, but at least he was trying, and that was enough for her.

Leaning her cheek into Benji's, she exhaled loudly. "You asked my dad to marry me?"

He chuckled as he nodded. "I thought that would mean a lot to you."

"You thought right."

"Yeah. I'm kinda smart."

"Eh, kinda," she teased and he smiled, nibbling at her jaw.

"So, you ready for today?" he asked, holding her as she moved the eggs around in the pan. Her eyes cut to the file her father had given Benji, the one with all they needed to shut Rick up, and she nodded.

"More than ready."

But when she saw Rick enter the Mexican restaurant, her gung ho attitude was nowhere to be seen.

Nope, nothing but nerves.

That is, until Benji's hand slid into hers.

When she looked over at him, he smiled and she let out a long breath. "We've got this."

She nodded as she looked back. Rick's eyes widened as he came to the table. "I thought I was meeting you."

Lucy nodded. "Well, seeing as how he's my fiancé, Benji wanted to be here."

It was obnoxious of her, but she wanted Rick to know that she had not only found love, but also a love she was going to have for the rest of her life.

Rick scoffed. "That didn't take long."

Benji smiled. "When you know, you know."

Rick just shook his head as he sat down, leaning back in his chair and watching them. "Okay, so what is this about?"

"Well," Benji said, leaning on the table, his gaze on Rick's. "I wanted to say I don't appreciate you manipulating Angie into making that video—"

"I'm not talking about that," he said, cutting Benji off, his eyes narrowing. "We can discuss it in court."

Lucy's nails bit into her palms at his callous attitude as Benji slowly nodded. "Fine, since you were so gracious to show us what evidence you are bringing to court, we wanted to show you ours. You aren't the only one who can hire a PI."

When Benji slid the file across the table, Lucy loved the look of pure fear that settled in Rick's eyes. "What's that?"

"A file on Amy Masters, who lives in Franklin with your twin boys. You'll find it to be very thorough. It also has information on how you've been taking money out of your mom's account and your personal account with Heidi and depositing it into Amy's account for your children. Pictures of you going to see said children, who are only maybe three? Children who would have been conceived while you actually were still married to me..." Lucy said slowly, Rick's eyes meeting hers. "There is a statement from Amy where she tells the PI that you work in Nashville a lot and can't always come home to her and the boys. That you two haven't gotten married yet because you are in the middle of a nasty divorce with your ex. Funny thing, it was as true when she got pregnant as it may be now."

Rick opened the file to see a picture of him sitting on a bench with Amy, their boys playing in the sandbox nearby. He shut the file and looked back at them. "So, you're blackmailing me? I don't show the video and this goes away?"

"Oh, no," Lucy said, feigning surprise. "Never. We are just reminding you that if you show, we show. While, yeah, it's gonna suck getting out of the fucking custody mess you caused, everyone will know that you are not only married to Heidi with a daughter the same age as the one you're fighting over, but you also have a girlfriend with twin boys that your *wife* knows nothing about."

"I mean, the video is bogus anyway. All it will cause is an investigation and I'll be exonerated in the end. But the fact you are putting money into another account without the knowledge of your wife or your mother is stealing, fraud even. I'm sure that won't go over well, especially if they press charges," Benji added and Rick's eyes narrowed.

Looking away, Rick sucked in a deep breath and shook his head. Lucy watched as he thought over his words, and she wanted to laugh how the cocky asshole was shaking in his boots. She was disgusted by him. She always knew he was a bad guy, but she had thought there might be a good guy underneath. She was wrong. So wrong, and as she watched the man she had loved at one point in her life struggle, all she could do was feel sorry for him.

He was pathetic.

When she looked over at Benji, he smiled, leaning over to kiss her temple before whispering, "We're okay."

She nodded. "We are."

When she looked back, Rick was watching them, venom in the depths of his blue eyes. "I hate you," he said, looking at Lucy, his eyes dark and full of malice. "I hate who you are, that you trapped me." He paused and Benji went to say something, but she held her hand to his leg, stopping him. "I don't like dealing with you. I want you to disappear more than I can even tell you. Your family has been a problem since the beginning, and now you have this guy you want to marry... Yeah, I'm done."

Her brows pulled together. The feelings were mutual, but what was he saying? "Done?"

"Yeah, listen, I don't care anymore," he said, sitting up and holding their gaze. She wasn't sure what he meant, but her heart dropped to her stomach as she watched him. "I hate doing this with you. Always fighting and having to see your smug face 'cause you think you're better than me. So, you know what? Do you want her?" he asked Benji, and Benji looked confused at the abrupt change in topic.

"Want who? Lucy? I've got her."

"No, Angie. You want her?"

Lucy looked bewildered as Benji nodded. "I mean...yeah. Yes, I do."

"Then take her," he said simply, like he was giving away a dog and not his firstborn. "I don't have the money for child support, obviously. And I was hoping if I got custody of her, boom, you'd be paying me. But now this is getting insane. My mom is saying she doesn't want me to fight anymore, and I just don't have the cash flow for it. The kid doesn't even like me. So if you want her, and you're cool with taking her, I'm honestly done."

Lucy's heart stopped as her eyes narrowed. "You put me through this, put Angie through this, so you could get child support money? For a child you don't even want?"

He shrugged as he held her gaze. "I don't like you. Anything to ruin your life is fine with me."

"But hurting a child, your child, in the process... That didn't matter?" she asked, tears spilling over her cheeks as she held his gaze. But Rick just shook his head. How could he do this? Who was this man she had made a child with?

This filth.

"It's over. I don't care," he said simply and then he stood up. Clearing his throat, he took their file, almost like he thought they didn't notice, before saying, "I'll see you Thursday, and we'll get the ball rolling."

"On what? What do you mean?" she asked.

"Come on, Lucy, keep up. I'm giving up my rights. I don't want her. I don't want to pay for her. I don't even want to deal with her. I'll always love her—I guess I'm supposed to—but she doesn't like me. She likes that guy. So you guys go ahead, be a happy little family."

She gasped as she looked up at him, unsure what the hell was really going on.

"Wait, are you serious? Just like that?" Lucy asked, her heart almost cracking her ribs it was beating so hard.

"What, you don't believe me?" he asked. He grabbed a pen from a passing waitress before taking a sheet of paper from the file. They watched as he wrote something and then signed it, laying it on the table. Tapping the file to the edge of the table, he nodded at them. "That's that. See you guys Thursday."

And then he walked away.

Like it was nothing.

Like he hadn't just agreed to give up his flesh and blood.

Reaching for the piece of paper, she read it through tear-filled eyes.

On Thursday, I, Rick Hart, will give up my rights so that Benji Paxton can adopt Angela Lynn Hart.

And then there was his signature and the date. That was it. Wide-eyed, she looked over at Benji. "What?"

He looked at the sheet, shaking his head. "Really?"

"Did that just happen?" she asked and Benji gulped beside her.

"I'm not a hundred percent sure, but I think he just gave me Angie. Like, actually, *gave* her to me," he said, his voice breaking as her body went numb. Looking over at her, he smiled. "She'll be mine. Like, I'll be her dad. Her real dad—she'll have my name."

Her jaw was slack as she held his gaze, unable to process this. Who just gives their kid up like that? But then…who the hell cared? She wanted Rick gone, and he'd be gone. But above all that, Benji would be Angie's dad. Well, if he wanted her.

"You want her, right?"

"Fuck yeah," he laughed and then his face lit up, tears flooding his sweet, gray eyes. "Lucy, we'll be a real family. All of us. One."

As her tears rolled off her jaw and onto her lap, she cupped his beautiful face. Her heart was in her throat. She couldn't believe it. While she hated Rick with everything inside of her, she could honestly kiss him for making Benji this happy. For giving him everything he ever wanted.

What Lucy wanted.

A good man to love her daughter.

Their daughter.

Around the lump in her throat, she whispered, "We've always been a family, but now it will be official."

Covering her hands with his, he looked deep into her eyes. "Officially complete."

As their mouths met and Benji pulled Lucy into his lap, she couldn't believe that, at one point in her life, she didn't think she could ever love someone, that a man could complete her. As her mouth moved with Benji's, her heart slamming in her chest as his slammed back, she believed it. She believed that two lost souls had become a full one, no longer lost but together. And she believed with everything inside her that nothing could ever break them apart.

Her life was finally beginning.

And what a life it was about to be.

Epilogue

Four months later

Everyone had come.

At least, the people who mattered to him.

As Benji looked around the room, Lucy's family—well, his too, now—stood front row, while his core Assassins teammates and their wives sat in the rows behind them. The room was full, a packed house. Even Lucy's dad was there. It wasn't just because he was their lawyer, but because they wanted him there. They wouldn't have gotten here if it weren't for him.

As Angie wiggled between them, her fingers laced with theirs, Judge Walker looked them over and smiled. It had been Angie's idea for all three of them to wear his hockey jersey, with his name on the back but her number. She was very insistent about having her number, not that Benji minded. He just wanted this day to come.

The day he became a father.

Again.

But this time, he wasn't some drunk the way he had been for Leary. No, he was going to be a good, solid father who would love Angie soberly until his dying day. It wouldn't be easy—he knew that because he was in love with her mother, the most headstrong pain in the ass he had ever met—but he wouldn't change a thing about her. He loved them both, and he was ready to start their lives together.

"Now, I have a petition here for the adoption of Angela Lynn Hart by

Benjamin Walter Paxton, is that correct?"

Mark stood beside Benji and nodded. "Yes, sir."

"Funny turn of events. Not that I'm complaining," the judge said, his face lighting up, and he wasn't kidding. Rick hadn't lied when he said he'd sign over his rights. Before the judge could even ask him if he wanted to consent to the new parenting plan, he'd volunteered that he wanted to give up custody, his rights, and everything to Lucy, as long as he didn't ever have to pay child support. The judge agreed for good reason, and Benji still couldn't believe it.

But he was fucking thankful.

Because that's where their story began.

As easy as it was to get here after Rick was out of the picture, the waiting game was what almost killed Benji. He would be lying if he said he wasn't scared, freaked out that, at any moment, Rick could change his mind, come back, and ruin everything. But they hadn't heard a peep out of him. Hadn't seen him or anything. It was like he fell off the face of the earth. It was ridiculous, but in a way, he didn't care. He'd wanted Rick gone, and he was gone. Now he just wanted to adopt his Angie.

And he was.

"Now, Angela, who is this man that is standing beside you?"

Angela beamed up at him as she swung their hands back and forth. "He's my dad."

Everyone aww'd behind them as Benji's eyes started to cloud with tears.

"Good, so you know that this man is your father. That it will be as if you are his flesh and blood?"

She nodded. "Yup. He's my dad."

Benji swallowed hard as the judge nodded, "That's right. Now, Mrs. Paxton, do you agree to this adoption?"

Before Lucy could answer, though, Benji heard Autumn in the back. "Did he say Mrs. Paxton to Lucy? Are they married?"

But Lucy just grinned, nodding her head as she swallowed. "Yes, sir, I do."

"And, Mr. Paxton, it is your wish to adopt Angela Hart?"

He almost couldn't speak his throat was so tight, but then she glanced up at him and grinned. A tear rolled down his face as he nodded, his voice hoarse as he said, "I want nothing more than to do that, your honor."

Angie giggled as she bounced on her heels, and when Benji met Lucy's love-filled gaze, his heart ached. They had all been so excited for this day. It was the big event of the year, especially since the Assassins had lost in first round of the play-offs to the Blackhawks. This was something to look forward to. While he was disappointed that he didn't have a run at the Cup, he was happy to have time with his girls.

The whole summer off while Lucy worked.

She was designing like crazy, and they had already decided she would need a bigger place before the New Year. As much as he hated to see her go from the backyard, he understood and was excited for her. Angie had done great in school, excelling in her classes, and she was awesome on the ice. She was the next Baylor, he decided, and just thinking of Baylor made him smile. She had announced her retirement the month before, and while he was bummed to see her go, he couldn't wait to meet the little bundle of joy she was carrying. Autumn was convinced it was a miracle baby, and everyone else agreed. They were all excited.

The way a family should be.

His family.

As Benji looked from Angie's profile to Lucy, he couldn't help but think of Ava and Leary. How he was going to make them proud by loving these two women with all the fierceness in the world. The guilt was still there in the background at being so happy, but he decided that was something he'd have to live with because he wasn't living without his girls.

As they signed the paperwork the judge had given Mark, Benji's hand shook so badly, but he was able to get his signature on the paper. He couldn't help but grin at Lucy as she signed too. They even had Angie sign below their names, and when she looked up at them, the future in her eyes, Benji had to do everything to keep it together.

When Mark handed back the paperwork, the judge stamped it and nodded, looking up at Benji, Lucy, and Angie.

"I'm going to metaphorically take off my judge's robes here for a second, since I know you to be good, Christian people. The greatest contribution to the kingdom of God may not be something you do, but someone you raise. And I truly believe that a family is God's masterpiece. Benjamin, you are getting the gift of something truly special. A beautiful young lady who you will help mold into an adult who will mirror you and your wife," he said. He paused as lips curved, and Benji's body broke out in gooseflesh. He swore he heard Autumn ask once against if the judge had said wife, and he almost looked to Lucy. Hadn't she told her mother that they had to get married for this to happen? Before he could, though, the judge captured his gaze. "I am very proud of the three people I see in front of me, and I will never forget this case. I pray that you live long, happy lives—and that the teenage years don't drive you into the ground."

They laughed, Benji's face hurting from smiling so hard as he looked down at Angie. As much as he wanted to believe she would be a great teenager, he would never forget the story of Lucy Sinclair as one. Or hell, himself.

They were doomed.

But he didn't care as long as he was with Lucy, being doomed together.

"So let's get this started, huh?" the judge asked and they all grinned up at him.

Benji actually held his breath as he squeezed Angie's hand.

"By the power vested in me by the state of Tennessee, I approve this adoption by Mr. Benjamin Walter Paxton of Angela Lynn Hart, who will now be known as Angela Lynn Paxton. May God always be with your family."

Before his gavel could even hit the desk, Benji had Angie in his arms and she let out a whoop of excitement, hugging him tightly. Kissing her hard, he squeezed her as the room broke out in applause. Pulling back to look at him, she grinned, her green eyes twinkling as she asked, "So you're, like, really my dad now, right?"

"Really."

"And we're a family, right, Mom?" she asked Lucy as Benji wrapped her up too.

"Yes, honey, we are," Lucy cried, leaning against her husband.

"Cool," she decided, and they laughed, probably to keep the tears at bay.

"You know what that means, right?" he asked and Angie beamed.

"We're going to Disney World!"

"Yup."

"Yay!" Angie cheered as Benji's eyes flooded with tears.

Lucy eyed him. "But the real question is are we sleeping in the castle?"

"Pfft. I'm Benji Paxton, the leading scoring defensemen in the league—"

"No, you're not," Lucy said.

"On the Assassins?"

"Nope, Jayden is," Angie said, and he thought that over.

"Fine. Of course we are, because I paid a lot of money to do it," he decided, and that had Lucy cracking up as Angie wrapped her arms around him, kissing him hard on the cheek. He was grinning from ear to ear as they started toward the back where everyone was waiting. But before they could even get that far, Autumn stopped them.

"Lucy Lane, did you marry this man and not tell me?"

Laughing, Benji looked over at Lucy. She pointed to her mother. "Well, you see…what had happened was… We couldn't finalize the adoption unless Benji was her stepparent. So we got married," she said and Autumn's eyes widened.

"You mean to tell me like you did before, like Jayden, like Jace, you ran off and didn't give me a wedding? Lucy! What in the world?"

But Lucy held her hands up. "I swear, I am having a big ol' wedding later. We just wanted to be complete, Mom. You can't be mad at that, can you?"

Autumn paused, her eyes narrowing, and while Benji knew she was annoyed, she wasn't mad. She was too happy to be mad. River wrapped his arms around her and beamed at them. "No, sweetheart, we can't. Congratulations."

"Thanks," she said, looking up at him. "We're pretty happy."

"We are," he agreed as he looked out at the crowd. Shea and Elli Alder grinned back at him, with Jordie and Kacey Thomas beside them. Everyone he loved was there. His teammates, his family, all of them grinning, so proud and supportive. He couldn't have gotten through the last couple months without a lot of them—but most of all, he couldn't have done it without Lucy.

Looking at her, he grinned as her eyes glossed over, and he whispered, "I can't believe this."

"I can't either," she admitted, going up on her toes and kissing his jaw. "I love you."

"I love you too."

"I love you both!" Angie declared and that had everyone laughing before she wrapped her arms around him, kissing his cheek once more.

And as he held Lucy and Angie in his arms, his heart still beating like mad in his chest, a feeling of wholeness came over him.

Benji Paxton finally had it all.

A NOTE FROM
TONI ALEO

So what did you think? Did you love it? I know I did. Benji is up there with Shea for me. He was just such a refreshing guy to write. And Lucy? God, I love her. Angie too. My sweet little girl who was based on my daughter, whom I love more than anything. When I came up with the premise of this book, I wanted to give the single moms out there hope. I know a lot of baby daddies like Rick, and I hate that. I hate the stress it puts on good women who are just trying to be good moms. It sucks, but don't worry, the man of your dreams is coming. And he's gonna love your kids like he loves you.

So thank you. Thank you for reading Rushing the Goal and for being a constant supporter of my series and of me. It means the world to me.

I have a great team of people behind me and they know I love and appreciate them, so I won't say that here.

Now, I know you are curious as to what I have coming up. I have a lot. I have a full writing year ahead of me, but right now, I don't know what I'm putting out next. So make sure to join my mailing list or follow me on Facebook for all the up-to-date info!

Again, thank you. I couldn't do all I do without your love and support. It doesn't go unnoticed, and I love you so much. Thank you.

Love,
Toni

More books from
TONI ALEO

Assassins Series
Taking Shots
Trying to Score
Empty Net
Falling for the Backup
Blue Lines
Laces and Lace
A Very Merry Hockey Holiday
Overtime
Rushing the Goal

Bellevue Bullies Series
Boarded by Love
Clipped by Love
Hooked by Love

Taking Risks
Whiskey Prince
Becoming the Whiskey Princess.

Standalones
Let it be Me

Make sure to check out these titles and more on Toni's website:
www.tonialeo.com

Or connect with Toni on Facebook, Twitter, Instagram, and more!

Also make sure to join the mailing list for up to date news from the
desk of Toni Aleo:
http://eepurl.com/u28FL

Made in the USA
San Bernardino, CA
08 December 2016